# SPARROW RISING

# SPARROW RISING

K.A. EMMONS

# SPARROW RISING



Cover Design | Illustrations: Abbie Emmons
Typesetting: Enchanted Ink Publishing

ISBN: 978-1-7340146-5-5 (E-book)
ISBN: 978-1-7340146-6-2 (Paperback)
ISBN: 978-1-7340146-7-9 (Hardcover)



W W W . K A E M M O N S . C O M

# PROLOGUE

*I CAN'T DO THIS.*

*I can't do this.*

*I can't do this.*

The words followed the beat of my footsteps as I paced the containment cell. I searched the emptiness around me, flattening my palms against the wall, closing my eyes.

I imagined Keegan in the cell just beside this one; I imagined his hands pressing against mine from the other side. I could feel his presence as though he were still there.

There was no turning back now—I had to do this. My agreeing to marry Aaron had saved Keegan's life.

*God, I hope he's safe. I hope they all are...*

I felt as though I were standing at the edge of a precipice with no other choice but to jump. Fear swelled in my chest, pounding against my rib cage like cold, angry waves.

*I can't...*

In my mind, I could see the clearing in the woods I so often returned to in my dreams. I could see those wings spread out against the swirling clouds, the hawk soaring above me.

"I can do this..." I whispered, drawing a slow, deep breath. "I *can* do this..."

In the distance, I heard footsteps echoing down the hall, nearing the cell door. They halted. A few beeps. The door opened.

"Sparrow." Aaron's smooth, deep voice filled the small room and echoed off the walls.

I turned to find him standing in the doorway, dressed in a black RGM uniform instead of civilian clothes, red stripes pinned to his breast pocket and a black beret covering his crew cut. His eyebrows were furrowed over his dark eyes as they probed mine. After a long moment he sighed and squared his shoulders.

"You ready?" His voice was softer but resolved.

Matching his confident posture, I stepped forward, yielding a single nod.

He slid off his black backpack and held the strap out to me. "Get changed, then."

I unzipped the bag and reached in to pull out a black uniform that matched Aaron's.

"They've given you a new name and an honorary rank for the time being too," he informed me, a little hesitation in his tone.

"What name?"

"Sparrow Turner."

My jaw set. "In their dreams."

"Sparrow." He sighed. "Just play the game, all right?"

"What happened to running?" I whispered, looking him square in the eyes. "What happened to escaping all of this together?"

He leaned closer, his voice low. "It's going to take time... and a lot of patience."

I searched his eyes. "Don't let them buy you with rank and power,

Aaron—what is any of it worth without freedom? You're not one of them."

He studied me for a long moment, the expression on his face unreadable. "You have to trust me on this, Sparrow."

My gaze sank back down to the black uniform jacket in my hands. I swallowed back a wave of nausea.

"I'll be waiting in the hall," he continued, backing out of the cell. "Get changed. Everyone's assembled."

I gave a single nod, peeling off my worn shirt and pulling the fitted black one on over my head.

*KEEGAN*

The Homestead had been all I'd ever known, and then, just like that, it was gone: consumed in flames and reduced to ashes.

I felt numb as I followed Cub through the wilderness. Every step I took, every mile I walked, every mountain I climbed and valley I crossed only reminded me that I was getting farther and farther away from Sparrow.

I could still hear her voice on the edge of the wind: *I don't love you... I never have. I never will. I could never love someone so dedicated to being a slider.*

Each word stung like venom.

I thought I'd read her mind that night, through the cell wall. But now I couldn't help but wonder if I'd just wanted to hear her say that she loved me so badly that I'd imagined it... that they'd been *my* thoughts and not her own.

*Had I made it all up in my head? Had any of it been real?*

As the days passed, we journeyed farther from Yellowstone and up into the craggy mountains of Section West. Snowy, rocky peaks reached up to crack the pink dawn sky, carving out valleys and reflecting in the lake that sprawled at the base of the mountain range. If everything hadn't been dead, it might have been beautiful. The trees looked like wind-whipped skeletons, reaching desperately for deliverance that hadn't yet come. For the first time I was beginning to question whether I was the one who was supposed to bring that deliverance. I felt incapable—gutted.

It was getting harder and harder to continue as Cub sprang nimbly from one rock to the next, coaxing me farther up into the mountains.

I knew we had to get Sparrow back. Whether she wanted to be back or not, she needed to be. She had no idea who she was—but I did. Hawk was her mother, and Icarus was her father, and until they returned, she was all that we had of them. She carried their blood in her veins. If the RGM destroyed her, we would lose everything we had fought so long and hard for. She was in a den of wolves, and it was only a matter of time until...

I slowed to a halt on a rocky plateau, shielding my eyes from the sunlight as I gazed out over the landscape sprawling for miles in all directions. It seemed that no matter how far the valley went, the light went farther, leaving nothing untouched.

*How are we going to get her back?*

I took a deep breath, closing my eyes and running a hand back over the stubbly side of my head where the wolf's teeth had given me a close shave. My skin was completely healed, but my hair had only just begun to grow back.

I perched on the edge of the rocky plateau, ignoring Cub's pleading yips for us to press on. There was a thousand-foot drop yawning beneath my feet as they dangled over the edge of the sheer rock slab. When I didn't budge, I felt the nudge of Cub's thick, fuzzy head as she came up behind me, perching beside me at the cliff's edge. I turned to look at her. She gaped up at me questioningly.

I wiped away the tears that had begun to gather in my eyes and reached over to run a hand down her soft coat. For a while we just sat there in the silence.

Then, behind me, I heard a voice.

"Keegan?"

*SPARROW*

The uniform scratched against my skin as I followed Aaron down the long, sterile hallway and out into the fresh air. The morning sun was shining, and the courtyard was crowded with personnel lined up in formation and flanking both sides of the dirt road. Bask was waiting at the end, standing at parade rest beside the RGM officer who would be acting as an officiant.

My steps lagged as I took it all in, my stomach twisting into knots. Aaron took a few more steps before pausing to look back over his shoulder. Raising one dark eyebrow, he extended his hand. I took a deep breath and grasped it. Time seemed to slow down with every step. I felt numb as we halted in front of Bask and the officiant.

Bask's face was devoid of expression. He scanned me up and down, as if I was a puzzle he was trying to solve. I swallowed and lowered my gaze to the ground as the officer stepped forward. His eyes were slate gray, and his bald head was covered in a black beret.

Aaron's fingers were still intertwined with my own as the officer began to speak.

"Corporal Price, raise your right hand and repeat after me... I, Aaron Price."

"I, Aaron Price." His fingers tightened a little around my own as he raised his other hand.

"In the presence of this assembly."

"In the presence of this assembly."

"Legally bind myself to Private Sparrow Turner in the alliance of marriage."

I swallowed, turning to look at Aaron. He was staring straight ahead.

"Legally bind myself to Private Sparrow Turner in the alliance of marriage."

"To further the cause of the RGM," the officer continued, "to increase its capacity and strongholds, and to create new alliances in its favor."

The more Aaron spoke, the sicker I felt.

"Private Turner." The officer directed his attention to me now. "Please raise your right hand and repeat after me..."

*I can't.*

*I can't...*

I squared my shoulders. Bask was still watching.

"I, Sparrow Turner."

"I, Sparrow..." I trailed off, my throat tightening. "Turner."

"In the presence of this assembly..."

"In... in the presence of this assembly..."

I could barely hear my own voice over the ringing in my ears.

"Legally bind myself to Corporal Aaron Price in the alliance of marriage."

I opened my mouth, but no words came out. I felt the heat of Aaron's gaze as he turned to look at me. My focus slipped back to Bask. His dark eyes still drilled into mine; his thick arms were crossed over his chest.

I closed my eyes.

"Private Turner?" the officer's now muffled voice prompted. "Repeat after me: legally bind myself to Corporal Aaron Price in the alliance of marriage..."

I pulled in a shaky breath, locking eyes with Aaron.

## *KEEGAN*

I turned at the sound of my name, scanning the craggy incline until my gaze caught on a familiar figure farther up. As he pulled off the hood of his gray cloak, I could see that Dad's blond hair was a stark contrast against the earthy rocks and boulders. Even from here, I could see the relief in his green eyes.

Jumping to my feet, I scrambled up the rocky slope, Cub at my heels. Dad met me halfway and threw his arms around me. He grasped the back of my head and embraced me.

"Thank God you're safe." His voice cracked, tears in his eyes. "Did you...?"

"I found her. But... I couldn't... she didn't..." I stopped, unsure how to even begin. "They captured me too, Dad. But then they released me."

"And Sparrow?"

I stared at him, my voice bottled up in my throat.

"Keegan."

"I... I tried, Dad, but she... she told me that she wanted to stay." I forced the words out. "That she was in love with one of the corporals—who just happens to be a slider himself, with powers of invisibility. She told me to leave and never come back—that she never wanted to see me again. That she could never be who you wanted her to be."

The color drained from Dad's face.

"What are we going to do?" My heart sank. "Dad, we have to go back. We have to—"

"No." Dad cut me off sternly. "No."

"We can't just—"

"They're baiting us, Keegan. We cannot fall into their trap."

"But what about Sparrow?" My voice rose and echoed off the cliff side. "What if they kill her?"

"There's a far greater chance that they will if we attempt to attack their base. They'll have us right where they want us—and then they won't have any reason to keep her alive."

"So what do you expect us to do?" My voice cracked. "Stand by and—and do *nothing*?"

Dad folded his arms over his chest, then turned and walked to the cliff's edge, pausing there, looking down on the valley, towards the endless blue horizon.

"Dad." I drew a shaky breath. "She told me she was... she was going to marry him."

Dad didn't say anything. Didn't move. He just stood there for a long moment in silence.

"I can't let her do it," I continued, speaking more to myself than to Dad. "I can't just stand by and let her throw herself away! Dad, can't you see that—"

"You must!" Dad's booming voice cut me off, tears rolling down his cheeks as he turned to me. "For now, Keegan, you must!" He clapped a hand on my shoulder. "We cannot risk them finding out who she really is..." I fought back tears as Dad looked me square in the eyes. "It will take time, Keegan... and something more than what we can give."

He started slowly up the rocky trail, and I set off after him. "And what would that be?"

"Her parents." His reply was ragged as he wiped his tears away with the back of his hand. "We need to find them."

"But how? We have no idea where they are or what happened to them. If they were still on Earth, Hawk would have come to you by now."

"We'll find her," he said. "Both of them."

"Where do we start?" I asked.

Dad didn't reply; instead, he gestured ahead, down a jagged path leading to the forest below. I could see the peaks of tents among the trees.

He turned to look at me, heaviness mingling with the hope that wouldn't die in his eyes.

"We start by building a new home," he said.

*SPARROW*

"I legally bind myself to Corporal Aaron Price in the alliance of marriage." The words rushed off my lips like a flood when a dam finally gives way. "To further the cause of the RGM... to increase its capacity and strongholds, and to create new alliances in its favor."

I felt like there was a vise tightening in my chest. Tears burned in my eyes.

The officer made a gesture, and a younger soldier stepped forward, a tray in his hands with a silver cup on it. He halted in front of the officer and took the cup from the tray. He extended it to Aaron.

Aaron took the cup and brought it to his lips. I watched as he sipped, swallowed, and then handed the cup to me. I froze.

"Take it, Private Turner," the officer insisted.

*I can't...*

Forcing my hand forward, I curled my fingers around the cool steel vessel. It was filled with deep red liquid. I swallowed a mouthful of it. It tasted like fire, and it burned my throat. The officer retrieved the cup from me and set it back down on the tray.

"Corporal Price and Private Turner," he announced. "You are now husband and wife."

My stomach sank as everyone began to clap. I felt Aaron's hand slide back into mine and give it a gentle squeeze.

*Husband and wife.*

The words echoed in my head. I could hardly believe them.

Bask extended a hand for Aaron to shake. "Welcome back."

His voice was flat and unreadable. His eyes were narrow as he studied the air in front of him, searching for the man only I could see.

After a moment of hesitation, Aaron grasped Bask's hand and gave it a firm shake.

The exchange sent chills down my spine. I knew Aaron was just playing "the game," as he had called it. Still, even after the crowd had dissipated, I couldn't shake the cold, terrified feeling that gripped me from inside, tightening like a vise.

Bask granted us both a leisure day, passing me a knowing look before he left us and then stalking back across the courtyard to his office. I turned to look at Aaron; his eyes followed Bask.

"Come on," he said finally. "Let's go."

We walked back to Aaron's lodgings in silence. He opened the door and held it for me.

I slipped past him and into the shack's dim interior. Faded light shafted in through the smoky glass, igniting particles of dust like fireflies around us. Aaron closed the door and leaned back against it. His rigid persona seemed to melt away.

"We won't be here that much longer," he said. He stepped forward, meeting me in the middle of the room. "Bask will move us to better lodgings soon."

"I don't want better lodgings," I answered quietly, looking up into his face. "I just want to get out of here."

Aaron's eyes lowered to the faded floorboards. "It's just going to take time, Sparrow."

I pressed my forefinger and thumb to my eyelids, trying not to let the tears spill down.

"Hey." His voice was hushed, soft like his warm hand as it came to rest on my shoulder. "Hey, it's okay..."

Aaron folded me into his arms, and I collapsed against his chest, wrapping my arms around his torso. I sobbed into his jacket, my fingers curling around fistfuls of rough fabric.

"Shhh." He kissed the top of my head, stroking a hand over my hair. "It's okay..."

I shook my head, my face crumpling. "No... no, it's not. Nothing is..."

He drew back, holding me at arm's length. "We're going to get out of here, Sparrow." His voice softened to a whisper as he looked into my eyes. "I promise."

I sniffed back tears, searching his eyes. Sensing my uncertainty, he pulled me closer. His forehead gently made contact with mine.

"I promise," he repeated. I felt his breath against my lips.

I nodded slowly, reaching up to rest one hand on his cheek, stroking my thumb over his soft, freshly shaved jaw. "Okay," I whispered. "Okay..."

He leaned in and kissed me. I felt frozen for a moment, but the warmth of his lips slowly melted the feeling away. I softened, moving my lips over his. His hands slid down to my lower back, and he pulled me in closer.

Tears spilled down my cheeks. In my mind, like a faded memory from a dream, I could still see that pink sunset sky. I could still make out the light glistening on the surface of the lake. I could still see Keegan's eyes. I could still taste his lips and feel his skin.

I drew back.

"What is it, Sparrow?" Aaron asked quietly, caressing my face with his thumb.

"Nothing," I answered.

He gently tucked a strand of hair behind my ear.

"I just..." I swallowed, trailing off. "I want to take things slow."

Aaron's eyes probed mine. "We don't have to do anything you don't want to do, Sparrow," he replied quietly. "I didn't marry you for that."

"I know..." I dried my eyes with the backs of my hands. "You married me to protect me from them."

"No." He shook his head. "I married you because I'm in love with you, Sparrow."

I lifted my chin and met his gaze, studying his face.

"We're going to be okay." Aaron stroked my cheek with the backs of his fingers. "We're going to find a way out of here. I promise."

# 1

*SIX MONTHS LATER*

"ARE YOU SURE?"

This had to be the fifth time she'd asked.

"Yes, Kateri. I'm sure." I ran my hand back through my long hair. It had taken a long time for the hair on the side of my head to grow back after the wolf attack. It was about four inches long on one side of my head and about twelve on the other, with the exception of the small braid that grew longer than the rest of my hair.

"I'm tired of my hair being two different lengths." I squinted out over the landscape sprawling beneath us. "It reminds me of things I would rather just forget..."

I felt Kateri's warm fingertips brush against the nape of my neck as she gathered my hair back over my shoulders.

"Plus, it looks stupid," I added, attempting to lighten the mood.

"It doesn't look that bad."

I scissored my first two fingers together, and she hummed a little laugh.

"All right, all right." I felt a gentle tug as she straightened a handful of my hair between her fingers. The snip of shears followed.

Again and again, locks of my hair tumbled to the ground, blending in among the blanket of golden pine needles. I stared out at the valley below, watching as the nectar of a new day slowly spilled over the mountain peaks to bathe all that lay below it.

"I wish we could heal more of this place," Kateri whispered. "Like we did back at the Homestead."

My stomach knotted at the mere mention of our old home; my brain instantly flashed back to images of flames rolling from the roof to the sky. I pinched my eyes shut.

"We can't risk being seen from the air," I said. "We are in hiding, after all."

Kateri stepped around the stump to stand in front of me, combing her fingers back through my hair. "Have you spoken with Sensei? Do you know what he's planning next?"

"Not yet, no. He transported out this morning for the school in Algeria. He said he'd be back in a couple of days."

Kateri continued cutting my hair in silence for a few moments. She paused to gently brush fallen strands off my cheeks.

"Can I ask you something, Kateri?" I said after a while.

"Mm-hmm."

"Do you ever wonder if we should just... I don't know." I blew out a sigh. "If we should just leave too?"

"Leave Section West?"

I hesitated, then yielded a nod.

Kateri snipped the scissors a few times, then paused. "No, not really. I like it here. There's only one place more beautiful than Yellowstone, and that's the Tetons."

I couldn't help but become aware of the looming mountains behind us when she said this. I turned to glance over my shoulder, my gaze tracing the rocky peaks that rose above us.

"It would be a bit more beautiful if we weren't living in constant fear of being discovered by invisible RGM forces," I added.

Her hands gently cupped the sides of my face as she straightened my head to face forward again.

"We would never do anything good if we waited around for the conditions to be perfect, Keegan," she responded, her soft brown eyes focusing on the scissors in her hand. "We're the ones who are going to change this place for the better, not the other way around."

We were only about a quarter of a mile away from were we lived now—what we all called "the shelter" because that was basically what it was: a large canvas tent camouflaged with branches and leaves. It was tucked away in the foothills at the base of the mountains, inconspicuous among the thick rust-colored forest.

"We'll get her back somehow, Keeg." Kateri's quiet voice pulled me out of my thoughts. She knelt in front of me as she analyzed my hair. "I think you know that."

I lowered my gaze to the ground. "Do you know how many plans we've tried that have failed, Kateri? Do you know how many times Dad and I have gone back there and tried to figure out ways to get in—to get her out of there?" I dragged a hand over my face, a vise tightening inside me as I rehashed everything that had happened. "I'm the only one who can read minds, so I'm the only one who can even see in there, and they've tripled security—transporting into that place could end in disaster."

"But you guys haven't gone back in months—"

"Because it's too dangerous," I cut in. "We were this close." I held up an inch of air between my fingers. "*This* close to getting caught last time. We can't risk being identified and followed. We could all be killed."

Kateri dusted off my head and took a step backward to study her handiwork. "That doesn't sound like the faith-filled Keegan I know."

I stood up, brushing myself off and running a hand back over my now much shorter hair. "I think he burned down with the Homestead."

Dad had sectioned off the back quarter of the shelter for an office of sorts. The dirt floor was covered with sealed jars filled with flora samples from the surrounding area. Cushions were positioned around a long strip of canvas that acted as his space for writing and analyzing his findings. An abundance of maps, charts, and notations were pinned to all four canvas walls: maps of the area, of Yellowstone, and of the space in between. There were also dozens of sketches and notations of what I'd seen when I was in the District: names, numbers, buildings, conversations—it was all there, covered in notes and questions and ideas.

I walked steadily around the perimeter of the canvas room, scanning each map and every chart, finally pausing to stare up at one particularly messy one that I had drawn myself.

The District... or at least, what I'd been able to piece together.

It was difficult to believe six months had passed. *Six months.*

I pinched my eyes shut, trying to push away the painful memories that hung like fog over my mind, along with that same tormenting question:

*Is she all right?*

We were running out of ideas—and time. The RGM forces were growing stronger by the day. Meanwhile, we lived in hiding, unable to use our abilities for anything beyond growing and fostering plants inside the shelter.

Dad had been right all along: what Sparrow needed was Hawk and Icarus. Wherever they were.

"Where on earth could they be...?" I whispered, running my fingers over the map. "It's been so long... Why have they stayed away so long?"

"Who?"

I glanced over my shoulder just as Preston brushed aside the canvas flap and stepped into the room. His face was covered in a few days' worth of stubble.

"No one," I muttered, turning back to the map in front of me. "Nothing."

"The patriarchs?"

I rubbed a hand over my face and nodded.

"Whoa. Your hair is..."

"Short?"

"I was going to say non-feral," Preston joked. "But that works too." He walked the perimeter of the room, gazing around at the walls. "Have you ever heard the stories about Hawk and Sensei Fin?" he asked.

"She was his best friend—*is* his best friend," I corrected myself.

"Yeah, but honestly, it's always sounded like it was more than that to me..."

I shot him a glance. Preston stooped to pick up a jar that held Dad's pens and some hawk feathers. He looked at me.

"I think Sensei and Hawk have a special connection," I agreed. "I really don't understand it."

"But if it was so special, why hasn't she returned?"

I thought about it for a moment, then shrugged. "Good question."

He set the jar back down on the canvas mat and walked over to me. He rubbed the back of his neck as he stared up at the wall. "If Sensei can't find them... it's hard to imagine who could."

The same thought tormented me, too. Dad never talked about Hawk and Icarus's disappearance like it was something permanent, or anything to worry about. The way he spoke about them would make anyone who didn't know better think that they'd be stopping by that afternoon. I didn't understand that about Dad—why wasn't he worried? The patriarchs were gone and so was their daughter, yet he never despaired.

Sometimes I was jealous. I wondered what it felt like to live without being eaten alive by your own thoughts and fears every day. To live with certainty that everything would turn out right.

"Where are Lara and Areos?" I asked.

Preston jerked his head in the direction of the flap he'd entered through. "Outside."

I nodded, beginning to step away.

"Keeg, wait." His eyebrows furrowed over his amber-brown eyes as he studied me for a moment. "Are you okay?"

I nodded. "I just... I need to be doing *something*."

Preston squared his shoulders. "I'm here to help—just tell me how I can."

"There's nothing you can do right now, Pres." I sighed. "In truth, I don't even know what I'm supposed to be doing."

"Well, when you do figure it out, you know where to find me." His eyes were earnest as he spoke. "Don't think I don't realize how much in your debt I am—you're the reason I have Janna back. Without you—"

I shook my head. "I did what any one of us would do. We're all in this together."

"But that's my point: none of us *could* have done what you did," he replied. "I hope you realize that."

I didn't answer. His eyes remained connected with mine.

"We're going to get her back, Keeg," Pres went on, his voice firm with resolve. "I know we will."

"I know, Pres," I said, turning to push open the canvas flap, and let myself out into the larger part of the tent. "I know."

Janna snagged Preston as soon as the flap had closed behind him. In the main living area, Myung was sprawled out on a cushion on the floor with her nose in a book.

"Where are Raf and Kateri?" I asked.

Myung continued reading.

"Myung?"

She sighed irritably and glanced up. "What?"

"Where are Raf and Kateri?"

She tipped her head in the direction of the shelter entrance. "Outside somewhere. I think."

Slipping out of the tent, I spotted Raf immediately, a stone's throw into the shade of the forest, centered in front of a target he'd nailed to an old, dead oak.

I crossed my arms and watched for a moment as he twirled a knife in his hand, took aim, then threw. It spun end over end in the air before nailing into the target with a satisfying *thwack*. A weak grin tugged at the corners of my lips.

"He's gotten good, hasn't he?" A familiar voice broke through my thoughts.

Kateri stood by the corner of the shelter, a knife in one hand and a long, straight, slender stick in the other.

"He has," I agreed, walking over to her, still watching Raf out of my peripheral.

"He's had a good teacher."

I shrugged, stopping beside her. "A mediocre one at best."

Kateri rolled her eyes and whacked me with the stick.

"Have you seen Lara and Areos?"

"They went for a walk to the edge," she replied, passing the blade of the knife over the stick, sharpening the pointed end with each pass. "I think Lara's trying to enjoy her time with him while it lasts."

Since Dad was often transporting out to other schools, he'd asked Areos to transfer from Section C to help us re-establish our own place of training here in the Teton valley. He'd arrived only a week prior, and Lara hadn't seen him in months. Needless to say, we tried not to follow them when they went off for a walk together.

"Hey, Keeg," Raf lifted his hand in a wave, walking over. The sunlight tangled in his thick, curly hair. He was almost my height, and his voice seemed to be on a roller coaster of octaves. "Want to throw a few?"

"Another day, Raf. You did great, though." I slapped him on the shoulder and shot Kateri a look. "I'll be right back."

Venturing deeper into the pines, I started down the familiar path I'd taken earlier with Kateri. My fingertips tingled as I skirted around towering pines and old white oaks. Their bark had long since rotted away and fallen to the earth to create a breeding ground for mushrooms—the only form of life that seemed to be able to flourish around here.

The woods were nothing like the forest that surrounded the Homestead. They were dull and gray and sick—and silent. There were no chirruping crickets, no singing birds. No scuttle of rabbits or squirrels hiding in the brush. The only sound to cut through the quiet was the soft thuds of my bare feet against the dry ground.

I closed my hands into fists, trying not to think about healing the trees. Trying not to think of all the things we were supposed to be doing.

*If only Janna hadn't told them where the Homestead was... if only she hadn't talked...*

But I couldn't blame her. I'd felt just as much fear as she had that night in the District—God, it felt like ages ago, now.

I slowed to a stop at the edge of the woods. In the distance I could already make out two figures standing at the edge of the plateau where the hill rolled down to the valley. Lara's arm was around Areos's waist, and his rested over her shoulders. Areos was tall with blond hair that was even lighter than Lara's. I couldn't remember the last time I'd seen two people look so happy together.

Areos turned to glance at me when I stepped out of the woods.

"Ah, Keegan."

"Hope I'm not interrupting anything," I said, shooting Lara a teasing look. She laughed.

"Not right now, anyway," Areos jested dryly. "Everything all right?"

I nodded. "I was wondering if you'd had a chance to discuss our next course of action with Dad before he transported out?"

A look of hesitation passed through Areos's eyes as he frowned. "Lara and I were just talking about that."

"Yeah?" I turned my attention to Lara. Her long blonde hair was pinned back in a bun, and her cheeks were pink. She nodded, that familiar look of hesitation on her face.

"What is it?" I asked. "What are you guys not telling me?"

"Our only hope is to somehow figure out what happened to Icarus and Hawk," Areos answered. "They're going to be the key to getting Sparrow out of there—to shutting this whole thing down. We can't do it without them."

"So, what—we just stand around here?" I asked, my tone a little sharper than I'd intended. "She's still trapped there—God only knows what they may be doing to her!"

Areos took a level breath, looking me in the eyes. "Yes, Keegan, I know, but from what you reported"—he paused—"it sounded like that was what she wanted. She may even have had chances to get away if she'd tried, but—"

"No." I shook my head, backing away.

"Fin's always had trouble with—"

"He doesn't know her like I do!" I blurted. "None of you do."

Lara stepped forward, placing a hand on my arm.

"What Areos means is that she may not come back willingly, Keeg," she explained softly. "You yourself said that she wanted to stay... and if everything she told you is true, she could very well be married by now."

It was nothing that I hadn't already thought about a hundred times, but it still sent a lead weight sinking into my stomach.

"We just have to be careful with how we go about this, Keeg..." Lara's green eyes were intense as she studied me. "All of our attempts to rescue her haven't worked... and we risk blowing our cover every time we get close. We need to focus on finding Hawk and Icarus," she finished quietly. "We'll talk to Sensei when he gets back in a few days."

I swallowed hard, jerking my head up and down in a shallow nod.

"And though it might be difficult for you to accept," Areos continued, his voice quiet, "sneaking in to save her may be the very last thing that Sparrow wants."

# 2

A STEADY *BEEP, BEEP, BEEP* SLOWLY PENETRATED MY consciousness. The sheets swished beside me, and a moment later the alarm stopped.

I rolled over, blinking my eyes open. Soft gray morning light filtered through the windows at the far end of the room to spill across the floor. Aaron sat on the edge of the bed, his back to me. I could see his muscles flex under his elaborate tattoo as he stretched. I lay motionless for a moment, silently watching him. He stood up and stretched his arms overhead now, crossing the room to open the top drawer of the sleek white dresser beside the window. The soft white curtains stirred in the gentle breeze, brushing against his deep brown skin. He took out a pair of black uniform pants and pulled them on over his boxers.

I closed my eyes when he turned around, pretending to still be asleep. A moment later his quiet footsteps drew closer, and I felt the mattress shift beneath his weight.

"Sparrow."

After a pause I rolled over on my back, looking up at him. His fingertips brushed over my cheek.

"Good morning," he said softly.

I reached up and took his hand in my own to give it a gentle squeeze. "Good morning."

I sat up slowly and pushed back the sheets to slip my legs over the side of the mattress. I stood, smoothed my crumpled T-shirt and made my way over to the dresser while Aaron pulled on his boots. I opened a lower drawer and took out the same RGM uniform I always wore, pulling it on over my underwear and zipping it up to my hips.

"Did you sleep all right?" Aaron asked.

I nodded, pulling a fresh shirt over my head. "You?"

I turned just as he finished lacing up his boots. "I always sleep well when you're beside me." He stood and started for the kitchen. "Coffee?"

I blew out my lips. "I'll need it."

Aaron walked out into the kitchen, and I followed, pausing for a moment when I reached the mirror to give myself a once-over. I ran a hand back over my short, RGM-standard pixie cut and zipped my uniform up a little higher. No matter how much I slept, the dark circles beneath my eyes never seemed to go away. It had only been six months, yet I felt as though I'd aged five years. The burgundy, triangular insignia on my breast pocket signified my rank as corporal. Aaron had been promoted to sergeant.

Pulling myself away from the mirror, I followed Aaron out of the bedroom and into the kitchen. He opened a cabinet and took out a bag of coffee. I stopped at the white marble island in the center of the room and hoisted myself up to sit on the edge. I studied the phoenix tattoo reaching up to his neck and the other on his opposite shoulder blade: claw marks.

"Doesn't it feel like we just had an appointment with Dr. Nakamura?"

Aaron scooped out some of the rich, earthy grinds. "Last month, yeah."

"Why do they keep interrogating us like this?"

"Because they see us as a valuable resource to them." He poured some water into the pot and set it on the single burner. Then he turned and walked over to the counter where I was perched. "Things are getting better," he said quietly. "Think about where we were six months ago and look at where we are today, Spar. They don't trust us—not yet. But they will."

"They ask the same questions every time... and every time I feel like they see straight through me, no matter what I say." I bit my lip, glancing down. "They expected me to be pregnant by now, Aaron. They're going to find us out eventually."

Aaron was thoughtfully silent for a moment. "The RGM can force us to do a lot, Spar. But not that."

His warm lips pressed gently against my forehead in a kiss. I lifted my gaze to meet his and studied his face for a moment, from the small lines across his forehead to his dark eyebrows, to the troubled frown resting on his lips.

"Does it bother you?" I asked quietly.

He tipped his head back to look at me. "Do you need to ask? Sparrow, you're my wife... That's all I've ever wanted, and it's enough for me." His voice was sincere. "I don't care what other people think. What we do is no one's business but ours."

"It's all the RGM's business, Aaron—you and I both know it. Everything we do, everything we say... whether or not we have sex. It's all part of their plan." I drew an irritated breath, stroking my fingertips across my forehead. "God, I just want to get out of here..."

"You know Bask's tripled security, don't you?"

"Of course. Everyone does."

"How easy do you think it would be to escape?" Aaron's voice lowered to a whisper. "And what do you think they would do to us when they caught us?"

The coffee began to percolate on the stove, filling the silence.

"I don't know," I finally answered quietly. "I... I don't know."

"Have a seat." Dr. Nakamura motioned to the sleek stainless-steel bench. "Let's chat."

*Chat.* That was what he called it every time. But it was more like an inquisition.

I closed the door behind me and straightened my jacket, crossing the room to perch on the edge of the examination table. I took a shaky breath and rubbed my sweaty palms along my thighs.

"How have you been feeling?" he asked, running a small, silver wand over my forehead and then over my chest. It made a series of bleeping and clicking noises.

Dr. Nakamura was tall and clean-shaven, with short black hair and glasses. He had to be in his mid-thirties, and he perpetually wore a frown.

"I feel fine," I answered. "Never better."

He nodded, not replying. He checked my pulse and blood pressure, then, seeming neither satisfied nor concerned, he sat down on his swivel stool, folding his hands on his lap and looking at me sternly.

"Are you getting along with your comrades?"

"Yes, just fine."

"I understand that your job has been an irregular one because of your unique position."

I ran my tongue across my lips and nodded hesitantly. "My job is mostly to undergo tests and interviews."

"And to provide intelligence," he added.

My stomach churned as I forced another nod.

"Do you like working with Bask?"

"He's all right." I was lying through my teeth. "We work together fine."

"Good... good. He seems to be pleased with your progress."

I pushed on a fake smile.

"And what about your husband, Sergeant Price?" he asked, bending his leg to rest his ankle on his knee. "How's your marriage going?"

His voice seemed to fade off as my mind reeled back over the past several months. It was still so hard to process the word "marriage"—to accept the fact that I was actually *married*. It had taken me weeks to get used to sharing a bed and months to adjust to living together. Unbeknownst to the RGM, we'd never gone further than a kiss.

"Our marriage is going really well," I said, attempting to inject my voice with some enthusiasm. "We get along really well, and we enjoy being together."

"Great. Are you both supportive of each other's work?"

"Absolutely," I replied.

"And what about your love life?"

"I could use a little more sleep, but I'm not going to complain."

"Excellent," he responded blandly, spinning back around to face the slender monitor protruding from his desk. "As you both know, your fertility tests came back looking great, so it's just a waiting game now, really. You both know it's in the RGM's interest to produce more sliders for our fighting forces—sliders who won't need to be captured and indoctrinated into our system because they will have been born into it. You and Sergeant Price would be helping us break new ground."

A sinking feeling settled inside me. I didn't say a word.

"Not to worry," he said, pecking away at the keypad. "I am a little surprised that you aren't pregnant already, given the results of your and Price's fertility tests. But these things can take time."

I wiped my sweaty palms on my thighs. "What if it just doesn't happen?"

"I wouldn't jump to any bleak conclusions yet." A few more clicks and then a sleek, high-tech scanner spat out a few pages. Dr. Nakamura stapled them together and handed them to me. "Here is some information on the subject that you may find helpful."

I took the papers and gave him a brisk nod. "Great. Thanks."

"Report to Bask now." The doctor stood and opened the door for me. "And I'll see you back here in a month."

Once outside, despite the smoky air, I felt like I could breathe again. I descended the steps and paused for a moment, folding up the papers filled with scientific jargon on baby making and tucking them into my back pocket. Squinting into the sunlight, I scanned the District.

There were twice as many soldiers as there had been when I'd first arrived. Apparently, authorities higher up the chain of command had been so pleased with Bask's accomplishments that they'd granted him more forces to work with, better equipment and, of course, more funds. There were guard towers on every side of the District now, and new barracks for the soldiers.

It was torturous, watching their means and methods getting better and stronger—because of *me*. The more equipped they were, the harder it would be for Aaron and me to finally escape when the day came. A day that seemed to grow more and more distant.

Pushing myself onward, I marched to Bask's office. Aaron was already in the room, though Bask was looking and speaking in the opposite direction from where Aaron actually stood.

"Ah, Turner. Good." Bask waved me farther into the room. "Come in."

I closed the door behind me and walked several paces to stand beside Aaron.

"How did your appointment go?"

"Fine, sir."

"Good. Excellent." He sifted through a few papers before pulling out one in particular.

"Over the past year we've analyzed your various abilities and run a myriad of tests," he began. "We know you can see the invisible, channel, and heal." I watched his eyes carefully as he extended the paper toward me. "Now I think it's time we began to put those abilities to good use."

*Analyzed*. That was how Bask described the long, hard hours of enduring test after test and interrogation after interrogation. They often locked me into one of the sterile white cells and forced me to channel orbs. What they didn't realize was that I was still a fledgling, and it was difficult to do any of these things on command, and when I couldn't produce the results they expected, I was punished with additional workloads.

Aaron, too, had more responsibilities now as a sergeant. He went out on more missions and patrols than ever, but his main duty remained the same: to stay healthy so that they could continue to draw his invisible blood, the main ingredient in the serum they injected their forces with and doused the entire District in.

I stepped forward and took the paper from his hand. It was a large list dotted with black-and-white photos. Names and bounties were listed beneath each, similar to the one I'd been given when I was first captured.

"We've located one of these sliders." Bask's voice punctured my thoughts as he reached over to tap one of the photographs. "And this time, you will accompany us on the capture mission."

My gaze shot up. "What? No. No, I can't! I—"

Bask's dark eyes leveled with mine. "Why not, Turner?"

"I... I just..." I could barely think straight, let alone answer. "I can't—"

"Am I mistaken in believing that your loyalty lies with the RGM, Turner?"

I swallowed back the bile that had risen to my throat. "No, sir, you're not, but I..."

My voice tapered off as I turned to shoot Aaron a look of desperation, hoping he would come up with something to save the situation. Instead, I found him staring straight back at me, his arms crossed over his chest as he waited for me to answer our commander.

"Think carefully before you answer, Turner," Bask cautioned firmly. "Knowing that I have the power to promote you or terminate you with a single command"—he paused and stared at me, unblinking—"will you or will you not accept this mission?"

I looked down at the paper Bask had given me. Circled in ink was a grainy photograph of a young man with steely eyes and tousled dark hair. There was a hefty bounty beneath his name.

And his name was Icarus.

# 3

I AWOKE WITH A START, DRENCHED IN SWEAT. I GROPED in the darkness, trying to make sense of where I was and what was happening. Reality seeped in like steady rain, and I slowly became aware of the canvas mat beneath me, the roof of the shelter above me, and the soft inhalations of Preston and Rafael asleep on either side of me.

Rising to my feet, I pulled on a pair of jeans over my boxers, strapped on my holster and slipped outside. The sky was a dusty predawn blue, dotted with faded pinpricks of stars. I walked into the forest a ways before stopping. The cool, early morning air brushed against my chest. I took a deep breath.

The same nightmare plagued me every single night: every word she'd said... the way she'd felt in my arms. Her skin under my fingertips.

I swallowed back a bitter feeling as I made my way to the target nailed to the pine tree where Rafael had been throwing the day before. I backed up a ways, stopping when the distance was sufficient. I slid a knife out of my shoulder holster, twirling it in my fingers for a moment, focusing on the target ahead. I counted my breaths, my heartbeats, slowly opening my fingers to allow the knife to levitate in my open palm. Warmth radiated from my center and into my hand, vibrating through the skin on my palm. I took aim and threw.

The knife hurtled through the air, spinning again and again, then nailing into the center of the target. Without hesitation I snatched another from my quiver and threw.

It sliced into the wood alongside the first.

I drew another, tossed it into levitation and blasted it forward. Another dull *thwack* pierced the early morning silence.

I curled my trembling fingers into fists, pressing them to my eyelids.

*Why can't I just stop thinking about her? Why can't I stop…?*

"Keegan."

My eyes snapped open. I turned and looked over my shoulder to find my father standing beside a large oak. He wore a thick wool cloak and watched me with curious eyes.

"Dad." My voice came out a little taken aback. "I thought you wouldn't be back for a few more days."

"I finished everything I needed to. They had everything else in hand." He walked up to stand beside me, examining my slashed target for a moment before turning to cast me a probing look. "The dreams?"

I swallowed and nodded. "Do you ever wonder why they never came back?" I finally asked, my voice quiet. "Do you ever wonder what happened to Hawk?"

Dad nodded slowly. "Not a day goes by that I do not search the sky for the silhouettes of her wings, or listen for the sound of her voice on the edge of the wind." His green eyes lifted to the swaying treetops overhead. "I know what it's like to miss someone so much that it doesn't even feel like you're missing someone else, but simply who you used to be with them, because that person is so much a part of you," Dad continued, his voice raw. "It's like a wound that won't heal."

I walked to the target and pulled one of my blades from the bullseye. "You know, if you'd said this a few months ago, I could have agreed with you.

But now..." I shook my head slowly, resting my hands on the faded trunk of the tree. "She fills my mind, Dad. Every moment of every day—but so does everything she said, every last word..." I yanked the second knife from the target and turned around to face my father. "It's like I can't feel anything anymore."

Dad studied me for a long moment, his eyes serious. "Did you expect your feelings to never change, Keegan?"

"If you truly have feelings for someone, shouldn't that be constant?"

"There's nothing constant about feelings," Dad answered. "They come and go like puffs of smoke on the wind."

I slid the knives into my holster. "Your feelings for Hawk never changed."

"There were times when Hawk and I disagreed with each other. Times when we fought like lions. Times when we didn't trust each other. Times when we didn't wait for each other. Times when we questioned each other— lit into each other..." His voice tapered off. "Other times, yes, we loved each other in a million different ways. But our feelings were never the constant thing, not ever."

I studied him, raising an eyebrow. "Then what was?"

For a moment Dad didn't reply. There was something distant in his eyes.

"I loved her, and she loved me," he answered simply. "And that's what kept us together."

I slid the last knife into my holster and straightened my shoulders. "If she loved you, then why didn't she choose you over Icarus?"

The question came out sounding coarser than I'd meant it to, but it didn't seem to bother Dad.

"Hawk and I both knew that there was a bigger purpose, for both of us. We loved each other, and we always will..." His voice trailed off, and then he gave a single nod. "But she loved Icarus too. She is a patriarch... I knew where her destiny lay, and it was not with me."

"And you were all right with that? With—with losing any chance you had of being happy, just so you could... what?" I gestured around us. "Live your life in celibacy out here in the middle of a dead forest? Well, I can't do that, Dad. Sparrow doesn't love me. She told me to my face that night before they released me. She told me that she could never love me like I love her."

"Keegan, I cannot explain to you what love is." Dad stepped closer. "But if it is real, whether she feels the same or not, it won't matter. It won't change your love for her."

My heart was thumping hard in my chest; my gaze sank to the ground as words jammed in my throat. I looked up as Dad set a hand on my shoulder.

"Come." He tipped his head in the direction of the shelter. "I have something to discuss with Areos and Lara, and I would like you to be there."

The swaying pines were now bathed in the soft pastels of dawn as the sun climbed the other side of the mountains. I straightened my holster and followed him through the trees.

When we reached the shelter, Dad pulled the canvas flap aside and held it for me. I paused for a moment, noticing the quiver of arrows leaned up against one wall. The long, slender sticks Kateri had been carving with her knife were now smooth, ornate arrows.

My lips curved into a smile.

"Keegan," Dad prompted, still holding the flap for me.

I snapped out of it, stepping forward and grabbing the canvas flap.

It was dim and almost empty inside except for Preston and Janna, who were sitting together on one of the floor cushions, kissing. Janna pulled away from Preston, startled, when she heard the canvas flap shut. I crossed my arms over my chest and shot Preston a look. He jumped to his feet.

"S-sorry, Sensei. We didn't realize anyone else was up."

Dad shooed them toward the door. "Away with the two of you. Go wake the others and start your daily tasks."

Preston grumbled a little, still teasing Janna as he chased her playfully out of the tent. Dad gestured for me to follow him to his office.

He slid off the pack he was carrying and rolled up the sleeves of his overshirt. "I have to confess that I didn't tell you the whole truth when I said I was going only to the school in Algeria," he began, dropping his stuff in a corner and beginning to pace.

"You didn't go to Algeria after all?"

"I did, but only for a few hours," he replied. "I then went to every single other school we have established to appoint new leadership."

I quirked an eyebrow. "New leadership?"

He didn't say anything for a moment, seeming lost in thought. Before he could answer, the canvas flap brushed aside, and Lara stepped in. She was wrapped in a blue cotton shawl, and her long, wavy hair flowed down over her shoulders. Areos trailed behind her.

"Morning," she said as they each took a cross-legged seat on one of the floor cushions.

Lara and Dad didn't say anything to each other, but from the glance they exchanged, I could tell that they both knew something that I didn't. I also couldn't help but notice that Dad's sudden return hadn't surprised them.

"We've spent the past several months looking for a way to get back into the District to rescue Sparrow," Dad began again, his green eyes scanning the maps and notations on the walls around us. "Each time, it's become more and more obvious that we need to find another way to go about this. The RGM has expanded their security, making their walls nearly impenetrable..." He paused, gesturing in my direction. "Walls only Keegan can see through by reading other people's minds."

I bit my lip, thinking back to the last time I'd used my abilities. We'd been such a long way away from the District, yet we'd encountered soldiers. Through the mind of the soldier I'd been able to tap into, I could see that we were miles from the gates—and surrounded by too many other security personnel to count. They'd seemed to come out of the woodwork, patrolling the surrounding forest and making it impossible to get anywhere near the looming gray wall that wrapped the prison camp.

I brushed away the sinking feeling in my gut, turning my attention back to Dad.

"We need to take a different approach," he continued. "Hawk and Icarus must be found. Not only do we need them, but they are their daughter's only hope of making it out of the District alive."

"Although there may not be much they can do, either," Areos added sullenly.

Dad shot him a look. "I do not pretend to have all the answers, Areos, but I have no doubt in Hawk's and Icarus's abilities. As Sparrow has grown older, it's become clearer and clearer to me that she needs them."

"She doesn't even believe that they exist, though," Areos countered.

"That doesn't matter."

"Keegan said himself that Sparrow told him she wanted to stay in the District," Areos argued. "She may even want to be a part of the RGM. What makes you think Hawk and Icarus can convince her otherwise—even if they could get that close to her?"

"Because they're her identity," Dad responded without hesitation, looking over at Lara to add, "You should know how that feels."

I glanced at Lara. She nodded solemnly, and a look of understanding slowly passed over Areos's face.

"Even when I was trapped inside the forces of the RGM," Lara said, "I knew inside that I was different... special. That I was meant for something more." She drew an unsteady breath, a distant look in her eyes. "And when I found Icarus, he affirmed it. He gave me hope, and because of that... I finally began to discover who I really was."

Areos nodded slowly and glanced from Lara to Fin. "Do you think if we found them, they would have some power to get through to her? To free her?"

Dad bowed his head. "I do think so, yes." His reply was solemn. "Which is why we have to act now—we've already wasted too much time."

"What do you mean?" I questioned.

"I mean that we have to find Hawk and Icarus before the RGM figures out who Sparrow is." Dad's voice gained momentum with his reply. "Which is why I am leaving you."

"Leaving?" I blurted, stunned. "What are you talking about?"

Dad took a seat on the ground across from me.

"I found Hawk once," he began quietly, a far-off look coming into his eyes. "The only thing that has prevented me from doing so again is my responsibility to my students. But now, I would be neglecting my responsibility to all of you if I didn't go."

I could tell that now was not the time to question my father. Even Areos remained silent.

I straightened my shoulders. "Let me come with you."

Without even considering the idea, Dad shook his head. "I need you here, Keegan."

"Why? Surely Lara and Areos can handle—"

"That's the thing, Keegan," Lara interrupted gently. "I'm... we're leaving."

My gaze shot to hers. "What? Why?"

"Areos has to go back to Section C," she explained. "And I'm going with him to help him run the school in Sensei's absence."

"Lara and I have discussed the matter in depth," Dad went on before I could say anything. "We've decided that you and Kateri should lead the group in our absence."

My eyes grew wide. "What? I—I don't know anything about—"

"You and Kateri both have shadowed Lara and me for many years now," Dad interrupted, his tone gentle but confident. "You both have been here longer than any of the other healers. You have plenty of experience, and you've proven yourselves again and again." He paused, his eyes probing mine. "You are no longer children. You have both reached maturity, and it's time for your responsibilities to reflect that fact."

I hardly knew what to say. I was reeling.

"Dad, I... I don't know if I'm ready to take all this on." My voice came out unevenly. "The last time I was responsible for the safety of the group, we lost Raf and Janna, and..." My voice cracked, and I stopped, sucking in a deep breath. "If someone else had been leading, maybe Sparrow would never have been captured."

I felt the warmth of fingertips against my skin as Lara reached over to put a hand on my shoulder. "You can't know what would have happened. Things could have been even worse..."

My jaw tightened as I pulled away from her. "There are things I could have done differently. I'm not going to lie to myself..." My eyes met Dad's. "But I trust your judgment much more than my own."

Dad's expression remained serious. "Were it not for my trust in both of you, I wouldn't be able to go."

I bowed my head, a lump forming in my throat. "Does Kateri know about this?" I asked.

"No, not yet," Dad answered. "I thought perhaps you would like to tell her."

# 4

"SHE'S STILL TOO MUCH OF A SLIDER, PRICE. SHE STILL HASN'T accepted the RGM way of life. I can feel the resistance when she steps into the room..." Bask paused, trailing off to lift the glass of whiskey to his mouth and take a long swig. "We need to make her one of us—to include her in more missions."

"Forcing Sparrow to do something she's not ready for will achieve nothing, sir," I argued. "She's my wife; I know her. I've spent the last several months learning everything there is to know about her. She resents being a slider every bit as much as I do, and she's ready and willing to serve—"

"Then she won't object to more assignments," he cut in. "She should be arriving at any moment to discuss exactly that."

The muscles in my jaw tightened. "What is it you want from her?"

Bask downed the rest of his alcohol and refilled the glass. "I want her to go out on the next hunt."

"For whom?"

My commander shuffled through the mess of scattered papers on his desk, finally picking up one in particular and thrusting it at me.

"See for yourself."

I walked forward a few paces to snatch the paper out of his hands. I scanned the rows of grainy black-and-white photographs until my eyes caught on the one that was circled in ink.

"Icarus?" I blurted, dumbfounded. "But he's—"

"One of the ringleaders, yes." Bask nodded and gulped his whiskey. "What better way to test her?"

I folded the paper in half, my palms beginning to sweat. "Where was he detected?"

"All the details will be discussed at the briefing."

"When is this mission to take place?"

"In three days."

I cursed inwardly, rubbing a hand over my jaw as I paced to one end of the room. I stood for a long moment, trying to think of what to say. Bask spoke before I did.

"Price, it's like training a horse. The only way to get it to obey is to break it first." He leaned back in his chair, folding his hands over his stomach. "Do you want a drink?"

I ignored his offer. "Let Sparrow get better acclimated before you task her with something of this scale," I shot back through gritted teeth. "I'll do it—let me go."

"There is no better way to acclimate a slider to the RGM than to make them turn their back on their own—to capture and kill their own..." He paused. "It worked with you, didn't it?"

My stomach churned as I strode back across the room to his desk.

"She isn't ready for this," I said sternly. "Wait a while—*please*." Desperation had seeped into my tone.

Bask stared straight ahead. "I'm tired of waiting, Price," he replied icily. "And unfortunately, we still find ourselves waiting for a lot of things."

"Such as?"

"Better utilizing Sparrow to capture the rest of her group who escaped our grasp at the Homestead," he began, numbering off on his fingers. "Better utilizing the two of you as a team to capture and kill rebellious sliders—and above all, having the two of you produce the RGM's very own slider forces."

I studied him for a moment. "You know I would like nothing better."

Bask frowned suspiciously. "Then why hasn't it happened?"

"Sometimes it takes longer when there's so much pressure to make it happen," I offered, trying to sound convincing. "We both want to start a family just as much as the RGM wants us to."

Bask's eyes twitched back and forth as he searched the empty air in front of him.

"You're hiding something from me, Price." His voice was like the hiss of a snake. "I can sense it."

"I am not, sir."

He grunted, a smirk tweaking his lips. "You'd better not be. Because if I find out that you are, I'll tell your sweet wife that you were the one who lured her back here—"

"Stop—"

"That Keegan had already been captured and locked up—that *you* had been the one to find him and lock him up. That there was *never* a chance of saving him. That you made it all up just to get her back here so you could have her for yourself—"

I slammed my hands down on his desk, grabbing a handful of papers and crumpling them in my fists. "If you tell her, I will *kill you*."

He stared hollowly ahead for a moment, expressionless. Then his lips slowly parted in a grin, revealing yellowed teeth.

"You wouldn't do that." He leaned back with his glass, draining the rest of it. "Not when I hold everything you value in the palm of my hand." His dark eyes glinted. "Including your wife."

My heart hammered in my chest. Swallowing hard, I slowly released the fistfuls of paper and backed away.

Before either of us could say another word, the door burst open, and Sparrow stepped inside.

"Ah, Turner, good." Bask gestured her forward. "Come in."

"I can't do it! I can't, I—*I can't…*"

A sick feeling sank in my stomach in spite of myself as I sat on the end of the bed, watching Sparrow pace the bedroom floor. She massaged her temples anxiously, scanning the room as if searching for a way out.

"I can't go out with them. I can't capture a slider—Aaron, why didn't you say something?"

"What was I supposed to say, Spar? *No?*" I sighed. "Look, when he informed me of his plan, I tried to convince him it wasn't a good idea, that you needed more time to acclimate, but I had to be careful. I didn't want to blow our cover. You know he already doubts your loyalty to the RGM."

Sparrow grunted. "And he believes you *are* loyal. God, I'm *so sick* of living a lie."

My gaze dropped to the floor. "Why don't you tell me how your appointment with Dr. Nakamura went?"

She sighed, walking over to the bed. "They asked me a bunch of questions about how I like my work, how I'm adjusting, how I like being married to you."

I perked an eyebrow. "How *do* you like it?"

"We get along, don't we?" Sparrow closed the gap between us to fold her arms around my neck. She just hung there for a minute, seeming to hug me more out of exhaustion than anything else. "They want me to get pregnant— to use us as breeding stock for the RGM."

"Yes, I know. Bask talked to me about it too." I gently ran my hand over her back. "But we knew they were suspicious about us back when they first gave us fertility tests."

"Which came back without any issues." Sparrow sighed. "Do you think Bask knows that we've never…"

"Never had sex? No. I've assured both him and Nakamura that we have a normal marriage and that it's just a matter of time. They have no reason to doubt it."

Sparrow grunted a laugh. "No reason to doubt it until now, you mean?" She drew back to look me in the face.

For a moment I just studied her. Her dark brown hair was trimmed down to a standard RGM cut, her skin was tanned from the summer sun, and her dark eyebrows arched as she studied me intently. Her lips were turned downward in a thoughtful frown.

Every time I looked at her, I was reminded of how beautiful she was, how lucky I was. Every time we went anywhere together and I noticed how many guys looked at us—at her, really, since they couldn't see me—when I saw the jealousy in their eyes, it made me realize that I had *everything*.

But everything hung by a thread. A thread that could break at any moment.

"Sparrow." I slid my hands gently down her arms. "They only know what we tell them. Bask thinks he's the one in control, but he's not—*I am. I own* him, Sparrow. I control him. He would be *nothing* without my blood—he knows that. What is true for Bask is whatever *I* decide is true for him... He can't control us. He can't control *you*."

A troubled look stirred in her eyes. "But what if he finds out? What if he—"

"He can't force you to have sex with me, Sparrow. I would never let that happen," I cut in gently. "If you begin to feel that you love me—"

"I do care about you, Aaron," she interrupted. "And in my own way, I do love you."

"I know you do... but you know what I mean, Spar..." I tilted my head to the side, giving her a look. "If you ever want to go there, I am yours. I always have been. I always will be..."

I leaned a little closer, slowly, carefully. Her dark eyes remained connected with mine, but then slid down to my lips as I drew closer. My fingers caressed her cheek. My lips were nearly touching hers when I stopped.

"May I kiss you?" I whispered.

I felt Sparrow nod, her forehead making slight contact with mine.

I let my mouth merely graze against hers. I waited until I felt her begin to reciprocate before moving my lips slowly over hers. They were full and soft and sweet. Intoxicating. I drank her in like water, cradling her face with one hand and letting my other slide to her lower back.

Finally, we drew away from each other.

"Sparrow, you're going to have to go out on this next mission with them," I began softly, looking into her face, circling my thumb over her cheek. "I'm sorry, but there's nothing I can do."

Sparrow looked at me for a moment before giving me one last kiss. "It's not your fault," she whispered, stepping away.

I felt a pang of guilt as the warmth of her lips faded, leaving a cold feeling across mine. She said something about coffee as she turned and walked out of the bedroom and into the kitchen. I didn't say anything; I just sat there for a moment with the ghosts of her words seeming to hang suspended in the still atmosphere.

*It's not your fault.*

I dropped back onto the mattress, staring up at the ceiling, numb.

*She has no idea.*

# 5

"WHY?" PRESTON'S DARK EYEBROWS FURROWED. "WHY would you leave now, when things are more dire than ever, Sensei?"

When we had all gathered in the main room for an evening meal, Dad filled the rest of our group in on the plan: that he, Lara, and Areos were all leaving Section West.

"All of this—living out here in hiding, having to suppress so much of our powers—is temporary. I hope you know that this is the case," Dad answered, looking around at all of us. "Sometimes we have to step out of our comfort zone and do something that may not even make sense in order to accomplish what we are truly meant for. I am doing this for all of you."

Kateri leaned forward on her knees beside me. "Finding the patriarchs, you mean?"

Dad bowed his head in a nod. "We are not meant to live so long without them. Sparrow's situation reflects this," he explained, a far-off look in his eyes. "There is a void without Hawk and Icarus."

For a moment there was silence. Then Janna spoke up.

"Sensei, with all due respect," she began slowly. "They've been lost to us for a long time... What if they..." Her voice trailed off.

"Janna," Dad replied softly, "a wise soul once told me that nothing is ever truly lost..." He paused and glanced at each of us. "Hold on to that."

"And what happens in the meantime?" Myung spoke up now. "With you, Lara, and Areos all gone—who leads us?"

Out of the corner of my eye I could see Kateri seated beside me; I could feel her eyes on me as she passed me a glance.

"I've asked Kateri and Keegan to be in charge of making sure everything runs smoothly in our absence," Dad explained. "Respect them as brothers and sisters, but in truth I want all of you to stop searching for someone to elevate as a leader or teacher."

"What do you mean, Sensei?" Rafael questioned from the opposite end of the mat, where he sat beside Lara and Areos. "You are our sensei—you've taught us everything. You've raised us."

"Yes, that is true—but the answer lies within the question, Rafael," Dad replied. "I *have* raised you... but you are no longer children." He laid a hand on his chest. "You will find a constant teacher within."

"Our hearts?" Preston questioned.

"What resides within your hearts," Dad replied. "Your source... your true self. The limitless beings all of you really are; all that is and all that can be." His eyes drifted to mine. "It is already inside you. I am here only to remind you to look inside yourself."

Dad's words stayed with me, echoing in my mind long after everyone had dispersed. I went to the overlook and sat down on the old tree stump, losing myself in thought as I stared out over the expanse beyond the trees, turning his words over and over in my mind.

It still felt surreal: the idea of leading while Dad was away. I couldn't shake the feeling that I somehow wasn't fit for it after what had happened. It had been a miracle that we'd even gotten Raf and Janna back... Sparrow was still living with the consequences of my actions.

I pressed my eyelids shut, rolling the tension out of my neck and shoulders, breathing deeply. I felt like a vise just kept tightening inside me.

The soft pad of footsteps snagged my attention. I caught glimpses of Lara's golden blonde hair as she made her way towards me among the groups of pines.

"Are you meditating?" she asked quietly when she entered the clearing.

I shook my head, and a moment later she sank down on the stump beside me.

"I'm sorry I didn't tell you about it before, Keeg," she began gently. "I wanted to, but I knew that Fin needed to be the one to tell you."

"I know," I replied quietly, looking out at the soft dusky sky. "You don't need to apologize."

"You just seem a little upset about it."

"To normal people we must seem so strange... We all look around the same age, yet you're hundreds of years older than me." A weak smile tugged at one corner of my mouth. "To the outside world you look like my sister, and in some ways you are. Yet you raised me right alongside Dad. You taught me how to throw knives, how to levitate and channel—how to talk to girls. Since Dad rescued me that day when Galway fell, you've been like a mother to me, and I—I guess..." The lump in my throat strangled out my voice as tears stung in my eyes.

"It's not going to be forever, Keeg," she said softly. "Just until your dad finds Hawk and Icarus."

"I know," I said. "I know, but..." I stopped, choking up.

Lara bit her lip, tears welling in her own eyes. She folded an arm around me, kissing the top of my head. A tear escaped my eye to flow down my cheek.

"I'm afraid of screwing everything up like last time, Lara," I whispered at last. "I'm afraid that something will happen again—something even worse."

"Keegan, listen to me." She drew back, lifting my chin so that my gaze met hers. "You were not to blame for what happened. You need to let go of the guilt you feel so that you can help prepare everyone for what will happen next..." Her tone was soft but firm. "This is all we have, Keegan. This moment, *right now*. Focus on that."

"But Sparrow..." I stopped, my voice crumpling as I spoke her name. My eyelids sank shut. "She's not here, and it's my fault..."

"We can't change other people," Lara answered quietly. "As much as we may wish we could sometimes, the only real change comes from inside. You have to let go of feeling responsible for what Sparrow thinks about herself. There is only one person you can control, Keeg. And that's you. You, and those thoughts of yours. Don't just let yourself wander aimlessly through this life—take hold of it by the horns." She tapped my forehead. "Use that mind. Be the leader I know you can be," she said gently, blinking back her own tears. "That's how you can help Sparrow... That's how you can help *everyone*."

I stared at the ceiling of the tent, listening to Cub breathe peacefully beside me, her thick, soft coat brushing up against my skin with each of her inhalations. She smelled like soil and fresh air. I stroked my fingers gently over her fuzzy head.

With the dawn, Dad, Lara, and Areos would be gone. We would say goodbye, not knowing how long it would be before we would all see each other again. The thought felt unbearable.

Massaging the stiffness out of my neck, I stood, slipping out of the shelter and into the warm blanket of darkness enshrouding the forest. The moon was ripe on the horizon, and the shadows of the trees fell across the dewy ground. In the clearing ahead, I could make out the shape of a familiar figure.

Kateri lay stretched out on a thick quilt, bathed in the moonlight, and staring up at the faded stars. She didn't stir as I walked quietly over and sat down beside her, hugging my knees to my chest and craning my neck to peer up at the night sky.

"Isn't it beautiful?" she asked softly.

I glanced down at her.

She lifted one hand from the soft blanket to gesture toward the starry dome above us. "Even when they are lost in the light of the moon, their starlight doesn't fade," she went on quietly. "They still shine."

"Mmm." I nodded slowly. "And when the moon is dark?"

She ran a hand back through her wild dark hair, which spilled out like a veil around her head. "That's when they shine the brightest."

I sat there for a moment longer, my arms looped around my knees as I stared up at the sky. Then I lay down beside her. "I know my dad trusts us, and I trust you more than anyone," I began, my voice barely a whisper. "I'm just... I'm afraid of what could happen."

"Because of losing Sparrow?" Kateri rolled over to rest her head on her arm, the moon casting shadows over her warm brown skin as her deep eyes seemed to probe mine. "Do you still love her?"

The question startled me. I took a breath to reply, but I couldn't find the right words.

"I know that you loved her when she first came here," she continued gently. "I saw a light in your eyes whenever she walked into the room. You looked at her like she was the sun..." She trailed off. "You looked at her the way I look at you," she said finally.

I felt a fluttering in my chest, as if I'd swallowed butterflies. I stared at her for a moment, rendered speechless in the wake of her words. Everything seemed to melt away—the trees, the wind, the moon, the stars. The only night sky was in her eyes.

"Kateri, I..." I faltered, sighing. "I... I did, once, you're right, but now I..."

Kateri waited, her eyes soft and understanding.

"But now," I began again, "I know that Sparrow and I were never meant to be."

Kateri didn't say anything right away, but I could feel those dark eyes reading my mind. "Sometimes we still love someone," she said, "even if we're not meant to be—"

"No." I felt my jaw clench as I shook my head. "No. I don't feel anything for her anymore, Kateri. I just feel... I feel..." I paused, letting go of a sigh. "I feel empty. Like I'm not even who I was before she came here."

"None of us is the same as who we were, Keegan," Kateri responded quietly. "We've each changed. You don't have to be who you were before. You only need to be true to who you really are inside, the one who Sensei believes you can be."

I lay there for a moment, watching the light from the moon sparkling in her eyes.

"And what if I fail?" I whispered at last. "What then?"

Her eyes scanned my face. "You cannot fail to be someone you already are, Keeg," she answered quietly. "The stars do not strive to become stars... They simply shine."

I didn't have a response to that. I just stared at her, wondering how she always knew exactly what I needed to hear. In her presence, I felt like my gift paled in comparison to everything she possessed.

"We're going to be fine, Keegan," she finished in a whisper. "We can do this... I know we can."

# 6

I SAT ON THE EDGE OF OUR BED AND STUDIED THE LIST OF wanted sliders Bask had given me. I couldn't stop staring at the photograph of Icarus, studying every line, every shadow, every feature of his face.

His intense eyes seemed to pierce my own, crowned by tousled dark hair. His sharp jawline was covered in stubble, and his lips were parted, as if in mid-sentence. There was something beyond mere color swirling in his eyes. There was something else, something like gold hidden away in a mineshaft. There was a *mystery*.

It was so strange to be looking at a picture of someone I hadn't even believed was real for so many years. It was even stranger to know that in a couple of short days it would be my job to help hunt him down and bring him into the RGM's custody.

The front door opened and shut hard, startling me out of my thoughts. Folding the paper, I stood and tucked it into the front pocket of my pants. I walked out into the kitchen just as Aaron came in from the entryway on the opposite side of the room. A tired smile curved across his lips when he saw me.

"Hey, Spar."

I slowed to a stop at the kitchen island, tracing my fingers along the cool metal surface. "Hey."

Aaron pulled off his beret and tossed it onto the table, crossing the room to take a glass out of one of the cabinets and fill it with whiskey.

"How was your day?" I asked.

"Fine," he replied. "Just patrols."

"Yeah? Whereabouts?" I probed.

"The forest. The place where the Homestead was."

My stomach sank at the word 'was.' It was still so unbearable to imagine the sweet, weathered cabin, surrounded by gardens and flowers, destroyed by flames and reduced to rubble. It was hard to remember why I'd hated it so much when Fin had first taken me there; it was hard to remember anything beyond how dear it all had become to me.

"And?"

Aaron shrugged, draining the glass. "Just routine. We didn't expect to find anything." He set the glass down and turned around to look at me, a knowing look in his brown eyes. "Don't worry, Sparrow, please. I wouldn't keep anything from you."

I blew out an anxious sigh. "I know, Aaron. I know you wouldn't. But in the morning, I have my briefing with Bask... There's no way I'll be able to make it through without exposing what I really feel."

"Spar, you've been doing—"

"No, no. I haven't been," I objected before he could finish reassuring me. "I've been struggling this whole time, Aaron. You of all people should be able to see that. It makes me sick to think of helping them—to consider how much I have already helped them by allowing them to study my powers..."

I rubbed a hand over my forehead, feeling a sick sensation starting to churn in the pit of my stomach.

"Aaron, we have to get out of here... We have to at least *try*. We need to just trust that everything is going to be all right and grab hold of the first opportunity we have to run—"

"Sparrow, I've already told you, we can't just *leave*," he returned firmly. "Can't you see what's happening?"

"All I see is the RGM getting more and more powerful because of us!" My voice rose, choked and ragged. "I can't take it anymore! I can't just stand by and watch them take it all back, piece by piece! I can't—*I won't*!"

Aaron's jaw tightened as he stepped closer, his eyes locked on my own.

"Sparrow, we are *surrounded*... If you weaken now, if you break, we will both regret it. And every single other slider—those people you call family?" He left only a few inches between us as he lowered his voice. "They will all be made to pay for it sooner or later."

I studied his hard expression. "You still talk like you're one of them... like you *want* to be here—like you don't want to leave."

Aaron's gaze was unflinching. I could feel his breath on my face as he drew a shaky inhale and let it all back out again.

"Sparrow, you have no idea how hard I have to work at keeping it together every single day—to keep the act going..." His eyes narrowed to resentful slits. "I'm the one powering this place—every unit in the District, every prisoner. I've made them what they are. If they didn't have my blood, they wouldn't have anything."

"Doesn't that make you want to escape all the more?"

"Of course it does," he answered emphatically. "But we have to bide our time. We can't lose our heads this far into the game—we have the power to bring the RGM to its knees, Sparrow—do you realize that?"

"What are you talking about?"

He lifted a finger to his lips, leaning over my shoulder to whisper in my ear.

"What happens when someone becomes addicted to a substance, Sparrow?" he asked. "When you try something and get hooked... when you just can't seem to stop chasing the next hit..."

My eyebrows knitted together in confusion as he drew back to look at me.

"Dependence," he concluded. "It's one of the most vulnerable positions you can be in, Sparrow. It keeps you awake at night—it keeps you sweating. This realization that you've become so entangled that you cannot even contemplate a life without it. A life without it seems like death; it is inconceivable. You would rather not exist than exist without it." He paused, staring at me. "We are the RGM's addiction, Sparrow."

I swallowed hard as Aaron searched my face.

"And if we stay," he continued, "if we wait... we have the ability to poison them with it."

"And in the meantime?" I asked. "What do we do, Aaron? Just let them slowly drain the life out of us? Let them hunt and kill other sliders—*assist* them with it?"

He didn't answer; he just stood there staring down at me with that same unreadable expression in his eyes.

"I'm sorry, Aaron." I crossed my arms over my chest and slowly shook my head. "I can't do it anymore."

"You have to, Sparrow. You don't have a choice!"

"You were the one who told me that I didn't have to! You were the one who told me that we were going to get out of here—that you wanted to! That you were on my side!"

His face hardened. "I *am* on your side, Sparrow. Which is why I'm telling you that you have to do this—they're not asking you to kill him; they're just asking you to help find him."

I spat a cynical laugh. "Oh, *just* that—what do you think they're going to do with him, Aaron? Have him over for coffee? I can't go along with it. I can't help them capture Icarus..."

Aaron's gaze snapped back to mine. "The RGM knows he's a ringleader. That's why they want him."

"And that's exactly why we need him."

"We, as in...?"

"We, as in the *sliders*—the anomalies, the protectors of Earth, Aaron, of whom you are one no matter how much you seem to fight it sometimes."

Aaron's jaw hardened. "I will never be one of them. I am not going to lie to you and tell you that I'll just accept it."

"Icarus didn't kill your father, Aaron."

Aaron just stood there, staring down at the space between us.

"Sparrow, I don't want them to find Icarus or kill him either..." he began quietly. "But you know as well as I do that if you don't go, our cover will be blown. They'll know how you really feel... that you're not loyal to the RGM. They'll figure out what you really are—and you should expect no mercy from them. Not if you interfere with something of this magnitude."

I swallowed back the tight lump that had begun to form in my throat. "Aaron, if you love me, you'll try to prevent this from happening."

His eyes leveled with mine. "Sparrow, do you think I actually have the power to do such a thing?"

I stepped closer, reaching up to gently place a hand on his cheek. "You had enough power to make them let Keegan go."

One of his eyelids twitched as he scanned my face; something I couldn't read swirled in his dark eyes. Finally, he leaned in and kissed me softly on the lips.

"I'll see what I can do," he whispered. "I'll try my best."

# 7

I STEPPED INTO DAD'S OFFICE, PULLING THE CANVAS FLAP shut behind me. The sudden disturbance was enough to make him turn away from the map on the wall that he was studying. He was already wearing his pack and carrying his long hiking stick in one hand.

Crossing the room, I clasped him in an embrace.

"I'm sorry," I said simply, stepping back. "I'm sorry for the way I spoke to you yesterday. It was wrong of me to question you."

Dad shook his head. "Questioning is the way of the student, Keegan. Question everything, even me... even yourself," he added, straightening his pack, looking me in the eyes. "Your heart, your motives. Your desires. Question *them* too, Keegan."

"I will, Dad," I said quietly. "I promise."

Dad clapped me on the back, and together we walked out into the morning sunshine. Everyone had assembled in the clearing just beyond the shelter. The same clearing where Kateri and I had lain out under the stars the night before. I spotted her right away, locked in conversation with Lara. She was gesturing with her hands, smiling, and saying something I couldn't quite make out. Her long, dark hair was pulled into a loose side braid, and a colorful woven poncho was draped over her shoulders.

For a moment I didn't hear anything beyond her distant laughter. Then I turned my attention to Dad.

"There isn't enough time for me to convey just how much each of you means to me, and how much I believe in you," Dad began. "I hope that you already know this within yourselves. Believe in yourselves... Rely on each other. Work as one body with many moving parts; do not compete against one another, but flow together like water surging toward the same ocean." He paused, glancing around at all of us. "And remember, I am always with you."

With that, Dad slowly made his way around the circle, embracing each of us. I noticed him place something into each student's hand, closing their palm to a fist before I could catch a glimpse of what it was. When Dad stopped in front of me, he lifted my hand and reached into his pack for something.

"It will not be long before we see each other again," he said quietly. "But until then, lead with bravery and faith." He placed something soft and light into my hand, curling my fingers closed around it. "Lead yourself... and by doing so, you will lead others."

I opened my hand when Dad let go. Resting in my palm was a soft brown feather that faded gradually to bright white at the tip. I looked up at him questioningly, but he only offered a subtle smile.

"Ask Kateri to tell you what it means," he said quietly.

I gazed over his shoulder to the place where Kateri was standing. She was examining something in her own hand. I bowed my head in a nod. "I just wish I was coming with you to find her."

"I know you do," Dad said, studying my face. "And it means more to me than you realize."

I pushed on a smile. "If anyone can find her, it's you."

Dad dipped his chin in grateful acknowledgment and stepped back. He stood in the middle of the clearing, waiting while Lara and Areos made the same rounds, saying goodbye to everyone. Lara cursed me quietly for making her cry when we hugged, and then we all watched respectfully as they filed out of the clearing and trekked into the thicker part of the woods to transport. No one spoke until they were fully out of sight.

Janna turned to face the rest of us. "So... what do we do now?"

There was a moment of tense silence. I could feel the burn of everyone's gaze as my mind raced for an answer.

"We carry on." Kateri spoke up after a moment. "We train in secret, just as we have been. We keep getting stronger, and braver, and more confident in our own abilities so that we are ready when Sensei and the patriarchs return."

Janna toyed anxiously with her thick, wavy hair. "*If* they return, you mean."

I stepped forward now, sliding the feather carefully into the front pocket of my pants as I shook my head. "No, she means *when*. Sensei didn't leave this open for debate—they *are* coming back. Things *are* going to change. Kateri's right... We need to be preparing ourselves for everything that will come. Does anyone think we're actually going to stay here in hiding forever?"

There was a hesitation. Then Myung raised her hand.

I rolled my eyes. "Come on, guys, seriously."

Preston spoke up. "I guess we're all just kinda tired of having to keep our abilities a secret. I know I miss bending light—especially when I'm surrounded by a forest that needs it."

"And water," Rafael added.

"Well, I can still use my ability," Myung interjected, crossing her arms over her chest. "Making music is something that can easily and safely be done indoors, where I belong and where everyone is safe from the RGM's detection."

Preston slowly clapped.

Kateri stepped forward before Myung could retort. "Great point."

I turned to look at Kateri, practically able to see the ideas swirling in her eyes as she glanced at the forest around us.

"Right now, we are trying to evade the RGM's detection," she began slowly. "We don't want to blow our cover, especially with Sensei and Lara away... We don't want to give them anything that could potentially help them track us down—they know who we are, and they're still looking for us, I'm sure. But just because we have to live in hiding right now doesn't mean that we can't be... well, who we are," Kateri continued. "Raf, you want to channel water—Janna too."

Raf nodded eagerly as Janna glanced up.

"Then do those things. Make a pond in the shelter," she concluded. "Keegan can grow some trees. Preston, you can give them the light they need."

"Trees in the shelter?" Preston looked about as puzzled as I felt. "The clearance might be a little bit of an issue, Kateri."

"Small ones, then," she persisted. "Fruit trees. Flowering trees. Ones that will fit indoors."

She gestured toward a still skeptical Myung. "Myung will create musical wind for the leaves to dance in, and a song for the trickling pond."

"What about you?" Rafael piped up. "What about your own abilities?"

"Oh, don't worry, Raf." Kateri smiled. "I'll be providing the butterflies."

I couldn't help but smile.

Kateri had rescued the day and our newly christened leadership within the group. Though there was actually fewer of us now, the shelter buzzed with more activity than it had in months. For a while, it was like everyone forgot about why we were really out here, and that Dad was gone.

Though it wasn't my natural tendency, Dad had taught me how to channel growth well enough to make growing the trees Kateri had requested no task at all. Preston worked with me, tossing an orb of warm, white light from one hand to the other, then blasting it up into the fresh green growth as each cherry tree and lanky birch sprang from the ground below to spiral up to the ceiling.

"Don't give them too much light, Pres, or they'll send the roof crashing down," I joked, dusting off my hands as I stepped back. "I don't know why we didn't think of this before. I mean, yeah, we've been training... but not on this scale." I paused, looking around at the vivid, green terrarium the shelter was fast becoming. "This is what we should be doing."

Preston massaged the light between his hands and nodded. "It's no wonder Sensei left her in charge. Why he chose you, though..." He shot me a teasing glance and shrugged his shoulders.

"Hey, I'm trying my level best to keep up with her, all right?" I snorted. "I'd like to see you try."

He glanced at me over his shoulder. "No, thanks. I think I would need a machete to hack through the chemistry between the two of you."

"Between Kateri and me?" I repeated, shrugging it off. "No. There's nothing like..." I trailed off, the previous night flooding my brain. It was impossible to shake off Kateri's open, honest words.

*"You looked at her like she was the sun... You looked at her the way that I look at you..."*

I blew out the rest in a sigh. "I don't know, Pres. It's too soon."

Preston thought about it, his expression no longer teasing but serious. "It's been six months, Keegan."

"That's nothing," I countered quietly as my gaze came to rest on Kateri. She stood beside Raf by the pond that now occupied a quarter of the shelter. Raf dangled one hand into it as it filled with rich, turquoise water. When Kateri wasn't looking, he lifted his opposite hand and shot a splash of water her way. She gasped and started laughing.

Preston came up alongside me, following my gaze.

"You don't have to punish yourself for what happened to Sparrow," Preston said, keeping his voice low.

"It's not that," I said, and then debated whether I should even continue. Whether I even knew *how* to continue. "It's just that..."

"You still feel something for Sparrow?"

"I know that it's over with Sparrow. She told me that she didn't love me," I said quietly. "That she wanted to marry that bastard Price. That she could never love someone who embraced being a slider like I did. She told me that flat out—that she didn't love me and never had. I'll never be with Sparrow,

Pres. Even if she left him and came back to us—no matter what, it's never going to happen between us."

Preston looked puzzled. "What makes you so sure about that?"

I couldn't tell him—I'd promised Dad I wouldn't tell a soul. Even if I could, I was fairly certain that Preston wouldn't believe a word of it.

Hawk and Icarus *had* to be found—not just because they were patriarchs, but because they were Sparrow's *parents*. I doubted that anyone would believe that. I only believed it because I knew Sparrow better than anyone...

Or at least that was what I had believed.

I stepped back, pulling out of my thoughts.

"Nothing, Pres," I answered, something hard and final making its way into my tone as I drove out the ghosts. "Everything between Sparrow and me is done—finished."

He looked at me for a long moment, then nodded slowly. He glanced back across the shelter at Kateri.

"Then don't be afraid of what might be there for you now, Keeg—*who* might be there," he responded quietly, stepping around me to the next tree and reigniting the bright orb in his hands. "Sometimes the one we've really been looking for has been in front of us the whole time."

# 8

I WAS WIDE AWAKE BEFORE DAWN THE NEXT MORNING. Before Aaron. Before the rest of the District. Everything was absolutely silent.

I listened to Aaron's deep, unconscious breathing beside me. He'd come back from his impromptu meeting with Bask late that night, too tired to talk when I'd asked how it went. He'd brushed away the question, untied his boots, angrily stripped off his uniform and collapsed into bed, leaving me to face a restless night alone.

I'd tossed and turned and wondered. Wondered how the conversation with Bask had gone, wondered what had been said, wondered if it had all gone up in flames and that was the reason Aaron hadn't wanted to talk about it.

I rolled over to my side, facing Aaron. His face was soft and expressionless, like a slate wiped clean by the cold, numbing depths of sleep. His long eyelashes lay softly against his dark skin, and his lips were parted slightly.

That face... It was so wild. Even after being with him all this time, reading him felt like trying to predict which path a tornado would take. Sometimes he was the stillness; sometimes he was the storm. I hated to admit it, but I felt like we were alike in that way. It scared me.

Knowing he didn't have any duties he needed to report for before noon that day, I slipped out of bed without waking him and tiptoed to the dresser. I dressed silently and stepped into my boots. I padded softly into the kitchen and checked the time.

0600. Enough time to start coffee for Aaron.

I scooped the rich, earthy substance into the pot and filled it with hot water. It was one of the only rituals we'd developed as a married couple—one of the few things we had together that were normal. When he was up before me, he made the coffee and had it waiting for me; on mornings when I was awake first, I did the same for him.

Maybe that was why I held on to the habit. Maybe I liked having one normal thing.

Zipping on my jacket, I left the apartment. I descended the metal staircase with as little noise as possible and made my way briskly across the District. Everyone was beginning to rouse. The doors to the prisoners' lodgings were beginning to open, and skinny, sunken shadows of what had once been soldiers stepped out into the light of day. I felt their wandering eyes on me as I strode down the middle of the street. One of them let out a long, low whistle as I walked past.

When I reached Bask's office, I rapped firmly on the door.

A pause, then a voice spoke.

"Come."

To my surprise, Bask wasn't stationed at his desk like he normally was. Instead, he was seated in one of the large, overstuffed leather armchairs in front of the fireplace. I raised an eyebrow.

"Turner, come in." He gestured for me to step farther into the room, then indicated the other armchair. "Sit."

I crossed the room without a word and carefully took a seat on the edge of the soft leather chair.

Bask didn't say anything; he just sat there gazing into the snapping fire in the hearth beneath the massive mounted bison head. He held a glass of whiskey in one hand; the other was draped comfortably over the arm of the chair. His jacket was off, his hair was untidy, and he was way too relaxed.

Something was off.

"How are you this morning?" he asked.

"Well, sir. And yourself?" I returned, watching him carefully.

He raised his glass in my direction before draining it. "Never better. Let me get you something to drink."

I put up a hand. "No, thank you."

Nevertheless, he stood and walked to his desk. "Has your husband not taught you the customs of the RGM, Turner? It is a gross insult to refuse a drink from a superior officer."

"I mean no disrespect, sir. But I was under the impression that I was here for a brief on the next mission," I explained. "Did Sergeant Price discuss—"

"Yes, yes, he did," Bask interrupted. "We'll get to that."

I heard the clinking of glass and then liquid being poured into a metal cup. He returned a moment later with the cup in his hand, which he extended to me. When he didn't back down, I took it from him, gritting my teeth. When he didn't sit down, I realized what he was waiting for.

Bringing the cool metal rim to my lips, I took a hesitant sip. It was warm and sweet across my tongue. I looked down into the cup, swirling it slightly. "What is this?"

"A favorite of mine." He began to smooth his mustache as he sat down again. I was surprised that he hadn't gotten himself another drink.

"Your husband met with me last night, yes." He circled back to my earlier statement. "He seemed to think you were a little concerned about the mission—that you didn't feel ready to go out yet."

I nodded, bringing the cup to my lips again. "Yes, sir."

"Why is that, Turner?" he asked.

The gears were spinning in my mind as I scrambled for an answer. I bought myself a little more time as I took another sip from the cup.

"I'm inexperienced. I feel like I would be nothing more than a hindrance—and that's the very last thing I would want to be with something as important as this, sir," I responded. "Sergeant Price would be a much better candidate for the task."

Bask studied me for a long moment, not saying a word, continuing to smooth his mustache.

"Yet we have tasked *you* with this mission, Turner," he countered. "Icarus is a very powerful slider... If we could capture him, we could have the rest of the sliders begging at our feet for mercy... That is what you want, isn't it?"

I swallowed, unable to look away from his dark eyes.

"I know how you feel, Turner," he continued, his voice softening. "Don't think that I don't. We all had a first time... a first mission... a first kill. It's perfectly normal to feel nervous."

I listened, a sick feeling swirling in my middle. Impulsively, I drained the rest of the liquid from the cup.

"But you will get over it," Bask went on, leaning forward. "Do you know why, Turner?"

I shook my head.

"Because you are a member of the RGM." His voice was soft but level. "Look at me."

I lifted my eyes to meet his. They suddenly didn't seem as dark; in fact, they were a bit blurry. My gaze shifted down to the cup in my hand; a warning flag flashed in the back of my mind. I was beginning to feel nauseous, and my thoughts were slow in coming, as if they were moving through water.

"Turner, look at me."

Blinking, I gradually lifted my gaze to meet Bask's again.

"You are a loyal member of the RGM. You are a soldier."

I nodded slowly. "Yes, sir."

"You are here not because we captured you, but because you *want* to be... You hated being a slider—you hate it still..." He leaned forward on his knees, the light from the flames flickering over his face. "But we've redeemed you. You are redeemed because you are one of us now."

Automatically and without thought, I nodded again. "Yes, sir. Yes, that's... that's true that I still do hate being a slider..."

"Why do you hate it, Turner? Why have you *always* hated it?" he questioned with emphasis.

"Because... because I..." My voice sounded muffled. "Because I've always wanted to just... to just be n-normal."

"Oh, Turner." He sighed. "You are more than normal—you are an elite member of our forces now. You belong with us."

I squinted at him, turning his words over in my mind. "You really think so?"

He nodded, getting to his feet. "I know so." He took the cup out of my hand and walked over to his desk again to refill it. It took a minute for me to process what he was doing.

"I really shouldn't drink any more," I protested, my words tumbling out over each other.

Bask didn't respond. He poured more liquid into the cup and handed it back to me.

"Thank you," I heard myself say, my words sounding foreign, as though someone else had spoken for me.

"Turner, you're going to be a great soldier. I can promise you that," he went on, watching me carefully as I took another drink of the sweet liquid. "You just have to trust me completely."

"Yes, sir."

"In order to do that, I need you to believe me..." He trailed off, looking at me intensely in the firelight. "To believe what I tell you."

"Yes, sir," I answered. "I... I believe you, sir."

I could hear the faint sound of a warning siren in my mind, but somehow, I couldn't stop myself from listening, from agreeing—from hanging on his every word. It was as if someone finally understood me.

"You hate sliders... You want to go out on this mission." He softened his voice. "And more than anything, you want to capture Icarus."

I nodded, wiping my mouth with the back of my hand. "Yes, sir. For so long I've had to live under his shadow... under *their* shadows..." I shook my head. My throat was starting to feel tight. Tears began blurring my vision, but I didn't even try to stop myself from crying. I felt like an open book.

"It's okay, Turner," he told me, his tone sympathetic. "You can tell me."

*No... no, don't... Don't tell him...*

Thoughts flashed through my head like broken radio signals through a haze of static.

"I've... I..." I stuttered and faltered, swallowing back a dizzy feeling. "I've been disloyal to the RGM," I blurted, a tear rolling down my cheek. "I haven't helped in all the ways I should... I have been doing the opposite. I've been trying to find a way to escape. Aaron and I both have..."

He smiled a little. "You don't want to escape, Turner."

I drained the rest of the cup, a strange heaviness settling inside me; my limbs felt awkward and cumbersome, and my tongue had become like lead in my mouth.

"You love the RGM."

"Yes, sir," I agreed, wiping my tears. "I was wrong. I... I do love the RGM."

"You are prepared to give your life for it."

"I... I am prepared to give my life for it."

"Everything you care about is *here*, Turner," he continued. "Everything that you hold dear. You have everything that you could want. Loyal comrades, friends, a loving husband..." He trailed off. "You do love your husband, don't you, Turner?"

I leaned back, the empty cup slipping out of my hands and falling to the floor. "I do love him, yes..." I said thickly. "He's everything I've ever wanted..."

It was strange, hearing myself admit something so intimate, but it was like I couldn't stop myself. Everything he said felt like a mere affirmation of things I hadn't realized I already thought and felt.

"You are both madly in love. Anyone can see that."

"Yes. Yes, we are." I couldn't help but smile, thinking back to Aaron's face earlier that morning. How handsome he was.

"You both want to have children."

"Yes, we do," I agreed.

"You are excited to spearhead this movement together—breeding the first generation of RGM sliders."

I nodded. I felt a pang of guilt in the pit of my stomach as I looked down. Bask said nothing for a moment, but I could feel his eyes studying me.

"Turner, what is it you're not telling me?" he asked.

I didn't respond. I thought of Price, his sleeping face. His bare chest as it rose and fell. He began to overtake my thoughts.

"Nakamura is confused as to why you haven't become pregnant yet, Turner," Bask continued. "Are you keeping anything back from him?"

Again, I felt that same alarm rise inside me. I couldn't understand what it meant. I couldn't understand why I was hesitating.

"I am your commander, Turner. I am your *friend*." He leaned closer, looking me in the eyes. "You can tell me everything."

I swallowed, trying to feel my way through the shroud of fog that hung over my mind.

"We haven't..." I began slowly. "We haven't had..." I cleared my throat. "We haven't had sex yet."

Bask's eyes hardened as I spilled my guts.

"I told Aaron that I didn't love him... that I didn't want to have sex with him because I couldn't think of him that way. I loved Keegan."

"But you *do* think of him that way, Turner," he replied firmly. "You're passionately in love with Aaron. You love *no one but* Aaron."

I nodded, blinking back tears. My mind drifted back to Aaron, to his face as I'd observed him lying there in bed.

He was right... I *was* madly in love with Aaron. *Why did I not see it before? Why didn't I understand my own feelings?*

"You won't hold yourself back anymore, Turner," Bask continued. "The next time you see him, you will desire him, and you will give yourself to him. You will not hold back anymore."

My thoughts drifted to Aaron as he spoke. I shook my head, tears dripping down my face. "I won't hold back."

"Very good."

"And I will go out on this mission." I sat up a little straighter, gripping the arms of the chair to pull myself to my feet. "I will help to capture Icarus."

"Very good, Turner."

Slowly rising to my feet, I wiped back the tears that were once again welling in my eyes. "God, I don't know why I've been like this—why I've been so stupid. I'm sorry."

"There's no need to apologize, Turner," Bask replied gently. "It's not *your* fault."

For a moment I looked at him with bleary eyes, wondering what he meant by that.

"All you need to know is that you will meet us in the courtyard this evening at twenty-one hundred, Turner. You will be given instructions then," he explained. "And I know now that I will have no reason to mistrust you."

I straightened up and shook my head. "No, sir. Of course not, sir."

Bask studied me up and down for a moment and then smiled. "Very good. You are dismissed."

Relieved, I left as fast as possible. I could barely think—barely breathe. I felt dizzy and light-headed and, well, *in love*. I couldn't believe I hadn't realized it before; I couldn't remember *why* I hadn't. It somehow felt as though everything before my conversation with my commander had been an illusion.

Now I was finally awake.

The ground trembled and roared as the geyser erupted, filling the factory with the necessary steam to power it for the next several hours. Dodging prisoners and soldiers, I made my way across the District. I pounded up the stairs to the apartment, biting back a smile that had crept across my lips without my awareness of it.

Aaron looked up when I stepped into the kitchen. He stood at the stove, pouring himself a cup of coffee. He smiled weakly.

"Hey," he greeted me. "How'd it go?"

He wasn't wearing a shirt, just boxers. The warm morning sunlight cast shadows over his abdomen rippled with muscles.

"It went great," I answered, slowly crossing the room.

Aaron quirked one thick, dark eyebrow. "*Great?*" he reiterated dubiously. "Your meeting with Bask went *great?*"

I nodded. "I'm all set for the mission tonight. To find Icarus. We gather in the courtyard tonight at twenty-one hundred."

He stared at me hard, slowly setting the coffee pot back down on the stove. "And you're okay with that?"

I nodded, blushing. "I feel ashamed for how I've acted. I haven't been loyal to the RGM. I haven't been loyal to myself—I haven't even been loyal to you."

The puzzled expression on my husband's face didn't change as I walked slowly around the kitchen island and came to a stop in front of him.

"Sparrow, are you okay?" he asked, taking a sip from his mug before setting it down to approach me. "When I spoke with Bask last night, he... he said he was going to force you..." His deep, amber-brown eyes were filled with concern as he scanned me up and down. "Sparrow, did he hurt you?"

A smile found my lips as I shook my head. I placed a hand on his chest and looked up into his eyes. "No, he didn't hurt me."

Aaron gazed at me for a moment, as if my face were a puzzle. His dark eyes sparkled in the morning light.

"What do you mean you haven't been loyal to the RGM, Sparrow?" he said quietly. "What do you mean that you haven't been loyal to yourself?"

I opened my mouth to speak, but my brain was still too foggy for words. Looking into his eyes, it was like something in me began to reach a boiling point. I couldn't hold it back any longer.

Taking his face in my hands, I pressed my lips to his. Chills spread rapidly over my skin as I kissed him. His lips were soft and tasted like coffee. At first, I kissed him slowly, gently, then gradually with more and more passion.

When I finally pulled away, I was breathing hard. So was he, his eyes still trained on mine.

"Sparrow, I..." he said haltingly, wrapping his arms around me. He kissed the top of my head and let his warm lips rest against my hair. "Are you okay?"

I drew back to look at him. "What, I can't kiss you?"

Aaron smiled, surprised. "Of course you can kiss me."

His voice softened as he leaned in and kissed me again. This time I melted, forgetting everything. I felt like there was a caged bird inside me, beating its wings, longing to be set free. At the same time, I still heard the faint cry of a siren in the back of my mind... words that made no sense:

*Turn back.*

I couldn't think. I couldn't understand what it all meant. I only felt the fire burning in my core as I kissed Aaron and he kissed me.

My lips parted wide, and my arms entwined around his neck. Reaching down, he wrapped his hands around my thighs and lifted me off my feet, holding me in his arms. I wrapped my legs around him, and for a few moments there was nothing beyond that—the places where our skin touched, where I grasped him and he held me.

Finally, dizzy and breathless, I pulled back, looking into his eyes. Slowly, like ice melting, he set me gently back down. Wordlessly, I took him by the hand. He said nothing, letting me take the lead.

Guiding Aaron across the kitchen, I pulled him into the bedroom and shut the door behind us. I led him over to the bed, and he sat down, bringing himself to my eye level. He scanned my face for a moment, then pulled me into another kiss. I reciprocated, starting to push him backward, but he stopped me suddenly. He held me out at arm's length, looking into my eyes. That same questioning look of concern still lingered on his face.

"Sparrow, are you...?" His soft voice faded as he studied me. "Are you sure? You seem so different."

Barely comprehending a word he said, I looked at him for a long moment before replying.

"I love you, Aaron," I whispered. "You're my husband, and I... I'm in love with you." I gently moved his hands down to my waist, my eyes still locked with his. "I want to."

Leaning in to kiss him again, I unzipped my jacket and peeled it off, tossing it to the floor. Aaron's eyes softened as his hands slid under my shirt, pulling it over my head and casting it aside. His hands wound around my waist; his skin felt warm against mine. In one swift motion, he lifted me off my feet once more and pulled me onto his lap, drawing me in like he couldn't get me close enough.

Without any more questions or doubt, like a wave swelling, cresting, and breaking, we became one.

# 9

"KEEG, CAN I ASK YOU SOMETHING?"

I didn't answer. My gaze was locked on the target that was nailed to the oak tree. I tunneled my focus, shutting out everything other than the splotch of red paint in the center of the target. I took a steady breath, holding the smooth blade in levitation before taking careful aim and finally hurling it forward.

It spun audibly through the air, whirling end over end—nailing into the center of the target with a satisfying *thwack*.

I blew out a shallow sigh, stepping back, and turned to Rafael. He stood a few feet away, shirtless and wearing a holster filled with knives. His blue eyes studied the target, and he gave me an approving nod.

"Go ahead," I told him.

I stepped to the side, giving him some room to center himself with the target.

"Do you think it was the right decision?" he asked. "For Sensei to leave? To go and look for Hawk and Icarus?"

"It's not really my place to say—to decide," I answered him. "I trust Sensei... a lot more than I trust myself."

"Sensei trusts you, though." Raf drew a knife from his holster. "Why else would he have left you and Kateri in charge?"

He had a point.

"I think it was the right decision," I admitted. "I think we've spent too long in hiding from the RGM. We need the patriarchs to return."

"Yeah, Sensei made it sound like they were the only ones who could bring Sparrow back." He positioned his grip. "Like that's the reason we haven't been able to get her back—because they're not here."

I felt a pang in my chest; I shook my head. "I think Sparrow hasn't come back because she doesn't want to, Raf," I replied. "None of us, especially the patriarchs, are to blame for that. I believe that they may be able to persuade her to come back, yeah. But whether she will come of her own free will or not..."

"But why them?" He pressed the question. "What do they have to do with Sparrow? She's no different from the rest of us..."

I sighed and tipped my head in the direction of the target. "Just throw already, would you?"

Pursing his lips, he turned his attention back to the target ahead, the only splash of color among the otherwise bleak, gray backdrop. Casting the blade into levitation, he shot it forward. It nailed into the target several inches to the left of my own, just skirting the red area.

Raf blew out a sigh, wiping the sweat from his upper lip where faint stubble that he refused to shave off had begun to develop. He shot me a sidelong glance.

"Critiques?"

I studied the position of his blade for a moment as I sidled up alongside him.

"When you float the blade, just let it happen. Don't rush it... I know it feels like it's just going to drop if you don't do something with it fast enough, but it won't," I explained, drawing a knife of my own to flip it a few times, letting the razor-sharp blade slice easily through the spaces between my fingers. "Anything you're thinking about, anything you're holding on to, you have to let go of all of it. You can't hold on to two things at once..."

Gradually I unfolded my palm, and the blade lifted into the air to hover. I held it there, letting Raf observe. "That's what will stop it from shaking," I continued quietly. "To think of nothing else beyond allowing the blade to float... telling it gently what path it will take. Not commanding it, not getting frustrated—working with it, just as you would work with any other living thing."

I lifted the knife a little higher, and Raf stepped to the side. I narrowed my eyes, focusing on the target once more.

"I don't know why I question Sensei," he said quietly, his mind clearly still stuck on our earlier conversation. "I guess I just..." He fought with the words for a moment before slumping his shoulders and biting his lip. "I'm just worried about Sparrow, Keeg. I still have dreams..." His voice quieted. "Nightmares about being in that horrible place; I know what they're like..."

My throat tightened. The blade spun a little faster above my palm.

"If it wasn't for her, I never would have gotten out of there alive." His voice cracked. "I can't stand that I'm just—just sitting around, hiding here, doing nothing while she's trapped there."

"She wanted to be there, Raf." My voice came out a bit rougher than I had intended. "She told me so herself."

"You can't really believe that, Keeg. My god—you saw the place for yourself!" The volume of his voice quickly escalated. "You know full well that that couldn't have been what she really wanted! They were forcing her—making her say things she didn't mean! You can't believe—"

His words were cut off as the knife dropped back to my hand, blade first. Slicing through my skin, it spun forward and thrust through the air, careening past its target and into the tree just above Cub's head. Roused from her sleep, the cougar scrambled to her paws to give the knife a cautious sniff before sauntering over to check on me.

I sucked in a startled breath, staggering back and gritting my teeth as I clamped my hand over the gash.

Raf's eyes went wide. "What happened?"

"Nothing!" I exploded. "I—I lost focus, that's all…"

Rafael said nothing else, though I could still feel the intensity of his gaze as I continued applying pressure to my wound.

"Look, maybe you should finish practicing alone," I said at last, my voice hoarse. "I'm—I have too much on my mind. I'm losing focus."

Rafael studied me for a moment through squinted eyes before leaning down to stroke a hand over Cub's back. "No worries. Sorry if I—"

"It's not you." I put up a hand. "It's… it's not you."

I took a deep breath and rolled the tension out of my shoulders, forcing a weak smile for his sake. "Sorry I snapped."

"Don't worry about it, Keeg," he said, waving it off. "You should take care of that cut."

I nodded, taking a few steps backward before turning around and walking out of the clearing, letting my expression fall only when I was no longer facing him.

My heart pounded in my chest, and my feet were like thunder as I made my way through the forest. At last, I came to the clearing where the trees spilled open to overlook the sprawling valley below. I walked to the edge and took a seat on the old tree stump. Taking a deep breath, I pressed my eyes shut and tried to silence my thoughts.

*Healing… focus…*

*"I can't stand that I'm just sitting around, hiding here, doing nothing while she's trapped there…"*

With Raf's words echoing in my mind, I pulled my thoughts back to the gash on my hand. I tried to coach myself to relax, to channel light from my core, to allow it to turn into healing.

My mind drifted back to that night in the woods, by the fire with Sparrow, when I'd taught her to heal. When I'd let her heal my wounds after the cougar attack. With my eyes closed, I could still sense the warmth of the fire on my skin. I could still feel the soft tips of her fingers. I could still hear her voice.

*God, why can't I just forget?*

My mind reeled back to my conversation with Preston earlier that day.

*"... She told me that flat out—that she didn't love me and never had."*

*"... But what about you? How do you feel?"*

*"Everything between Sparrow and me is done—finished."*

That was how I'd answered.

That was what I'd said.

But I was lying to him and myself—and I *knew it*.

Drawing a long, steady breath, I massaged my forefinger and thumb over my tired eyes. I could feel the warmth of the ripe evening sun on my face as it cast its rusty red shafts over the surrounding foothills.

The sound of soft footsteps approaching caught my attention.

I didn't look up or open my eyes as Kateri sat down beside me. Gently, her arm brushed up against mine.

"I was wondering where you'd gone," she said quietly, her gaze fixing on the blood seeping through my fingers. "What happened?"

"Just a scrape." I belittled it, peeling my fingers back to reveal a cut that looked much worse than it felt. "I lost my concentration, and the knife slipped."

Without another word she took my hand in hers, closing it between her soft, warm palms.

"Why haven't you healed it yourself?" she asked softly.

"I just..." My voice faded. "I couldn't..."

I trailed off as my gaze slid up from Kateri's hands to her face. Her eyes were closed. She was focused on healing my hand.

"You were incredible today," I whispered. "I know why Sensei chose you... You bring us together even when it seems like everything is breaking apart."

"He chose you too," she said, opening her eyes again to look at me. "Sensei gave you something, didn't he?"

With my free hand, I reached into my pocket and took out the feather Dad had pressed into my hand before he left.

"He said to ask you about its meaning," I began softly. "That you would know."

Kateri gazed at the soft brown and white feather between my fingers for a moment before a smile curved over her lips. She gently resumed caressing my palm with her fingertips.

"It's an eagle's feather," she explained softly, the sunlight illuminating her brown eyes. "They represent all that is brave. All that is strong. Eagles soar higher than any of us; it has been said that they carry messages to us from the heavens, because that is where they dwell. It means that the giver believes you to be worthy of it. To be brave... strong..."

Kateri closed her eyes again, her long, dark eyelashes pressed to her cheeks as her hand moved slowly over mine, her fingertips like fire against my skin. I could feel the energy radiating from her hand and into mine, pulsating gently through my arm, flooding my veins.

Something inside me felt weightless as I stared at her. For a moment, my heart pounded in my chest—for a moment, I hesitated. Something inside me seemed to whisper: *Don't.* But there was something else beyond that voice. Something stronger.

As if some force I couldn't see was pulling me, I leaned slowly closer. The warmth of her face glowed against my skin as my lips gently captured hers. I felt her draw a surprised breath, her eyelashes fluttering open against my cheek.

My lips pressed against Kateri's. I wanted to draw back, to look into her eyes, to make sure this was okay. But these fleeting thoughts were eclipsed by the feeling of her hands slipping out of my own, her fingertips cupping my face. A soft, murmured sigh rolled from her lips and filled my mouth, and she pulled me closer.

Everything inside me ached, ignited. I brushed my fingers back into her long, wild hair and kissed her deeper. Kissed her like I was lost and she was the North Star.

When I finally drew back, I was breathless. Gently, I took the eagle feather in my hand and tucked it into her hair. Her eyes drifted over my face. For a moment I did nothing—still lost. Then Kateri took my face in her hands again and pulled me in, pressing her lips to mine.

A fire burned within me. Wrapping my arms around her, I felt like I was drowning, sinking deeper and deeper into something I'd never experienced before. Her hands slid down to my chest, pushing me backwards. The soft earth caught us as I rolled backward, spreading out on the soft ground.

The shape of her body melted over mine. Her hair spilled over my face like a curtain, blacking out the world, leaving only us—only her. Only that moment of my hands on her waist. Hers on my cheeks as she kissed me with the kind of passion that made me forget who I was.

My fingers tangled in her hair; my lips parted over hers; my hands wanted her closer.

I rolled her to the side, gently kissing her face, her neck. I could feel her pulse, the warmth of her breath. I felt intoxicated, like I was out of my mind.

For an instant my mind flashed back to what felt like another life—a sunset, a lake, the warmth of Sparrow's lips against my own. The fire inside me reaching for the flames within her.

A bolt of pain like a knife cut into my chest.

I pulled back, breathing too heavily to speak. For a moment I just lay there, my fingers drifting through her hair, my forehead resting gently against hers.

"I've loved you since the day I met you, Keegan," Kateri said softly.

I didn't know how to respond except to kiss her again. It was getting more and more difficult to stop.

"I'm sorry," I said, my voice shaky. "I... I'm getting carried away."

"Don't be sorry," she whispered. "It's..."

"Hmm?" I kissed her. "It's what?"

She hummed a little laugh. "It's nothing I haven't imagined before."

My lips curved into a little smile. I sprawled out on my back beside her, my head light and my heart pounding like a drum in my chest. For a moment neither of us said a word.

The sun had slipped below the purple horizon. Soft shades of lavender and gray had washed away the streaks of crimson and gold, leaving us in blankets of soft semidarkness.

*Sometimes the one we've really been looking for has been in front of us the whole time.*

I didn't want to live in the darkness anymore, lost in the overwhelming shadows of what Sparrow and I had once been, grieving the loss of her. Truth was... I couldn't.

I felt as if I was standing on the edge of something... Of what, I wasn't quite sure. But I knew it was time to let go.

I rolled to my side, wrapping Kateri in my arms, resting my face in the curve of her neck. For a moment my thoughts spun with the fevered rhythm of my heart.

"Kateri..." I finally managed a whisper. "Can I ask you something?"

"Hmm?"

My heartbeat picked up. I didn't reply—I couldn't. Finally, she rolled over onto her back to look up into my eyes.

"Yes, Keeg?"

I pulled in a deep breath. "Will you marry me?"

# 10

'I SLOWLY OPENED MY EYES, UNSURE OF WHERE I WAS, OR what time of day it was. I rolled to my side and felt a warm arm slide around my torso, and then Sparrow's lips on my neck.

"I was wondering when you were going to wake up," she said quietly, stroking her fingertips over my back. "I have to go soon. It's nearly time."

I rolled over to face her, pulling her in for a kiss before she could escape. "Five more minutes."

Sparrow laughed against my lips, kissing me.

I still could hardly believe that this was my wife, the same Sparrow who had only yesterday been so frantic to escape the RGM's grasp. She seemed like an entirely different woman: one who was loyal to the RGM, who had no desire to run away, and who was eager to love me as her husband.

I'd been suspicious at first, but those doubts had quickly melted away along with everything else when Sparrow had kissed me and told me that she loved me.

For the first time since marrying Sparrow, I began to feel as though this might *actually work*. Maybe Sparrow finally *was* beginning to turn against the sliders. Maybe she *had* finally fallen in love with me.

I couldn't imagine what had taken place in her meeting with Bask to cause her attitude to change so drastically. I certainly intended to find out. But for now, I kissed Sparrow back, wound my arms around her and pulled the sheets up over our heads.

I felt lighter than I had in years as I dressed and then grabbed a quick bite to eat with Sparrow in the kitchen. It felt so weird yet normal at the same time to be sitting across from her at the table, having easy conversation. It felt like everything I'd imagined being married would feel like.

Sparrow's smile was contagious. We talked and ate, checked our respective watches, and then headed out. As we walked down those dirty streets together for the first time, it didn't really matter that no one could see me but her. She reached over to give my hand a squeeze when we reached the courtyard, where she was meeting the rest of the team.

"I'll see you when you get back." I gave her a reassuring smile as our hands separated.

She returned the grin over her shoulder as she strode away. "Not if I see you first."

I stood there for a moment, watching her stride confidently away.

She was like a different person. How was it *possible*?

I squared my shoulders and set off in the direction of Bask's office. I walked in without knocking, closing the door behind me. Bask looked up, his spectacles sliding to the end of his nose.

"Ah, Price," he greeted me. "Did you see your wife off?"

"Yes, she just joined the others in the courtyard," I affirmed. "Now that we're alone, are you going to let me in on how we even discovered Icarus's whereabouts?"

"As to that, none of us are quite certain," he replied, lifting a cigarette to his lips. "We detected activity in the forest around the Homestead site. Suspecting it to be someone from the group of sliders that Sparrow is from, we conducted a thorough search."

"And found?"

"A man in the forest whose description matched that of Icarus."

My brow furrowed. "Why was he not simply apprehended, then?"

Bask stroked his chin thoughtfully for a moment. "Icarus is a powerful slider. It's best to fight these people with their own kind—fire with fire, hmm?"

"That never seemed very logical to me."

Bask let out a raspy chuckle before taking another long drag. "These people do not live by logic, Price. They follow a strange kind of instinct—you must know that."

My jaw hardened. "I've long since shed my slider skin. I am a soldier and nothing more; I know nothing of the anomalies of Earth or their strange ways."

"But you are married to one."

"Sparrow is one of *us* now," I replied, matter-of-fact. "It seems I was wrong to suspect that Sparrow wasn't ready for this mission."

Bask exhaled a long stream of smoke. "It would seem so."

"Did she seem at all... *different*... when she spoke with you?" I questioned, trying to be subtle. "She seemed so..."

"Don't worry about her, Price."

"I'm not worried about her." My voice hardened. "I trust her completely."

Bask tapped the end of his cigarette, sending flakes of ash drifting to the floor. He took a shot from his flask. "Is there anything else, Price?"

There was: a hundred things. I wanted to know exactly what he had said to Sparrow and she to him. But I knew full well Bask would tell me nothing I didn't already know. It made no difference that Sparrow was my spouse—what Bask had told her was between her and him.

For now, I would just have to accept that Sparrow's change of heart was genuine, and that, when it came down to it, it might have had nothing to do with her and Bask's meeting at all. Maybe I was trying to piece together two completely unrelated things.

"No, sir, there's nothing else." I cleared my throat and reset. "I'm headed to the clinic from here."

"For what?"

My brow furrowed. "The usual, sir. Blood extraction."

Bask took a long sip of smoke. "Yes. Yes, of course."

I stood there for a moment, then turned and strode to the door and let myself out.

The District was alive with activity when I stepped outside. Sparrow was gone, and so were the other soldiers who had been with her. Prisoners were carrying massive logs down the dirt road toward the factory. I stood there for a moment, watching them.

I could still remember how long the days had felt when I was a prisoner. Never-ending. Each moment a hell all its own. They were disposable; I was not. They contributed little; I was literally the lifeblood that kept the place going.

I'd come so far.

I pushed forward, crossing the District to the infirmary, where Dr. Nakamura was waiting for me.

"Price," he greeted me when the door opened, "come in. Have a seat."

It was all motor skills at this point—no thought involved. The cool steel examination table, giving the doctor my arm when he asked for it. Waiting as he felt around with his finger for the right vein to plunge the needle into. I barely felt the sting anymore.

"How are things, Price?" he asked eventually, slowly pulling back the plunger, coaxing clear liquid from my veins.

"Fine. Why do you ask?" I shot back.

Nakamura pressed his lips into a thin smile. "I was just passing the time, Price. I know Turner just departed on her first major assignment."

"She did."

"I know how that can be. The worry that can come with—"

"I'm not worried." I cut him off. "Not in the least. We're both confident in what we do, and happy to be of service."

Nakamura fell silent as he retracted the needle and placed it on the tray. "Of course."

I was bullshitting, of course. Naturally, I *was* concerned about Sparrow, her strange behavior and how she would react when bluntly faced with the reality of having to capture one of her own—one whom the sliders revered as a founder. It had been no small thing to capture Icarus. In truth, I was jealous; why hadn't *I* been chosen?

But that jealousy was eclipsed by a much stronger feeling: fear of how she might react.

I snapped out of my thoughts moments later when another needle pierced my skin. My focus snapped to Nakamura, confused.

"Isn't it usually just three?" I questioned as he pulled back the plunger.

"I'll be taking six today, for convenience," he said. "We won't need you back in for another week now."

"Did you discuss this with Bask?"

"Bask is the one who gave the order."

He'd mentioned nothing to me.

"But what about overdrawing?" I asked.

"The most you'll feel is a little dizzy," he promised me. "Just take it easy for the rest of the day."

Nakamura scribbled my next appointment into his tablet and told me when to come back. I felt dizzy and sick to my stomach as I left.

My mind was filled with Sparrow as I headed back across the District toward the apartment. Where was she now? What was she doing? Was this just a trap to push her to the brink?

Bask believed I'd converted Sparrow. Sparrow believed I was on the sliders' side. I was a different person to each of them, and it was vital that no overlap occurred. Bask needed to believe that Sparrow was a loyal convert and that I'd been the hero to recruit her. Sparrow needed to believe that I was a rebel looking for an opportunity to escape.

It all hung by threads.

Threads that, with one misstep, could break.

And send my world crashing down around me.

If Sparrow revealed her true feelings, Bask would know that I'd been lying about her. If she blew it now, everything we'd built would go up in flames. The truth was, I didn't care what Sparrow felt about the RGM. I *needed* her. After being with someone who could actually see me—and who actually, finally loved me—I couldn't give that up. I *wouldn't* give that up.

I mumbled a prayer to a god I didn't even believe in as I stumbled up the stairs to the apartment.

*Let her be okay; let her get through this. Let her be strong. Let this change in her be real. Let her be one of us...*

I shouldered open the door and staggered inside, slamming it shut. Falling back against it, I leaned there for a moment as the room swirled around me. I felt a strange, prickling sensation that an unseen presence was in the room.

Swallowing back the dizzy feeling tingling in my head, I stepped cautiously forward, crossing the small mudroom. I sidled up against the wall, listening.

Nothing.

*Silence.*

My hand drifted down to the pistol at my hip. I pulled it from its holster and lifted it to a ready position, my finger sliding forward to rest on the trigger.

The sound was barely audible, but there all the same: *breathing.*

For a moment I stood there, listening. Then, in one fluid motion I stepped out from the cover of the wall, bracing the pistol out in front of me. Seated at the table was a cloaked figure, a hood pulled up to conceal the face.

"On the ground now!" I ordered, my finger tense over the trigger.

The figure remained still for a moment before slowly looking up, the light shifting over his shadowed face to ignite his features. An old black man with wrinkled skin and a white beard. His steady gaze locked with mine.

My eyes widened, and my stomach tightened to a knot, along with every other muscle in my body.

"Aaron." His deep, quiet voice formed my name.

I felt frozen. The pistol began to tremble in my sweaty grip, fear swelling in my gut.

"Turn back, Aaron." His voice was level, haunting. "Turn back before it is too late."

In a gut reaction I squeezed the trigger, holding it down and emptying my magazine. A series of loud cracks pulsed through the room.

When the room stilled once more, I found myself standing there alone. Just me, an empty chair, and a spray of bullet holes punched into the wall.

# 11

WE MOVED THROUGH THE FOREST LIKE GHOSTS, OUR
boots making little sound against the soft ground. When we grew closer to
the Homestead, I activated the speaker inside my helmet to speak to my commanding officer, Ishaan Anand.

"How close are we to the last area he was spotted?"

All I could see of him was the black helmet in front of me, his shield
pulled down like mine.

"Not far," he answered. "A few miles past the ruins."

There were seven of us, each a glowing green figure across my night-vision screen. They wove ahead through the trees and into the clearing. The
commander and I followed suit, entering the clearing after them.

The blackened remains of the Homestead loomed in front of us. My
boots crunched over pieces of shattered glass scattered across the ground. It
was difficult to take my eyes off the remains of the log cabin that had once
been my home.

Confused feelings twisted in my gut as I carefully skirted around the rubble. I squinted ahead, keeping my head on a swivel as we moved forward.

A shrill screech cut through the night like a warning call. I froze, my gaze darting up to the treetops. Anand continued forward, unfazed.

I paused to scan the treetops warily.

"Turner." Anand jerked his helmet toward the thick, dark woods ahead.

I jogged to catch up, jumping over a few charred timbers. We continued in silence. I listened carefully for anything beyond the chirruping crickets and occasional purr of a whippoorwill. I couldn't seem to brush away the sick feeling swelling in the pit of my stomach. I almost jumped out of my skin suit when Anand grabbed me by the arm and pointed ahead.

"There."

That was all he said. Everyone else had taken cover behind trees, their weapons drawn and at ready positions. I sank back behind a thick tree trunk beside Anand, my heart rising to my throat as I scanned the forest ahead.

Between the oaks, a small mound rose from the ground like a knoll. But I could tell through the crystal-clear night vision my shield afforded me that there was something unnatural about it. My heat sensor caught on a pile of warm coals gathered in a circle near the structure.

"That's it?" I whispered.

"Affirmative."

"What do we do now?"

He lifted one black-gloved finger to the sleek front of his helmet. He waited a moment before whispering a reply.

"We wait."

We crouched there, observing in the silence, watching for any sign of life or movement.

Another long, shrill screech rippled through the quiet. This time, I shot an anxious look in Anand's direction, my heart beating faster. He shook his head.

Like a memory from a dream, a blurry vision of wings against a churning gray sky flashed through my mind. I squeezed my eyes shut and tried to stay focused.

"Move."

Everyone surged forward at once, and with Anand beside me, we surrounded the small shelter constructed between the grouping of trees.

Soft clicks sounded around me as everyone flicked their weapons into firing mode. I followed suit, and Anand motioned with his finger for me to proceed as we had planned.

Sucking in a nervous breath, I broke away from the circle and approached the shelter, dropping to my knees to brush aside the curtain of moss that covered the opening.

I clicked on the flashlight attached to my rifle's upper. The interior illuminated. It was empty. Just a worn dirt floor and walls constructed of branches. Nothing else.

Dropping back, I scrambled to my feet and shook my head. Anand cussed through my earpiece.

"Fall back," he said tersely.

I was halfway to him when I stopped dead in my tracks.

A long, low howl rippled through the trees. Instinctively I jerked around, scanning the forest. Dark shapes and shadows surrounded me, illuminated green in my shield.

"What was that?" A few soldiers' voices cut in and out over each other through my headset. I stood there, frozen, hardly breathing as I tried to answer that question for myself.

I couldn't see anything...

"Turner, fall *the hell* back," Anand seethed.

I turned back around and took a step toward him.

That was as far as I got.

Something blurred in my night vision—then two hundred pounds of sheer force barreled into me, sending me flying backward through the air like a rag doll. I impacted against the trunk of a tree.

Shaken, I bolted to my feet. Before me stood a massive wolf, its jaws open wide, its coat as white as the moon. It snarled and lunged for my helmet.

I threw myself to the side, rolling away just as gunshots exploded around me. I heard a bullet hiss through the air only inches from my head, impacting into the ground beside me, spitting dirt. My headset exploded with a chaos of frantic voices. I scrambled to my feet, firing—missing.

A blur of white—then what felt like razor blades sank into my shoulder as I slammed to the ground. An agonized scream roared out of my throat, hot tears filling my eyes. I drove my knee into the beast's belly, but it didn't budge.

A shot rang out. The wolf staggered, stumbling off me.

"Turner, move!" Anand's voice.

There was no way to fall back without circling around the massive, now wounded and angry animal. With the bullet in its flesh, it took off after me, its throaty growls and snarls pounding through my body as it pursued me, its paws shaking the ground under my feet as I sprinted.

I dodged a tree, leapt over a rock. Bullets whipped through the air, thudding into trees and the dirt ahead of me. I glanced back over my shoulder just as a stray round bit into my thigh, setting it on fire. My legs gave out from beneath me.

The wolf was on top of me in a heartbeat, sinking its claws into my back as my night vision flickered and went dead, leaving me in darkness as the creature's jaws snapped around my helmet. Its teeth shattered through the bulletproof glass as if it were nothing more than brittle plastic.

Roaring, it shook my head in its jaws until the helmet disintegrated beneath the pressure. With a furious snarl, it tossed the mangled remains aside and turned to stare down into my face, baring its teeth. I lay there staring up at it, frozen to the ground. The massive wolf recoiled, gathering strength, and lunged for my throat, jaws open wide.

Instinctively, my eyes clamped shut as I braced myself for the end.

For a moment the gunshots and the shouts and the pounding of footsteps faded from my hearing, leaving just me and the wolf.

Fearfully peeling my eyes open, I found the wolf standing over me, staring down into my face. Its shining blue eyes reflected what little illumination drifted down from the waxing moon.

It lifted its massive head, tilting it to the side as if curious. My heart lifted in my throat as it leaned closer, lowering its head to mine.

Then a bullet slashed through its chest.

My eyes widened as the massive beast stiffened and then slumped to the ground. I scrambled backward and leapt to my feet, only to fall back down again when my injured leg buckled. A strong arm immediately caught mine.

"What goddamn part of 'fall back' didn't you understand?" Anand shouted through his helmet.

I was too out of breath to answer. The sound of running footsteps filtered through the trees as the rest of our unit burst out of cover and gathered around the motionless wolf.

"Spread out—everyone," Anand ordered. "Search for footprints. Search for any sign of—"

"Icarus!" one of the soldiers shouted, cutting him off.

My eyes locked on the soldier, then followed his gaze. He was pointing to something on the ground—to the wolf.

To the wolf that was no longer a wolf, but a man covered in blood.

# 12

THE WOODS WERE DARK; SHADOWS ROSE FROM THE ground and stretched skyward around me. In the distance I could hear the sounds of footsteps.

Then something else. A long, low howl—so deep, so desperate, it seemed to rip the night apart as if searching for something within the darkness itself.

I slowly turned my head, scanning the dark forest, searching for the source of the sound.

There was a crashing in the brush behind me, and before I could even turn, pain exploded through my body as a crushing weight came slamming down on top of me, and the familiar sting of claws seared my chest.

A cry of agony rattled in my throat, but I couldn't hear my own voice. My eyes widened; a wolf stood over me. It was bright white, almost glowing. Its blue eyes drilled down into mine, and then, with a snarl, it lunged for my throat.

I bolted upright. My gaze swept my surroundings, my mind fighting to make sense of where I was. Sweat prickled over my skin.

Preston lay sleeping a few feet away to my left, and Rafael to my right. I could only vaguely make out their shapes in the soft, purple-gray wash of dawn. Neither of them stirred.

I slowly became aware of the pattering of rain outside. It pelted gently against the canvas sides of the shelter and dripped steadily from the branches covering the roof.

*The shelter... I'm in the shelter... It was a dream.*

Steadying my breathing, I brushed the blanket aside and quietly stood. Grabbing my holster at the door, I slid it on as I stepped outside.

Fog rose from the ground to skirt the trees, causing them to appear as though they were floating. Rain pelted my skin and rolled down my face.

*What did the dream mean? Why a wolf?*

A soft, shrill sound pulled me out of my thoughts. I stepped into the shadows of the trees, questioning for a moment whether I'd actually heard the sound or merely imagined it. I listened for anything above the sound of the pattering rain, craning my neck and scanning the treetops for any sign of life.

I walked on, and a short time later I came to the edge of the forest, the overlook point where Kateri and I had kissed the night before.

On the soft breeze came a lilting call, stopping me in my tracks. Curious, I walked to the edge of the cliff.

Far below in the distance, a black speck drifted over the trees, outlined against the mist. It dipped and moved, pulling itself through the air in a wide circular motion. Two outstretched wings.

"No way..."

The hairs on the backs of my arms rose as I stared out at the hawk, watching until, at last, it dipped below the tree line and vanished.

I was breathless by the time I reached the shelter. I slowed to a stop alongside the canvas flap.

"Kateri," I whispered. "Kateri, are you awake?"

After a pause, a familiar hand brushed the canvas aside, and Kateri stepped out, her long hair resting over her shoulder. She tipped her head in the direction of the woods. I followed her a few paces away from the shelter, stopping at a large oak tree.

"What is it?" she asked.

"I thought I heard a noise, so I walked into the woods. I couldn't tell at first if I'd just been dreaming, or if it was real. Then I heard it again—I saw it."

Her dark eyebrows rose. "Saw what?"

"A hawk of some sort… It was far off, but still… we haven't seen any sign of life since we first came here."

Kateri shook her head. "Do you think it could be…?"

"I have no idea, but I'd be lying if I said it wasn't the very first thing that crossed my mind."

"Do you think it has anything to do with the fact that Sensei left to search for her?"

I turned the idea over in my mind, visions of the hawk hovering in the valley below still dominating my thoughts.

"I don't know," I admitted. "But I can't help but feel like it might mean something."

For a moment we both went thoughtfully silent. Then I noticed a look on her face, the kind of look she only had when something had just occurred to her.

"What is it?"

"Back before…" She sighed, meeting my eyes once more. "Before Sparrow was taken, when we were hiding in the woods, Sparrow told me that she was having dreams of a hawk. She asked me what it meant when a hawk appears over and over in dreams."

"What *does* it mean?"

"It could mean many things… but to the Cheyenne, hawks are symbolic of protection from enemies," she explained quietly. "To see one in a vision or a dream can be a warning that there is unseen danger."

"What about seeing one in real life?"

Kateri brushed her fingers back through her hair, chasing away the raindrops.

"I don't know," she admitted. "But let's be on our guard."

I nodded, a million thoughts still churning in my mind. Kateri wrapped her arms around my neck, resting her head against my chest.

"Keegan, I've been thinking."

I stroked a hand over her hair, my chin resting gently on the crown of her head.

"Hmm?"

"Maybe we should wait to tell everyone—just until Sensei returns and things aren't so chaotic."

"When are things ever *not* chaotic?" I kissed the top of her head. "You're not having second thoughts, are you?"

She smacked me playfully in the ribs, pulling back to look up into my eyes. "What do *you* think?"

"What do I think?" I repeated the question, then shook my head slowly. "I *can't* think around you." I leaned in and pressed my lips against hers, kissing her slowly. "I want to marry you more than I can possibly describe," I whispered against her lips. "I don't want to wait to tell everyone—I *don't want* to wait to marry you."

She brushed her fingertips gently over my cheek. "I know. I don't either, but..."

"But?"

Kateri gazed up into my eyes. "We have a responsibility. Sensei trusts us. We can't allow ourselves to get distracted—not even by our feelings for one another."

I took a breath to protest, then blew it back out in a sigh instead. "Why do you always have to say the right thing?" I asked, half teasing.

She laughed, kissed me. "So it's settled, then?"

"Mmm."

"*Keegan.*"

"*Fine.*" I captured her lips once more, lingering there for a moment before pulling away to look down into her eyes. "We'll wait."

95

# 13

AARON MET ME AT THE GATE. THE FIRST LIGHT OF DAWN illuminated my bloody leg and chest.

"What the hell happened?" he asked, rushing forward to loop his arm around my torso.

"We apprehended the target," Anand answered for me, jerking his head in the direction of a stretcher covered in black cloth.

Aaron gave it a quick once-over. "Dead?"

"Severely wounded," I answered, wincing as my gaze drifted to the stretcher. "Better hurry up and get him into the infirmary."

Anand dipped his head in a nod, gesturing for the two soldiers carrying the stretcher to follow him. "We'll take him there immediately. The rest of you are dismissed."

The unit dispersed. I leaned on Aaron as we slowly followed the procession carrying Icarus. Despite the pain burning through my leg and chest, I couldn't help but stare.

I hadn't seen his face yet—his human face. It'd been too dark, and I'd no longer been in possession of my night-vision shield, thanks to the damage he'd done. I couldn't help but wonder what his human face looked like in person, having only seen it in the old photo the RGM had provided me with.

"You've been hit," Aaron pointed out, alarmed.

"It was dark—and that section of the forest was hot," I explained, my voice feeble. "I ran straight ahead of our force's frontlines. It was my fault."

"Thank God you weren't *killed*."

I nodded slowly, wincing. "The rest of the damage is from the wolf."

Aaron turned to face me, bewildered. "Wolf?"

I drew a painful breath, watching as Anand and the other two soldiers hauled the stretcher through the door of the infirmary and disappeared.

"It's... a long story."

I told Aaron the whole story, filling him in on everything that had happened since I'd left the District with the rest of the unit. I described the moment we'd found the shelter deep in the forest, and the grueling fight with the wolf that had ensued... the wolf that had been *Icarus*.

"He was in a shifted shape?" Aaron asked, sounding surprised. "That's something we've never anticipated... No wonder they've been able to evade us for so long. They're using alternate forms as cover. Very clever."

I nodded slowly, still trying to process it all myself. "If he hadn't attacked me, we probably wouldn't have apprehended him—he was moving so fast."

"Well, in that case, perhaps it was worth the battle scars," he responded quietly, taking a seat on the bed where I was lying to lift my injured leg into his lap. I watched as he carefully unbound the bandages the medic had wrapped my calf in barely an hour ago, when I'd limped into the infirmary. They had removed the bullet and taped me up... but Aaron was capable of much more than that.

He smoothed his warm hands over the bruised and bloodied flesh along my lower leg, drawing slow, deep breaths, then closing his eyes as he began to focus on my healing. Clean, healthy flesh was all that remained when he removed his hand. He moved on to my other wounds—these, from the wolf attack.

My lips formed a tired smile when he finally turned to look at me once more, sweat beading at his forehead.

"How did you learn to do that with no training?" I asked quietly.

"It's always come naturally. I don't know why," he answered, sounding almost ashamed. "Are you all right?"

I nodded. "I am now. Thanks to you."

Aaron's eyes grew serious as he studied me solemnly for a moment. "I'm not talking about your wounds, Spar. I'm talking about the mission. You captured the ringleader... You captured *Icarus*. Are you... are you reconciled to it?"

The question seemed somehow far off. It took a moment for me to even understand what he was asking. I reached out and took his hand in mine, tugging it gently until at last he smiled and pulled himself closer, leaning his body over my own.

I stroked the backs of my fingers over his cheek, cupping my hand around the back of his neck and drawing him into a kiss. His lips were soft and tasted like strong coffee and the faint remnants of nicotine.

"I'm not thinking about Icarus," I answered at last, my voice quiet.

Aaron's depthless eyes softened as he stared down into my face. He traced his fingers back through my hair, then gently touched his forehead to mine.

"God, I'm so in love with you, Sparrow." His voice was a whisper.

I pulled him closer, wrapping my legs around his torso. Aaron melted in my arms, his lips moving over mine.

I tugged off his shirt and tossed it aside, running my hands over his muscled chest and shoulder blades, pulling him closer, closer—like I couldn't get him close enough. A soft moan spilled past his lips, and his hands slid underneath my shirt. I pulled it off after a moment when he didn't, and threw it across the room.

My fingers explored every inch of Aaron's skin as I kissed his face, losing myself in the feeling of his hands on my body.

"Sparrow," came his breathless whisper against my cheek as he kissed me, then drew back to look into my eyes. "Are you sure?"

I nodded. "Yes," I replied softly, capturing his lips with my own once more. "I'm sure."

At first, everything was blurry. I felt dizzy, listless... as though I were floating in ether. Then, the fog in my mind began to clear around the shapes of those hauntingly familiar trees. I felt cold droplets of rain on my skin as a dark storm cloud churned over my head.

Shielding my eyes, I searched the sky for the outline of wings. After a moment, they appeared above me, materializing seemingly out of vapor. And with them came a voice so soft it almost wasn't there.

"Sparrow..." it whispered. "Run... run far away..."

Fear tangled in the pit of my stomach as I stood there, squinting up at those wings, a hundred questions I couldn't seem to give voice to burning in my throat. The soft, female voice spoke again:

"While you still can..."

My body felt frozen. My eyes widened as I tilted my face to the sky, gazing up at the dark, winged form circling above me.

As suddenly as it had appeared, it plunged downward toward me in a dark, chaotic blur that overtook me, knocking me to the ground. As it climbed away again, it uttered one last command:

"*Go!*"

My eyes flew open, and I bolted upright, gasping and glancing around frantically.

*Where am I? What's happening?* The questions pounded in my skull along with the migraine that was beginning to pulse there.

I was in our apartment—in our bedroom. In our bed. My fingers were clenched around fistfuls of sheets, and sweat dripped down my forehead.

The room was still; Aaron lay sleeping quietly beside me. Sunlight shafted through the window and glistened over his muscled shoulders. When I glanced down at myself, my heart froze. I was naked.

I clutched the sheets to my chest, my heart racing.

"Aaron? Aaron, what happened?" The question spilled out urgently, frantically, as I jumped out of bed. "Aaron, wake up!"

He startled awake, blinking as he sat up to look at me. "Sparrow, what is it? What's wrong?"

"W-w-why am I naked?" I demanded, grabbing my underwear off the floor where it was lying beside my uniform, which had been tossed there. "What happened?"

Aaron stared at me, looking as though he had been slapped. "What happened?" He echoed my question, sounding stunned. "What are you saying? Don't you remember?"

I pressed my eyelids shut, swallowing back a sick feeling. "No. No, I don't remember—I don't remember anything."

I heard a soft rustling as Aaron brushed back the sheets and stood. A moment later I felt the warmth of his hand on my shoulder. A lump forming in my throat, I looked up into his eyes.

"Did we... did we have sex?"

Aaron pulled in a deep breath, as though unsure of what to say. Finally, he nodded.

"No..." I whispered. "No, no, no, that can't be—"

"Sparrow, you're the one who started it—I asked if you were sure."

"Is this the only time we've had sex?"

A look of alarm filled Aaron's eyes. For a moment he couldn't speak.

"Aaron," I rasped, "please tell me."

"Tell me the last thing you remember."

"My... my meeting with Bask."

"Spar, that was a few days ago."

"What do you mean days ago?" My throat tightened around the question. "I just came from there."

"No, you didn't." The look in his eyes grew more concerned. "Sparrow, you just came back from patrol—you helped apprehend Icarus. You were gone all night. You were shot... How can you not remember any of that?"

"What?"

"Icarus was captured. He's being confined in the infirmary now. You were there."

I could hardly believe what I was hearing.

*Icarus has been captured? I... I helped them do this?*

The sick feeling in my gut intensified as a wave of nausea gripped my stomach.

"Aaron, you have to help me," I managed quietly. "If my meeting with Bask was a few days ago, then I literally cannot remember the last few days. Tell me what happened—please."

"Surely you remember some of it?"

"*None*. I don't know what's wrong with me..."

A look of uncertainty passed over his face. "Tell me the truth, Sparrow," he said softly, his voice strained. "Are you in love with me?"

My heart sank a little as I studied his face; his brow was creased with anxiety. I couldn't lie to him. "I... I do love you, Aaron... but not... like that."

"Then why did you tell me you did? Why did you tell me you loved me—that you wanted to make love with me—*why?*" His voice was a hot, desperate whisper.

"I—I don't remember saying that, Aaron. I don't remember any of it."

Without another word, he began pacing the room.

"Aaron, I'm sorry—"

"You said Bask gave you something to drink when you met with him?"

"I refused to drink it at first, but he made me take it."

Aaron slammed a fist into the wall, pounding it over and over again until the plaster gave way beneath the force.

"Aaron—Aaron, stop it!" I grabbed him by the arm. "Please, just stop!"

He clenched his head in his hands, collapsing to lean his forehead against the wall, breathing fiercely.

"Aaron, what is it?" I begged. "Please talk to me."

He jerked his arm away from my touch and strode out of the room. I watched him go, standing there in the doorway. He vanished down the hallway, slamming the front door behind him.

# 14

I BURST INTO BASK'S OFFICE AND STRODE ACROSS THE room. I snatched a glass bottle of what looked like whiskey from his desk and dashed it into the fireplace. It shattered over the logs, and the liquid evaporated in a whoosh of flames.

Bask leaned back in his chair and folded his hands behind his head.

"You finally puzzled it out, did you?" he asked, his voice sarcastic and calm. "Did she come down from the drug while you were in the middle of having—"

I didn't give him a chance to finish. I lunged forward and grabbed him by the throat, dragging him towards me over the desk, leaving a mere inch between our faces.

"What did you do to her, you bastard?" I hissed, spit flying out of my mouth. "Tell me!"

Bask choked, then cracked a smile. A soft click caught my attention, the cool muzzle of a pistol sliding up against my temple.

"I will decorate my walls with your brain matter, Price," he whispered into my ear. "Let go."

Sweat dripped from my hairline, trickling down my face. My fingers trembled around his reddening throat, unwilling to release, until finally, I jerked back.

Bask pulled the trigger. A bullet bit into my thigh.

Curses roared out of my throat as I doubled over, clutching my leg. Bask came around to the front of his desk, his pistol still aimed accurately at where I stood.

"Make one move and I will pepper the walls with bullets, Price—one of them will be bound to hit you, believe me," he seethed, lowering his voice. "You think you have the right to ask me what I did to Turner?"

I gasped for air, my eyes screwed shut in pain. "H-h-her name is *Sparrow*. Not Turner. Not any other goddamn name you give her—*she is not yours!*"

"No?"

"She's my *wife*—I love her!"

He chuckled dryly. "Ah, yes. But she doesn't love you and never has. In fact, she's in love with somebody else and always has been."

Sucking in a pained breath, I struggled to straighten back up. "That's... that's a lie."

Bask lifted a thick eyebrow, staring straight ahead. "Is it? Sparrow told me so herself. She told me that she was in love with Keegan, and that was why she and you had never had sex. She didn't want to have an intimate relation- ship with someone she didn't love."

"Keegan?" I repeated quietly. "She... Sparrow..."

"Yes, she told me so herself."

"That... That can't..."

"Oh, but you *know* it's true. You and I have both always known," he re- plied, circling slowly around me. "You knew it the day that she begged for his release, when she agreed to stay. You knew that she was sacrificing herself for him—you wanted me to believe that she was one of us... and you wanted her to believe that you were a rebel... that you wanted to escape too." He paused.

"Now, at last, I know where you stand, Price. You are whoever you need to be to meet your own ends. You think you hold all the cards in your hand."

He shook his head slowly, his finger still resting on the trigger.

"You are clever, Price. But you forget one thing." His voice hushed to a whisper. "I have not yet played *my* hand."

My hand shook, still clamped firmly over my wound. Warm, clear liquid oozed out between my fingers. I felt the cold muzzle of the gun press firmly against the back of my skull.

"You think that because you are married to Sparrow, you can somehow keep her from me—from the will of the RGM," he continued softly. "You cannot. Sparrow is more ours than she is yours—we can make her love you or hate you. We can make your marriage a fulfilled one, or we can make it one of deprivation. It's all within our power, Price: *we choose*, not you."

I swallowed back the lump that had formed in my throat. "She told me that she was in love with me."

"Mm, yes. Because I told her she was—that she loved you madly. That she wanted nothing more than to reproduce with you."

"You don't even see us as people, do you?"

Bask chuckled. "You're not people, though, are you? You and your wife are nothing more than filthy sliders."

Despite the cold, hard feeling sinking in my gut, my blood was coming to a boil.

"Do you think I won't take her side in this? That I won't tell her what's happened?" I shook my head slowly, gritting my teeth. "I will tell her *every-thing*. I will tell her what you've done to her, what you've done to us..."

Bask circled around to stand in front of me once more, squatting down to my level.

"I wouldn't if I were you." His voice came out ragged but quiet, his hot breath stinking of cigarettes. "Because if you do, I'm afraid I will have to tell Sparrow that you're the reason she was captured in the first place. That *you* were the one to lure her back here... in exchange for a few honorary perks."

Rage exploding inside me, I lurched for him, but he grabbed me by the shirt, quickly sliding his hands up around my neck. He stared into the place he now knew my eyes were.

"You will say nothing to Sparrow, Price," he whispered. "You will tell her nothing of the drug."

Tears of rage burned in my eyes. "What are you trying to do to her?"

"What *you* failed to do," he replied bluntly. "The drug opens her mind to suggestion. Whatever I tell her becomes truth to her—she will accept anything. It will ultimately make her one of us."

"You think you can do that with a drug? You can't artificially induce loyalty!" I shouted into his face, tears dripping down my cheeks. "You may think you know her—that you know me too. But I know her better—*far better* than you ever will. There's a fire inside her that you'll never be able to beat out!"

"Perhaps not," he admitted. "But finding out that her husband is also her captor?" He clucked his tongue. "Now, that just might throw some water on those flames."

With a rough jerk, he shoved me backward onto the floor.

"Besides, what would you know about loyalty?" he seethed. "You've never been loyal to anyone but yourself."

The room seemed to spin around me as I staggered to my feet, every part of my body tingling with numbness.

Sparrow loving me, our marriage, our life—who I thought we were and what I thought we could become... it was all an illusion. *None of it is real.*

Everything had hung by threads. Threads that could break.

Threads that had *broken*.

# 15

I COULDN'T STOP THINKING ABOUT ICARUS—I COULDN'T
stop Aaron's haunting words from echoing in my thoughts: *"Icarus was captured. He's being confined in the infirmary now. You were there."*

How was that possible? What on earth had happened to me? I couldn't
remember anything. Not the past few days, not capturing Icarus, not having
sex with Aaron—nothing.

I still couldn't believe we'd had sex—and that I'd been the one to initiate
it. What on earth had taken possession of my mind? I had no recollection of
any of it.

When Aaron didn't come back, I put on my jacket and slipped outside
for a walk. I stopped in the middle of the dirt road. The factory churned on as
always, belching out its billows of smoke and steam. I scanned my surroundings in search of anything out of the ordinary.

Tall watchtowers rose from all four corners of the enormous walled-in
area. Barbed wire crowned the top of the wall in razor-sharp spirals. Prisoners

carried logs on their shoulders, from the entrance gates to the factory. The ground rumbled softly beneath my feet.

Beyond the gates, in the distance, I could see ant-like soldiers here and there, patrolling the hills. Acting as guards to ensure that no one got in—and, more importantly, that no one got out.

I slowed as I came up alongside the familiar barred cellar window at ground level. It brought back all those strange and terrifying feelings that come when you're uncertain of whether you'll live to see the next sunrise. I would never forget what it felt like to be trapped down there in that cell.

Shuddering inwardly, I brushed the feelings aside. I was about to walk away when a sound from below caught my attention.

A soft, barely audible sound of a human voice.

I paused again, listening more intently. I cast a quick glance around to ensure that I wasn't being observed before kneeling down beside the window.

As my eyes adjusted to the darkness, I began to make out the shape of a man lying stiffly on the ground at the opposite side of the room. I still couldn't see his face, it was turned away from me, but I could see the crimson blood streaked across his chest and caked in his long, dark hair.

My exhale silently formed his name: "Icarus..."

Almost as if he had heard me, he stirred and moaned again softly.

Chills raced down my spine. I stood there and watched him in silence for a moment before forcing myself to move on. I halted when I heard the door to the infirmary swing open and slam shut. I fell back against the side of the building. A moment later, Nakamura came into my line of sight. I watched as he disappeared among the crowd of prisoners and armed soldiers patrolling the streets.

I crept around to the front of the building and up the steps Nakamura had only just descended. I tried the door handle, and it turned easily in my palm. Silently, I slipped inside and into the hallway that led to the labs and, eventually, to the dark, turning staircase that sank into the belly of the District: the place that no one ever wanted to go.

The ground was soft and muddy under my feet as I made my way through the twisting, turning rows of cells. My throat tightened as I came to the one that had once been my own. I slowed to a stop before those cold metal bars, peering into the dimly lit space within. Icarus was a mere shadow on the floor, a still and unmoving one. For a moment I just stood there, watching him breathe, trembling inside.

His wounds had been attended to, but he was still covered in blood, and already his body was as white as stone, as if death were slowly wrapping its icy fingers around him.

Almost as though he could sense my presence, Icarus stirred on the ground, turning slowly towards me. For the first time, I saw his face. His cheeks were drained of color. His eyebrows were thick and dark like the hair that tumbled over his bloodied forehead. His eyelids were tinged with purple, and his lips were dry and cracked.

But there was something else beyond all of that. Something that felt like looking up into the night sky, feeling a vastness swelling inside you, yet you can't explain why.

His lips parted, and he drew a shallow breath, letting it back out again in a whisper—something I couldn't quite make out.

Tears stung in my eyes. God, more than anything I wanted to break into that cell—to heal him if I could. To tell him about everything—to ask him every single question that had been burning inside me since I was a little girl. But there were cold metal bars between us.

Slowly, Icarus's eyes opened. It seemed to take him a moment to focus; then his eyes locked with mine.

"Hawk?" His voice was dry and brittle.

I swallowed, shaking my head. "No," I whispered. "No, I'm not Hawk."

He blinked a few times, then attempted to sit up, giving his body a once-over, as if to make sure everything was still there. "What happened? Where am I?"

"You're in a holding cell at District Firehole," I explained quietly. "An RGM prison camp."

Icarus leaned back against the wall. "And there I was finally beginning to think I was finished with the RGM."

I stared at him, that same, strange feeling still stirring inside me. He gave me a long, careful once-over before tipping his head back against the wall.

"You're the one, aren't you?" he asked, still looking at me.

"What do you mean?"

"Last night, out there..." he rasped. "You were the one I attacked. I remember those eyes."

"I... I was just sent down here to check on you," I fibbed.

"What are they planning to do to me?" Icarus asked. "If they think they'll get anything out of me, they're wasting their time," he said, his voice quiet but steely. "They would have been better off letting me die."

"So you're one of the patriarchs," I said quietly, almost afraid to speak the words. "The one all the sliders follow."

Icarus shook his head. "No. Not me."

"But you are—"

"Yes. But if you think I am someone they follow, you're wrong," he cut in. "We protect them, that's all. We protect the movement so that Earth can continue to awaken to the voice they should follow—and that voice is not mine."

"Whose, then?"

Icarus's blue eyes shifted to mine, narrowing a little. "The only one we ever truly answer to: the voice inside us."

*The voice within.* It was exactly what the old man had said.

"It's all right if you don't know what that means," he continued. "Your heart knows."

I studied his face, everything Fin had ever told me about my parents rushing back like a tidal wave.

"And... what about Hawk?" My question came out small and timid. "Where is she?"

"You're one of them—an RGM soldier." His blue eyes grew hollow. "Why would I ever tell you?"

Lowering my eyes to the floor, I made no reply. He studied me so intensely I could practically feel the burn of his gaze on my skin.

"I feel like we must have met in another world," he said softly, more to himself than to me.

The gravity of his statement finally sank in, and my heart skipped a beat as it finally hit me.

"You can see..." My whispered words were less of a question and more of an astonished statement. "You can see us—this place."

He slowly nodded. "Can't you?"

"Yes, but..." I glanced around, checking to see if any guards had appeared. Then I turned back to Icarus. "Listen, you cannot tell anyone that you can see—no one." My voice grew urgent. "There's only been one other slider who can see this place, and they... they never got out of here." My throat tightened around the words.

Icarus gazed at me curiously for a moment; then realization dawned in his eyes. "You?"

Fighting back the lump in my throat, I jerked my head in a single nod.

Wordlessly he rose from the ground, supporting himself against the cold stone wall. Staring at me as though he had just seen a ghost, he began to slowly shake his head.

"It can't be..." His words were barely audible as he stepped closer, finally coming to a stop in front of me, gazing down into my eyes.

My heartbeat quickened as he reached through the bars and gently took my face in his hands. A soft mist of tears clouded his eyes.

"It can't be..." he whispered again, his voice cracking now.

The lump in my throat prevented me from saying anything.

"*Sparrow?*" His voice was so quiet I was surprised I could hear it.

The tears I'd been holding back sprang to my eyes. Biting my lip, I gave a single nod.

Icarus stared into my face, awe and disbelief at war in his eyes, his hands still cupping my face. "I can't believe it." His trembling words were barely audible. "I... can't believe it..."

I couldn't speak; I couldn't think of words to say. There were none.

"We have spent our lives trying to find you again." He wiped my tears gently with his thumb. "We have never stopped searching."

"Why did you leave me?" I whispered. "Why didn't—why didn't you come back?"

"It seemed that no matter what we did, we could never get close to you. We would find only clues to where you had been," he explained softly. "As if... there was something keeping you always just out of our reach."

"*We?*" I repeated, my voice shaking.

Icarus bowed his head in a single nod. "Your mother and I."

*My mother.*

Like dark magic, the words seemed to break me out of a trance, pushing me away from Icarus. I drew back, wiping away my tears.

"Look, you have to get out of here while you still can," I whispered, sniffing. "Can you transport without a portal?"

"When I recover a little strength, yes," he answered. "I'll have to wait until my wounds heal a bit. I have no energy with which to conduct a transport—sliders can't do that without full, focused energy."

"Can't you heal yourself?"

Icarus sighed. "I used to be able to, many years ago... but then we lost you, and..." His voice faded, and he shook his head. "Grief is a force that weakens us, Sparrow. Grief and bitterness, they weakened me. I resented myself for leaving you—for not being able to protect you. That was my responsibility, and I failed. I failed myself, I failed Hawk... and most of all, I failed you."

I swallowed hard. "I... I haven't been able to heal either, since..."

Since that night when I'd told Keegan that I didn't love him. When I had told him to leave and never come back, hoping with all my broken heart that this lie would somehow save him.

"Since I lost someone I loved very, very much," I finished at last, my voice a cracked whisper. "Whom I love still."

Icarus bowed his head, his eyes filled with sympathy.

"Try your best to recover." I blinked back tears, looking him squarely in the eyes once more. "You have to get out of here. They want you and Hawk dead. They're going to get what intelligence they can out of you, and then probably use you to lure her here."

"They will not succeed. I have no idea where Hawk is—we were separated months ago, during a fight with the RGM." His fingers closed around the bars as he looked out at me. "And even if I could transport, I would never leave without you. When I regain my strength, we can get out of here together."

I shook my head. "I can't."

"Sparrow, you *have* to—we have to—"

"I *can't*. I'm... I'm married to one of the soldiers. He's a slider. He wants to get out of here as much as I do. We've been trying to escape..." I trailed off, that same lump taking shape again in my throat. "I can't just leave him."

"You're *married*?"

"Yes."

"Tell me about him—how it all happened, how you came to be here. It was not of your own free will..." His eyes probed mine. "Was it?"

"I-I can't talk now," I faltered, lowering my eyes to the ground. "I have to go."

"Sparrow, you have to leave this place!" Reaching out, he grasped my arm.

"It's not that easy," I interrupted, my voice hoarse. "You don't understand. You just got here, but I've been here for a long time. I know how things work. Aaron and I have talked about leaving, but it has to wait—we have to be patient and bide our time."

"For what reason?"

My jaw firmed. "We've both been hunted down and captured like animals. We aren't willing to endure that again. Aaron thinks we can turn things around—use our powers to eventually control the RGM."

Alarm filled Icarus's eyes as he began to shake his head. "You could sooner stop a hurricane in its course. We are not here to turn a failing system of evil around to make it good." His voice rose slightly. "We're here to awaken the world—to spark a movement all our own. And beyond these walls, it's already happening!"

I gazed up into his face, a thousand lonely nights filling my head. A thousand aches that wouldn't leave my chest.

I shook my head. Closed my eyes.

I could still see those wings. I could still feel that question that had been burning inside me since before I could remember.

"No," I whispered, my eyes narrowing. "I can't just leave Aaron here..."

The expression on Icarus's face was like a turbulent sea. His hand slid down to my own, his cold fingers closing around mine. I didn't want to cry again, but tears burned in my eyes.

"I'm so sorry," he said almost inaudibly. "I'm so sorry we couldn't find you... I'm so sorry."

I felt empty as I stared at him, numb. I jerked back, hurriedly wiping my tears. Without another word, I turned and strode back down the long, dark hallway. Leaving Icarus standing there.

<h1 style="text-align:center">16</h1>

A STIRRING FROM OUTSIDE THE CANVAS WALL OF THE shelter startled me out of my sleep. I could hear the high winds rolling slowly down from the mountains and through the towering pine trees. Their soft shushing willed me to keep my eyes closed, to surrender to the arms of unconsciousness once more, but when I heard the sound of quiet footsteps outside, I sat up and looked around. Preston was gone, and I suspected the footsteps had been his.

When I stepped out into the early morning light, my suspicions were confirmed. The air was cool and crisp, and fog hung low in the woods, skirting the trunks of the trees. I spotted my friend twenty yards off, gathering deadwood and adding it to the bundle in his arms.

"You're up early," I greeted him, coming up behind him and stopping to snatch a few sticks off the ground myself.

"So are you," he returned, shooting me a chiding look. "For an insomniac."

"I guess I've been sleeping a little better lately."

He shot me another look. "And would Kateri have anything to do with that?"

I laughed. "All right. All right, fine—yes. Kateri and I are... well, I asked her to marry me."

"Are you serious?"

"Why wouldn't I be?"

"Doesn't that seem a little..."

"I don't think it's rash. I think we're in love," I answered before he could say it. "What's wrong with that?"

"Nothing—nothing is wrong with it," he replied. "I wasn't going to say rash—I don't think it's rash."

"What, then?"

He bent down and picked up another stick to lay across the bundle in his muscular arms. Then his eyes switched back to mine. "Fast."

"Our feelings for each other are real."

"I'm sure they are. I'm just surprised."

I rubbed my fingers absently over the stick in my hand. "You're the one who said that maybe it was time for me to move on."

Preston considered it a moment. "True. But that's for you to decide, not me."

"Well, I feel like I finally am." My reply rushed out almost before he had finished speaking. "I realized I *do* love Kateri. I... I *am* in love with her." I picked up another stick. "I don't see why we should wait. Neither of us does."

"I can understand the feeling. But..."

"But?"

His expression emptied to a look of raw honesty. "Are you one hundred percent sure you've moved on from Sparrow?"

Something in my chest twinged.

"Pres..."

"I know. I didn't want to bring it up. It's just..." He rubbed the back of his neck. "I think you felt a lot for her. I think you and she... had something real. It wasn't just an infatuation."

I shook my head. "For her it was. She told me so when I was there—that night when I spoke to her before they released me. She told me she never really loved me—that it was just..." My voice cracked and faded.

I heard Preston step closer. He laid a hand on my shoulder.

"But it wasn't an infatuation for you," he said quietly. "That's all that matters when it comes down to it, you know. Not what she felt or didn't feel for you, but what *you* felt for *her*. And it seems to me you felt a lot." He paused. I could feel the sting of his gaze. "Are you sure you're being fair to Kateri? Are you sure that your feelings for Sparrow are really gone?"

At first, I couldn't find the words to answer him. In my mind's eye I could still see Sparrow's face. I could still see those eyes, those dark, night-sky eyes, lit up by the fiery reflections of the sunset.

"No," I whispered. "I will never feel those things for her again. Not after... everything. Not after all that's happened." I glanced up at him. "Besides, I don't think I'll ever see her again."

"Sensei is searching for Hawk, Keegan," Preston reminded me. "He truly believes that she will be able to help bring Sparrow back to us."

"*If* he finds Hawk, you mean," I corrected him. "I hope he does, Pres. Don't get me wrong, but they've been gone a long time. Just like Sparrow..."

Preston didn't reply. He watched as I piled a few more sticks onto the stack in my arms.

"I think you gave me the best advice anyone possibly could have," I concluded finally, straightening up to look at him. "It's time to move on."

That night we were all seated in a circle outside the shelter, around a roaring fire that sparked and popped, tossing golden specks up into the sky like confetti.

I leaned closer to whisper into Kateri's ear over the noise of the chatter around us.

"Are you going to say something, or should I?" I asked her teasingly.

Kateri's warm eyes met mine. Her lips slowly curved. She looked around at the semicircle of us and then cleared her throat. "Everyone..."

The chorus of voices halted one by one, in messy succession, as the attention of our small group turned to Kateri.

"I—we—have something we would like to share," she began softly. "Keegan and I are—"

"Getting married?" Rafael piped up.

I couldn't help but laugh. "Raf, you were supposed to let *us* say it."

For a moment there was a surprised sort of silence; then everyone spoke all at once. Questions that I couldn't make out, exclamations of surprise I could barely hear. "You're kidding!" "Really?" and "When?"

I let Kateri answer. Her voice was music, firelight dancing in her eyes.

My gaze wandered to the forest, toward the path that led to the lookout point. Somewhere beyond those valleys, Dad was looking for Hawk. Somewhere beyond those valleys, Sparrow was still a prisoner...

A sinking feeling filled my chest as I glanced over at Preston and found him already looking at me. There was a halfhearted smile on his face, but something else underneath it.

My gaze drifted back to Kateri as I pushed away the memory of what Preston had said. I listened to Kateri but didn't really hear what she was saying until Myung asked her a question.

"So what are you guys waiting for?"

I snapped out of it as Kateri looked from Myung to me, her eyes glimmering with both surprise and question.

"We couldn't possibly, not until Sensei returns," she began unsteadily, seeming to want me to pitch in. "I mean..."

I thought about it and then made a decision. "But we have no idea when Sensei will return," I said. "What's the point in waiting?"

Kateri's eyes didn't move from my own for a long moment as she seemed to make a study of me.

"I think Keegan has a point, Kateri," Janna joined in, shooting Preston a pointed glance. "What's the point of waiting when you know exactly what you want?"

I smiled, and Kateri blushed.

"Well," she said, her voice collapsing in a laugh as she shook her head, "I... How could we possibly perform the ceremony without Sensei?"

"We can still exchange promises. I already know Sensei would want us to do what we felt in our hearts we should," I answered. "But it's up to you."

Kateri's deep eyes studied my own until finally she smiled and said, "All right, all right."

I kissed her hand with a flourish and said, "One month from today, then."

The lively conversation around the fire that night slowly dwindled until Kateri and I were the last ones up. She leaned her head on my shoulder. For a while I watched the stars, beginning to wonder if she'd fallen asleep against me. The fire had long since faded to a few glowing embers.

Finally, she took a deeper breath and sat up to look at me.

"What is it?" I whispered. "Is something wrong?"

Kateri looked at me for a moment and then shook her head. She lifted a hand to stroke the backs of her fingers over my cheeks. "Nothing is wrong," she replied. "I just need to ask you something."

"Mm?"

"Are we... is this..." She stopped, closing her eyes. "Is this wise, do you think?"

"Is what wise?"

"Moving so quickly."

"Is it quickly?" I asked, unsure. "It feels like it's been forever."

"In a way, yes, it does."

"You don't want to wait either, then?"

She slowly shook her head. "No, but I want to be sure we're doing the right thing."

I leaned closer and softly kissed her lips, separating only enough to whisper: "How could loving each other be wrong?"

Kateri drew back just enough to look into my eyes. "If that's what you feel, Keegan," she answered quietly. "If you are sure that's what you truly feel."

It wasn't an agreement or a disagreement, yet, even after she had kissed me again and risen to her feet to slip away from the warmth of the fire and into the shelter, her words seemed to hang in the air like a mist.

# 17

I COULDN'T LEAVE AARON BEHIND. ICARUS DIDN'T understand that Aaron was the only reason I'd been able to get both Raf and Keegan out of the District alive—I owed it to him. Despite what Aaron said, he cared about the cause of the anomalies enough to help us as much as he had—enough to help me. What kind of person would I be if I abandoned him now?

But I couldn't tell Aaron who Icarus really was and why he wanted me to leave with him. I couldn't tell him that Icarus was my father because even though it wouldn't reveal anything new about Icarus, it would reveal enough about me to put my life in greater danger than ever before.

Icarus wouldn't leave without me. I knew by the look in his eyes he wouldn't.

Was it truly because of Aaron that I refused to leave? Or was it something else?

*"Why did you ever leave me? Why didn't—why didn't you come back?"*

My own aching questions resounded in my mind; I couldn't shake out of their cold vise grip. My soul was disquieted by the answers Icarus had given—they didn't make sense to me; they only swirled and muddied the waters all the more, leaving me feeling hollower than ever.

What troubled me even more was the gap in my memory—the things I still couldn't remember at all.

Now it was like a curtain had been drawn between Aaron and me. His eyes had been empty as he sat across from me at the table that morning, staring at nothing in particular. He'd picked at the food on the plate in front of him, not making eye contact.

"Aaron." I said his name softly, waiting for him to glance up. "Aaron, please look at me."

His gaze lifted reluctantly to connect with mine, as if it was burdensome to do so.

"Aaron, speak to me."

He didn't respond. He just stared straight ahead.

"Aaron, I know I hurt you—and I'm sorry," I began quietly. "I do love you... and I... I don't know what got into me that we—"

"Don't," he interrupted. "Don't justify it, Sparrow. I... I don't need to know why you did what you did, or why you might feel differently now. It makes no difference to me."

"Aaron, I know you're angry with me."

"I *was* angry—I still *am*, but not at you, I..." Aaron trailed off, drawing a narrow breath. "I understand more than you realize."

I lifted an eyebrow. "You do?"

Aaron nodded slowly. "You've been under a lot of stress lately, and stress can make people act in ways they never thought they would—for reasons they don't even understand."

"I... guess that's true, but... but I can't remember any of it, Aaron. It doesn't make any sense to me."

Aaron shrugged. "Why don't you go see Dr. Nakamura about it? You must have an appointment coming up with him soon, don't you?"

"I don't want to talk to him about it—they're only interested in one thing: making sure I get pregnant."

Aaron didn't say a word. He lowered his gaze to the table.

A cold, heavy feeling sank inside me. "You... you did this to me, didn't you?"

"Did what?"

"You and—and Bask—" My voice rose as I pushed back my chair to stand. "You did this to me, didn't you?" I said again, louder this time.

"Sparrow, calm down—"

"No, I will not calm down, Aaron!" I shouted back. "You drugged me, didn't you? You and Bask! You gave me something so that I would have sex with you and get pregnant! That's all this is about: the RGM's desire for their own anomalies. And you—" I slammed my hands down on the table, leaning closer to look into his eyes. "You helped them!"

A muscle in Aaron's jaw tightened. "Sparrow, I had nothing to do with it—it was Bask's doing, one hundred percent of it! I had no idea until that morning—when I punched a hole in the wall. I went to Bask's office. I made him tell me everything. And then he shot me."

"He *shot* you?"

"He shot me in the leg, and he told me that he could do whatever he wanted with me—whatever he wanted with *us*, Sparrow!" Aaron's voice went hoarse, his dark eyes burning into mine from across the table. "I love you, Sparrow! I would never do anything to hurt you—but the RGM... Rest assured, they are going to do whatever it takes to get what they want out of us—whether we cooperate or not!"

I could tell by the look in his eyes that he was telling the truth. A sick feeling churned in the pit of my stomach. Almost without conscious thought, my eyes lowered to my stomach.

*I can't be...*

I closed my eyes, drawing a slow breath. "Aaron, we have to get out of here."

"We will, Sparrow. We will, but—"

"No," I cut in firmly. "Not someday: *now*. We need to get out of here now. I mean it, Aaron. I won't stay here another day—I will leave with or without you."

"They'll hunt us down like dogs, Sparrow."

"Then let them! They can shoot me at this point—I don't care! I would rather die than go on living like this!"

"You don't mean that—"

"Yes, I do mean it, Aaron!" I cut him off, my voice turning to stone. "I mean it more than I've ever meant anything."

I could see the torture in Aaron's expression, in the lines that etched the corners of his eyes and his forehead. War waged in the darks of his eyes. Abruptly he rose, brushing back his chair and snatching his jacket off the back of it.

"Where are you—"

"Bask's office," he answered before the question was even fully out of my mouth. "There's to be an interrogation of the prisoner."

"The prisoner?" I repeated. "You mean Icarus?"

Aaron gave a single nod, zipping the black jacket up to his throat. "They say that with the patriarchs, if you kill one, the other will die too. But they can't seem to kill him."

"What do they plan to do?"

He glanced over his shoulder as he turned for the door. "We'll see."

I sat by the window, my head pressed to the cool, rain-streaked glass. The long dirt road was muddy, and the prisoners and soldiers who trod it were spattered from head to toe. At the end of the road, I could see the lab. I could see the basement window with the cold iron bars keeping its prisoners in and everyone else out. Bask strode down the road in the direction of the infirmary, a few soldiers flanking him. They marched up the steps and vanished into the building.

I closed my eyes. I could still see Icarus's face... the tears in his eyes...

I pulled in a steady breath, letting it all pour out again to bathe the windowpane in steam.

*What will they do to him?*

That same nauseous feeling rose in my gut. I stood, taking long, deep breaths.

I paced the length of the bedroom, trying not to think about the sick feeling still swirling in my middle, trying not to think about what could be happening to Icarus just down the road.

I paused mid-stride, my eyes catching on the slender screen that protruded from the nightstand. The clock and the calendar were displayed, with all of my and Aaron's schedule information entered into it. My eyes narrowed as I examined it for a moment, stepping closer.

With a swipe of my finger, I circled back a month, my eyes scanning the dates. I swallowed, the sick feeling only intensifying as I swiped back to the current month, double-checking the date.

*I'm late.*

My mouth ran dry. Crossing the room, I came to a stop in front of the mirror. My focus immediately drifted back to my stomach. My uniform was already a little tight around my middle. I'd noticed it a few days ago and figured it was just that time of month, but my period hadn't come.

My eyes locked on my own in the mirror, strange, dark. Terrified. Dark circles lay beneath my eye sockets; my dark brown hair was short and scruffy against my scalp. My skin was drained of color. I was a fragment of what I had once been.

I gently placed one clammy hand over my belly, resting it there for a moment. Squeezing my eyes shut, I took a few slow, deep breaths. I walked to the bathroom and snapped on the light. I opened a cabinet and took out a small, circular metal device. I turned it over in my hand for a moment, studying it.

I unzipped my uniform jacket and untucked my tank top. I hesitated for a moment, drawing a shaky breath; then I gently pressed the metal sphere to my slightly swollen abdomen.

I held it there as it softly lit up and began to scan my belly. I held my breath.

*Please... please... please...*

I glanced back into the bedroom, to the window and beyond it where the street lay, pointing the way toward Icarus's cell, where Bask and his men had disappeared. There was still no sign of life.

A muted beep drew my attention back down to the device in my hand as the pale blue light on the top ignited.

My fingers remained clutched around the device for a moment, tightening as I stared down at the light, unable to move, to swallow, to breathe. Tears blurred my vision. The device slipped from my hands. Covering my mouth with my hands, smothering silent sobs, I slid down the wall and crumpled to the floor.

# 18

THE INTERROGATION ROOM WAS BLEACH BRIGHT AND hazed with smoke from Bask's cigarette. He sat across from Icarus at a small metal table in the center of the room. Icarus looked like a dazed animal that had been dragged from its hole and pinned under those bright lights. His eyes were bloodshot, and his face was drained of color beneath his scraggly hair and beard.

I sat at the back of the room with two other security forces soldiers, watching and listening.

Bask asked Icarus questions and took notes.

"Were you and Hawk together at the time you were captured?"

Icarus made no reply.

"We have the power to have you executed, Icarus. Do you realize that?"

Icarus stared straight ahead. "Do *you*?" he said flatly.

My eyebrows lifted, my attention shifting to Bask to see how he would react. I noticed the back of his neck reddening.

"You have tried and failed to kill me," Icarus continued. "What makes you think you will be able to do so now?"

For a moment Bask didn't respond. I began to wonder whether this had stumped him. Then he cleared his throat.

"Icarus, when we find Hawk, we will kill her."

"What makes you think that you'll be able to?"

Bask struck Icarus across the face, sending him sprawling backward, his chair clattering to the floor. Suddenly, something that felt like sonar pounded against my body. A flash of white light radiated out from Icarus's body, sending Bask flying out of his chair and slamming into the bolted metal door. His cigarette rolled across the floor.

The soldier beside me jumped to his feet and held out a hand to him. "Sir! Are you all right, sir—"

"Get away from me!" Bask roared, slapping his hand away. He clawed his way up to his feet, swiping a palm over his thin greasy hair and straightening his jacket.

Icarus was already up and seated at the table again by the time Bask reached it. Undaunted by what had just happened, he leaned right across it once more and grabbed Icarus by the throat—only to lurch back an instant later, screaming in pain.

I caught only a glimpse of the palm of his hand, but it was all I needed to clearly see the bloody boils across the skin.

Icarus remained seated in his chair, staring straight ahead. Bask clamped his unscathed hand over the burned one, whirling around to throw an outraged glance in our direction. "Don't just sit there, goddammit—secure him!" he ordered, fuming.

The young soldiers who flanked me jumped to their feet and surged forward to grab Icarus by the arms. I didn't move from where I was seated. At first, Icarus seemed to submit; then, as one of the two soldiers whipped out a set of bands to tighten around his wrists, I saw Icarus's sharp eyes dart to the side.

He snapped his hands effortlessly out of the soldiers' grasps, pushing his arms out to the sides, palms open. The two soldiers went flying in opposite directions, crashing against the walls and falling to the floor.

Bask sat speechless, still clutching his wounded hand. Icarus slowly pulled back his arms to rest his palms on his lap.

I rose quietly, stepping over the limp legs of my comrades to circle around the desk and position myself behind Icarus.

Bask leaned closer, his jaw trembling, sweat sheathing his face. He stared into Icarus's eyes and drew an unsteady breath.

"Perhaps we cannot kill you, cannot kill Hawk..." he began raggedly. "But if you have a child... we will discover it. We will find it. We will track it down. We will make it suffer, and we will kill it before your very eyes."

Icarus's jaw tightened.

Bask waited a moment, seeming to gauge Icarus's response—or lack thereof. His narrow eyes scanned Icarus's face, and for a moment the only sound in the room was the quiet hum of the lights overhead and my commander's labored breathing.

Icarus didn't move, didn't speak. He seemed to have no idea that anyone was standing behind him. I drew my pistol from its holster and brought the butt of it down on the back of his head. He froze and then slumped forward onto the desk with a thud.

Bask stared down his nose at Icarus, his eyes narrowed to slits.

"What makes you think that Icarus and Hawk have a child?" I asked.

My commander gestured toward Icarus.

"Lift him back up."

I hesitated a moment, puzzled. Then, reaching forward, I took hold of Icarus by the shoulder and pulled him back up to a seated position in his chair; his head slumped listlessly on his chest. Bask waved me to his side.

Circling back around to the front of the desk, I halted alongside my commander and faced Icarus.

"Tell me what you see, Price," he said, his voice quiet but forceful.

I paused, giving Icarus another once-over. "I see a slider."

"No."

I glanced at Bask. Again, he gestured toward the prisoner.

I studied Icarus up and down. I stared into his face, glimpsing the features that were less noticeable beyond his straggly beard and long hair. His thick, dark eyebrows, the structure of his face, the lines of his nose, his lips hanging open.

"What do you see?" Bask asked.

I gazed into Icarus's face now with intent, a strange heaviness beginning to take shape inside me.

Bask leaned a little closer to where he sensed that I stood. "*Who* do you see?" he whispered.

I swallowed, unable to answer. Unable to think fast enough.

"No." My voice was a ragged croak. "No, no, it can't—there's no possible—"

"Think about it, Price—think carefully before you speak," Bask said, a strange note of excitement in his voice. "Think carefully."

My fingertips began to tingle, my throat running dry.

"Now tell me whose face you see when you look into his." I felt Bask's hot breath on my neck. "Tell me whose face you see, Price."

My mind raced back to the day Sparrow had told me that she had never known her parents, that they had abandoned her.

I swallowed, my throat tight.

"We have no record... no evidence that Hawk and Icarus ever had a child..." I responded carefully.

Bask seemed to consider this for a moment before slowly nodding and turning his gaze back to Icarus. "And no evidence that Sparrow ever had parents..." He paused, looking back in my direction. "Now, is that not the strangest coincidence?"

My heart began to beat faster; I didn't know what to think, what to say. It was all a whirling blur.

Bask shook his head slowly. "I always thought there was something... *something* about her, though I could never quite..." He broke off, rubbing his jaw. "My god, Price, do you understand what this means if it's true? Can you even glimpse it?"

I turned to face him. "My wife is not the daughter of the patriarchs. She is... she is..."

"She is what, Price?" Bask interrupted, scoffing. "You have no idea. You knew *nothing* about her when you married her—you only ever knew one thing: that she could see you!"

"And it was the only thing that mattered!" I exploded. "Do you think I *wanted* to deceive her? To—to lure her back here, to *lie* to her? To tell her that Keegan was here and that I would help her to rescue him? That—that we would all escape together? Do you think I *wanted* to lie to her? My god, it has eaten me up inside!"

Bask tipped his head back, still only half occupied with what I was saying. "Don't behave as though you are a victim in all of this, Price. You had a choice. You come and go as you please, and no one can stop you, not really." He paused. "Two choices were laid before you: a life in freedom with Sparrow, or a life of infamy within the ranks of the RGM, and you chose the latter. That's why you lured her here. That's why you lied to her. That's why you captured her and Keegan. That's why you beat him and killed him when I asked you to. You didn't even tell her of the drug and the influence it had over her simply because I commanded you not to. You did all of this, Price..." He tapered off, turning finally to look in my direction. "You did *all of this* because you chose to do it. You chose us over her."

My heart was hammering in my throat. My brain felt frozen yet ablaze. I stared straight ahead.

"Now another choice must be made, Price," Bask continued, his voice level. "Will you go and get your wife?"

My eyes shot to his. Bask stared hollowly into the thin air.

I turned and looked at Icarus again; his head was still collapsed against his chest.

I looked back at my commander. His unyielding face waited for an answer.

Swallowing back my heart, I surrendered.

"Yes, sir."

Bask dipped his head in a small, approving nod. That was all. I left the room and stepped out into the hallway. A ringing filled my head as I walked, each of my footfalls seeming more and more muffled as though I were hearing them underwater.

Outside, twilight unfurled across the District, though I barely comprehended the glow of the flickering lanterns that hung all around me, or the sounds of the prisoners' voices as the factory ground to a halt for the night. I saw only the building at the far end of the road, drawing nearer and nearer at an alarming rate that I couldn't seem to stop. Suddenly it was just before me; suddenly I was mounting the steps and opening that familiar door.

I stepped into the dark interior of our apartment, pausing a moment in the entryway, clutching the handle of the door, pressing my eyelids shut, forcing myself to breathe.

"Sparrow." My voice cracked as I spoke into the darkness. I waited and received no answer.

Stepping into the kitchen, I walked quietly through the room and into the next. Both were vacant.

The bedroom door stood open. I glimpsed a silhouette against the faint amber glow of the window.

I stopped in the threshold, supporting myself against it, drawing a feeble breath.

"Sparrow." My voice came in a cracked whisper. "You have to come with me. There's... there's something important we need your help with."

The figure didn't answer. Didn't move.

I stepped farther into the room. "Sparrow."

The figure slowly turned, revealing not the face of Sparrow but the haunting outline of another, shadowed beneath the hood of a cloak. My eyes widened, and every muscle in my body tensed as he lifted his hood, revealing piercing eyes that bored into mine.

"Aaron," a voice deeper than thunder intoned, "what have you done?"

I staggered back, turning, falling against the wall; I fumbled for the light switch, snapping it on. The bedroom illuminated.

There was no one there.

# 19

I PULLED ON MY JACKET AND HAT AND SLIPPED OUT THE door, skirting the row of buildings in the darkness. The sky was dim purple overhead, fading to the darkest shade of blue along the horizon.

I shivered into my coat, sprinting forward under the cover of the deepening night. Rain pelted down in large drops, further saturating dirt roads already engulfed with runoff. The flash of lanterns swinging from their hooks lit my way as I ran the length of the dank alley between rows of buildings. When I reached the end, I halted.

A couple of soldiers carrying lanterns marched through the courtyard, sending up splashes with each of their heavy boot-falls. Their voices were muffled by the thundering of the rain. Beyond them, the infirmary stood ignited by soft tungsten lamplight. I squinted, searching for the small, barred window to Icarus's cell.

I waited until the soldiers had marched into the distance to sprint across the courtyard and drop down alongside the window.

"Icarus," I whispered into the void. "Icarus, can you hear me?"

The rain pattered down to fill the silence. I reached through the space between the bars, feeling in the emptiness.

"Icarus, can you hear me?"

"He's not there, child."

I whirled around, stumbling and falling back against the side of the building. A dark figure loomed before me, barely standing out against the dark, smoky sky. My voice caught in my throat. A hand reached out, each wrinkle stretching across his weathered palm reflecting in the lamplight. The old man stood before me.

"He's not there. Come, we must speak quickly."

I reached up and grasped his hand, allowing him to help me to my feet again and lead me around to the back of the building, where we were concealed. He placed his hands on my shoulders as we stepped into the shadows, stopping me where I stood.

"You must leave, Sparrow—now. You must leave." His voice was even and serious. "They know. They have found out what you yourself are still unsure of."

"W-what are you talking about?"

"One need only look into your eyes to see the path of your origin, Sparrow," he replied, his gaze intense through the cold drizzle. "Do you need further evidence? Do you not glimpse it each time you look into the mirror? Do you not feel it with every breath you take? Do you not hear whispers of it on the edge of the wind?" He stepped closer, lowering his voice. "Does not all of creation cry out to you through every sense you possess? Does it not roar 'Awaken'?"

A warm feeling swelled within me as I stood there and stared into his face. I didn't know what it meant, but I knew it was there. And that was all that mattered.

"I'm pregnant," I said softly. My words were like white water the dam could no longer hold back. "I'm afraid."

"Which is why you must leave—and now," he answered firmly. "This child is what they've always wanted. They will keep you under lock and key, and once the child is born, they will use it for their own purpose—as a weapon of darkness."

"But that will not be for months."

The old man shook his head slowly. "It will be much sooner than you think, Sparrow; the RGM has altered you."

My throat tightened. "How do you mean?"

"It will not be long," he replied softly. "Maybe three months."

I swallowed hard. "Three months? Three months until the baby is born?"

"They injected you with a serum on each of your visits to the infirmary. It contained the ability to speed up the reproduction process." The old man took my hand. "You must escape, and you must escape now. You will not be able to conceal your condition for long."

I drew a shaky breath, pinching my eyes shut, trying to process all of this. "Aaron..." I whispered. "I can't just leave him here."

"You must."

I turned and looked up at him. "I have to see Icarus—I have to."

Before he could say another word, I wrenched away from his grasp and took off at a run. It was something I couldn't explain. I didn't expect anyone to understand, but something inside me needed... a confirmation.

I was carrying a child inside me who had a father, and if I was going to leave him behind without a word, then I needed to at least take Icarus with me.

*Was it that something inside me knew Icarus was indeed my father, just as the old man had said? Did I actually believe that, deep down?*

I wasn't sure. But I knew that Icarus was good, I'd glimpsed it in his eyes, and there was no way I was going to leave him in the clutches of the RGM. He'd promised that he wouldn't leave without me, and he'd kept his word.

I felt every bit as determined to keep my own promise: the silent one I had made that I would not leave him either.

I rounded the infirmary and crept up the steps, peeking into Nakamura's office before reaching out for the doorknob. The office was dark.

As quietly as I could, I let myself in. I padded silently across the room and into the hallway opposite, making my way down the long, cement corridor. I carefully rounded the corner—and then halted at the echoing sound of voices.

I collapsed back against the wall, breathing hard, droplets of rain trickling down my face. A dull, twisting pain stung in my abdomen. I bent forward, biting my tongue as my hand slid to my belly.

Breathing steadily, I forced myself to straighten back up, ignoring the pain. I inched my way closer to the door from which the voices seemed to emanate. I leaned my head to the side, straining to hear every muffled word through the thick iron door and bulletproof glass.

"You have no idea." The voice was Bask's. "You knew nothing about her when you married her—you only ever knew one thing: that she could see you!"

"And it was the only thing that mattered!" Aaron's own voice exploded. "Do you think I *wanted* to deceive her? To—to lure her back here, to *lie* to her? To tell her that Keegan was here and that I would help her to rescue him? That—that we would all escape together? Do you think I *wanted* to lie to her? My god, it has eaten me up inside!"

My insides suddenly felt hollow.

"Don't behave as though you are a victim in all of this, Price. You had a choice. You come and go as you please, and no one can stop you, not really." He paused. "Two choices were laid before you: a life in freedom with Sparrow, or a life of infamy within the ranks of the RGM, and you chose the latter. That's why you lured her here. That's why you lied to her. That's why you captured her and Keegan. That's why you beat him and killed him when I asked you to. You didn't even tell her of the drug and the influence it had over her simply because I commanded you not to. You did all of this, Price..." He trailed off. "You did *all of this* because you chose to do it. You chose us over her."

*No... no...*

My thoughts were dim and flickering like the flame of a candle at the end of its wick. I tried to swallow, but my throat was too dry.

"Now another choice must be made, Price," Bask said. "Will you go and get your wife?"

Every muscle in my body tightened, sweat beading on the back of my neck as I braced myself for the answer, my trembling fingers clenching into fists. The answer came in two flat words:

"Yes, sir."

I waited in the shadows until I heard the door of the lab open. A moment later Aaron strode by, his eyes hollow as he stared straight ahead, leaving the infirmary. I gazed after him, fully aware of where he was headed, still hardly able to believe that he was about to betray me—had been betraying me since he'd brought me here. And I'd been too blind to see it.

The door to the lab opened a second time, and two guards dragged a barely conscious Icarus out of the room and down the long, dimly lit hallway. I followed them like a ghost.

Icarus put up no resistance as the guards hauled him down into the belly of the District. I ducked into a dark adjacent hallway and waited, my back to the wall, listening as the guards unlocked his cell and threw him inside. I heard the jangle of keys and a click as they locked the door once again.

"If you're so powerful," sneered one, "then break yourself out of this cell—level this place to the ground! Show us what you've got. Save yourself!"

Icarus made no response. After a moment of snickering and jeering, the two guards departed once more, making their way back down the hallway. I could hear them nearing my hiding place. I held my breath as they walked past, disappearing into the darkness once more. I remained there for a moment, my back to the cold, damp wall and my heart pounding in my chest, until I was certain that I was alone again.

I sprinted to Icarus's cell and grasped the bars, thrusting my face between them.

"Icarus!" I hissed.

He was slumped against the wall, but at my voice his eyes opened. He struggled to his feet and made his way slowly to the cell door to close his hands over my own. His deep blue eyes met mine. "Sparrow, what are you doing here?"

"We have to go," I whispered. "They know that I'm your…" I trailed off, stopped. "They *know*."

Stunned, he took a step back and swallowed, his jaw set. "You're in grave danger, Sparrow. Does your husband know this too?"

"He was there, discussing it with them. He's betrayed me… many times." The words sank inside me like ice. "I didn't know until tonight, but I watched him leave to go find me—to bring me to the lab. To Bask."

"You must leave him behind."

"Yes. Yes, I know that now. He can't find out about…" I paused.

"About what?" he asked.

I drew a deep breath, hardly able to speak the words. I slid one hand to my stomach. "His child," I said quietly. "I'm pregnant."

Fury flashed in Icarus's eyes. In one quick motion, he flattened his hand against the lock on the gate. Sucking in a pained breath, he closed his eyes. The metal began to hiss softly—and a moment later, the lock burst. He swung the gate open and pulled me inside—into his arms.

He held onto me as though he would never let go, and I wrapped my arms around him. I could hear his heart beating in his chest, feel tears stinging in my eyes.

"Do you have enough energy to transport both of us out?" I whispered urgently as I drew back to look at him. "Are you all right to do this? You're still in pain. Have you healed enough?"

Icarus pulled my head back to his chest, placing a soft kiss in my hair. For a moment he didn't answer; he just held me.

"Trust me, Sparrow." His voice broke. "I'll save you."

Tears burned in my eyes as I held tightly to him—afraid in ways that I never had been before. Afraid because I was pregnant. Afraid because the man I had come to trust had betrayed me in ways I would never have thought possible—had killed the man that I loved. Afraid because the RGM knew something about me that they had never known before. Afraid because now… now *I knew it too*.

"Think of nothing," Icarus said softly.

My thoughts became numb, nonexistent. Slowly, my body became heavy, yet it felt as though I were floating at the same time. I could barely feel my arms around Icarus anymore, but I could still feel the warmth of tears trickling down my cheeks.

As everything began to fade, slipping away into a dark void, I heard the faint sound of his voice one last time.

"I love you, Sparrow."

I had the sudden feeling of having been pulled out of my body, completely displaced; I had no idea what was happening or where I was. For a moment I was lost in the ether, weightless and numb.

Then, abruptly, I fell back into consciousness. I felt ground beneath my feet and the palms of my hands—but it was different, colder. I was on my hands and knees on the ground. I slowly opened my eyes and looked up to find dark silhouettes of trees towering above me, spinning listlessly.

Squeezing my eyes shut again, I tried to steady myself; my heart was pounding in my chest.

A cool, soft breeze brushed against my skin.

I wasn't in the basement of the infirmary anymore. I wasn't in Icarus's cell—I was outside. I was...

*Free.*

"We made it," I whispered, my voice shaking. "Icarus, we—we made it—"

My words died in my throat as I opened my eyes and looked around.

Icarus wasn't there. I was alone in the woods.

"No." I clambered to my feet. "No—no, no, no! Icarus! *Icarus!*"

My voice trembled as I shouted into the cold darkness, spinning wildly about, searching the still, silent trees around me. But there was no sign of life.

"Icarus..."

*"Do you have enough energy to transport both of us?"* My question haunted me. *"Have you healed enough?"*

Tears welled and burned in my eyes as I stared into the darkness before me, the darkness where, only moments ago, Icarus had been. My arms felt cold now, no longer wrapped around him.

He hadn't had enough energy. Not for both of us... Just one.

His answer hung in the air like the voice of a ghost: *"Trust me, Sparrow. I'll save you."*

Pain cutting through my chest like a knife, I squeezed my eyes shut. Tears spilled down my cheeks as I crumpled to the ground.

# 20

THE DAYS PASSED AS STEADILY AS THE COOL WATER THAT ran in the streams. I was so tired of waiting. I had so much inside me, waiting to be set free. Sometimes I wondered why we didn't just leave—transport out of Section West completely and be done with it. Why were we there, if not to heal?

My conversation with Rafael still echoed in my mind.

*"If it wasn't for her, I never would have gotten out of there alive... I can't stand that I'm just sitting around, hiding here, doing nothing while she's trapped there."*

I'd replied, "She wanted to be there," as if I knew.

And I'd never forget that look on his face—the look he had given me. Half disbelief, half disappointment.

*"You can't really believe that, Keeg—you know full well that that couldn't have been what she really wanted!"*

No matter how much I tried, I couldn't seem to wash those words out of my mind; I couldn't seem to escape them. I knew how Raf felt. I couldn't stand waiting any longer, either. And that was exactly what I told Preston the following morning before the sun had even risen.

"Keeg?" he murmured, rubbing his eyes. He squinted at me through the gray light of dawn. "What's going—?"

I was crouched on the canvas mat beside him, riffling through my belongings with as little noise as possible, tossing things hurriedly into a rucksack. I lifted a finger to my lips before he could finish, shooting a cautioning glance in the direction of where Rafael was still sleeping, Cub curled up at his side.

"I can't wait for Sensei to return any longer." My tone was hushed but urgent. "I have to do *something*. If it is Hawk who must be found, then I can't just stand by—I have to be out there, helping Sensei find her."

"You have no idea where Sensei went, Keeg," Preston protested, looking a little more alert. "And he told you to stay here—you and Kateri both. He gave you each a place of responsibility."

"Kateri is more than capable of keeping things together," I replied, continuing to toss things hurriedly into the open sack. "I'm of no use here. I think Sensei's been waiting to see what I will do... and I know now that I cannot just stand by."

Preston studied me in the dim light for a moment, an expression on his face that I couldn't quite read. "Don't you trust him?"

"With my life," I replied without hesitation. "And he trusts me. I cannot—I *will not* let him down, Preston. If Sensei truly believes that it is Hawk who can bring Sparrow back, we *have* to find her."

Preston was quiet for a long moment, his lips pursed. "You're getting married in less than two weeks."

"What does that have to do with this?"

Preston shot me a firm, knowing look. "Come on, man, don't pretend. Not with me."

Heat flushed my neck as I understood his meaning. "I want to help get Sparrow back, Pres—of course I do. Not because I love her, but because I know who she—"

I stopped myself short before I blurted it out.

"She's one of us," I rephrased in a whisper. "I would do the same if it were you or anyone else."

Preston's dark eyebrows pressed together in the center of his forehead. Finally, he rendered a nod.

"What about Kateri? What are you going to tell her?"

I pulled in a slow breath, considering it for a moment. Then I yanked the drawstrings on the rucksack and looped it over my shoulder.

"Nothing," I stated. "I... I can't talk to her about this yet. It's nothing I can put into words, it's just something I have to do. But you understand me."

"Not really."

"You'll know better how to tell her."

Preston shook his head. "No. No, no, I am not telling her anything, Keeg. You tell her yourself."

"I can't—there's no time, and I know she'll want me to stay."

"Maybe that's what you should be doing."

"What?"

"*Staying*," he countered firmly.

"We've been hiding up in these mountains long enough, Preston—I cannot anymore," I answered firmly, rising to my feet. "I've had dreams of Hawk—dreams that I've seen her."

Preston's eyebrows rose in surprise. "When?"

"A while ago. And once, I woke up, and she was actually there."

"Have you told anyone?"

"Only Kateri."

He drew in a breath only to blow it out in a sigh. "You saw *a* hawk, Keegan," he protested. "There's no way for you to know that it was Hawk herself. You're going to leave Kateri without a word to chase shadows?"

"I know what I saw, Preston. It is for Kateri's sake—for all of ours—that I *have* to go." I made my way to the flap of the tent and paused there, one hand clutching the canvas. "Please tell her. Please try to explain."

Preston dragged a hand over his face as he pushed himself up to a seated position, passing me a weary look.

"There's never any stopping you when you've made up your mind, is there?" His question was a tired one. I could tell he didn't expect an answer. He gestured irritably for me to go. "Fine. Fine, Keeg. I'll tell her."

I bowed my head. "Thanks, Pres."

At this, Cub lifted her head, slowly opening her big greenish-yellow eyes to peer at me suspiciously. When she saw that I was opening the tent flap to step outside, nothing could hold her back. She bounded to my side. Thankfully, she was noiseless on her massive paws, and Raf remained asleep.

I shot one last look at Preston. "Tell her I'll be back in a few days," I whispered.

Preston frowned but surrendered a begrudging nod. "Fine. But you'd better be back here before the date, though—I won't make an excuse for you."

"Don't worry," I assured him. "I'll be back long before then."

Without another word, I slipped outside, letting the flap of the shelter shut behind me. Cub, as if anticipating my plans with some surreal intelligence, was already standing at the edge of the woods, watching me with her sharp eyes, waiting for me to follow. And I did... though not without pausing to look back over my shoulder at that little camouflaged shelter among the trees. I couldn't help but wonder if Preston was right. But in the back of my mind there was a burning sensation I could not ignore: there was a voice that tore me apart at the seams, and I could not disobey its command.

I couldn't explain it, not even to myself. And that was why I couldn't tell Kateri—how could I speak of something I myself didn't understand? I couldn't tell her even if I wanted to—because I would have to explain why, and I'd sworn to my father that I would never tell anyone who Sparrow really was: the daughter of the patriarchs.

She was made of stars and born from something far greater than I could understand. And despite what she said, what she thought, and perhaps even what she wanted... she was the missing key. Maybe she just needed to realize it. Maybe she just needed to be awakened.

Dad knew Hawk better than anyone—loved her. Had spent his life in silent, faithful service to her; in a way, he seemed every bit as bound to Hawk as Icarus was. The distance between him and the woman he loved had never prevented him from giving himself to her fully. In his heart, he was married to her, in a way, and because of that, I believed that he knew her better than anyone. He believed that she could help us get Sparrow back.

And so, I fixed my gaze straight ahead and walked deeper and deeper into the woods that lay ahead, blanketed in the thick fog that swelled from the ground.

I thought of Kateri as I walked away, pulling up the hood of my warm sweatshirt. In my pocket was the eagle's feather Dad had given me. The very same one I had tucked into Kateri's hair the night I had kissed her. The night I had realized just how much I cared about her.

Every little detail of that night seemed to fill my thoughts as I trod across the cold ground, my soft moccasins leaving footprints in the dew.

For the first time in a long time, I felt a sense of clarity. A sense of actually knowing what I was doing. I felt more myself than I had in the weeks I'd spent staring out at the valley sprawling below us, wondering what to do, wondering where Dad was, and whether I was doing the right thing. I felt like I was finally where I needed to be; I finally had a direction. Maybe it was because, deep down, I knew this was what my father wanted me to do.

As I left, I felt as if part of me stayed behind with Kateri. Part of me never left her. When I returned I would have so much to tell her, and doubtless she would have things to tell me too. Part of me wished we could race through time—already be married, already belong to each other. There was an anxiousness inside me that I couldn't account for, that I couldn't quite put into words.

But I pushed these thoughts to the back of my mind, focusing on following Cub through the dense forest.

I trekked down the mountain toward the valley sprawling below, the same place where I had seen the hawk swooping low over the woods a month earlier.

Making my way through the trees, I came to a stop alongside a large oak to peer up at the clear, cold sky.

I wondered where Dad had gone to search for Hawk, wondered whether or not he was scouring Section West, or whether he had transported out to look for her elsewhere. Where did he believe she was after all these years?

*Why didn't she ever come back?*

The question rang in the back of my mind as I continued through the forest. It was the same question that had haunted my father for many years, distressed him more than he had ever put into words. His unyielding devotion to Hawk never ceased to awe and confuse me in equal measure. He loved her still. Yet, it seemed, she was forever out of his grasp.

I swallowed back a tight feeling in my throat, continuing deeper into the forest until I was far from the shelter and the mountains. Until I was far from any sign of life.

Any life I could *see*, anyway.

# 21

"SPARROW..." I WHISPERED HER NAME INTO THE DARKNESS.

The steady, echoing drip of condensation coming off the walls was the only sound I heard in reply.

Sparrow's own face, once the sweetest tonic to my tortured mind, was no longer a comfort but a further poison, yet I couldn't escape it. I couldn't get her face out of my mind.

How was it possible that she was Icarus's daughter? How had I not seen it? She was the very offspring of the two beings who had doomed my fate, yet without her my life was reduced to dust.

I stared up at the ceiling in the darkness, stretched out stiff on the cold floor. I watched the shadows dance across the ceiling when someone trod past with a lamp and the light ventured in. I listened to the air fill and leave my lungs. When the ground did not tremble, there was a stillness unlike any I remembered: it was so quiet. The kind of quiet that keeps a haunted man from his sleep.

My voice ached in my parched throat as my lips formed the name that had once been the most beautiful word in the world.

"Sparrow..."

Cold, dark silence was the only response. Then, steadily, out of that stillness came a voice.

"Why did you not leave when you had the chance?"

I sat up, staring wildly around. In the shadows of the next cell, a figure sat with his back to the cold cement wall. I squinted, trying to make him out.

"If you had truly loved her, you would have escaped with her long ago," he continued. "It's your selfish ambition that has kept you here—it's the reason you are in that cell now."

I stood, walking to the barred wall that separated my cell from his. At the same time, he stepped out of the shadows, and I saw his face.

"Icarus?"

He tipped his head back, his sharp blue eyes peering through the darkness. With a jolt, I realized he was staring *right at me.*

"You..." My voice faded in my throat. "You can see me? That's... that's impossible. I—I knocked you out. You didn't even see me standing there—"

"I saw you," Icarus interrupted, his eyes locked on mine. "I chose to let you hurt me so I wouldn't have to hurt you."

"Bullshit—why wouldn't you defend yourself?"

"Because I don't need to. There's nothing you can do that would hurt me."

I stared at him, thunderstruck, as he stared back at me.

"How the hell is it possible that you can see me right now?" I said more quietly now. "I thought only Sparrow could."

Icarus shook his head. "The more you learn to see into the invisible parts of yourself, the more you can see of other people."

"I... don't understand."

"I was not always who I am today," he said. "I was more or less dragged into the anomaly movement. I didn't know if I even believed in it at first. Much like my daughter. Much like you."

My jaw hardened as I shook my head. "No. No, not like me. I don't believe in anything—I don't stand for anything. That's the reason you're in that cell. That's the reason Sparrow is gone. That's the reason I just killed a man. Because I'm not like you—I never will be."

Icarus didn't flinch. He just kept staring at me.

I wrapped my fingers around the cold metal bars, looking back at him.

"You know how she escaped, don't you?" My voice dropped to a hoarse whisper. "You helped her... I should have guessed. I'm surprised you didn't save yourself."

"I couldn't. I didn't have enough strength left. Only one of us was getting out of here."

"And you chose her over yourself?"

"That's what you do when you truly love someone," he replied steadily. "When there's nowhere to go, when there's no way out... When you find yourself at the edge of a cliff with no escape—you choose them. Because you love them. It's not even a question."

"So you sacrificed yourself for Sparrow... because you truly love her." I let out a miserable laugh, shaking my head slowly. "Whereas I, on the other hand, have used her... I've kept her chained here. I've lied to her, she doesn't even know it, but I'm the reason she was trapped here in the District. I wanted the power it would bring... but that power." I blew out a sigh. "It was all an illusion. She was the only thing that was ever real. Now I've lost her... and I will be hanged in the morning." Tears stung in my eyes. "I deserve it. I deserve to die... I was going to betray her. I was... I was about to do something I never thought I would do."

"We all have shadows, Aaron," he replied quietly. "Two wolves battling inside us: one of darkness, and one of light. It's never about eliminating one or the other... It's about which one we feed. Which one we follow. That's what makes the difference... that's what saves us."

"Yeah? And how the hell would you know?" I asked sharply. "I'm the reason you're here, Icarus! Do you get that? I'm the reason Sparrow has been through hell! I'm the reason all of this is happening. *I'm the reason.* Do you even know what that feels like? To be responsible for destroying the very person who means the most to you?"

Icarus stepped closer, the dim light reflecting in his eyes. "Yes. Yes, I do, Aaron. I know more of what you're going through than you realize. You're not like them, Aaron. You never were," he went on. "You have the potential to do something great. You have it within you to be the man my daughter believed you were... to be the father your child deserves."

My throat tightened. "You... you know that she's pregnant?" Icarus bowed his head. "Now I'll never see him... or her," I said, more to myself. "My own child, and I'll never see their face or hear their voice..."

"You are the decider of your own path... No one else can take that journey for you. You have it within you to follow the white wolf... The choice is yours, Aaron."

My eyes narrowed as I studied him, still clutching the bars between us.

"White wolf? What the hell does that mean?"

Icarus looked me square in the eyes—as if he could see straight through me, into my thoughts. Into my innermost being.

"When the time comes," he answered, "you'll know."

Before I could ask another question, a door slammed, and I heard the muffled clomping of boots approaching. I retreated to the back wall of my cell, sitting down on the floor. The footsteps halted abruptly just outside the barred door of my cage.

I could feel the sting of the guard's gaze as he searched for where I might be. Though I was bathed in the light from his lamp, he couldn't see me.

"Are you ready?" His voice boomed in the small enclosure. "I am giving you one last chance, Price," he growled. "I'm giving you one last chance to redeem yourself."

The corners of my mouth twitched toward a miserable smile. I shook my head.

"No," I managed at last. "No, there is nothing that could redeem me. Nothing in this world, anyway."

The guard grunted. "We have the power to execute you, Price. We can make that happen sooner rather than later."

"What can you possibly believe that I know?"

"Corporal Turner's whereabouts, as you were the one to aid her in her escape."

I glanced over at Icarus, my jaw tightening. He watched me in silence from the shadows.

I could tell the guard everything Icarus had just told me. Maybe they would lighten my sentence. Maybe...

I swallowed, squeezing my eyes closed.

*Sparrow*. Icarus had rescued her. She would be so devastated if anything more happened to him.

"I will tell you nothing," I whispered.

"You were commanded to retrieve her—and instead of bringing her to us, you helped her escape. And then you proceeded to commit the *greatest atrocity* a soldier can commit." Fury bled through his voice. "You knew what it all meant—when Bask told you Turner was Hawk and Icarus's child. She is the very key to finding Hawk—to luring her here if she would not come for Icarus's sake... Surely, she would have come to the aid of her daughter. We could finally have had them both in one place. We could finally have destroyed them!"

"What makes you believe you *will* be able to destroy them? When you're incapable of destroying even Icarus?"

"They are connected; the one keeps the other alive. Separate, they are strong, because the stronger one will keep the weaker alive. But if they are together, in the same place, then *we* are in control."

"And you think she would have come for Sparrow?"

"Sparrow is her own flesh and blood."

I swallowed, my jaw tightening. My voice crashed through the quiet as I repeated the words: "Bask would have killed her."

The words hung in the air like ghosts. The guard's face was dimly lit by the rusty glow from the lantern in his hand.

"Just as you destroyed our commander," he returned, his voice flat and icy, "you too will be destroyed."

## *ONE DAY EARLIER*

I felt rooted to the floor, staring at the place where the old man had been standing only moments earlier. I couldn't bring myself to move. The hair on the back of my neck stood on end as I gazed steadily around, searching for any sign of him.

Finally, managing at last to move, I ventured across the room, sweeping it with my gaze as I investigated further. Nothing seemed out of place.

"Sparrow?" I called softly, pausing to gaze all around me, not really expecting to see her, but terrified by a thousand prospects that churned in my thoughts.

Finally, something glinting caught my eye. On the bathroom floor lay a small metal sphere. Crouching, I lifted it and turned it over in the palm of my hand. I stared down at the device, wide-eyed, my heart in my throat. A streak of pale blue glowed across its tiny screen.

*Sparrow is pregnant?*

The little sphere trembled in my shaking hands as I studied it, drawing a slow, steady breath as my heartbeat quickened.

A sharp pounding on the door a moment later snapped me out of it. Jolting back into alertness, I looked around for a place to dispose of the device.

"Open up!" a gruff, muffled voice boomed through the door.

Racing across the room, I dug into the wastebasket that stood beside the bed, throwing the device in and burying it with handfuls of crumpled paper.

I hurried to the door and opened it. Two guards stood outside in the drizzling rain, rinsed in the shadows and the glow of their lanterns. One stepped forward, steel-faced, his eyes searching the empty space in a futile attempt to perceive where I was standing.

"You were commanded to retrieve Corporal Turner and report back to Commander Bask immediately," he barked. "Where is she?"

I opened my mouth, about to reply, when the guard shoved blindly past me, drawing his pistol at the same time. The other followed suit, surging full force into the apartment, which they found as empty as I had found it only moments earlier.

I stepped silently into the kitchen, watching them conduct their hasty search of the vacant apartment. When they found nothing, the guard who had first spoken stormed back in my direction.

"Where is she?"

A sick feeling churned in my stomach. "I don't know."

His cold gray eyes narrowed to slits, his gaze flicking back and forth. "Bullshit. You helped her escape, didn't you?"

I shook my head. "I didn't. I swear I didn't—"

He cocked the pistol and extended it in front of him, lips pressed together. "Don't say a goddamn word, you lice-bag traitor!" His gun was aimed accurately at where I stood.

I drew a trembling breath. "Please... please believe me. I came to get her, but she was gone!"

He snorted, a disgusted frown curling his lips. "Save your lies for Bask."

I let them escort me from the apartment without protest, hoping that if I made an effort to cooperate, it would somehow prove to my commander that I'd had no hand in this.

But as we crossed the District, I couldn't ignore the sinking feeling inside me. My eyes probed the darkness for some sign of her—a blur, a ghost—but the darkness didn't give her away; the night kept her a secret.

One of the guards shoved me into Bask's office, slamming me in the back with the butt of his rifle so that I staggered and fell onto my knees. I heard Bask rise from his desk, and a moment later I saw his boots halt in front of me, shining in the firelight. My gaze remained on the floor.

"Sir, we found him in his lodgings, but Corporal Turner was already gone," one guard began hastily. "Should we shut down the District?"

I didn't even need to look up at Bask to know that he was nodding. "Get everyone out there immediately. No one gets in; no one gets out. Secure the wall."

"Yes, sir!" Their boots clomped on the floor as they hurried out of the office.

My back still throbbed where I'd been struck. Bask waited until the door had slammed shut behind them to grab hold of the collar of my shirt and drag me up to my feet. His eyes flashed back and forth furiously, searching for me in the thin air.

"I asked you to bring Sparrow to me."

"Yes, sir."

"Yet she is not here." Bask's voice clenched to a hiss. "In fact, she is *gone!*"

I struggled for breath. "I went straight there—as soon as I left you, I went to retrieve her, but our apartment was empty! I can't—"

"You *can't*," he mimicked, chuckling. "Yes, Price, that is correct. You can't... You never could."

I scanned his face as he held me fast in his grip. It was crimson, sheathed in sweat, and his eyes were wild as they searched for mine.

"Sir," I choked. "Please believe me. I would have brought her here—I did not know who she was."

Bask's face contorted into grimace of further rage. "But now you do know. You know exactly who she is and what it means—that she could very well be the final straw, the one who could send the anomalies' empire toppling." His voice dropped to a livid whisper. "You knew she had just become our greatest weapon... that we could use her to destroy them and then destroy her too." He paused, and now his hardened, dark eyes stared directly into mine. "I was mistaken in thinking you were too dead inside to love; indeed, I wish you *were* dead."

He shoved me backward, hard, sending me stumbling over my feet to catch myself against the wall.

"Sir, please—believe me!"

"After all this time, after everything I've given you—after everything the RGM has given you—this is how you repay us, Price?" he growled, pacing the floor. "I gave you everything you wanted—I even let you marry the little bitch—and now, *now* you let your emotions for this slut cloud your judgment?"

My throat instantly tightened. Heat filled me from the inside as I slowly straightened, not taking my eyes off him as he paced, fuming, stroking a hand over his jaw.

"Admit it!" he bellowed, halting in the middle of the room, turning to face the direction where he had thrown me—though, unbeknownst to him, I was no longer standing there. "You helped her escape. This is *your* doing—you directly disobeyed my order!"

I barely heard. I watched as he grew impatient for an answer, angrily stepping closer to where I had last been. Lifting my hands, I let the heat that seemed to be boiling within me trickle steadily down the length of my arms.

"This is the last time," he snarled, reaching out for where he thought I was, grasping thin air. "This is the last time, Price—"

I clamped a hand down on his shoulder and wrenched him around, slamming him back against the wall and knocking the wind out of him. My free hand locked around his throat like a vise, my fingernails sinking into his reddening flesh.

"Yes, sir," I hissed, staring into his eyes as he sputtered and struggled to breathe. "This is the last time."

He fought against my grip, choking.

"You can't kill me, Price—you're too cowardly," he rasped, spit flying out of his mouth. "You're nothing without me; I made you what you are."

My jaw clenched, my lips twitching into a ruthless smile. "No..." I lowered my voice, leaning into his face as burning energy radiated from my hands. I could feel his flesh beginning to melt under my fingers, see his eyes growing bloodshot. "No, I made you what *you* are... I gave you everything you have. *I did.*"

A trembling, animalistic scream rattled in his throat, distorting and fading as a surge of lethal energy pulsed and radiated through my body and into his. I heard the crack of a bone; then his neck went limp.

I stood there, shaking, sweat trickling down my face as I watched the life go out of his eyes. I released him with a jerk, and his body dropped to the floor in a pathetic heap.

I stood over him, catching my breath. Then I wiped his blood off my hands and started for the door.

# 22

MY FINGERTIPS FELT ICY, AND THEY TINGLED WHEN I TRIED to move them. I hadn't opened my eyes yet, but when I breathed in, the cold stung my insides. I moaned, coughing, and rolled onto my back. Dry, rust-colored leaves made up my bed, and stark barren tree branches stretched out over my head.

I lay still for a moment, watching as they swayed in the gentle wind, seemingly unsure of what half-frozen creature was nestled beneath them.

Aaron had killed the only man in the world I had ever truly loved. Keegan's face filled my mind. Chills raced over every inch of my skin as I recalled his eyes. I still ached in a hundred places, and inwardly a wound still bled, a wound I myself had made when I'd told him that I no longer loved him—that I never *had* loved him.

I would never be able to look him in the face and tell him that it wasn't true, what I'd said—I'd lied in order to save him. I lied because I loved him more than any words could express. I loved him with all that I was—body and soul.

And now it was too late. He was gone.

As I lay there on the cold ground, staring up into the skeletal arms of the trees, I wanted to stay there. I didn't want to get up. I didn't want to keep going. I just wanted to stay there until the earth swallowed me up.

*Keegan.*

I pressed my eyelids closed. One hot tear escaped to roll down my cheek.

I forced myself to sit up. My legs felt like dead weight from the lack of circulation. I began to move them slowly, awakening them first and then my arms, noticing my exhales as they painted the crisp morning air.

I knew the RGM had destroyed the Homestead—I'd heard all about how it had been found abandoned and burned to the ground. But even if they had all survived and escaped before the RGM had gotten there... *where are they now?*

I needed Fin now more than I ever had in all my life. I needed him because I was afraid for my life—and for the life of the unborn child inside me. I needed him because I was lost in grief—overwhelmed by the darkness of it. Unable to conceive of a world without Keegan in it; unable to fathom who I was without him.

How on earth was I going to find Fin? And if I *did* find him... Would he even *want* me back—after losing his son because of me?

I brushed the thoughts away, trying to refocus. I had to keep moving—I couldn't think about anything else. The farther I got away from the area of Section West where the RGM resided, the safer I would be.

Leaning against the oak tree, I struggled to my feet. My body felt like lead. More than anything, I just wanted to curl back up on the ground and go back to sleep.

"No... no..." I said to myself. "Keep moving..."

I'd barely taken a step forward when pain rippled through my abdomen, sending me reeling forward onto my knees. Sucking in a sharp breath, I caught my lower lip in my teeth and wrapped my arms around my stomach.

The pain sizzled and then faded away. I remained doubled over, frozen for a moment in the silent wood. Lowering my gaze, I looked down at myself, my hands still resting on my now very noticeably swollen abdomen. I knew now why the old man had urged me to escape—why he had made it seem as though it were now or never.

The child that grew inside me was everything the RGM had ever wanted. If they had found out about my pregnancy, they would have locked me away in a lab by now. Which was precisely why I had to keep moving: they would be looking for me, and there was no way I was letting them find me.

Wincing, I forced myself to struggle back up to my feet, drawing a steadying breath.

Miles of faded earth passed beneath my tired, aching feet as I moved steadily away from the District. I zipped my black jacket up to my chin, shivering into my collar. It was thin and did almost nothing to keep me warm. The day wore slowly on, the golden sun riding high in the sky, cascading lower, and finally meeting the horizon again.

Finally, when I felt I could go no farther, I pressed my back to the trunk of a rough oak and slid to the ground, tipping my head back to drink in the cool air. I could tell I was at a much higher elevation than before; it was becoming more and more difficult to breathe easily. My calves burned from the constant uphill climb.

Every muscle in my body ached, leaving my limbs heavy and difficult to move.

Looking around at the woods washed in the golden glow of the sunset, I couldn't push away the regret that welled in my chest along with a sick feeling that came and went. The realization that I could have—*should have*—escaped so long ago. That the door had stood open before me for so long and I had been blinded, and by what? By love?

Of a kind, yes. But also by my refusal to let go of a fabrication I'd been spoon-fed and forced to swallow. The man I'd married, whom I'd stood and slept beside, had been my greatest enemy—the murderer of the man I loved. And I'd been his puppet. And now, inside me, his child grew at an abnormally rapid rate; though still unborn, he or she was also a victim of the RGM and their ruthless greed.

*If only I had escaped sooner... If only I had seen him for what he really was... If only I had known.*

I blinked back the tears, pressing my eyelids closed. I rested my hands on my aching stomach.

For a moment I listened to the wind as it brushed through the trees, swaying their barren branches. Beyond that was stillness. The sun's golden rays had faded to rust and shadows.

Then a soft snap cut through the stillness.

My heart lifted to my throat. Without moving even my head, I looked hastily back and forth, scanning the silent forest around me.

The breeze rolled gently down the mountains and through the valleys. Its chanting whispers faded, leaving the violent hammering of my heart to throb in my ears. I listened carefully. A soft snap came again, to my left. My gaze shot to the place where the sound had come from, but saw only craggy oaks and splintering pines. And then I saw a darker shape among the trees.

My eyes widened, fire rushing through my veins as the figure split into two—the shadows of two men. Coaching myself to remain calm, I carefully pulled myself back behind the tree, concealing myself in a clump of dead bushes.

The soft thuds of footfalls came into earshot. There was the snapping of an occasional twig and the crunch of leaves. I held my breath. More footfalls, then hushed voices.

"You really think he got this far?" asked one.

There was a long silence. Thud, thud, pause. I peered out at two legs standing in the clearing I'd only just been resting in.

"With him, there's no way to know," a familiar voice replied. *Anand.* "He could be out of Section West by now..."

His boots resumed their soft thudding as he crossed the clearing and again paused, resting his hands on his hips.

"But no matter what, we have to find him. Price is a traitor."

The other soldier rustled open a map. "What about finding Turner?"

I waited, breathless, for Anand's response.

"Both are of equal importance," he replied firmly.

"But Price is one of our greatest assets," the other soldier protested. "Without his blood we return to the world of the visible."

My throat tightened at the mention of his name, my gaze flashing back and forth between the two RGM soldiers.

"Yes, without his blood..." Anand agreed, tilting his head to the side. "But not necessarily without *him*."

"How do you mean?"

I waited for the answer, my heart pounding in my chest.

Anand didn't answer right away, almost as if he knew he'd said too much already. He rubbed a hand over his jaw, seeming to deliberate for a moment before finally speaking again. "Why do you think Bask was harvesting three times as much of his blood as we normally do?"

The other soldier looked up from the map in his black-gloved hands. His eyebrows pressed together. "I didn't know that we—"

"Our commander was a mutator before he came to us," Anand cut in. "Remember that."

"B-but he's dead."

"He shared his plans up the chain of command long ago," Anand replied. "Do you really think he would have remained beholden to Price forever?"

"So they've made the formula synthetically?" the soldier puzzled aloud. "So if we—*when* we find Price, what do we do with him? If he's no longer needed..."

Anand just stood there for a moment. "You know your orders, Lieutenant. You know how we deal with traitors."

The soldier didn't respond. Anand made a quick gesture with his hand. "Come on. It'll be dark soon. Let's get moving."

Without another word the soldier accompanying Anand folded up the map and followed his commander deeper into the woods. I remained as still as stone until their voices had faded from earshot.

*Bask is dead, and Aaron is missing?* I could hardly dare to believe it.

How could all of this be possible? How could it, when I'd heard them consorting together? I'd overheard their conversation in the infirmary. Aaron, despite everything he'd so desperately wanted me to believe, was undyingly loyal to the RGM—Bask had spelled it all out, had made him face up to the fact that he was only lying to himself if he believed anything otherwise. Bask had ordered him to murder Keegan, and he'd done it without question—letting me believe I'd saved his life. My sacrifice had been for nothing.

Bask was dead. Aaron was missing—being hunted as a traitor. *Why?* How could it possibly be true that Aaron was now on the run from the very military to whom he'd pledged every portion of his allegiance?

Slowly, wincing from the pain in my abdomen, I crawled out from my hiding place. I scanned the woods carefully, remaining low to the ground. I could still see the outlines of the two men fading in the distance. I breathed a sigh of relief when they finally faded altogether.

But if they were searching out here for Aaron... was I really as alone as I felt?

I swallowed back a hard feeling in my throat, turning to look over my shoulder. Only dead trees loomed behind me as the twilight crept in. Only trees.

I lay curled in a tight ball in the shelter of a hollow oak, trying my best to escape the cold that suddenly seemed more bitter than ever. I tried to channel warmth into my hands, wrapping my trembling arms around myself, but my efforts were useless.

My teeth chattered, and faint spurts of pain echoed through my head where my temple rested against the cold, hard ground. My heavy limbs ached, and I couldn't feel my fingers anymore. I curled tighter, snuggling as deep into the hollowed-out tree as I could.

I gazed up through the rotted-out top of the tree, where only a few scraggly branches remained reaching skyward. Beyond them, a deep onyx sky stretched over the forest like a canvas, pinpricks of silver the only contradictions to the darkness. Even these tiny beacons of light grew dim as my eyelids sank shut. I drifted and descended into the dark until I became steadily one with it.

Ghostly shapes fluttered against the darkness, soft plumes of feathers. Wings that circled high over my head. Eyes that watched me. A voice that I had never heard before.

*Please let me in...* A voice so soft I could barely detect it came and went like the currents of wind. *Please don't push me away... please let me find you...*

The voice was soft and feminine but weighed down with grief. Each time it spoke, the words repeated, and each time with more bereaved fierceness.

*Please... please let me find you. Please stop pushing me away...*

*Please...* The word repeated over and over each time the winged creature circled above my head. *Please...*

Abruptly, a shriek tore me from the arms of the dark and into the light of day. The soft white rays of morning shimmered through the gray fog to rouse my senses. Through the hollow trunk I could see the pale blue sky stretched overhead.

I closed my eyes again, my heart beating swiftly.

I'd had the dream of the hawk so many times before but had never heard the voice.

I slowly pushed myself up into a seated position, brushing the dead leaves and pine needles out of my hair with trembling fingertips.

Had I heard the voice because I had finally met Icarus? Because part of me somehow knew, deep down, that Hawk was my mother? The RGM was scouring the forest for me: even that bloodthirsty militia must have believed that I was their daughter.

*But do I truly believe that?*

Swallowing hard, I pushed this haunting question to the back of my mind as I stepped cautiously out of my place of hiding and started into the woods.

*Please let me in.*

# 23

SUNLIGHT REACHED THROUGH THE TREES WITH LONG, golden fingers. The cool morning air made me all the more grateful for my very large, furry sleeping partner. There had been a time when Cub had slept in my arms. Now, she was fully grown, and it was the other way around: I slept with her thick, furry limbs wrapped around me like an encompassing blanket while she snored in my ear.

I lay there for a moment, my mind wandering, subconsciously searching for someone else's thoughts in the endless stretch of forest. Finally, I detected something—no, more like a *hint* of something. Like a ghost, it was there and gone in an instant.

Rolling to my side, I lifted silently to my feet to squint into the fog and shadows, scanning the woods for anything other than the looming trees.

I stepped into the shadows a little farther, listening with my mind.

The silence ebbed and gave way to the gentle breeze and then to silence again. With Cub at my heels, I wove my way through the stands of pines, my fingertips brushing against their moss-covered bark. Then, abruptly, I stopped.

The same all-encompassing sensation of uneasiness seized my senses, diverting my mind directly into someone else's.

*We have to find him... We have to find both of them. My god, we're as good as dead if we return empty-handed...*

The stream of thought was there and gone, but close and clear.

*We have to... I have to...*

Cautiously inching around the trunk of a pine tree, I peered at the dense woods around me, searching for a source—searching for the possessor of the mind I had inadvertently begun to read. I saw nothing beyond the still trees.

I spun slowly, narrowing my eyes, searching for even the slightest of motions among their long shadows. I moved carefully to the next tree, then the next, watching, listening with every sense.

Something brushed against my leg.

I spun around, my adrenaline skyrocketing. Cub lifted onto her hind legs to plant her massive paws on my shoulders, lapping my face with her tongue.

Breathing a sigh of relief, I nudged her down. I glanced over my shoulder again to give the silent woods one last glance. I could hear nothing now; no thoughts tapped into my mind.

Finally, surrendering to the fact that whatever had been there was gone, I turned and followed Cub farther into the woods.

As I walked, I pondered the snatches of thought I'd detected in my mind, trying to puzzle them out.

*We have to find them...*

Find whom? Who were they—and who were they searching for?

Chills traced my spine as the inevitable occurred to me: there was a reason I hadn't been able to see them.

"Could it really be...?" I murmured to myself, stroking my fingertips over my forehead. "Would RGM soldiers be this far from the District?"

I listened intently, becoming all the more aware that if there were invisible troops scattered throughout the woods, there was no way to know whether or not my next steps would lead me right into their hands. I needed to keep my mind open and alert.

I cupped my hands around my mouth to make a hushed howling sound, signaling for Cub to follow me into a thicker part of the woods—the direction from which I'd heard the thoughts.

Soldiers, out here, searching for someone—two someones. *Who?* With each of my footfalls against the golden ground, the words seemed to echo with greater strength.

*Who?*

*Who?*

*Who?*

My first thought was of Sparrow, because it could be of nothing else.

Were they looking for Sparrow?

That would imply that she was no longer in the District. It would imply that she had escaped. *Has she escaped?* How would she have gotten away—and why?

There were too many unanswered questions for me to assume anything. I couldn't even be one hundred percent sure that the mind I'd read was that of an RGM soldier from District Firehole, though everything seemed to point to this.

The best-case scenario would be to find the soldier again and tap back into his stream of thought; the worst-case scenario would be if I bumped into him by accident.

I kept my mind on high alert as Cub and I wandered deeper and deeper into the thick, foggy woods.

The rest of the day was uneventful. I never detected the soldier again.

I sat with my back to a tree, gazing up at the darkening sky, my mind a mess. I felt like I was being pulled in two separate directions: my thoughts wandered back to our base camp in the Tetons—back to Kateri. I wondered how she had reacted to the news when Preston had explained why I had left. I prayed that she would understand.

The other side of my heart filled with Sparrow like floodwater, sinking deeper and deeper into a sea of seemingly unanswerable questions.

Was she the one they were looking for? Where was she? How was she? Did she ever think of me?

Cursing under my breath, I stood again and began to pace, rubbing my jaw. I forced myself to think about something—anything—else.

Until the long, shrill call of a hawk cut through the silent woods.

I halted in the midst of the trees. Cub's ears flattened against her head, a low growl rattling in her throat as her discerning eyes scoured the tree canopy.

I took a few careful steps forward into the clearing ahead, scanning the sky for a sign of the wings I'd seen first in my dreams and then again in the distance that morning, soaring through the fog rolling in the valley, vanishing as swiftly as it had appeared.

I spun slowly, searching the treetops, opening my ears—my mind. For a moment I began to wonder if I'd imagined it until Cub crept up alongside me and halted, grumbling a low growl, her neck stiff as she crouched and stared straight ahead. I followed her gaze to the opposite side of the clearing. All the muscles in my body froze.

A dark outline of a figure stood silently among the shadows of the pine trees. Their face was all but hidden beneath the shade of a long cloak that veiled their form, revealing only the tip of a nose and the outline of red lips.

Almost as if being pulled by magnetic attraction, I stepped forward, my gaze transfixed.

"Who are you?" I whispered.

The figure didn't answer. They stood there, still and silent. I shushed Cub with a flick of my finger as she growled softly.

I stepped closer as the figure drew nearer to me, meeting me halfway, my bare feet stepping softly over the blankets of golden pine needles. The figure was female, I could see now. I could feel the searing intensity of her eyes as she studied me from beneath the hood that hid her from my prying gaze.

"Who are you?" I asked again.

Hands like those of a ghost lifted slowly to draw back the hood. I saw that one finger was marked by a black band. My eyes widened as I stared into frighteningly familiar dark eyes. So similar to the ones I'd gazed into a thousand times before.

Her face was beautiful but fierce, and she wore the steady, unflinching demeanor of someone who had witnessed both the most profound love and the most violent war. Her eyes narrowed as she studied me.

"You're Fin's son, aren't you?" she asked.

For a moment, I was too overcome by the familiarity of her face to provide an intelligent answer.

She quirked a slender eyebrow, giving me a quick once-over.

"Y-yes, I-I am. I'm Fin's son," I stuttered finally. "Keegan."

Warm recognition came into her eyes.

"Fin," she repeated softly, as if it were the only thing she had really heard. "My god, after all this time—all these years of searching... Is he with you?"

I shook my head slowly, my gaze still fixed on her face. There was absolutely no mistaking that this was Hawk. In some strange way I actually felt closer to Sparrow just looking at her.

"No, Dad's not with me. He doesn't even know I'm out here," I answered. "He left weeks ago to look for you."

Her eyes locked with mine once again. "For me?"

I nodded.

"How long has he been looking for me?"

I was about to answer "about a month," when I paused. "Honestly? Since you left... Since you asked him to take Sparrow."

At the mention of her daughter's name, a distant look came into Hawk's eyes. For a long moment she stared at me without saying another word.

"I can't believe it's you." I studied her in disbelief. "Fin's never given up hope that you would return. Sparrow was... she was captured by the RGM.

We've tried everything to get her back, but..." I trailed off as a lump formed in my throat. "We haven't been able to get anywhere near her. They've posted guards everywhere and increased their security tenfold, and... we haven't been able to get her back."

"Captured." Hawk repeated the word as if it were poison. "No... no, it can't—"

"Dad believes that you and Icarus are the only ones who can get her out of there," I cut in. "The only ones who can bring her back to us."

Hawk drew a narrow breath, shaking her head. "Where does Fin believe I've been all these years, Keegan?" Her voice lowered to a whisper. "Can you tell me that?"

"Dad... Dad never really talks about it," I answered softly. "I think it... hurts him."

That same distant look remained in her eyes.

"Hawk, please come back with me," I said at last.

"No." The answer flew out of her mouth. "That won't be possible. Not if you wish for her to return to you—not if you're hoping she finds you again." A shadow of fear passed through her eyes. "No, I have to stay away, don't you see? We left Sparrow behind in order to protect her. The RGM wanted to find her more than anything—they wanted to *destroy* her. It was too dangerous for us to be anywhere near her..." She trailed off, her voice quieting. "For years we were in war zones until, finally, it seemed safe enough to come to her again." She stepped closer, words tumbling out now. "But we couldn't find her. No matter how hard we tried—no matter how much we searched for her and Fin..."

"You and Icarus have both been looking for Sparrow?" I asked, stunned.

"Every time we think we're close to finding her... she's gone. We're always just a little too late." She drew an unsteady breath. "It's almost like some unseen force is keeping her just out of our reach, keeping her hidden from us."

Her voice faded. I waited for her to continue, but when she didn't, I reached out and gently touched her arm. Her eyes lifted to mine, a tear rolling down her cheek.

"Hawk," I began, "if you tell me everything, I *promise* I will do whatever it takes to get her back," I whispered, looking her straight in the eyes. "I *promise.*"

Hawk studied my face through tear-filled eyes. "You are so like your father," she replied softly.

My lips curved into the slightest of smiles, and I took her by the hand.

"Come on," I said. "It's going to be dark soon. Let's find shelter for the night, and then we'll talk... about everything."

# 24

BLOOD DRIPPED FROM MY HANDS AS I TORE THROUGH the brush, my lungs groping wildly for air as I sprinted through the overgrowth. I dodged logs and boulders that were only partially visible in the semidarkness that enshrouded Section West.

Gunshots exploded behind me, spraying the trees with bullets. One tore into my shoulder.

I bit back curses, dropping behind a craggy slab of stone. More gunshots pounded through the air, followed by the thundering of encroaching footsteps. I waited, listening, as they drew nearer.

As they closed in, I lifted my hands to my chest, bringing my palms up to face each other, leaving only a few inches of space between them. Warmth rose from my middle and rushed down the length of my arms.

It came so easily, losing myself to something that had been stirring inside me for so long. Finally letting it out felt so natural, finally allowing myself to use my abilities, as I had watched Icarus do. I had him to thank, in part, for the courage to finally take the life of the man who had for so long manipulated me, stripped me of everything that mattered.

I was worth nothing to them now, not even for my blood. My god, no wonder they'd harvested so much of it. The RGM had been watching and waiting for this: for me to finally lose it. Bask had only kept me alive for that purpose—that and the hope of breeding his very own army of sliders, trained to kill and do his dirty work. With Sparrow gone, both these purposes had been extinguished.

And now Bask was gone: his own experiment had finally turned on him—had finally brought him back to all he ever really had been: nothing. I felt no remorse about having killed him, or for killing the guards who had stood in between myself and my escape.

The RGM was wrong about one thing, however: they hadn't failed in creating a new slider who would soon come into the world. And that slider bore not only his mother's blood but mine too. But they would never know this—not now that Bask was cold in his grave. I would find Sparrow, and she and I would escape this place forever. Now that Bask was dead and the game was over, she was all that I had left. She and the child she carried inside her.

I sank back into the shadows and watched and waited until the soldiers finally darted past the rock I was hidden behind. They saw nothing as I took aim and merely opened my hand, letting the energy radiate out of my palm like deadly surges of electricity.

There was an ungodly shriek, the kind a dying animal would make. Then the first soldier dropped to the ground as if someone had nailed him there. Another soldier ran to his side. I opened my palm again, energy surging from my body to kill the other two soldiers.

In silence, I rose from the place I'd been crouched in hiding and continued walking, leaving three bodies sprawled lifelessly behind me, the flames in their lanterns still flickering, the only light to contradict that dark, dark night.

I walked straight ahead, deeper into the woods. Unable even to process what had transpired in the past several hours, I kept my mind fixed on

Sparrow. I knew that if I tried to understand what had happened—what I'd done—I would go out of my mind.

Because somewhere inside me I knew that I'd lost everything. I'd lost the most important parts of who I was, so much so that if I could have stood outside my own body, I wasn't sure I would recognize myself anymore.

Bask had battered me for years, tortured me, tested me, murdered my only friend, and I'd withstood it all without complaint—paradoxically, with a sick desire for punishment. My reasoning had been that if I was a slider, I deserved punishment. I deserved all of it. Yet one word—one shot of venom directed towards Sparrow—had made nonsense of all my efforts and agony.

He'd degraded the woman I loved, and I'd murdered him. It was strange, the little things that could rise and become one's own undoing.

All I had left was Sparrow.

As I trudged through the night, I zipped my jacket up to my chin, trying to brush aside the questions that returned to haunt me. Questions I wouldn't be able to answer until I found my wife and asked her myself.

*Why did she leave? What caused her to leave? What forced her to risk everything only to escape? Did she know that Icarus is her father? Is he the reason she left? Or did she go because she knew what would come next—what would happen to her?*

I felt completely numb as I trudged onward, shivering into my jacket, allowing the light of the waning moon to guide my crooked path through the dead and dying forest. One thought plagued me more than the rest, a thought so heavy my mind could barely withstand its weight:

Had she somehow overheard? Had she... had she somehow known my part in all of it? Had she known that I'd been about to betray her?

I almost couldn't believe it myself. Had I really been about to do that? Would I really have handed her over to the wolves just like that?

"No," I whispered, my lips trembling and numb as I walked. "No, I would never betray her..."

I shuffled to a stop, checking over my shoulders, making sure I was still alone. Of course I was. It was just me out there; the moon and I and those strange, heavy words lingering in the air like cotton-thick fog.

*I would never have betrayed her...*

No, I wouldn't have. I would find her, and I would tell her that. No matter why she had left, I would do whatever it took to track her down and tell her that I would never have done that. I would tell her that I was hers—above all, I was hers.

And she was mine.

# 25

# KEEGAN

"EVERYONE ALWAYS SAID THAT I TRAINED YOUR FATHER. I guess in some ways that is true," Hawk trailed off. "When he came to the Dimension, like many of the anomalies, he was a little apprehensive about what he was capable of doing. But he was never afraid of it... More curious than anything else."

"You taught him to control his abilities?" I asked.

"Mm-hmm." Hawk paused a moment. "Which seems so little in comparison to what he taught me."

We'd taken refuge in the shadow of a looming oak. Exhausted from the long day's journey, I'd stretched out with Cub alongside me for warmth. Hawk had remained seated at the base of the massive tree, her face tipped toward the sky and the moonlight reflecting in her eyes.

"How do you mean?" I asked softly. "Wasn't Dad less experienced than you?"

Hawk was thoughtfully silent. "That would depend on what sorts of experience you refer to. Maybe I was more well versed in my own abilities, yes. But when it came to kindness, gratitude, patience... love?" She shook her head slowly. "There he always had the upper hand. For every one of those things came as naturally to him as breathing."

I studied Hawk for a long moment in the pale light of the moon.

"Dad told me that he loved you," I told her. "He told me that he loves you still."

Hawk sat there, gazing up at the sky.

"You said that if you came back to our camp with me, that Sparrow wouldn't be able to find it," I went on in a whisper. "That you believe that she... that she's somehow pushing you away?"

Hawk seemed to think about it for a moment. "I've only been able to get close to her in dreams. When she's asleep. When that fighting spirit inside her has quieted. That's the only time I can get close to her."

"You see her?" I repeated, a little surprised. "In her dreams?"

"Sometimes, yes," Hawk replied quietly. "I know that she is wandering, lost somewhere, but I don't know where."

"Lost? Not imprisoned?"

"If she was a prisoner, she is no longer," Hawk answered. "In her last dream I spoke to her. I..." She drew a deep breath. "I begged her to let her father and me find her."

"Where *is* Icarus?" I asked.

"I don't know. I don't know where he is," she answered. "We've been traveling separately in areas that are densely occupied by the RGM to avoid detection. But I feel... I feel him. No separation can sever the connection between us. I think he may have seen Sparrow." She paused. "But I'm afraid of what that means if she was imprisoned, as you say she was."

I nodded slowly, rubbing my forefinger over my brow. "She was. I know that she was... I was... I was there."

I felt Hawk's attention turn to me.

"You were there? At the District with her?"

"I tried to get her out. That was why I was there..." I swallowed. "She told me that she wouldn't leave. That she had never..."

Hawk waited a moment. I could feel the intensity of her gaze even in the darkness. "That she had never...?" she prompted me.

"That she had never loved me," I went on, deciding to be completely honest. "That she was in love with one of the soldiers—a slider himself."

"You're in love with Sparrow?" Hawk asked, almost as if viewing me through new eyes because of this new piece of information. "I didn't realize—"

"I'm not. Not anymore," I quickly assured her. "I'm in love with someone else..." My voice tapered off, my mind wandering through those woods and back to the shelter tucked away in the peaks. "I'm getting married, actually."

"Then I'm happy for you," she said quietly.

"Thank you," I said, but the words fell flat. A strained silence filled the space between us. I tried to think of what to say next.

"So you really won't come back to the camp with me?" I asked. "What if it's true—what if Sparrow really did escape? What if that soldier I told you about earlier really was searching for Sparrow? If she's wandering out here, don't you want to find her?"

"With all of my heart," Hawk answered without hesitation. "But if she is searching for you, her only hope of finding you is for me to be a million miles away."

"I still don't understand that," I confessed. "How would your presence deter her?"

Hawk rose soundlessly and walked a few paces through the moon's milky illumination, coming to a stop at the edge of the clearing. She stared out at the woods without answering for several moments, her long cloak pooling around her ankles.

"Sparrow's heart is hardened towards her father and me." Her voice was raw. "But above all, me. She believes that I abandoned her—that I wanted to leave her. That I didn't try to find her."

"I don't know if it's that," I said. "I don't know if Sparrow believes in anything at all. Especially in you or Icarus; Dad has taught all of his students about you and Icarus from the time we were initiated—Sparrow more than anyone." I sighed. "Maybe she doesn't quite believe in herself."

Hawk nodded slowly. "We all have belief in something. Even our doubts are themselves beliefs. Sparrow has made an image in her mind of who she thinks she is and who she thinks we are, and whether it is true or not, that is what she lives by; everything in her life aligns with it. All that she accepts as true, she draws into her life, and all that she doubts..."

"All that she doubts, she pushes away," I finished for her.

Hawk knelt on the ground beside me. "Return to your father and the rest of the students, Keegan," she said quietly. "Tell him everything I have told you. Tell Fin that he cannot find someone who does not want to be found."

"Are you referring to yourself?" I questioned. "Or to Sparrow?"

"Maybe I'm referring to the both of us," she answered. "Sparrow will find what she is looking for. I know that she loves Fin as she would a father. If I return with you, she will never come back to Fin."

"You think she would feel that Fin betrayed her somehow?"

"Something like that..." Her eyes were still distant and glossy. "It's a hard thing to explain, Keegan, the things that can happen inside a person when everything feels torn apart. When they feel forsaken. Sparrow is not ready to see me. I hope one day that she will be, that she will let me come to her, but that time is not yet."

"Then what do you propose?" I asked. "Dad and I have tried everything—you were all we had left! That's why we have been searching for you!"

"You're wrong, Keegan," Hawk replied. "I am not all that you have left. You yourselves are what Sparrow has left—you are her family."

"You *really* don't understand," I argued. "Sparrow hated us when she came to the Homestead. She never wanted to be part of any of this. For a while I had begun to believe that maybe she finally did begin to feel like she belonged but... but then..."

I couldn't finish. I wasn't sure how to.

"All I can tell you, Keegan, is that, despite whatever happened between you and Sparrow, she is out there... She's searching for what she lost." She touched my shoulder gently. "You. Fin. Her family. This isn't about me, Keegan. It's about her... and you."

My eyes narrowed curiously. "Me? I have no idea what to do—how to help... I don't—"

"You don't need to understand," she interrupted quietly. "Just return to Fin and tell him everything." She stood, taking a step back, scanning the woods once more. "Do you remember how I told you of a connection between myself and Icarus?"

"A soul split in two," I responded. "Yes."

"Be the light that guides her. You don't need to search for anything or anyone else, Keegan." She pulled her hood up over her head. "You don't need to look anywhere other than inside yourself."

Questions swelled in my throat. I was about to ask what she meant, and how I could possibly be the answer to bringing Sparrow home, when a soft snap cut the silence around us.

My adrenaline spiking, I spun around to scan the woods behind me, peering through the semidarkness. I saw nothing with my eyes and heard nothing with my mind.

After a moment I turned back to face Hawk.

"Did you hear—" I stopped abruptly.

Hawk was gone. All that stood before me were miles of silent, empty woods.

# 26

FOR THE FIRST TIME THAT I COULD REMEMBER, I DREAMED about my mother. Not the hawk form, but the human form. I could hear her voice, the same one I'd heard in the dream I'd had the night before, except this time there was a face to accompany the voice. A face I couldn't quite make out, but a face nonetheless. An outline of a face veiled in a mist I couldn't see past. Dark eyes like my own peered down into mine, pleading with me.

"Sparrow," whispered the smooth, rich voice of the figure leaning over me. "Sparrow, wake up."

I felt the warmth of a hand on my forehead. Though my eyes were already open, I felt as if I still couldn't see.

"But I'm awake…" I replied, or tried to. I couldn't tell whether I'd spoken within the dream or outside it. "I'm awake…"

The warmth of the hand slowly faded, leaving a cold I felt more keenly than before. I opened my eyes. Trees loomed above me in silence.

I had no will to move. I couldn't. I couldn't feel my limbs or my fingers. One hand lay on the cold, hard ground; the other rested lifelessly on my swollen abdomen. Though it had hardly been a month, I looked around four months pregnant. Like Aaron, I had been reduced to one of their experiments. The RGM had never tried this before. I was the first.

It was hard to say whether it was the cold or the fear that kept me lying there, stiff, listening to the breath wash in and out of my lungs. Despite the old man's reassuring words, I couldn't help but wonder as I lay there, pain wringing through my torso, if I really would be all right. If I really would live through this.

For the first time I began to really feel as if my life was slipping away from me. As if I could feel it passing through my fingertips, and no matter how much I tried to grab hold of it, I couldn't.

My mind reached back to the night Icarus had transported me out of the District. I couldn't forget his last words to me, the way his warm arms had faded away to nothing, leaving me alone in the middle of the woods. It had felt as though something had been torn away, as though my heart was hollow.

There were so many things I'd wanted to say to him—so many questions I'd wanted to ask. I wanted to know who he was. Not whether he was as powerful as I'd always heard he was. Not whether he was one of the patriarchs, one-half of the Splitsoul. I wanted to know whether he was my *father.*

*Is he?*

I pushed the thoughts away as hot, angry tears began to sting my eyes.

Turning carefully onto my side, I pressed myself up into a seated position, sitting there for a moment. I took in my surroundings, focusing on drawing long, steady breaths as I attempted to ignore the pain slicing through my middle.

The sky was cloudless, and the forest was silent and golden around me. Shafts of nectar-yellow light cut down through the empty arms of the trees and bathed the ground.

Supporting myself against the trunk of a bark-stripped pine, I lifted myself carefully to my feet. Squinting through the light, I began to debate which way I should go. The truth was, I had no idea where I was going.

I had no choice but to keep walking, keeping my senses open for any sign of soldiers that were in pursuit of me or Aaron.

It was still hard to believe that Aaron could be out here in the woods with me.

Why were they searching for Aaron? Why had he left the District? The questions kept running through my mind again and again. Maybe it plagued me so relentlessly because deep down I knew there could only be one reason for his disappearance.

He was looking for *me*.

Part of me knew it, but every other part of me was too terrified to admit it.

Why would he have forsaken everything in order to come and find me? In overhearing his and Bask's conversation, it was made perfectly clear to me where his true loyalties actually lay. Not with me—not even with the RGM, not really. His only loyalty was to himself.

Perhaps the rest of the RGM had finally turned on him now that Bask was dead. Still, the snatches of the soldiers' conversation I'd caught didn't add up in my mind.

I kept trudging through the forest, my eyes wandering through the treetops to the bright blue sky overhead, interrupted only by the occasional passing cloud. I watched and listened, drinking in the sounds that filled the forest—listening to the silence and anything that might be hiding beneath it. I sensed no sign of life until, in the distance, light sliced through the trees.

I paused for a moment, squinting into the distance. The trees thinned and opened up to a meadow lit golden and red. In the distance I could detect soft thuds, the disruptions of movement.

I tucked behind a tree, hiding for a moment, listening. I was unsure of what I was listening to, but I was certain of one thing: there was something in the meadow. Something or someone.

For a moment I wondered if I'd stumbled onto the soldiers again.

Leaving my place of hiding, I slipped back out into the open, one hand resting on my belly as I walked quietly among the trees, nearing the place where the forest ended. Sucking in a tentative breath, I reached out a trembling hand and pushed aside the brush to step out into the meadow before me.

Massive, familiar shapes filled the golden, living meadow. Big brown eyes turned to meet my own. Soft, visible breath lifted from large nostrils like plumes of steam.

My fingertips traced my lips as I bit back a smile, a lump forming in my throat.

For the first time in days, I knew exactly where I was.

Moving forward into the meadow, I couldn't help but stare, pausing to spin slowly, taking in the creatures around me. A herd of buffalo grazed peacefully in the tall golden grass, and fuzzy brown calves frolicked around their mothers, the sunlight igniting the outlines of their shapes to create a sort of halo around them.

I watched in awe, my thoughts reaching back to the day Keegan and our group had encountered this meadow. It had been a valley of death then, and I hadn't even cared. Keegan had lit into me—gotten right in my face and told me how wrong I was to think that the death of the herd didn't matter.

I sank to the ground. A lump formed in my throat as I watched the buffalo moving gently through their one place of safe haven, the last herd in the world. A herd that had once been reduced to skeletal monuments among dead grass that was now miraculously covered with blossoming daisies and wild roses. It all seemed so unreal, so like a dream that I actually expected at any moment to awaken and find that it had all been just that: a dream. Perhaps even my escape from the District was all part of the dream. Maybe I was still actually there.

If that was the case, I didn't want to wake up again.

One of the buffalo, the largest of the herd, lumbered gently over to me, snorting and leaning closer to sniff the top of my head. I stiffened out of instinct, but then slowly reached out a hand and placed it on his broad, soft face. His long eyelashes lit up against the warm sun.

The lump in my throat only hardened as my eyes traced the rugged yet gentle frame of the creature before me: a being that had nearly been reduced to myth.

As if the softness of my touch had proven to him that he could trust me, the looming creature before me took a step closer, bending his head until it was pressed to mine. His thick, soft coat brushed my forehead. Reaching up, I wrapped my arms around his face, leaning against him. Tears welled in my eyes and spilled down my cheeks as I squeezed them shut.

With a soft moan the buffalo settled to the ground, not turning his face from me. I embraced him and wept.

Keegan filled my mind and soul. There was not one part of me that didn't feel torn in two.

I knew where I was now. I was close to the Homestead, or whatever was left of it. I had to make my way there and search for any clues as to where they had gone.

*But what clues would there possibly be?* They would have left no trace, or else the RGM would have found them.

My eyes heavy, I lay down in the grass alongside the massive, warm body. Daisies swayed around my head as I gazed up through their petals.

My eyelids lulled shut, and everything else seemed to fade away.

A gunshot yanked me from the darkness of sleep. I bolted upright, then flattened against the ground.

Someone had just fired a shot into the meadow.

My throat tightened. A cautious grumble vibrated in the throat of the massive buffalo beside me, who still lay at my side. I felt the air part around him as he moved, clambering to his feet to gaze around at the rest of the herd. And then he threw back his head and let out what could only be described as a roar.

I crawled through the grass, pulling myself along on my elbows, lifting my head just enough to see over the grass and heads of wildflowers. I swiftly scanned the perimeter of the meadow, taking note at the same time of where the sun rested in the sky. Harsh light streamed directly down to bleach the field.

Another shot exploded in the silence. The ground thundered as the rest of the buffalo scattered. Mothers bellowed to their calves, who shrieked in reply. And then I saw him: there, at the edge of the meadow, half-hidden behind a tree stood a figure clothed in RGM uniform.

He lifted his rifle to his face and took aim—at the buffalo just beside me.

In pure, thoughtless reaction, I lifted to my feet in a swift motion and threw myself in front of the massive, gentle head that had only moments before caressed me. I spread my arms wide like wings that were bulletproof.

A crack rippled through the air, and my legs flew out from underneath me.

I landed on my stomach, which already pulsed with pain. I heard frantic shouts in the distance. The buffalo thundered away, leaving me lying there in the grass.

*Keep moving, keep moving—fast.*

I lunged to my feet as the world rocked around me, staying as low to the ground as I could. The grass whipped against my legs and arms. I heard nothing beyond the ringing in my ears as I reached the opposite side of the meadow. The bark spattered off a tree just ahead as a bullet grazed it.

I sprinted into the woods, searching for a place to hide. Distantly I began to hear the rumbling bellows of the herd, but even those noises faded away as the gunshots continued. They were close now.

They were just behind me.

I ran as hard and as fast as I could until I thought my lungs would burst, all the while throwing glances over my shoulders, trying to see how far away they were.

Not a hundred yards behind me the brush swirled, and shadows dipped and blended with the barren branches of the trees until suddenly their dark uniforms were no longer a camouflage. The forest abruptly burst to life under my feet, as if I'd just passed over the border between the valley of death and the land of the living.

I began to realize what it meant. *This part of the forest is alive.* I quickened my pace as I ran, pumping my legs harder and harder as I wove through the trees.

The meadow where the buffalo rested… the woods after it… I knew what came next. I was no stranger to this part of the woods.

My hands tore at the branches of trees and slashed through the thorny brush. My eyes darted back and forth, taking in my surroundings until finally I could see where the trees thinned out in the distance.

I shot a quick glance over my shoulder. I could see movement in the distance behind me.

The ground that passed beneath my feet was soft and familiar. Just ahead I saw where the trees opened up to the familiar glade where the Homestead stood. I crashed through the brush and emerged into a clearing, slamming to a halt as my heart sank to my feet.

Where four walls made of thick logs had once stood, there were now only jagged, charred remains. The roof had collapsed in on the rest of the house, and the windows had all shattered. The door had blown off its hinges.

Fevered shouts from close behind yanked me out of my thoughts.

My heart lunging to my throat, I ducked through the doorway and into the ruins of the Homestead. Picking my way cautiously through the debris, I came to a tight pocket where the upstairs floor had tumbled down, its plaster and beams lying jumbled against the sturdy first-floor wall. I slid into the little cave-like space, peering out through the tiny cracks between the floorboards, watching the space where the front doorframe used to be.

A bolt of pain surged through my leg, causing me to look down for the first time. A bullet had sunk into my left thigh, and my pants were soaked through with my own blood. I sucked back curses, squeezing my eyes shut and leaning my head back against the charred timbers behind me. Outside, the voices drew closer.

"She came this way," someone bellowed. "Search the premises—look everywhere!"

The command was followed by the frantic thudding of footsteps. I held my breath as they circled slowly around to the back of the house.

"Where the hell did she go?" one of them muttered angrily.

My heart pounded in the back of my throat as I listened to his footsteps drift slowly over to the doorframe. The soldier's shadow passed over the debris inside. I could practically feel the burn of his gaze as he scanned the demolished interior.

"Nothing in the barn," the other soldier announced, passing the exact opposite side of the wall I was leaned against. "She probably went deeper into the woods."

I could still see the shadow of one of them standing there.

"What do you think?" asked one of the soldiers.

"I think she could be in there."

"In there?"

"There's enough space for a body."

The soldier grunted. "Not mine. If you want to crawl in there, fine—I don't feel like having that pile of shit come crashing down on me."

"Fine. Stay here, then."

My throat tightened as one of the soldiers crunched through the charred wood and ash. Wood clattered as he tossed pieces of it aside, hunching down to make it through the door. Then, with a creaking groan, everything began to shift.

"Whoa, whoa!" yelled one of the soldiers outside. "Get the hell out of there!"

Grunts and curses followed as the soldier retreated, then came an overwhelming crash.

I frantically shielded my head. It took everything inside me not to cry out as the demolished structure shifted, snapping the beams that I'd been hiding behind in two. A cloud of ash exploded around me, and something heavy landed on top of my legs.

Tears welled in my eyes. Ash filled my lungs as I gulped for air. What felt like fire coursed through my veins.

Everything rumbled and settled to a mere trickling sound like sand spilling down through the cracks.

And then there was silence.

"Come on." I heard the soldier's voice. "There's no way in there—not even for a snake like Turner. Let's go."

My teeth sank into my lower lip as I fought to keep quiet and still. I listened as their footsteps thudded slowly out of earshot and back into the woods.

I waited a moment before even daring to move. Ash burned in my eyes as I made a motion to move my legs. I couldn't.

Pinned down on my back, I tried to pull myself up into a sitting position. I couldn't move.

Above me, peeking through the battered, burned beams, was the open sky. I could feel my blood draining from me, soaking my clothes.

I listened for any sounds, but I heard nothing beyond the wind as it whispered through the beams.

I WOULD BE LYING IF I SAID I WASN'T TOTALLY PISSED AT Hawk for leaving me high and dry like that, after I'd just spent the past several hours relaying to her just how much Dad believed that she was our last hope for saving Sparrow.

She was stubborn, mysterious, pretty, and hard to understand—proof alone that Sparrow was her daughter, if there had ever been any doubt. No wonder Dad was in love with her.

I still couldn't understand why Hawk believed that Sparrow had escaped the District. How could she know that for sure? Could I really place my trust in that?

Hawk seemed to believe that Sparrow resisted her presence like a repelling magnet, pushing her away, in essence. But how could she push away someone she didn't even believe in?

It didn't make sense to me, but one thing was clear: Hawk was gone, and it was up to me to find Sparrow.

The next day was spent plodding through the seemingly endless woods alongside Cub. I knew there were soldiers out here searching the woods for someone—two someones. I knew that Hawk believed that Sparrow had escaped the District.

*But did she?* I had no idea what to believe, but I stayed as alert as possible as I trekked through the dense woods, wading my way through the brush. I stopped at the base of a maple tree, tipping my head back to stare up into the bright, lush leaves.

My fingertips traced over the damp bark as Cub padded to a stop alongside me. "We're in the part of the forest that we healed. We must be close to the..."

I didn't finish that. It was too painful to speak the words.

"Come on," I called to Cub, nodding in the direction of where the woods turned gray again. "Let's head back."

Cub's ears flattened against her head as she lowered her nose to the ground, sniffing the soft soil. I was about to give her a gentle prod with the side of my leg when I followed her gaze. There were footprints on the ground.

I dropped down beside Cub to examine the footprints more closely, resting my arm on her thick, soft coat. Boot prints for sure—two sets. Ahead, I spotted another set embossed into the dirt, the markings of heavy boots, still, but these were smaller than the others. One foot dragged a little. A little farther ahead there was a faint trace of something splotched on the ground alongside them. I dropped to a squat, pressing my fingers to the substance. A tight sensation made its way into my muscles and throat as I stared down at my fingertips. They were stained with blood.

Rising to my feet, I began to follow the prints, my gaze sweeping back and forth across the ground. The farther I walked, the more the footprints seemed to drag, the more faint streaks of blood I found. I quickened my pace, pushing past the brush and into a clearing.

The stench of ash still hung faintly in the air. The skeletal remains of the Homestead loomed ahead.

I swallowed back the tightness in my throat, forcing myself to take a step forward. The footprints disappeared into the charred, crusty fallout surrounding the burned-up ruins of the Homestead.

I stepped farther into the clearing with caution, scanning the area for any sign of life. When I listened, I heard nothing but the soft padding of Cub's paws as she trotted ahead and began sniffing around the wreckage. I stopped dead in my tracks, a sudden wave of dizziness pulsing through my head.

*I can't... I can't anymore...*

Someone was out here—I could feel their thoughts, flickering like a flame being snuffed out. It was there and gone so fast I wasn't even sure if it had been there at all.

*Forgive me.*

The flickering stream of thought faded.

I rubbed my fingers over my forehead. "Come on... come on..."

I tuned into my mind's power, pacing back and forth in front of the house, straining to hear it again. I circled around the back of the Homestead to the barn. The door stood open, and it was empty.

I bit my lip, venturing to the edge of the woods on the opposite side.

"Come on," I whispered, scanning the forest floor for any sign of footprints that had continued onward. "Please give me more than that... please..."

There were no prints continuing into the woods. As I circled, I finally came across the two large sets of tracks, but nowhere did I see the limping, bloodstained ones.

That was when I realized that Cub was no longer beside me.

I circled around to the opposite side of the remains of the Homestead. I found Cub crouched alongside the partially demolished exterior wall, sniffing the ground furiously. She didn't budge even when I came to a stop alongside her.

"Hey." I nudged her away. "Come on, we have to keep looking."

She didn't lift her head.

"Cub." I spoke a little more firmly now. "Come."

Reaching out, I grabbed her by the scruff of the neck and gently tugged. She whirled around and snapped her jaws. I lurched backward, cursing. Cub clawed furiously at the ground, scooping away pawfuls of dirt and ash.

My heart rate began to quicken as my gaze traced the wall. With my bare hands I dug away at the burned soil, adrenaline beginning to course through my veins. Finally, I grabbed hold of the charred log at the bottom and gave a firm pull, prying it until it splintered in half with a hollow crack.

Dropping to my stomach, I blinked and squinted into the dark space.

"Sparrow?" I called into the void. "Sparrow, are you in there? Can you hear me?"

No reply came. I reached one arm through the opening and felt around over the jagged shapes of the splintered, burned wood and rubble. Then my fingers brushed the softness of flesh: a human hand.

I held my breath as my fingertips traced over ones that I would have recognized anywhere.

"Sparrow!" My voice splintered as I grasped her hand. "Sparrow, can you hear me?"

Still, there was no response from the darkness. Nothing beyond an ominous groan as what was left of the structure began to creak and shift.

Reluctantly letting go of her hand, I pulled myself backward, straightening up to reach back into my rucksack and grab my hatchet. Raising it above my head, I brought it down on the wall, hacking away at the small hole I'd made. Cub still dug feverishly at the ground, doing her best to aid my efforts.

The next log split, and I tossed it aside, hacking immediately into the one above it. I swung the hatchet up over my head and brought it down again and again and again. The scent of ash filled my nostrils; chips of blackened wood flew every which way.

The structure shifted and groaned again, louder this time, sending pieces of rubble from close to the top of the pile tumbling down into the demolished interior.

Casting the last burned log aside, I dropped down again and crawled inside. I could barely make out the shape of Sparrow's body pinned under a fallen beam. Sweat trickled down my face as I fought to free her from the debris, lifting another fallen beam from her right arm.

Another foreboding rumble echoed through the tight space.

Shimmying behind her, I slid my hands under her arms and dragged her, crawling backwards out of the space and taking her with me. Outside, I jumped to my feet, lifting her lifeless body in my arms, and quickly put as much distance as I could between us and the crumbling ruins.

Seconds later, a deafening crash roared out from behind me. Clouds of dust billowed past my legs.

Dropping behind a large oak, I wrapped Sparrow in my arms, shielding her head and face from the fallout as what remained of the Homestead collapsed to the ground. A blast of ash and dust blew past us.

I could feel Sparrow's faint exhalations on my face. The spaces between my fingers filled with her soft hair as I cupped her head in my hand, holding tightly onto her until the dust had finally settled.

"Sparrow," I whispered, shifting carefully forward to lay her gently on the ground. "Sparrow, can you hear me?"

My attention snapped to her thigh: she was bleeding. I pulled a blade from my holster and carefully went to work, cutting away the fabric to expose the wound. It looked as though she had been struck by a bullet. I slid my palm over it, applying pressure and closing my eyes.

My heart was caught in my throat, and my hands were shaking.

In a moment I felt the contact of metal in my palm. Drawing a deep breath, I opened my eyes, examining the bullet in my hand. It was covered in blood, and that alone was the only reason I could see it. Sure enough, just like the last one Kateri had taken from my own shoulder, I could only feel it. The bullet was invisible.

Dropping it into the pocket of my flannel overshirt, I leaned back over Sparrow, examining her leg and searching for signs of any other wounds. That was when I noticed that she was pregnant.

"Sparrow," I whispered again, gently, sliding a hand under her torso to lift her into a seated position. "Sparrow, can you hear me?"

Her face was as pale as ice. The wound had completely healed, leaving only clean, normal-looking flesh to peek through the ripped fabric.

I lifted her into my arms and carried her, keeping my senses open, listening for the sounds of other footsteps or voices in the forest. Cub had already bounded ahead into the woods. I followed, carrying Sparrow in my arms, her head pressed against my chest.

"You're safe now," I told her, kissing the top of her head gently. "It's going to be all right. I promise... it's going to be all right."

Too drained of energy to transport, I cursed myself for not covering more miles on foot. I found us a sheltered hiding place: an old oak tree with mangled, far-reaching roots that bent and curved to create an almost enclosed circle in the shadow of the bare, scraggly branches overhead.

Cub stretched out at the base of the tree, allowing me to use her as a pillow as I laid Sparrow down on the ground.

Exhausted, I spilled onto the ground beside her, catching my breath for a moment, my eyelids pressed closed. Without even thinking about it, I reached out and took her hand in my own, clasping it gently, sliding my fingers into the empty spaces between her cold ones.

For a moment I just lay there like that, my eyes closed, the side of my face resting in Cub's soft coat, Sparrow's hand in mine. My thumb made slow circles over the top of her hand.

When I opened my eyes, I could just make out her closed ones in the waning gray light. Her dark eyelashes stood out against her pale cheeks. I could see the beginnings of her jaw outline; she was so thin.

I lay there for a long time, just watching her gently breathing. Her lips were pale and slightly parted. Her chest rose and then drifted downward again with her every shallow inhale and exhale.

A lump formed in my throat as I scanned her face, caressing the palm of her hand with my thumb.

My mind wandered back to that night by the lake. The night I had finally admitted to her how I felt; when I'd kissed her. She'd been so full of life...

I closed my eyes again, the lump in my throat tightening. Lifting her hand to my mouth, I pressed the backs of her fingers to my lips. She drew in a deeper breath in her sleep and began to shiver.

I watched her for a moment longer before slowly letting go of her hand to sit up and unbutton my flannel overshirt. I gently slipped one hand beneath her torso, pulling her closer. I tucked my shirt around her and folded her into my arms. I tucked my chin gently into the curve of her neck and closed my eyes.

For a moment I forgot where we were. I forgot who I was. I forgot everything.

# 28

THE LAST THING I REMEMBERED WAS SAYING THAT I WAS sorry. Keegan's face, which filled my mind as I whispered the words.

*I can't anymore... Forgive me.*

I'd let go, thinking it was the end and that the darkness closing in around me was death. I was pinned under rubble and unable to move my limbs. Unable to heal my wound. Unable to escape.

Lying there, half conscious, I began to realize how much I regretted. How many things I wished I had done differently. But of all these sorrows, the greatest of them all was the fact that I would never see Keegan again—his death was all my fault. I would never see his face or hear his voice or his robust laugh again. I would never again see the way he ran his tongue over his lips when he was concentrating, or trace the wrinkles that formed at the corners of his bright eyes when he grinned. I would never get the chance to tell him that I was sorry. I had told him so many lies just to keep him safe—to get him out of that hell I'd thrown myself into. The worst part of all was that he hadn't escaped. All this time I'd believed that my incarceration was a sacrifice so that Keegan could live, but Aaron had killed him anyway.

It was my fault. And the last thing he'd heard from me was that I didn't love him. And now I would never get to tell him how much... how long... how *fiercely* I'd loved him. So I'd whispered *forgive me* into the darkness.

I stirred, beginning to awaken, my lungs reaching for air, sputtering, coughing. I blinked my eyes open and then closed them again. Light filtered through blurred leaves.

I slowly became aware of the softness beneath me. I was warm, warmer than I had been in a long time. There were blankets over me and even more layers of them beneath me.

I reached up to rub my eyes before making a second attempt at opening them. As my vision began to clear, I realized that I was no longer outside. I was in what looked like... a *tent*. There were soft canvas walls and a ceiling made of the same material. There were plants growing everywhere, like in a greenhouse. Vines clung to the fabric walls and draped from the ceiling, small trees grew in the corners, and wildflowers sprang up from seemingly everywhere in between. I caught the scent of wild roses.

I ran my tongue over my lips, letting my heavy eyelids fall shut again. I could hardly feel my arms or legs I was so tired.

After a moment I heard footsteps.

"Sparrow?" A soft female voice. "Are you awake?"

Drawing a feeble breath, I peeled my eyes open again. Kateri came into clear focus, wrapped in a brown shawl, her dark hair parted in the middle and flowing over both her shoulders. She quickly crossed the space to the place where I lay, kneeling down beside the cushions I was sprawled out on and setting a tray beside me.

"I thought you might be awake by now, so I brought you a little something to drink," she explained gently. "How are you feeling?"

My head was still spinning. I squinted at her, unsure of what to think.

"Am I dead?" I managed to say.

Kateri set the tray down and straightened up. She looked puzzled, then smiled gently. She placed a hand on my shoulder.

"You're not dead, Sparrow," she said. "You're safe. Keegan found you in the woods. He brought you here."

I stared at her. "Keegan? Keegan is... He's alive?"

Kateri studied my face for a moment before slowly nodding. "He escaped the RGM, Sparrow. He's been here with us for months—"

"But Bask—Aaron—I—I overheard them..." My words tumbled over each other. "They said he'd been killed."

Kateri shook her head. "It was Keegan who found you in the ruins of the Homestead. Keegan who *saved you*, Sparrow."

It was too much to take in. Hot tears filled my eyes as I stared at her, my heart wild in my chest. I pressed my hands to my face, and the tears came.

"Shhh, shhh. It's okay... It's okay, Sparrow," Kateri soothed. "You're safe. It's going to be all right."

I rubbed my fingers over my eyelids, trying to process it all. "Keegan..."

"Yes, Keegan found you."

"When? How long have I been asleep?"

"He found you yesterday. You've been unconscious. You're at our base camp in the Teton mountains, where we've been hiding ever since they burned down the Homestead."

I tried to sit up, but my head started spinning.

"Hey, take it easy," Kateri said quietly. "Let me help you."

She grabbed a colorful fabric cushion from a stack and brought it over to slide it behind my shoulders. Pressing into the palms of my hands, I hoisted myself up into a seated position, leaning back.

"God, I'm so tired," I mumbled. "What happened?"

"No one's sure. Keegan said you'd been shot in the leg," she explained. "But he healed you, of course. You were hiding in the ruins of the Homestead back in Yellowstone. He thinks you were being pursued."

*Keegan.* I still couldn't believe it. He'd escaped after all. Aaron hadn't killed him—Aaron had ignored an order to kill him.

I closed my eyes to keep the tears from streaming down my cheeks.

"By RGM soldiers." I dipped my head in a shallow nod. "Yes."

Kateri looked surprised as she reached for the steaming cup of tea on the tray. "So you remember?"

"Bits and pieces." I tried to take the cup from her when she offered it, but nearly dropped it. Kateri caught it before it spilled and lifted it carefully to my lips for me. "I never saw Keegan. I don't remember anything that happened since crawling into the wreckage of the Homestead."

The spicy-sweet liquid warmed my throat as I swallowed a mouthful. Then I leaned back again to look at her.

"I remember being with Icarus," I continued, my voice a whisper. "At the District."

Kateri's eyes grew wide. "Icarus? He was in the District?"

I nodded slowly. "More than that... I helped capture him. I didn't know what I was doing. I was under the influence of a serum. My memory of those few days is completely blacked out." I pinched the bridge of my nose, squeezing my eyes shut. "I'm so ashamed..."

"Sparrow, you cannot think like that." Kateri placed a hand on mine. "It wasn't your fault—you were a victim of an RGM weapon. That's nothing to be ashamed of. It was not your doing."

"Yeah, but sometimes I wonder... what if there was something I could have done?" My voice trembled. "It was because of me that he ended up trapped there, and I couldn't even..."

My voice faded in my throat.

*I couldn't even save him. He saved me.*

"Couldn't what?" Kateri asked gently.

I swallowed, shook my head. "Where is Keegan?"

Kateri didn't answer right away. She looked down at the cup in her lap and then set it on the tray again. "He went to the lookout. I'll let him know you're awake. Would you like to see him?"

My heart beat a little faster at the very idea. But when I looked down at myself—down at my swollen belly—I remembered the last time I'd seen him: the night I'd told him that I didn't love him and never could. And now I was married to someone else—someone I'd told him I was in love with—and I was pregnant with his child. I couldn't imagine what he thought of me.

"No." My voice came out quiet. "I should try to rest. I'm so tired."

Kateri rendered an understanding nod. "Still, I'll let him know. I'm sure he'll want to see you now that you're awake."

I had no idea if she knew the full story or not. I pressed my lips into a weak, forced smile and nodded. I knew she was just trying to be nice.

Kateri gave me a reassuring smile as she rose to her feet. "Everything's going to be all right now that you're here, Sparrow," she told me gently. "You'll see."

Exhausted, I slept. When I awoke, it was to a voice whispering, "Knock, knock?"

I peeled my eyes open. Preston hesitantly pushed aside the canvas flap to peek inside, his expression uncertain.

"It's okay," I mumbled. "You can come in. I don't bite."

The look on his face grew more assured, his usual wise-ass grin taking shape once again. "Since when?"

I smiled wearily. "Oh, shut up."

Preston crossed the small area to sit down on the edge of the cushions beside me.

"How are you feeling?" he asked, leaning his elbows on his knees and clasping his hands together. "You look like hell."

I laughed a little. "I feel like it too."

"Kateri told me that you saw Icarus," he began. "That he saved you from the District?"

I pulled in a long breath, only to let it back out in a tired sigh. "Icarus was shot... beaten by the RGM soldiers. He didn't have enough strength to transport both of us out of there... He told me that he did, but he didn't. I only found out when—"

"When you opened your eyes and found yourself alone?"

I nodded. "Icarus is still back there... He was hurt and in a lot of pain—I could tell. That's why he couldn't transport... He didn't have enough power left." I swallowed the lump in my throat, memories from that cold, dark night in the woods flooding my mind. "God knows what they're doing to him now."

The look on Preston's face was grave as he seemed to consider it. "I still can't believe they let Keegan go."

I didn't say anything. I just kept staring at the pattern on the blankets, a lump forming in my throat.

"Sparrow?" Preston asked quietly.

My gaze shifted up to his soft brown eyes, stinging tears beginning to cloud my own. I shook my head.

"They were going to kill Keegan... but Aaron promised me that if I married him, the RGM would let Keegan go. So I lied to Keegan and told him that I wanted to be there—that I didn't love him. That I never had. I promised Aaron that I would marry him in exchange for Keegan's release—" My voice broke off, interrupted by a sob. "But Aaron was ordered to kill Keegan anyway—I overheard him saying as much, but Aaron must have disobeyed. He must have kept his promise to me after all."

"Oh god, Sparrow," Preston said softly. "You sacrificed yourself for Keegan's release?"

I nodded, tears spilling down my cheeks. "I knew there was no other way..." I sucked in a sharp breath, sniffing back tears. "I know the RGM. I know what they're like... I know what Keegan's like too... I knew he'd come back for me if I didn't break his heart. That was a risk I wasn't willing to take."

"He tried. He and Sensei both have tried many times to get you out of there," Preston explained. "But the RGM forces have grown so strong, they couldn't get anywhere near you."

"Good," I said. "I didn't want them to."

"Has Keegan seen you? Have you told him any of this?"

I shook my head. "No, he... he hasn't come to see me. I don't blame him..." I bit my lip. "He must hate me."

"He doesn't hate you, Sparrow."

I wiped the tears from my cheeks. "Where is Fin? Why hasn't he come to see me?"

"He isn't here. He's away—searching for Hawk," he answered. "Sensei believed that finding her and Icarus would be the answer to getting you out of there…" He paused, exhaling a long sigh. "Now Icarus is trapped there too."

"When do you think he will return?"

"Knowing Sensei? When he finds Hawk."

It was like salt in a wound, hearing her name. Thinking about Fin, whom I needed so much right now, out there looking for my mother.

"How is Keegan?" I deftly changed the subject.

There was something hesitant in Preston's eyes, but before he could answer, the canvas flap burst open.

"Sparrow!" Rafael rushed in, knelt and wrapped his arms around me. "You're back!"

I hummed a weak laugh and slid an arm around his back. "I'm back, Raf. My god, what happened to that scraggly boy I used to know?"

He grinned and pulled back to look at me. "How are you feeling? How did you get out of there?" His eyes lowered to the place where the blankets covered my swollen belly. "When are you—"

"Raf," Pres cut in, giving him a playful nudge, "relax. Sparrow's been through a lot, and I don't think she's in the mood for an inquisition."

I pressed my lips into a tired smile. "It's all right. I don't mind." I gently placed a hand on my stomach. "I'm not sure exactly when, Raf…"

"Boy or girl?"

"How am I supposed to know?"

"I know, I know, but your best guess."

Despite the seriousness of the situation, I couldn't help but smile.

"Hmm." I leaned back into the cushions a little. "Girl."

"I hope it's a boy. That would be so much cooler—it would be like having a little brother."

I quirked an eyebrow. "What's wrong with a little sister?"

He shrugged. "Nothing. But I'll need someone to hang out with once Keegan's married."

Preston whacked his arm. "Raf."

"Ow. What?" Rafael's thick dark eyebrows knitted together. "Didn't you tell her about—"

My stomach dropped as my eyes locked on Preston's. "Keegan is... getting married?"

Preston shot Rafael a disgruntled look. "Raf, I think Janna needed a hand with chores."

"They're already finished."

"Then go see if she needs help with something else," he said firmly. "Please."

Rafael sat there on the opposite side of the cushions, looking confused, but when Preston didn't budge, he gave a labored sigh and got to his feet. "All right, all right, fine..." He paused in the doorway to give me a small wave, which I returned with a weak smile. When he had disappeared outside, my smile vanished as quickly as it had come.

"I was going to tell you," Preston began. "I just... I wasn't sure where to be—"

"So instead, you just let me go on and on about how much I..." I pressed my fingertips to my forehead. "It's Kateri, isn't it?" My voice cracked a little.

Preston slowly nodded.

I pressed my eyes shut, not saying a word.

"Since you've been gone, she and Keegan have gotten really close," he explained gently. "I could tell that Keegan liked her... I told him it was okay to move on. But I didn't expect everything to happen so... fast, I guess."

I drew a deeper breath, looking up at him. "When are they exchanging their promises?"

"In about a week."

A silence crept in between us. I had no idea what to say. There was a sick, cold feeling sinking in my chest. Finally, Preston gently placed a hand over mine.

"Sparrow, you have to tell him."

I stared down at the pattern on the quilt. "Tell him what?"

"Exactly what you told me—be honest with him about what happened: you did what you did to save his life. You stayed so he could go free."

"And reopen old wounds that have clearly healed for him?" I shook my head. "Kateri is far better for him than I could ever hope to be, Preston. If anything, I'm glad that my absence has caused him to see that."

Preston's eyes were serious. "You would let him marry Kateri without knowing that you're still in love with him?"

"If Keegan is in love with her, it wouldn't matter anyway, Pres. Don't you see?" I sighed. "It's better this way. Promise me you won't breathe a word of what I told you to Keegan."

Preston studied me, frowning uneasily.

I slid a hand over his. "Please. Promise me."

"It's not my secret to tell, Sparrow," he replied at last. "But I hope you change your mind."

"Thank you," I said softly, then winced as a dull, throbbing pain ripped through my gut.

"You okay?" he asked. "Should I get Kateri?"

I shook my head, reclining back into the cushions. "No. No, I'm just going to rest for a little while."

"You sure?"

I nodded. "Yeah. I'm just really tired."

Preston studied me for a moment, then rose to his feet and crossed the room. He paused in the doorway to look back at me. I gave him a reassuring glance, settling onto my back.

"We'll call a meeting as soon as you feel up to it," he said. "We'll discuss everything."

"Yes," I replied quietly. "Yes, we will."

I closed my eyes and kept them closed until I heard him leave. Then I opened them again and stared hollowly up at the fabric ceiling stretched out over me. The sun was high in the sky, and it washed down through the leaves on the trees, sending their shadows dancing across the canvas.

My vision blurred as tears filled my eyes and rolled down my cheeks.

# 29

I WOUND BACK MY ARM AND THREW. THE BLADE FLASHED through the rays of afternoon sunlight and thudded into the thick trunk of a pine tree.

I grabbed another knife from a nearby stump and threw it.

Another flash, another thud.

I took another and tossed it into levitation, focusing first on the knife's handle and then on the place where I wanted it to impact. It swayed gently in the air before beginning to tremble, slashing forward at dizzying speed to impact into the exact spot I'd focused on.

Another flash, another thud. Again, and again, and again I threw until finally I held the last knife in my hand. I gritted my teeth and slashed it to the ground, dropping down onto the tree stump beside me. I leaned forward to rest my elbows on my knees, rubbing a hand over my jaw. I stared ahead into the woods.

After a while I heard footsteps, and then a familiar hand slid into my line of sight, holding a knife by its handle.

"Yours, I think?"

I reached out and grasped the handle. "Thanks."

Kateri sat down beside me. "Something wrong?"

I looked down at the blade in my hands, shaking my head slowly. "No. No, nothing is wrong."

"Sparrow's awake."

I made no response as I ran my fingertips absently over the blade.

"Preston's in there talking to her now," Kateri continued. "I thought you would have been the first in line."

I turned to glance at her questioningly. "How do you mean?"

She pulled her shawl more tightly around her shoulders, giving a little shrug. "You loved her once."

"In the past," I reminded her.

"Yes, but you still care for her, don't you?"

In the blade I could see the reflection of my own green eyes staring back up at me. "Of course I still care."

"She told me that Icarus is in the District."

I turned and stared at her. "What?"

"Sparrow helped capture him. The RGM forced her to take a serum that put her under their mind control. She had no choice, and now... he's trapped there."

"Icarus? Trapped at District Firehole?" I shook my head. "I don't believe it—how is it even possible for them to hold him there?"

"Sparrow told Preston that it was Icarus who helped her escape. He was badly injured. He didn't have enough strength to transport out himself, but he saved her..." Kateri trailed off, looking out into the woods. "Icarus must have figured out that she was a slider."

I turned the blade in the palm of my hand.

*Or... that she was his daughter.* That was what Kateri didn't know—no one did except me.

Kateri drew a quiet breath, twirling the tassels on her shawl between her fingers. "I'm so glad you found her, Keegan. God only knows what she's been through."

I nodded slowly. My thoughts were filled with Sparrow—dragging her out of the rubble, carrying her to safety. Sleeping beside her, kissing her fingertips. She had been the first thing I'd seen when I'd opened my eyes that morning. I'd lain there, holding her in my arms. The shape of her body fit mine so perfectly, her back pressed to my chest, my face resting in the curve of her neck. My arm that held her had been completely asleep, prickling with pins and needles, but with the other I'd reached over to check her pulse and brush the hair away from her face. It had been so hard to believe that she was actually there. It was so hard to believe that I was holding her in my arms.

With a few hours of sleep, my strength had returned. I'd shaken Cub awake and gathered my things, lifting Sparrow into my arms once more. I'd closed my eyes and focused on the shelter in the Tetons, vividly meditating on the imagery until I opened my eyes to see Cub frolicking ahead toward the canvas structure in the distance.

"I wonder what Icarus said to her," I whispered. "How he found out who she was…"

My voice faded. I could feel Kateri's eyes on me.

"Why don't you ask her?"

I glanced at her, wondering if she could see straight through me to the hurricane that was brewing underneath. Then I looked back down at the blade in my hand. At the reflection of my own eyes staring up at me.

I stood there, gripping the canvas flap tightly in my clenched fingers. I took a deep breath. I couldn't get the words out.

"Kateri?" Sparrow's soft voice came from inside the shelter.

I pulled in a shaky breath and pinched my eyes shut. *God, why am I so damn nervous?*

"Sparrow, i-it's—it's me."

A short silence elapsed. I pulled the fabric aside and leaned in. My heart lifted to my throat as soon as my eyes met hers.

"Is it okay if I come in?" I asked gently.

Sparrow was sitting up, one of Kateri's brightly woven shawls wrapped snugly around her shoulders and pillows propped behind her back. Her hair was wild, messy, and falling into her dark eyes. For a moment I just stood there and stared at her, forgetting what I was doing.

Sparrow stared back at me, looking as lost as I felt, before nodding.

Swallowing back my heart, I stepped farther inside, standing there like an idiot, frozen.

Sparrow didn't say a word. Faint voices drifted in from outside.

"How are you feeling?" I managed.

Sparrow didn't reply. I began to wonder if she would answer at all.

"Would you sit beside me?" she asked quietly.

The same stupid, dizzy feeling rose inside me as I crossed the room and lowered myself down beside her.

Sparrow gently reached across the soft blankets, her fingertips brushing against my own. A tear rolled down her cheek.

God, something inside me snapped. I closed the distance between us, wrapping my arms around her, taking her hand, filling the spaces between her fingers with my own.

She wrapped an arm around me, her face resting in the curve of my neck.

"I thought you were dead," she told me at last. "I thought he killed you."

"He was going to, but I told him if he lied to you, you'd be able to see straight through him—that you would know if he'd killed me. That if he really wanted your heart"—my voice faded—"he would never break his word to you. He fired a shot into the air."

"Keegan," she said, looking up at me. Her eyes glistened with tears. "I can't stay here."

"What are you talking about? Of course you can—you'll be safe here."

"They are looking for me, Keegan," she insisted. She sounded exhausted, spent. "He is..."

"He?"

"Aaron."

My blood ran cold at the very mention of his name, and I lowered my gaze from hers once more.

"You married him," I said, "didn't you?"

"I did."

I closed my eyes, drawing a steady breath. "You love him still?"

Sparrow didn't respond right away. "He was going to hand me over to them, Keegan. He was going to let them kill me because they found out who I really am—that I'm Icarus's daughter."

"How did they find out?"

"I think they saw the similarities..."

"And Icarus?" I asked. "Did he know who you were?"

Sparrow bit her lip, blinking back tears as she nodded. "Yes. Yes, he recognized me... even though he hasn't seen me since I was born. It was like... it was like he could see through me—straight to my heart. And I helped *capture* him, Keegan. My own father... It was *my* fault. They drugged me—I had no idea what I was doing. I couldn't even remember it afterwards."

My jaw hardened. "Aaron did that to you?"

"No, not him—his commander. But Aaron... lied to me about so many things." Her voice was strained. "When I found out I was pregnant, I knew they would never let me go..." She shook her head slowly, her dark eyes distant. "It was the reason they wanted me there in the first place."

"They wanted you to have children?"

"To raise as their own force of sliders. Yes."

"Do they know that you're pregnant?"

"I left that same night," she said. "Icarus said he would save me... He transported me out."

"What makes you think Aaron's looking for you?"

"I heard soldiers in the woods—I was hiding from them in the brush. They were looking for me and Aaron. He must have left District Firehole after I did, and now the RGM wants him dead as much as they want me back."

"They would never kill you even if they did find you. Not now that you're pregnant."

"No, they would just lock me up for the rest of eternity," she concluded. "I would rather die."

I studied her for a moment, wondering where to begin. "Sparrow, I have to tell you something. The only reason I found you out there in the woods was because I was already out there... looking for Hawk."

Her dark eyebrows rose. "Hawk? But Preston said that Fin was—"

"My dad is out there searching for her too, yeah. But... I was sick of waiting around. I had to do something myself, so I left..." I paused. "And I found her."

"*What?*"

"Or rather, she found me," I went on. "She came to me in the woods one night. We talked about—"

"Wait—no. How...?" Sparrow cut in. "How is that possible?"

"My dad has believed that she's been close by for a long time now. That's why he went out looking for her. No one understands him—I can't say that I do either, but it was like he could sense her presence... like they were tied together in some mysterious way..." I looked at her. "Kind of like..."

I stopped myself before I could say it: *us*.

Sparrow stared into my eyes for a moment. Something inside me was aching to pull her into my arms.

"Sparrow, your mother told me that she and Icarus have been searching for you—for years now."

"Icarus said the same thing."

I narrowed my eyes curiously. "And you don't believe them?"

"I... I don't know what I believe, Keegan. Why didn't she come back with you?" She pulled away. "If she's been looking for me for so long, then— then why didn't she return with you?"

"She told me that she couldn't—that if she came back to camp with me, her presence would repel you. She said she saw you in a dream... that you had escaped the District, and the only way you would be able to reach us again was if she was as far away as possible." I paused. "Did you have a dream about her, Sparrow?"

Sparrow didn't answer right away. She looked down, swallowing hard. "I can't talk about this, Keegan—I can't talk about her."

"Why not?" I asked, not about to drop the subject that easily. "Sparrow, she's your mother. You met Icarus. Surely you must realize that he's—"

"Yes," she cut in, her voice firm. "Yes, I do. Which only makes it hurt more—to know that they are real, that they do exist, that I am their daughter, yet they haven't... she hasn't..." Sparrow's voice broke off. She shook her head. "I don't want to talk about this anymore. You must have more important things to do."

"Nothing more important than being with you."

"I'm sure Kateri wouldn't agree," she replied quietly.

A muscle in my jaw twitched as I swallowed. "Kateri told you?"

"No, Rafael did."

I sighed. "Sparrow, I... I don't know what to say—"

"You don't owe me an explanation, Keegan. I'm happy for you," she said. "You have to move on and so do I—I can't just stay here and wait for the RGM to find me."

"No, no, Sparrow. You have to stay, at least for now. Until Dad gets back," I protested. "We'll protect you. There's no other option."

"Keegan, you don't understand what you're asking."

"I don't care who's looking for you. I'm not afraid of Aaron—or the RGM."

"It would put every single one of you in danger, Keeg."

"They'd have to get through me first." I looked down at her hand, her fingers still entwined with my own. "Do you really think I'd give you up that easily?"

"No," she answered. Something stirred in the darkness of her eyes. "No, I'm sure it took time for you to do that."

My heart stuttered on its next beat, comprehending her meaning. My jaw tightened a little. "A lot longer than it took you, I think," I answered.

Tears glossed Sparrow's eyes. For a moment she just sat there stiffly. Then she pulled her hand away from my own.

"I need to rest," she said.

I sat there for a moment, my eyes probing hers, searching for answers to the questions I couldn't ask. The questions I didn't know how to ask.

Finally, I stood and walked away.

# 30

*"YOU LOVE HIM STILL?"*

I'd wanted so badly to say no—to tell him the truth. Everything inside me wanted to blurt out: *No, of course I don't love him. I love you. I have always loved you.*

When he'd stepped inside the tent, I wanted to hold him, to hug him, to run my fingers through his now much shorter hair. To kiss his lips. To breathe him in. To love him so hard, because I was bursting at the seams with all of the warring emotions inside me.

I love *you*, Keegan. *Always.*

Instead... I'd changed the subject. It was like holding back a raging river to keep the truth down inside me. Especially with my arms around him, with his hand in mine.

I told him that I needed to rest. I wanted him to leave me alone. I didn't want him to see me cry, lose it. Because I was going to.

I rolled over onto my side and lay there in the silence, listening to his strong footsteps fade out of earshot as hot, empty tears rolled down my cheeks.

I felt like I was bleeding inside. His words ran their fingers over my brain, digging their nails in until it hurt to think.

I lay there, my fingertips making slow circles over my belly. A nudge from inside me responded to my touch. Glancing down at my stomach, I spread my palm, taking the feeling in: he was kicking. Or she.

For a moment I forgot about Keegan and everything else, overwhelmed by the fact that there was an actual *human being* inside me.

I pulled in a deep breath, closing my eyes, resuming the small circular motions with my fingertips.

It was strange how a child I'd never wanted or dreamed I would have suddenly made me feel like I wasn't a lost cause. Like I wasn't as alone as I felt, even if Keegan and I were done.

I had a child inside me. I wasn't alone.

"It's okay," I whispered, a warm tear cresting my lip and rolling down my chin. "We're gonna be okay... I promise I won't let them find you."

The truth was, I had no idea how I could stop that from happening. The RGM was out there combing the woods for me. They wouldn't give up on Aaron or me that easily.

I needed to speak with Fin. Why was he out there looking for Hawk when *I needed* him?

"Here—drink this slowly. Just a little sip."

I sat up and took the cup from Kateri's hand. I lifted it to my lips and closed my eyes as the warm steam drifted against my face. I took a small mouthful of the sweet liquid and swallowed. "Has everyone gathered?"

Kateri nodded. She sat on the edge of the cushion, wrapped in a warm wool shawl. "Keegan and Preston built a fire outside."

"A fire?" I questioned, alarm rising in my voice. "What if someone sees?"

"It's okay," she quickly assured me, placing a hand on my leg. "We're safe up here in the mountains."

I drew a steady breath and turned to look back at her.

"Raf told me that you and Keegan are getting married," I said, forcing the corners of my lips to turn up in a weak smile. "I'm so happy for you."

A blush brightened Kateri's cheeks, and she smiled back at me. "Thank you."

I didn't know what to say next, so I drank down the tea. She took the cup from my hands when I was finished.

"Let me help you outside," she said, offering me her arm. "Take it slow."

I didn't need to be told twice. My head was already spinning as I brushed back the covers and got to my feet.

We made our way over to the firepit, which sat a little way out from the shelter itself. Keegan sat by the fire, colors from the flames bathing his skin and shadowing his face.

Myung slid over to make room for me beside her on the blanket she was sitting on. Kateri kept hold of my arm, trying to assist, but I assured her that I could manage.

I settled down on the blanket beside Myung, and Kateri made her way over to Keegan. He slid his arm around Kateri when she sat down beside him. I tried to ignore the stab of pain in my chest.

"Sparrow." Preston's voice diverted my attention. "Why don't you tell us what happened?"

I looked at him through the firelight. "Me?"

He nodded, his warm amber eyes glowing in the light from the flame. "Tell us what you've been through."

I stared at him for a moment before my gaze shifted back to the fire. I ran my tongue over my lips, contemplating where on earth to even begin.

"I... it's so hard to know where to start. I helped capture Icarus." I lowered my gaze to the ground. "I can still hardly believe it."

"It wasn't your fault," Preston was quick to remind me. "They were using a weapon against you, Sparrow."

"I know, but still." I pinched the bridge of my nose, shaking my head. "I can't stop thinking about him. I can't get that image of him in a cell out of my head... He was injured. Beaten."

"When was he captured?" Myung asked. I could feel the intensity of her gaze.

"About a week ago," I replied. "I thought maybe Sensei would have some idea of what we should do—how we could get him out of there. We can't just leave him there—we have to do something." I glanced up at Keegan. "Do you think you could... do you think you could find Hawk again? If anyone could save him, it would be her."

"'Again'?" Kateri raised an eyebrow, turning to look at Keegan. "Keegan, you found Hawk?"

Keegan's eyes met mine from across the fire as everyone fell silent.

Then it hit me: he hadn't told anyone else yet.

Everyone exploded into questions at once; a tumult of voices rose and fell over each other.

"Why didn't you say anything sooner?" That was the question that surfaced when everything else had stilled. It came from Kateri, who gazed at Keegan with curious eyes. "You've seen Hawk?"

"She appeared to me in the forest," Keegan answered, though his eyes remained focused on mine. "I told her that Sensei has been searching for her, that he believed her to be the only way of getting Sparrow out of the District. She told me that Sensei was wrong, that there was nothing she or anyone else could do to save Sparrow—that it was in Sparrow's hands."

My jaw grew tighter as I listened to Keegan, a lump forming in my throat. I stared at him, feeling something burning deep in my middle.

"Does she know that Icarus is at the District?" Preston asked.

Keegan nodded. "She sensed that he was there."

Preston exhaled a long sigh, shaking his head in disbelief. "It's been so long... and suddenly, within a few short days, the two of you have seen the patriarchs." He nodded between Keegan and me. "Did he realize you were a slider, Sparrow? Is that why he transported you out of there?"

For a moment I didn't respond; then I nodded slowly. "Yes."

It was only scratching the surface of what the real answer was, but I couldn't tell them. I'd locked it all away for so long that I wasn't sure I could get the words to cross my lips even if I wanted to.

My eyes lifted from the flames, and I found Keegan already looking at me—through me. He knew.

I quickly looked away.

"This serum." Janna spoke up. "Why did they—"

"Because I wouldn't submit," I answered before she finished. "Because they will break whomever they keep within those walls."

No one spoke for a moment.

"Did they experiment on you?" Janna asked timidly.

A sick feeling sank inside me. I knew I wouldn't be able to hide it for too much longer. I didn't want to tell *anyone* about the abnormal nature of my pregnancy, never mind *everyone* and all at once.

"No, Janna, they didn't experiment on me." I took a shaky breath, rising to my feet. Kateri jumped up to help, but I lifted a hand to stop her. "I think I need to rest now."

I slipped away before anyone could stop me. The lump in my throat only intensified as I trekked back toward the tent. I blinked back hot, angry tears as I stepped soundlessly behind the shelter and walked a few paces into the forest. Stopping at a pine tree, I pressed my forehead to the rough bark, trying to silence the whirlwind of thoughts within me, biting my lip to keep from sobbing.

Memories of every story Fin had ever told me about my parents seemed to whisper in my ears.

I looked slowly up at the sky, leaning against the tree for support, gazing up at the moon. It was half visible over the crest of the mountain, cool white with a haze around it as if it were a holy thing. A tear trailed down my cheek.

For a while the only sounds were those distant voices rising from the fire. It was easy to pick out Keegan's voice from the rest. He spoke for only a moment before falling silent.

Something rustled softly behind me.

My breath caught in my throat. I whirled around, muscles tensing.

The moon lit up the forest, casting long, gray shadows of the tree trunks over the mossy ground. I held my breath, listening, my eyes darting back and forth as I squinted into the shadows.

Everything was still. Not even a breeze stirred.

Drawing a quiet breath, I kept my eyes on the woods as I walked backward a few steps. Then I bumped into something—*someone.*

I gasped as I spun around. Keegan stood in the dusty shadows of the moonlit trees. I pressed a hand to my chest and closed my eyes, steadying my heart.

"Where are you going?" he asked.

I took a small step back, putting a little space between us. "Nowhere. I just... needed a moment to myself."

"You're crying..."

I wiped my cheeks. "No, I'm not."

He reached up and grasped my hand, his warm fingers curling over my own. I looked up into his eyes.

"You know they're both real now, Icarus and Hawk... I can see it in your eyes that you finally believe it was all true, everything my dad ever told you about yourself and who your parents are," he said gently, stepping closer. "So what is it you're so afraid of?"

I studied him for a moment before drawing a shaky breath. "For a long time, I really thought I was Fin's daughter... that he just hadn't wanted to admit that he had been with a woman and that I was really his." I sniffed and gave a miserable laugh. "For a long time, I wished that was the case because it was less painful than accepting that Hawk and Icarus were my parents..."

"Why was that more painful?"

"Because it would mean that they *had* abandoned me. And that they weren't coming back."

"Your mother *is* looking for you, Spar," he said. "She has been for years. And your father—he *found you.*"

"No, no—I found *him*, Keegan, and I never should have!" Fresh, hot tears welled in my eyes. "He's in far greater danger now than he was before, and it's *my fault. Mine.*"

Keegan's deep green eyes glittered in the moonlight.

"Sparrow, let me ask *you* something... Do you really think one of the patriarchs, one of the Splitsouls between which the universe exists, could *really* be captured by the RGM against his will?" He slowly shook his head. "I think he laid down his powers to find you, Sparrow. Even if that meant letting you capture him... letting the RGM put him in chains." He smoothed his thumb over the back of my hand. "He would do anything to get you back... They both would. Don't you see that?"

I stared at him, a thousand questions stirring inside me.

*Icarus had known all along? Icarus had laid down his life, his powers, his freedom... for me? Could that be possible?*

"Then why haven't I seen Hawk?" I said, more to myself. "She appeared to you, Keegan... Why didn't she appear to me?"

"Hawk told me that she has appeared to you in dreams. She said she's tried to communicate with you that way—to speak to you," he said. "She told me that's the only way she can seem to reach you. Is that true?"

I swallowed hard. I remembered the many times I had dreamed of those dark wings stretched out against the sky, circling over me, protecting me.

*Sparrow...*

That voice. *Her* voice.

"Yes," I answered quietly. "Yes, I have had dreams of her. She has spoken to me."

Keegan was still holding my hand; his warm fingers filled the spaces between my own.

"Sparrow, Hawk told me that every time she and Icarus have tried to get close to you, it was almost as if some type of force was trying to keep you apart."

"I... I don't understand." My voice faded in my throat. "I don't understand how that's possible."

Keegan fell silent for a moment, looking down at the palm of my hand. "Do you want to know what I think?"

I nodded.

"You were hurt, Sparrow," he said. "You were lost... so you retreated inside yourself because you thought you would be safer behind the walls you built... Believe me, I know." His eyes pierced mine. "That night when we were out in the woods together... the night Raf was captured, and I, uh... I broke down. I cried... and you held me?"

I nodded. "I remember."

"That was the first time I had ever really come out from behind my own walls, Sparrow," he said. "And *you* helped me do that."

My gaze lowered to the ground, tears rolling down my face. "Keegan, I... I don't know how..."

He lifted my chin, his fingertips brushing gently against my cheek. "Your heart knows, Sparrow."

I stared into his eyes, lost for a moment in the warmth of his touch, his closeness. My eyes traced the features of his face, the shape of his lips.

"Keegan, I..." My voice broke off. "I missed you *so* much."

Keegan gazed into my eyes, pulled me closer, then wrapped his arms around me. He kissed the top of my head, smoothing a hand over my hair.

"I missed you too, Sparrow," he whispered.

For a moment, he just held me. I could hear the beat of his heart in his chest, feel his warm breath on the curve of my neck. Tears rolled down my cheeks.

"Sparrow." He drew back gently. "I wish I..."

My heart pounded in my chest as I stared into his eyes. His gaze traveled over my face, pausing at my lips. He leaned in.

Then a distant voice called his name.

Keegan hesitated. "I'll... let you get some rest," he said quietly, pulling away again.

I swallowed, feeling frozen for a moment before finally taking a step back. I gave a single nod.

"You should get back to the fire," I told him softly. I took a few steps toward the shelter, pausing to look back at him. "Goodnight, Keegan."

He gazed at me for a moment before stepping back into the shadows. "Goodnight, Sparrow."

# 31

THE FOOTPRINTS STOPPED AT THE ASHY REMAINS OF THE Homestead. I knew beyond the shadow of a doubt they were Sparrow's.

I scanned the clearing for any sign of the soldiers I knew were pursuing her—the same soldiers who were pursuing me. There was no sign of them. I stepped out of the shadows and into the clearing. That was when I realized I was not alone.

There was a cougar circling around the side of the demolished Homestead. I froze in my tracks, staring ahead. It couldn't see me, I was certain of that, but whether it could catch my scent was a different matter.

I kept silent, stood statue-like at the edge of the clearing, watching it carefully to see what it would do and whether it would react to my presence. It was fixated on something underneath the house, sniffing and digging at the foundation of the ruins, keeping its nose to the ground.

I slowly lifted a hand, my focus locking on the animal as pulsating, invisible energy traced its way up through my arm and into my palm. I had just taken aim when a new figure rounded the back of the house and stopped beside the cougar. I could hardly believe my eyes.

It was Keegan. Keegan, the man Bask had ordered me to kill—the man Sparrow loved.

Here he was, standing not fifty yards away. The energy wavered in my palm, heat radiating from the pit of my stomach. Everything inside me wanted to watch him die.

I was about to let go of the energy in my hand, pierce his body, nail him to the ground where he would forever lie. I was about to let go of every ounce of rage I had inside me.

But then I heard him say her name, and I stopped.

"Sparrow!"

I watched, as still as stone, as Keegan dropped to his knees and started to examine the side of the charred building. He said her name over and over again, and each time he said it, his voice carried a little more resolve.

When the rubble began to shift, he drew an ax and started hacking away at the logs that made up the side of the charred remains. He was through the wall within the span of a minute. I watched as he crawled into the void, disappearing. I held my breath, my fingers still tingling.

A moment later he reappeared, with Sparrow in his arms.

Her invisibility had worn off, allowing Keegan to see her. God, I wished she were truly invisible like I was, that no one on earth could see her except me.

But he could see her. He held her in his arms, and he ran, the cougar at his heels.

I watched them carefully, tracking them as I moved swiftly through the woods after them. I couldn't help but notice Sparrow's swollen abdomen, unmistakable evidence of the child she was carrying inside her. *My child.*

I watched as Keegan tore the fabric of her pants and healed a gunshot wound on her leg. He attempted to wake her, but she would not be roused. Finally, he lifted her from the ground once again.

I could have acted then. I could have killed him and taken Sparrow.

But I didn't. Instead, I watched. Instead, I followed.

They walked for hours and hours. I spent the night close to where Keegan stopped, lowering her to the ground by a big old tree. I sat not twenty yards away, staring him smack in the face. If he'd been able to see me, he would have seen hate in my eyes.

Still, I said nothing as I watched him lying there with my wife in his arms. I did nothing when he took her hand in his own and kissed her fingers.

Killing him then and there would have been easy, too easy. Because the thing was, I didn't just want him anymore. No, *sliders* had done this to me—I was a fugitive now, and it was *their* fault. It was that old man's fault—and the fault of every single anomaly he had helped train. Killing Keegan would bring only a moment of satisfaction.

I wanted to keep him alive for now. I wanted him to lead me back to the rest of them.

*I wanted to destroy every single one of them.*

I tried my best to stay awake, but my eyelids grew heavier and heavier each time I forced them open. Finally, they closed.

When I lurched awake, the first thing my eyes locked on was the vacant place where they had been, where they were no longer.

Cursing, I jumped to my feet, frantically scanning the ground for footprints, circling around the trees, my own footsteps becoming increasingly erratic as I searched for theirs. I found nothing.

I picked the most likely direction, a faint footpath through the trees, and began to walk, trudging ahead, running a hand over the stubble covering my scalp.

The same suffocating fear kept hitting me over and over and over again. What if I never picked up their trail again? What if I never found her? What if I never saw her again...

What if no one ever saw *me* again?

She was the only one who ever could. She and, perhaps, the child inside her. *My child.*

I swallowed hard, pressing the heels of my hands to my temples.

*No... no, she can't be gone... She can't be...*

I picked up my pace, walking faster, trying to think, trying to push all the ghosts out of my head, pounding my temples with my fists.

I sprinted through the trees, thrashing through the dead brush and overgrowth. Every footstep felt like I was falling, like the ground was pulling itself out from underneath me.

"Aaron."

The sudden voice over my shoulder sent me sprawling, my face slamming into the dirt.

Blood oozing from my lip, I rolled to my back and shot my arms straight out in front of me, blitzing the trees and the underbrush with bolts of energy. I scrambled upright, backing up against the trunk of a tree, bracing myself there, scanning the woods. It all felt unreal, like a fever dream.

My eyes darted back and forth, searching for the voice that had spoken. I had no doubt in my mind to whom it belonged.

Energy quivered in my hand as my gaze flashed back and forth, searching for the dark cloak among the shadows of the trees, for those eerie, clear blue eyes peering out at me from under the shadow of his hood.

I strained to listen past the ringing in my ears, blood dripping from my lip.

The forest blurred around me as I turned, looking for the old man. But the woods were empty and silent.

I don't know how long I stood there before I finally forced myself to keep going. I kept checking over my shoulders every few seconds, straining my ears, expecting to hear the voice again. Expecting a hand to clap down on my shoulder. Expecting to fall on my face again. But I heard nothing more than the rhythmic crunches and thuds of my footfalls and the pounding of my own heart.

It was getting dark when I came to a wide-open meadow. Stars were beginning to appear in the sky, and in the twilight, I could make out the looming mountains in the distance.

A heavy hopelessness filled my gut. The vast, silent landscape before me had begun to echo my darkest thought—*Give up*—when something in the distance caught my eye.

Like a freckle among the unending blankets of the night as it rolled out over the mountains, there was a soft, orange glow.

Barely there. A tiny spark of space between the mountain peaks. I held my breath, taking another step forward to stare and squint, wondering for a moment if I was imagining it.

No, it was there. Flickering and faint, but there: a flame. A fire up in the mountain pass.

I dragged one shaking hand over my lip and jaw, wiping off the crusted blood with my shirt. I pressed on, keeping my eyes fixed straight ahead on the faint glow.

# 32

I COULDN'T SLEEP THAT NIGHT. I TOSSED AND TURNED on the ground until the faintest hints of dawn tinged the sky. I rose before anyone else stirred and brushed back the canvas flap to step out into the crisp early morning air. I made my way past the targets and into the glade where Preston and I had felled two dead trees for wood the day prior.

I grabbed the ax from where I'd left it leaning, bringing it up to rest in the crook of my shoulder. I scanned the fallen tree, then straddled its trunk, swinging my leg over the leaner part at the top. I swung the ax down on one of the dry branches, hacking away at the wood. Those hollow thuds were the only sound in the otherwise silent forest, as the blade of my ax dismembered the giant.

I paused between branches and scanned the ghostly trees standing around me like watchmen who had frozen in the night. I was transported back to the night that Hawk had appeared in the woods. It was still so fresh in my mind, so vivid, I felt like at any moment I would see her standing there among the shadows, just like she had that night.

She'd been right. She'd been right about all of it—about Sparrow and Icarus and almost everything else. Except for me. She thought I'd been Sparrow's guiding light, someone who would help Sparrow find her way. But I wasn't sure I could be that after last night... I wasn't sure I could trust myself anymore.

God, the way Sparrow had looked at me. The way she had felt in my arms. For so long, I'd ached to be close to her again—just once. And now she was here.

Did she still love him? That question kept repeating in my thoughts.

So many emotions had stirred within me. For a moment it was like I had forgotten everything—everyone. Even Kateri, as painful as that was for me to admit. For a moment she'd been so close... The warmth of her breath on my skin. I'd almost...

I took off my baseball hat and wiped my face on my sleeve. I cursed.

"There you are," a lilting Irish accent interrupted the silent forest.

For a second, I thought I'd imagined the voice. I turned to find Lara standing there, her lips curved in a warm smile. I swiftly met her halfway in an embrace.

"I thought you and Areos were in—"

"I was, and Areos still is. I just thought it was high time for a visit." She pulled back to hold me out at arm's length, giving me a once-over. "So why are you out here venting your anger on this tree?"

I blew out a sigh. "You seen Dad?"

"He hasn't returned?"

"No. He must still be looking for Hawk," I told her. "I need to find some way to locate him and tell him that I already found her."

She raised an eyebrow. "Hawk or Sparrow?"

"Both."

"Are you serious?"

"I set out about a week ago to look for Hawk myself. I was going stir-crazy just sitting around here, waiting for Dad to come back. I couldn't do it anymore."

"And you *actually* found her?"

I nodded. "Actually, Hawk found me. She appeared to me out of nowhere. Talked in riddles just like Dad does; it pissed me off so much."

A slight smile twitched at the corners of Lara's lips. "So she's back at the shelter?"

"Not... exactly."

"But I thought you said you found both—"

"I did, but..." I sighed the rest out. "Sparrow is here; Hawk isn't. Icarus is in the hands of the RGM, and Sparrow is... She's pregnant."

"Pregnant?" she repeated, eyes wide. "So she married the soldier?"

I nodded solemnly. "She wants to leave us—says they're looking for her and that her presence here will endanger the rest of us."

Lara frowned, her sharp green eyes already scanning the forest in response. "She could be right."

I tilted my head, giving her a look. "You know full well I'd never let her go. Not when I know who she is. Not when she's one of us, whether she likes it or not," I countered. "Besides, where would she go? There's not that much time before she has the baby."

Lara pinched her lower lip, nodding thoughtfully. "I could take her back with me."

"What, to Section C?"

"Why not?" she questioned. "She'd have Areos and me to look after her until she delivers her child."

"Yeah, but Section C is a war zone."

"And *this* isn't? They burned the Homestead to the ground, Keegan. They beat all of you back—out of Yellowstone and into the Tetons. They captured three of you, nearly four, and now they have Sparrow."

"They don't have Sparrow—we do."

"You may have her, Keeg, but do you really *have* her?" She lowered her voice. "She may love that soldier, you know. She may want to give birth to this child and return to him as soon as she can. We don't know her, Keegan, not really. No one but your father seems to. Have you really thought about where her loyalty may lie?"

I pulled in a long, steady breath, studying her face. "Yeah. Yeah, I wonder about it all the time."

Lara's green eyes narrowed as she studied me in return. "You're in love with her."

I shook my head. "No. No, Lara, that's over."

"You're sure about that?"

Memories of the night before flashed through my thoughts, the way Sparrow's dark eyes had reflected the moonlight, the warmth of her fingers filling the spaces between my own.

"I'm... I'm in love with Kateri." I fumbled over the words. "We're actually exchanging promises in a few days."

"*What?*"

"I'm serious."

"You and Kateri?"

I nodded. "I don't really know why it took me so long to see how I felt about her."

Lara smiled, but I could see there was reservation hiding behind it, a bunch of questions she was still trying to figure out how to tactfully phrase. I beat her to it with the answers she needed to hear.

"Yes, I know it's fast, and we've talked about that—a lot. But we love each other." I gave a little shrug. "What's there to wait for?"

"Possibly nothing," she replied. "I'd just hate to see you rushing into something before your heart's truly ready for it. For both of your sakes."

"You're starting to sound like Preston now." I sighed. "Lara, I swear to you, I know how I feel about her."

"I trust you," she said at last. "And so does your father."

"And speaking of him," I said, shifting the conversation. "How do you propose we go about finding him? He needs to know that I found Hawk and that Sparrow is safe."

Lara nodded thoughtfully. "I have no idea where he is, Keegan. He didn't tell me where he was going."

"Which is a problem." I dug the toe of my boot into the ground. "Because he's the only one who's going to have any idea of how to go about this."

Lara went thoughtfully silent. "What about you?"

"Me?" My gaze snapped up from the ground. "What *about* me?"

"Why do you think your father left? Why do you think he commissioned Areos and me to take over Section C? Why do you think he left all of you way out here on your own?" She put a hand on my shoulder, looking me square in the face. "Your father left you here—all of you—because he believes in you. In who each of you truly is," she said quietly. "You are the healers of Earth. That's why he brought you here in the first place. Did you really think it was just to heal the forest?" She shook her head. "It was to heal yourselves. To help you to believe in what is already inside you."

Despite the truth in Lara's words, something within me still felt strangely heavy.

She stepped back. "Come on. Let's head back. I would like to speak with Sparrow and everyone else. I don't have much time."

I gave a nod. "I'll fill you in on everything Hawk told me on the way."

Lara spent a little time talking to everyone, but when she disappeared into the shelter to talk to Sparrow, she stayed in there for a while.

When I caught myself pacing, I went back out to the woods to finish cutting up the tree. Carrying an armload of the wood back to the shelter, I found everyone gathered around the fire. There was a vibe of apprehension hanging in the air because of Lara's sudden appearance.

I dumped the wood into a pile beside the fire. "I could use help with the rest," I announced, dusting off my hands. "There's plenty to be carried. Any volunteers?"

Kateri raised her hand from where she was standing over by the shelter. Preston followed suit, beginning to rise until Kateri made a subtle gesture for him to stay.

"Why do you think Lara is here?" Kateri came up alongside me as we made our way out of the glade and into the deeper part of the woods. "Did she hear from Sensei?"

I shook my head. "She knows as much about his whereabouts as we do. She just came to check in, see how we all are."

"What did she say when you told her about Sparrow?"

"She was surprised." I glanced up at the treetops rising against the gray, overcast sky. "She offered to take her back to Section C with her—said she'd be safer there."

"That sounds reasonable." When I didn't respond, she took my arm. "Isn't it, Keeg?"

I blew out a slow exhale. "Yes... and no. Section C is a nightmare right now. You heard how Areos talked about it."

"But surely Lara wouldn't suggest that Sparrow should go there if—"

"I know—I know. But Lara's just afraid that Sparrow might be right— that her presence here might compromise our position."

"And... you're *not* afraid of that?"

I slowed to a halt and turned to look at her. Her deep brown eyes narrowed uneasily.

"Of course I am, but what are the chances of that ever occurring when I transported back with her? There are no prints to follow. No one would be able to track us."

"It's not like you transported that far," she countered. "You walked all day from the Homestead. That would have already put you very close to where we are."

I glanced down at the ground. "What do you think we should do?" I asked.

A troubled look etched itself on Kateri's face; she crossed her arms over her chest, then stepped closer and reached up to brush her fingertips over my cheek. Leaning in, she kissed me, and her lips felt like fire on mine.

She drew back, looking up into my eyes again. "That's what I think."

I smiled and kissed her again.

"I think you're right." She paused. "Well, *probably* right."

"That Sparrow is safer here with us?"

"Yes, and that the chances are low that they would ever track her when you left them with no set of prints to follow," she replied. "Even if you did walk part of the way."

"We were still a ways out," I assured her. "I could only see the mountains in the distance."

Kateri nodded as we resumed walking through the trees. "Did you tell Lara about your encounter with Hawk?"

"Yes, everything. Just in case she sees Dad before I do."

"Why did you not tell me about it?" Kateri asked. "Before you told everyone else last night... before you told Sparrow."

I felt the back of my neck grow warm. "I thought she should know first. I mean, my entire search for Hawk was for the sole purpose of getting Sparrow back."

Kateri didn't respond. I slowed to a stop, then turned and took her face in my hands, brushing her hair back away from her face. "I'm sorry I didn't tell you first, and I'm sorry I didn't tell you about my plan before I left to look for Hawk, but I... I didn't want to worry you."

Kateri looked at me for a long moment in silence, an unreadable look lingering in her eyes. "When have I ever tried to stop you, Keegan? When have I ever told you to go against what your heart is telling you?"

"Never," I answered, my voice raw. "I'm an ass."

She nodded. "Kiss me again."

I smiled. Pulled her in by the waist this time and moved my lips over hers. It was so easy to forget everything for a moment; when I was with Kateri, reality seemed to wash away.

"I think you're right," Kateri said, pulling back a little. "I think she should stay. I think that it has all happened for a reason—her coming here, you seeing Hawk. I wonder, though... Why Hawk? What does she have to do with Sparrow?"

Standing there, staring down into her eyes, I wanted to tell her everything—the truth about Sparrow and who she was and why I felt so strongly about all of it. I wanted her to know.

But I couldn't. I'd given Dad my word—I'd sworn I would never divulge her identity to anyone. Not even Kateri.

Finally, I looped an arm around her, and we continued walking. "I really couldn't tell you, Kateri."

## 33

LARA SAT ON THE END OF THE CUSHION AND LISTENED intently to my story: I told her everything that had happened at the District and, more importantly, how I'd escaped. That Icarus had saved my life.

"Icarus was kind to me. He spoke as though he had always known me. Has he?" I was almost afraid to hear the answer. "Has he always known me?"

"Sparrow, what do you think Fin has been trying to tell you all these years?" Her eyes locked with my own. "Do you think he was lying to you? If you didn't believe him, why on earth would you believe it from my lips?"

I stared at her, unsure of what to say.

"Sparrow." She placed a hand gently on my knee. "I know who you are. I know both your parents—they saved my life. I have no doubts about you—I have nothing but faith in your identity, but unfortunately faith cannot be given. You'll have to find that faith for yourself, Sparrow. No matter how much evidence I lay before you, I cannot *make* you believe."

I pressed a hand to my forehead and drew a narrow breath. "I know. I know, Lara. You're right. I just... I just—" Tears began to well in my eyes. "What do you think Fin would say if he were here?" I said miserably. "What would he think of me now?"

My gaze lowered to where my hand rested on my belly.

"He would tell you what I have just told you," she replied, her voice gentle but unwavering. "And he would tell you that he loves you."

I swallowed, pinching my eyes shut. "Lara, I'm so scared," I whispered. "I don't know what's going to happen to me—if they're going to find me. If *he's* going to find me."

"Aaron?"

I swallowed and nodded. "I'm afraid that I'll lead him here. That I will endanger everyone because of my presence here—that something will happen to Keegan."

"Keegan can take care of himself," Lara said, trying to put my fears to rest. "As for the others... I share your concerns. I told Keegan that I could take you back to Section C with me—"

"Would you really? I would be so grateful—"

"Keegan would have none of it," she said, glancing in the direction of the shelter door and pressing her lips together thoughtfully. "Keegan's not himself lately."

"I think he's more himself than he's ever been," I contradicted. "He's finally marrying Kateri. I think everyone knew she was right for him—except for him. Until now..." I wiped my cheeks with the backs of my hands. "I'm glad to see him finally happy."

Lara frowned, running her fingers back through her tangled blonde hair. "Are you sure you've reconciled to the idea?"

I nodded without hesitation. "And Keegan has no right to tell me whether to stay or go," I went on, resolute. "I *want* to go."

Lara studied me for a moment, then gave a slow nod. "If you want to come to Section C, you are more than welcome to. Areos and I will do all that is within our power to keep you safe, but we cannot promise. Section C is still a very high-risk zone for sliders."

"I don't care about risk," I said. "Not for myself, anyway."

"You have more than yourself to consider now, Sparrow," Lara reminded me gravely. "When are you due?"

I didn't know—I had no idea. My abdomen ached and felt even more swollen today than it had the day before, though I hoped to God no one noticed this but me.

"In a couple of months," I answered softly.

"Did he... were you..."

I shook my head. "No. He didn't force himself on me, Lara."

"Do you love him?"

I didn't reply right away. Aaron's face came to the front of my mind. He had once been my only comfort in that hellhole, his face now represented darkness itself.

"Love had nothing to do with it," I said, pressing my eyelids closed. "You should know that nothing in the RGM is done for the sake of love: not marriage, not sex, not the creation of a child..." I trailed off, my voice cracking a little. "I want to return with you to Section C."

"And Keegan?"

"Will be happy," I said, resolve settling in my voice like iron. "The best thing in the world, for both of us, would be for neither of us to see the other again."

"Are you certain of that?"

I could feel the burn of Lara's gaze as she studied me. "I've never been more certain of anything." I swallowed back the lump in my throat. "What's important now is to get Icarus out of there. That's what I have to focus on— regardless of whether he's my father or not."

"What about Hawk?"

The abrupt question only increased the tightness in my throat. "What about her?"

"Surely Keegan must have told you that he saw Hawk, spoke with her."

"Yes. Yes, he told everyone," I responded quietly. "Lara... Keegan seems to think Icarus allowed me to capture him. That he and Hawk would do anything to find me again."

"And you?" She raised an eyebrow. "What do you think?"

"I... don't know what to think." My voice was barely audible now. "I don't know what to believe anymore."

She patted her hands on her knees, drew a breath and rose. "You can come to Section C."

"Thank you, Lara... When do we leave?"

"Not until after Keegan and Kateri exchange promises," she said. "I wouldn't miss being there for anything."

My heart faltered.

"After that, I'll transport back to Section C alone, discuss all of this with Areos, and get things ready for your arrival," she concluded. "Until then, you'll stay here."

I hated the idea. It was almost everything I had hoped that she wouldn't say.

"How long will it take until things are ready for me to move there?"

"A couple of weeks at most." Lara crossed the room and paused at the door. She pressed her lips together and looked back at me. "Sparrow, there were days that I lived through where I thought the darkness would never end, but I promise you it does," she told me quietly. "And it will."

I nodded, forcing a smile.

With each passing day it became easier and easier to get out of bed. Kateri let me borrow clothes that were loose enough to fit comfortably.

This morning, I woke up before any of the other girls and tiptoed softly around the cushions scattered on the ground, slipping outside into the dim light of dawn. It was a cold, foggy morning. Everything was soft in the pale early light. I paused for a moment where the remnants of the fire from the night before still lay, smoldering faintly. I closed my eyes and listened.

Venturing into the woods a short distance, I made my way to a tree that had a target nailed to its trunk. I paused in front of it, examining all the places where the blades of Keegan's knives had slashed through. My fingertips brushed over the battered surface.

In a few days he would be married. And I would be gone.

I squinted ahead as the first rays of sunlight began to spill down over the folds of the mountain. Through the trees in the distance, I could see a clearing, a sort of void that seemed to stretch on into the distance.

Shooting a quick glance over my shoulder at the shelter, I crept a little deeper into the forest, making my way towards the clearing. At the far side of the clearing was a ledge that fell away to a sheer-drop cliff.

Far below was a valley, and beyond that another forest. The sky was robin's-egg blue, clear and uninterrupted by even the faintest of clouds. Far in the distance was Yellowstone.

I knew Aaron was out there somewhere.

I emerged from the tree line and stepped carefully into the clearing, then sat down on a large weathered stump that stood monument to a tree that had been felled long ago. I hugged my thick wool shawl more tightly around me, staring out into the void below, losing myself for a moment.

My thoughts found their way back to Icarus, to that time we had spoken. I could still remember that look in his eyes... how he had looked at me like he'd known me.

Keegan's words echoed on the edge of the gentle mountain breeze: *"I think he laid down his powers to find you, Sparrow. Even if that meant letting you capture him..."*

I leaned forward on my knees, shivering, riffling my fingers back through my hair. I didn't know what to think anymore.

I hated feeling like there was nothing I could do, but... there wasn't. I was pregnant and running from the RGM; there was no way for me to help Icarus. I couldn't go back there—Icarus wouldn't want me to. All that remained was for me to leave—to finally get out of Aaron's and the RGM's range of detection. Despite what Keegan and Kateri seemed to believe, this place, though hidden up in the mountains, was not beyond their reach. They had no idea how much danger they could be in because of me.

Besides that, I didn't know how much longer I could bear to be close to Keegan. Every time I was with him, every time he looked into my eyes, I was afraid he would read my mind, know exactly what I was thinking and how deeply in love with him I still was.

"Sparrow?"

My breath caught in my throat. Keegan stepped out from the shadows of the trees and into the clearing. His hair was tousled, and his shirt was only partially buttoned.

"What are you doing all the way out here?" He studied me through curious green eyes.

I quickly looked away. "I could ask the same of you."

"I come out here most mornings."

I heard his footsteps as he drew closer, and a moment later he sat down beside me. His arm brushed against mine. We sat there in silence. Words burned the inside of my throat.

"How are you feeling?" he asked at length.

I drew a shaky breath. "Better. Better than I was..." I turned to look at him. "Thank you. For last night... for being so patient and kind, and... *Thank you.*"

I didn't want to cry, but letting the words out caused a lump to form in my throat. I pressed my fingertips to my eyelids as tears began to blur my vision, and my throat grew tight.

I could feel Keegan's eyes on me. "Hey, it's okay," he whispered, wrapping an arm around me. "It's okay, Sparrow."

I couldn't speak. Weak and tired, I leaned on his chest. He tucked his chin over the crown of my head.

"I wish Fin were here," I told him. "I don't know what to do. I know I need to leave, but part of me feels like a coward—like I should be doing something to save Icarus... He saved me, Keegan. I would have died there if it weren't for him."

Keegan was silent for a long moment, smoothing my hair gently with his fingertips.

"I wish my dad was here too..." he said at last. "I wish I could talk to him. He always knows what to do... what the right thing is. I wish I could recognize truth as easily as he does."

"I think you're more like him than you realize, Keegan."

He shook his head; I felt the stubble on his chin catch in my hair. "I feel like a hurricane inside, Sparrow."

He hesitated, almost like he wasn't sure whether he should say anything else. I could hear the pounding of his heart in his chest.

"Can I ask you something?" he said at last.

I nodded, and he pulled back to look me in the eyes.

"That night, when you told me..." He paused, sighing the rest out. "Sparrow, when you told me that you loved him—that you had never loved me... Did you mean it? Truly?"

His voice was so raw and honest, his eyes reaching into mine, searching for some honesty in me. God, I wanted to just tell him.

"Keegan, please... don't make me answer that."

"Sparrow, I saw what he was like." He took my hand in his. "He was a monster. He would have killed me—he *wanted* to. I could see it in his thoughts."

"There's nothing about Aaron's character that I wasn't intimately acquainted with. There's nothing you can tell me about him that would surprise me." I looked out over the valley below us, avoiding his eyes. "Keegan, there's... there's nothing that would make me happier than to... than to just be friends again."

Keegan didn't respond. I could feel his eyes on me.

"I told Lara that I want to go back to Section C with her," I continued, trying to steady my voice. "I hope you won't fight me on this."

"I can't promise that—I don't think it's a good idea."

"And putting all of you in grave danger *is*? Keegan, you just acknowledged yourself that Aaron is a monster, yet—" I gasped, doubling over and grasping my stomach as pain sliced through me like a knife.

Keegan grasped my shoulders. "Sparrow, what is it? Are you all right?"

I could barely hear him as he repeated my name. Then, like a strange and sudden fog lifting, the pulsing pain passed.

"I-I'm fine," I said quietly. "Really."

"Bullshit."

"No, really. That happens from time to time," I insisted. "Don't worry, I'm not going into labor or anything."

"I'm *not* worried about that. I'm worried about *you*." His hand was suddenly on my cheek, turning my face to look at his serious, searching eyes. "Are *you okay?*"

I didn't know how to reply. The answer was no: no, I wasn't. The truth was, I didn't want to leave just so that I wouldn't be reminded every day that I had lost Keegan. I needed to get to Section C because I had no idea if I would even survive having the baby. The RGM had never before done what they were trying on me. I didn't know if I would live through giving birth, and that was the last thing I wanted Keegan, or anyone else, to know. I didn't want to be treated differently, as if I were made of glass and about to shatter.

But looking into his eyes and lying to his face was easier said than done.

"I am fine," I said at last. "I will be fine if you just let me leave. Let me start afresh somewhere else."

"You say that as if I actually have the power to stop you," he said. "If only that were the case."

There were so many things I wanted to say, but there were no words to describe what I felt. The feelings inside me made mockery of spoken language when I looked into his face. It wasn't just that I felt in love with him. No, it was so terrifyingly beyond that I could scarcely give it a name: it was like discovering a new world—one so real it made this one seem as if it were made of vapor.

The skin of his palm burned against my cheek.

"You know I want you to stay, Sparrow," he told me softly. "But if... if leaving will make you happy, then..." He paused, sighing. "If it will make you happy, I will help you however I can."

# 34

"WHAT DO YOU THINK OF THIS?"

I turned away from the open flap of the shelter, where I stood staring out at the gently falling rain.

A long dress made of soft woven fabric hung from Kateri's fingertips. She scanned my face, and then her lips formed a little smile. "You didn't hear a word, did you?"

I shook my head. "I-I'm sorry. I was lost in thought."

"About?"

"Nothing, really." My gaze shifted to the garment she still held in her hands. I stepped closer and ran my fingertips over the soft fabric. "You'll look beautiful in anything," I said, then held back a grin. "Or nothing."

Kateri gave my arm a little smack, but I laced my arms around her waist anyway, brushing aside her hair to kiss her neck.

"Keeg."

"Mmm?" I rested the side of my face in the curve of her neck. "What?"

She drew a deep breath, continuing to brush through the fabrics laid out on the table in front of her.

"You're distracting me."

"How?" I asked softly, then kissed her neck again. "Like that?"

She laughed and spun around in my arms. She looked up into my eyes and smiled, lifting onto her toes to press her lips against mine. Then she pulled away. "Keegan."

"Mmm?"

"You seem distracted. What's bothering you?" she asked softly, the tone of her voice revealing that she already half knew. "Sparrow?"

"Sparrow?" I drew back a little, rubbing the back of my neck. "What do you mean?"

"Lara told me that she'll be returning to take Sparrow back to Section C with her as soon as she and Areos get everything ready."

I nodded. "Sparrow's convinced that her presence endangers us. Lara told me that she agrees."

Kateri's eyes followed me as I began to pace. "What about Sparrow? Have you spoken with her?"

I dragged a hand back through my hair, gazing absently down at the dress on the table. "I—yeah. Yeah, this morning, actually."

"What did you say to her?"

*When you told me that you loved him—that you had never loved me... Did you mean it?*

That was what I'd said. I hadn't been able to stop myself—the words had rushed out of me like crashing waves, desperate and aching, and I didn't even know why... I was afraid to admit why.

"Keeg?"

I squeezed my eyes shut, clearing my throat. "Uh, what?"

"What did you—"

"She said that she wants to go," I interrupted, my voice a little frayed. "She wants to start over."

Kateri lifted the dress and looked at it for a moment before folding the fabric over on itself. "I can understand that. Can't you?"

"Yeah," I lied. "I totally get it. I just... I just don't know if it's the right choice."

"She'll have Lara and Areos."

"Yes. But..."

"But?"

"Dad brought her *here*..." I ran my fingertips over the table. "I just feel like that was for a purpose."

"Sometimes a purpose may only last for a season," she said quietly. "Perhaps that purpose, for her, has been fulfilled."

"How?" I said, more to myself than to her, walking over to the tent's opening. "How can it be, when..."

When she still didn't believe who she was, not really. Wasn't that why Dad had brought her here in the first place? What had we accomplished?

She was still at war inside.

I couldn't believe that this was the right thing, not when I'd met her mother and seen the look in her eyes. Not when I knew the truth about Sparrow.

More than anything, I wanted her to stay... I couldn't give up on her. *God*, part of me just couldn't let her go.

"I told her I wanted her to be happy," I said, staring out at the gentle rain. "I want her to find the kind of happiness I have found with you. But still... Something about the idea of her leaving just feels... wrong."

Kateri was quiet for a moment; then she came up beside me. She looked out thoughtfully at the rain for a moment before turning to look at me. "Have you?"

"Have I what?" I asked.

"Have you truly found happiness?"

Studying her face, I brushed a strand of hair off her forehead, my fingers taking their time across her skin. I nodded and leaned my forehead against hers.

"I have," I whispered. My lips touched hers as I spoke. "I love you, Kateri."

I could feel Kateri's lips form a smile against mine. She gave me a soft, brief kiss, and then let her lips linger there. I could feel her restless thoughts.

I pulled her into my arms, running my fingertips back over her smooth, soft hair. I stared ahead, my mind drifting as I listened to the wind beyond the shelter walls.

The rain lasted into the night. Everyone stayed up late together in the main section of the shelter, talking and listening to Lara's stories about Section C. Kateri sat beside me, snug under one edge of the same blanket that wrapped my shoulders. Sparrow sat beside Lara. She barely said a word. Her hand rested on the curve of her belly, her fingers moving in gentle motions now and again as if this was a means of communication between her and the unborn slider inside her.

Why had I asked her about that night—whether she really loved Aaron? Why hadn't I just let things be? Was I still so hurt over the fact she loved him? I was happy. Kateri and I were getting married; we were moving on... But still, something inside me writhed in torment when I looked at Sparrow.

Was it because I was jealous of him—of that asshole she was married to? Was I jealous because he had done everything I'd ever dreamed of doing with Sparrow—marrying her, building a life with her... making love with her? *God*, it had been such a narrow miss... If things had been different, maybe I would be sitting beside her. Maybe the child inside her would have been mine and hers...

She looked up and caught me staring at her.

I looked away, refocusing on Lara, pretending to be engaged in whatever she was talking about.

That night I lay awake for hours, staring up through the darkness. My mind drifted back to that morning, when Sparrow and I had sat talking together on the edge of the escarpment.

Why couldn't I stop thinking about her? Was it because we'd once been so close that it still felt natural to want to touch her? I didn't want it to feel natural. I didn't want it to feel any way at all. I loved Kateri—I could see myself with her. She and I had something so... *real*. I couldn't lose that. There was never any pretense with her. We were cut from the same cloth; we knew the contents of each other's heart because we were both made of the same earth, sunlight, and wild wind.

Yet, it was because of that wild wind that I felt *so restless* now.

Maybe it was better this way, that Sparrow went her way and I went mine. Maybe it would be better.

But if that was true, why was I still awake? Why did the very idea of her leaving have me wearing a hole into the hard ground with all my tossing and turning?

Why did everything feel so wrong if everything was so... right?

I wished the night were gone—that it would speed up and that the five days standing between Kateri and me would melt away. I wished that I were already hers and she were already mine. I could see her when I closed my eyes, wearing that yellow dress, with flowers caught in her hair.

I wanted to be there already.

Instead, in sleep's cruel absence I lay in the darkness and thought about Sparrow. We'd talked yet said hardly anything. Maybe that was why my hands had found her face, holding it like it was the sun.

I just wanted her to know who she was—I wanted her to see who I saw when I looked at her. I wanted to be there for her, and I was afraid of losing her.

But, in a way, I think she wanted to be lost.

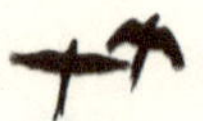

I woke up late the following morning. It had been nearly dawn by the time I'd finally drifted off to sleep. Kateri, Myung and Preston were at the fire. Rafael was standing a ways off in the woods, Sparrow by his side. I could see him gesturing wildly with his hands, the way he did when he was stoked about something.

I caught faint snatches of Sparrow's laughter on the soft wind. It was the first time I'd heard her laugh since her return. I smiled, watching the two of them for a moment, before a hand clapped down on my shoulder from behind me.

"I've been thinking," Lara said, in a determined voice. "I have enough time before you and Kateri exchange promises. I can go to Section C and make preparations for Sparrow's arrival and still be back before your wedding."

I turned and looked at her. "I'm still not convinced it's a good idea that she leaves."

"Sparrow needs stability right now, Keegan—safety."

"I know, I know." My eyes wandered back to Sparrow and Rafael. "But I just..."

"And the baby? Do you expect her to have it out here in the woods? Hmm? Without anyone experienced here to help her?"

"Of course not. But you could be here."

"I *can't*, Keegan. You know that. I have to get back to Section C, and you and I both know that Sparrow will be better off there."

Nothing inside me wanted to admit that she was right, but after a moment I gave a grudging nod of agreement. "Yeah... you're right."

"You'll be married by then anyway," she added. "You'll be too busy with other things to even notice anything else."

I gave her a weak grin. "Yeah. Yeah, I guess that's true."

"I'll be leaving shortly—breakfast first." She folded me into a hug, patting me on the back. "I want you to know that I'm proud of you and Kateri. You've proven yourselves spectacularly—you make a great couple."

I closed my eyes, hugging her back. "I wish I could say I haven't been distracted. I wish I could be the kind of leader Dad's always been—so focused."

"Not all leaders are made of mountains, Keegan. Some of them are stormy seas, but with good hearts."

I grunted a laugh. "Yeah? Like who?"

She pushed me out to arm's length, looking me square in the face. "Icarus."

She gave my arms a little squeeze; then she walked off toward the fire to join the others. I stood there for a moment, thinking about her answer. My eyes drifted back to the woods. Rafael was throwing knives at the targets now, and Sparrow was watching. She clapped when he hit the bullseye. The gentle breeze ruffled her dark hair, brushing strands of it into her face. She was smiling. Tearing my eyes away, I glanced back at the fire. Kateri was locked in conversation with Lara.

Before I realized it, I was making my way through the trees, toward Sparrow. I came up on the other side of the tree she was leaning against.

She glanced around at me, then looked back at Rafael. We both watched him in silence.

"You've gotten great at this," she congratulated Raf when he'd thrown the last of the knives in his holster.

He cast her a wide grin before he dashed over to start pulling the blades out of the wooden target.

"You taught him well," Sparrow told me quietly.

I turned and looked at her. Her head was tipped back against the trunk of the tree, and wisps of dark hair fell across her face. I dragged my gaze back to Raf.

"Sparrow," I said finally, not really sure how I was going to finish that sentence.

"Mm?"

I shifted my weight to the other foot, stepping incrementally closer to the place she was standing. "I... I guess I just..."

"Okay, you want to give it a try?" Raf cut in, striding back over to Sparrow. He saw me and raised a hand in greeting, then turned back to Sparrow. "Or is that too much with—"

"Pssh." Sparrow brushed off the question, snatching one of the knives playfully out of his holster. "Being pregnant doesn't mean you can't throw knives."

She walked over to the place where Rafael had stood moments ago, then opened her hand and tossed the knife into a levitation. It twirled there, hovering just over her palm as she took aim. Her fingertips shook a little as she moved her hand, and then she sent the blade hurtling forward, rotating a couple of times before driving itself neatly into the center of the target.

Rafael let out a low whistle. "You're the one who's gotten good, Spar."

She stepped aside, motioning for Raf to reclaim his place. "I had a good teacher, same as you. And many opportunities to use what I learned during my time at District Firehole."

"Yeah?" Raf asked, stepping up to tug a blade free from his holster. "Like when? I bet you have a million stories to tell."

Sparrow's smile instantly washed away, a distant look springing to her eyes. She shook her head slowly. "No. No, nothing worth telling, Raf," she answered softly. "You remember what it was like."

"Yes, but..." He sent another blade careening through the air. "But I *saw* nothing. You saw it *all*, Sparrow—but you never talk about it."

Her eyebrows knitted together. "I told you, Raf. It's not worth talking about."

He turned to look at her. "I always told Keegan that you didn't want to be there—that you stayed because you had to, because you had no other choice."

I straightened and took a step toward him. "Raf."

"He said you loved Aaron Price," he continued, ignoring me. "I told him that you would never betray us, but he didn't believe me."

"Raf." This time I spoke his name more firmly. "I didn't—"

Rafael spun around to face me, so tall now that he was at eye level with me. "Yes, you did. You told me that she wanted to be there—you said she told you so herself! I was the one who argued with you. I was the one who told you it wasn't true, that she would never, *never* want to be there..." His voice trembled, his eyes flashing with an anger I'd never seen in him before. He stepped closer to me. "That's exactly what you told me, isn't it?"

"Rafael, that's not what..." I trailed off, my eyes shifting from his to Sparrow's. "Why don't you ask Sparrow what she told me the night I left?" I finished finally, looking back at him. "Why don't you ask her why she wanted me to leave?"

Rafael turned sharply to look at Sparrow.

She remained frozen, then nodded. "Yes, Rafael. Keegan is right."

"No." Rafael shook his head. "No, Sparrow, I don't care what you say. I know it's not true!"

"Rafael, listen to me!" Sparrow's voice rose. "I told Keegan to leave because I... because *I wanted* him to leave. I wanted to be with Aaron."

"I don't believe you," he shot back. "I don't believe a word you say, Sparrow."

Sparrow closed what little distance remained between them, grasping him gently by the shoulders and looking him square in the face. "Well, you should, Raf."

I swallowed the tight feeling in the back of my throat. Raf slowly pulled away from her. Tears glistened in his blue eyes as he turned to throw me a glance.

"Raf." I started toward him, but he quickly put up a hand, starting back toward the shelter.

Sparrow watched him go, standing frozen where she was. She didn't meet my gaze; she just stared hollowly after him.

"Sparrow, I—I'm sorry. I didn't mean..."

Sparrow didn't respond—or give me a chance to finish. She turned and walked out of the clearing, striding into the woods, away from the shelter. I stood there and watched her for a moment, watched the distance grow between us—like it always did.

*Like it always did.*

I took off after her.

"Sparrow." I yelled her name as I jogged to catch up. "Sparrow, wait! Please..." I fell into step beside her. "Please stop."

She didn't wait, didn't stop. Didn't even look in my direction.

"I just—you don't understand. I just wanted Rafael to know that it wasn't like I'd abandoned you there. It wasn't like I'd given up." My words spilled over each other. "I just wanted him to know that I hadn't lied to him, that you had—"

"That I'd wanted to stay?" She stopped short, turning to look me straight in the eyes. "That I loved Aaron—that I married him and wanted to have a family with him?" She gave a short, bitter laugh. "There are things that happened in the District that I could... I could never—*would* never tell him, Keegan..." Her voice cracked. "Things I would never even tell *you*."

She turned to keep walking, but I caught her by the arm. "What things?"

"Let—let me go!" She struggled to pull her arm away.

"Sparrow, what things?" I gently grasped her arm with my other hand. We struggled against each other for a few steps until finally I pulled her close. My forehead touched hers.

"Sparrow," I whispered, "what things?"

She wrestled against my grasp, pushing against my chest for a moment before she suddenly relented, one of her hands resting over my heart. I let go of her, pulling away just enough to see tears spilling down her cheeks.

"I had to marry Aaron," she said. "I had to do what they said, or..."

"Or?"

Her lips trembled as she squeezed her eyes shut. Shook her head. "I—I cannot. I—"

"Sparrow, please."

"I cannot tell you, Keegan. I never will," she gasped, pushing me away, staring at me through her tears. "But if you think it's what I wanted—if you think I *wanted* to marry Aaron, if you think I wanted to live in fear of being attacked and raped by soldiers, of being experimented on or killed by the RGM, if you think that I wanted to get pregnant with his child?" Her voice broke. "If you think that's what I *wanted*?" She shook her head slowly, biting back a sob. "Then you don't know me at *all*, Keegan."

Everything I was about to say faded in my throat, leaving me speechless. I stood there staring at her staring at me through tears.

Then, without another word, she whirled around and left me standing there. I watched her vanish among the trees, leaving me alone once more, the ghost of the feeling of her skin lingering on the tips of my fingers.

*My god, what have I done?*

A soft noise in the brush startled me out of my thoughts. The hairs on the backs of my arms stood on end.

I glanced around for a moment, but there was nothing there. A gentle breeze hushed through the woods.

I walked back to the shelter and said "nothing" every time Lara and Kateri asked what had happened. I forced myself to pretend I was fine. I was the furthest thing from fine.

# 35

"SPARROW—SPARROW, WAIT! PLEASE..."

Sparrow continued straight ahead as if she hadn't heard.

"I just—you don't understand," Keegan called after her. "I just wanted Rafael to know that it wasn't like I'd abandoned you there. It wasn't like I'd given up. I just wanted him to know that I hadn't lied to him, that you had—"

I watched them progress toward where I was crouching, hidden in the dark shade of the dead trees. Sparrow slammed to a halt and turned to face him, her eyes ablaze.

"That I'd wanted to stay?" Her voice rose, shattering the stillness. "That I loved Aaron—that I married him and wanted to have a family with him? There are things that happened there that I could... I could never—*would* never tell him, Keegan. Things I would never tell *you.*"

She tried to leave, but he grabbed her by the arm. "What things?"

"Let—let me go!"

"Sparrow, what things?"

They struggled in a way that pulled them in closer to each other. Finally, Sparrow was pressed up against him. He leaned into her as if he couldn't get close enough, speaking to her in a low voice that I could no longer hear from where I watched. But I didn't need to hear whatever it was he said.

No, I could see the expression on my wife's face. I knew the look in her eyes.

Finally, she shoved him away.

"I cannot tell you, Keegan. I never will." Her voice was hot with anger. "But do you think it's what I wanted? Do you honestly think I *wanted* to marry Aaron, that I wanted to live in fear of being attacked and raped by soldiers, of being experimented on or killed by the RGM? Do you think that I wanted to get pregnant with his child?"

My heart sank in my chest. My fingertips began to tingle with heat, but I closed my fists.

"If you think that's what I wanted, then you don't know me at all, Keegan."

With tears in her eyes, she left him standing there alone.

My fingertips trembled though they were still locked into fists. My eyes fixed on the back of his head, the tangled red hair.

Slowly, my right hand eased open; my fingers uncurled. Hot white energy flickered faintly over my open palm.

With the only person who could see me gone, I lifted to my feet, raising my arm, clutching the soft, pulsating ball of energy in my hand as I did. I leaned forward, a little too far. The brush rustled against my leg, making a sound just audible enough to catch his attention.

He turned, his green eyes wide, dilated, behind wisps of red. He was like an animal with senses surpassing that of a normal human being—even a slider.

I let my mind go quiet so that he could not sense me there. I knew better than to think too loudly in his presence.

I extended my arms in front of me, positioning myself, taking silent aim at the middle of his forehead as he turned now to face in my direction. Had he possessed Sparrow's unique abilities, he would have seen me standing there, not fifty feet from him, holding enough power in my hands to render him lifeless right then and there.

Instead, his eyes scanned the thicket around him like a frightened rabbit.

My fingers still trembled, clenched around the orb that seemed to pulse with the pounding of my own heart. I watched his eyes, wondering what Sparrow loved in them. Envying him. Hating him.

I wanted to let go; my fingers were already beginning to loosen.

His eyes narrow as he stared, his gaze now fixing directly on the place where I stood. The wind began to blow.

His eyes softened once more, his broad shoulders relaxing. He had just attributed the rustling sound to this—the wind. It was nothing; it was the wind.

It could have been his last thought. I watched him stare into the woods, then in the direction Sparrow had taken off in.

Did Sparrow truly love him? I knew that she didn't love me—I'd always known that... but did she love him? Would she truly choose him in the end, when he was in love with someone else?

If I killed him, I could make that choice for her. But I would never know what she would have chosen herself.

If I let him live...

My gaze bored into his back as he slipped away among the trees. I lowered my hand to my side, breathing for the first time in a while. Watching in silence as the wind whistled through the dead brush.

If I let him live, Sparrow would choose. She would have to watch him marry someone else and forget about her. I would find her at her most vulnerable. And we could escape together—before she ever dreamed of going to Section C.

She would see that I would never betray her. I never *had* betrayed her.

The woods became my home, the ground my bed and the sky my roof. I slept in the base of a hollowed-out tree. It kept me warm enough that I didn't freeze to death as the nightly temperatures steadily dropped. Each morning when I awoke, more frost bathed the ground than on the day before.

Some days I would just lie there in the tree, listening for the voices of the soldiers. I never heard them, but occasionally, far off, I could hear Sparrow's.

I was only about a hundred yards behind their shelter. She thought me miles away, but I was never far from her.

Why had she left me behind? That question still burned like an ember in my brain, and only one terrifying answer made any sense at all: she had overheard. That night, before I'd killed Bask, she'd overheard us talking in that room with Icarus. She'd heard everything, and she knew that I'd never been who she thought I was.

Either way, I could never go back to the RGM, not after... all of it.

This girl I saw through the patches of leaves, drenched in sunlight or bathed in the flow from the dancing flames, the woman who carried my child inside her—she was all I had left in the world.

I could have claimed her whenever I wished it—but I didn't wish it. I wanted her more than anything, but I wanted *her* to want *me*... Otherwise it was all meaningless.

I had once tasted ecstasy, had felt her hands as they trickled over my body like the cool rivulets of a waterfall, had once been intoxicated by her scent and the sensation of her. I had once known the heaven of her desire, and now all else was hell.

Keegan didn't love her—didn't want her. Even worse, he desired someone else. Now Sparrow would know what it felt like: to desire someone who doesn't want you. The most strange and terrible kind of darkness.

But in that darkness, I was there. I would wait for her to want me.

And when she did, I would save her.

# 36

"SPARROW?" PRESTON LIFTED TO HIS FEET FROM THE OTHER side of the fire as soon as I emerged from the woods. "Sparrow, what is it? What's wrong?"

My gaze locked with his as I passed him. Walking as quickly as I could without breaking into a run, I made my way to the tent, throwing open the flap. Finally, alone within those canvas walls, I fell to my knees, unable to bear it any longer.

I buried my face in my hands, light-headed, gasping for breath. Tears filled my eyes, but I was unable to weep. I didn't have that much left inside me.

Something deep in my core just wanted Fin; I wanted to be held in his arms like when I was a little girl. I just wanted to hear his voice softly hushing me, telling me that everything would be okay. I just wanted everything to be okay.

*Where is he? Why isn't he here?*

Didn't he understand? I didn't need my mother; I needed *him*. He was all I had ever needed—a mother, a father, a brother, a friend—all in one person, one golden heart. Hadn't I always told him that he was my world?

I squeezed my eyes shut behind my trembling fingertips, whispering his name through sobs.

"Fin..."

"Sparrow," a soft voice said through the canvas, "can I come in?"

I shook my head, face still cupped in my hands. "Go away, Preston."

I heard the sound of the canvas moving aside and, a moment later, footsteps. I felt the warmth of a hand on my back as Preston knelt down beside me.

"Sparrow, it's okay."

I shook my head, remaining where I was, stiff and shaking with misery.

"Sparrow, please tell me what happened," he said quietly. "I promise I will do whatever I can to help you."

Slowly, I straightened up, my fingers still pressed to my eyelids. I shook my head slowly. "There is nothing... nothing you can do, Preston."

"Is it Keegan?" he asked.

Finally, my hands fell away from my face.

"Sparrow, why not just tell him?" He clasped my hand in his own. "You cannot let him go into this marriage blind to how you truly feel—"

"It doesn't matter how *I* feel—Keegan isn't promising himself to Kateri because *I* no longer love him. He's promising himself to her because *he's* in love with her, and my feelings for him won't matter—and shouldn't."

"No..." He paused. "But his feelings for *you* should."

I froze, staring at him. "Keegan loves Kateri. I know he does. I've seen it in the way he looks at her."

"He does love Kateri, in a way. I just think the roots of the love that you and he had still grow inside him, deeper than he realizes." He sighed. "I know Keegan, Sparrow—he is my brother."

"Preston, don't." I rose slowly to my feet, stepping away. "Don't say that—don't say anything more, please."

"Do you think it's easy for me to say these things, Sparrow?" He kept his voice low. "I love Keegan and Kateri. For so long I thought... I thought their being together would bring them the happiness they deserved. But when you came back, something changed. I saw it in his eyes. He might not know it, but it's obvious he's still in love with you—"

"Don't say these things, Preston, please!" I whirled around to face him. He was still kneeling on the ground. "Do you even understand how much it hurts?" Finally, my tears began to fall.

Preston's deep amber eyes studied me. "Why not just speak to him?"

"Because I know that he would truly be happy with Kateri. They're so much alike—cut from the same cloth. He would be miserable with me. We're too different..." I swallowed back the lump in my throat. "He'll be happy with her. Even if he does feel something for me, which I very much doubt, it will fade. He'll have real, true, lasting love with Kateri. You and I both know he will."

"What about honesty?"

"It's not my place to be honest." I pressed my lips together, shook my head. "If Janna was in love with someone else and not you, would you jeopardize her happiness just because of what you felt?"

Preston studied me for a moment without answering.

"You know you wouldn't," I answered for him. "Because you care about her too much to do that."

In the silence, voices from the campfire drifted through the canvas, inaudible snatches of Keegan's voice among them. I swallowed and dried my cheeks with the backs of my hands.

"I appreciate you, Preston." I spoke softly. "I appreciate you thinking of me."

Preston's dark eyebrows remained furrowed, that same, sad look in his eyes. Then he sucked in a breath and got to his feet.

"I wasn't just thinking of you," he said quietly. "I was thinking of *all* of you. It's not fair to Kateri if Keegan's heart isn't really free."

He got to his feet. He didn't try to hug me; he just stood there with his arms out wide for a moment to see if I wanted one. He was one of those types who could make even the most miserable person smile, I swear.

Of course I wanted one. I wrapped my arms around him and buried my face in his chest. He was so much taller than me.

"Things will be better this way, Preston," I said.

"You sure?"

I couldn't answer, so I just nodded.

There was only one day left.

Lara had gone to Section C to speak with Areos and make preparations for my arrival. Everything else carried on as usual. Everyone had their daily chores. Mine, I was always told, was to rest, but I was so tired of resting; it gave me too much time to think, and that was the deadliest thing of all.

It was late afternoon when Janna, Myung, and Kateri gathered in the girls' side of the tent. Myung had made fresh tea over the fire, and Janna held something wrapped in fabric in her hand.

"You didn't have to give me anything!" Kateri reminded her, unwrapping it. "Your presence tomorrow is gift enough."

They had pulled the floor cushions into a rough semicircle on the floor. The sunlight poured in through the roof, dappling the ground in pools of warm yellow. Steam rippled up from the iron kettle as Myung poured the fragrant tea into mugs. She shot me a glance, then tipped her head in the direction of where they all were seated.

"Sparrow, come and have a cup."

Kateri turned to look at me, then sidled over to make room for me to sit beside her and patted the cushion. "Yes, Sparrow, please."

I was sitting on the edge of my bed, wrapped in a blanket. I tried to ignore the aching pain in my back and belly as I pressed my lips into a weak smile and rose to join them.

I sat down beside Kateri and carefully took the cup from Myung's hand, hoping to God that the warm tea would help ease the grating pain inside me.

I sipped it slowly, watching Kateri's hands as she unwound the bundle, which contained a necklace made from smooth stones Janna had pulled from the river.

"I thought it might go well with your new dress," Janna told her, smiling proudly.

"Try it on," Myung chorused.

Laughter and insistence ensued. Finally, Kateri surrendered. She retrieved the dress she had made and slipped into it, looping the necklace over her head. Janna made her turn around and wove her long, thick hair into an elaborate braid.

Kateri made a face when she was finished, feeling around the back of her head to try to identify what Janna had done to her. She glanced from Myung to me and then spun around again, fingering the braid.

"I don't know. What do you both think?" she asked us. "It's not very... me, is it?"

"Only you can be the judge of that," Myung responded.

The sun traced ribbons of light through Kateri's hair and cascaded over the folds of fabric as she turned and looked down at herself.

"I wish we had a mirror." Janna bit her lip and glanced around as though one would appear.

I swallowed back the pain still coursing through me. "You don't need a mirror." I spoke up finally. "You look beautiful. Keegan will love you no matter what you wear."

Kateri looked at me over her shoulder, an expression I couldn't quite read passing over her face for a moment before her lips curved into a smile.

"I hope you know how happy I am for you," I continued quietly. "For both of you."

Kateri looked at me for a moment in silence, then bowed her head in a nod. "Thank you, Sparrow."

Janna started to unbraid her hair. "What about after the wedding?" she asked. "Sensei left both of you in charge—how will you have any time to get away together?"

"We'll figure something out. No matter how much we care for each other, our greatest responsibility is here, with all of you," Kateri responded. "And when Sensei returns, maybe we'll get a few days to ourselves—"

Myung grunted. "*If* he returns."

"We will establish where we will go from here," Kateri went on, as if Myung hadn't spoken. "We cannot live in hiding forever."

I swallowed a mouthful of the tea. As the conversation drifted on, I rose and slipped away.

As soon as I had ventured from the shelter a little ways, I gritted my teeth in pain, leaning back against one of the trees. I could feel the tiny being wrestling inside me, as if it were in as much pain as I was.

I was reminded with every passing day, as the baby inside me grew at an alarming rate, that I was an *experiment*. At this point, dresses were the only comfortable thing I could wear. I looked seven months pregnant at least, and that was what everyone thought I was. In reality, it had been barely two months since I'd conceived.

I hadn't told Lara about the serum and the experiment. I knew I should have said something, but Lara and Keegan confided in each other, and even if she didn't betray me with her words, she would unknowingly do so with her eyes. And the last thing in the world I wanted was for Keegan to know what was really happening to me.

The truth was, if I didn't survive this baby, I didn't want Keegan to know why, and I didn't want him to know ahead of time that that was a risk. I would either survive, or I wouldn't. There was nothing anyone could do. I was terrified, but at least no one knew how much. That was my only consolation.

I closed my eyes and rested my head back against the trunk of the tree, breathing for a moment in the cold, still silence. Then I straightened again and walked on a little farther. I stopped when I came to a place where a tree lay dead in the brush, its branches hacked away and chopped into firewood that had been laid out to dry now that the rain had subsided.

I knelt down and turned a piece over to touch the side that had been facing down. It was still damp.

I flipped it over and set it back down so that the damp side was now facing the sky. I moved down the row, rising and then stooping again to flip each of the logs in turn. When I reached the last few, I found that they were dry enough to burn; I stacked a half dozen into my arms.

I straightened just as a figure stepped into the clearing. Keegan tossed up his hands in exasperation and hurried over. "What are you doing?"

I shrugged. "Helping."

"You shouldn't be lifting stuff." He slid his arms beneath the logs and took them from me, shaking his head. His fingers brushed against mine, and for a split second, he let them linger. His piercing eyes shifted to mine and stayed. "Let me help you, Sparrow," he said softly.

There was raw honesty in his deep voice as his green eyes searched mine. His jeans were ripped at the knees, and the knives he wore on his chest glinted through the top few buttons he hadn't bothered with. His cheeks were covered in stubble, and there was a streak of dirt on his forehead.

"Thank you," I said.

He straightened up and adjusted his burden, studying me for a moment, almost like he wasn't sure what to say or how to say it.

"Sparrow, the cliff's edge, where we spoke..." he began haltingly.

I lifted an eyebrow. "Yes?"

Keegan hesitated for a moment. Then he leaned in, lowering his voice to a whisper. "Meet me there tonight after everyone is asleep."

For a moment I was so surprised I didn't know what to say.

A thousand questions fired off inside me: why did he want to see me? What did he want to tell me?

Could I trust myself to be alone with him one more time without betraying how I truly felt? It was hard enough as it was, just standing this close to him, feeling the warmth of his breath on my face.

I knew I wouldn't be able to do it. I knew without a doubt that I should say no, that I couldn't meet him that night, alone, in the woods.

But everything inside me was on fire. And it was the fire that spoke.

"Okay," I said at last. "I'll meet you there."

# 37

GOD, IT SEEMED LIKE THE DAY WOULD NEVER END. I FELT sick, dizzy and unable to concentrate on any one thing. I cut up the rest of the tree and laid the wood out to dry, trying to sweat out the anxiety bubbling up inside me. Even being out in the woods was no longer the soothing balm it had once been.

I couldn't stop thinking about Sparrow, the way she had looked into my eyes when I'd asked her to meet me at the lookout point. The way she had said, "I'll meet you there."

*It had been so hard to walk away.*

I didn't see much of Kateri that day. There was always someone with her, always something she was doing.

Walking back to the shelter, I pushed aside the flap of our side of the tent and stepped inside. I pulled off my sweaty shirt and dropped onto one of the cushions on the floor.

"You look down for a guy on the brink of bliss," Preston jabbed from where he was seated on the cushion bed across from mine, scribbling in a notepad. "What's up?"

"Nothing," I lied. "I guess I just..."

"You're nervous about doing it for the first time?"

I laughed and shook my head. "Are you kidding? No."

"What, then?"

"I just keep..." *Thinking about Sparrow.* "Thinking about why Sparrow wants to leave so badly. Why now? I just..."

Preston didn't respond.

"I don't know why it bothers me so much," I confessed finally. "I can't put my finger on what exactly, but there's something strange going on."

"How do you mean, strange?"

"When I'm out in the woods, I get this strange feeling like... like we're not alone out here. It's impossible that those soldiers could have tracked us when Sparrow and I transported. There weren't tracks for them to follow."

"If soldiers had found our location up here, they would have made themselves known to us pretty forcefully by now."

"True." I nodded. "That's why it doesn't make sense."

"Maybe you're just..."

"Paranoid."

He chuckled. "That, and you just have other things on your mind right now."

I wasn't convinced. The uneasiness inside me was unrelenting.

"Yeah..." I said. "Yeah, maybe."

Preston looked back down at his notepad. I propped myself up on my elbows and shot him a look. He was bent over the page, but he wasn't writing anymore. I knew him—something was on his mind.

"What's bothering you, Pres?"

"Nothing," he said hesitantly. "I was just thinking."

"About?"

Preston bit his lower lip, seeming to debate whether he should tell me something. Finally, he just sucked in a breath and shook his head. "It's nothing, really."

"C'mon, Pres. There's clearly something you're not telling me."

For a moment his eyes remained fixed on the page.

"Pres," I began again, straightening up now to look him square in the eyes, "seriously, what is it?"

Preston's eyes locked with mine. "I promised her I wouldn't tell you."

"Who?" My heart rate quickened. "Promised who?"

I already knew from the look in his eyes exactly who he was talking about. He didn't need to say her name.

"What did Sparrow tell you?" I lowered my voice to a whisper as I leaned forward. "Please... *please tell me*. I have to know."

Preston studied me for a long moment, conflict in his eyes. "But, Keeg—"

"I don't care what you promised Sparrow—there's something going on with her, something she won't tell. It's... it's killing me to not know..." My voice faded in my throat. "And I used to know her better than anyone."

Preston blew out a sigh. "Sparrow's still in love with you, Keegan."

The words hit me like a tidal wave. "W-what?"

"She always has been—can't you see it in the way she looks at you?"

"She... she told you this?"

"When she first got back. Yeah."

I stared at him, still hardly able to believe what I was hearing. "Sparrow told me that she—"

"—loved that dick of a guy she's married to?" Preston cut in. "Keegan, she married him to *save your life*. That was the stipulation. That was what they told her—if she married Aaron, they'd let you go. That's why she did it—because she loved you... *loves* you." He paused, shaking his head. "She had to break your heart so you wouldn't go back for her. She knew you would, and she didn't want you to... She wanted you to be safe."

I rose to my feet and began to pace, swallowing the lump that had risen in my throat.

"Sparrow... sacrificed herself for *me*?" I ran a hand over my face, my palms beginning to sweat. "My god, why didn't she tell me? Why didn't she tell me?"

I stopped in the middle of the shelter, my back to Preston. My heart pounded in my chest.

Sparrow was in love with me? Sparrow had... she had married Aaron to save my life?

Why hadn't she ever told me? My *god*.

Hot tears welled in my eyes.

"She saved my life..." My voice was barely audible. "All this time, I thought she didn't love me... didn't want me."

"I wanted to tell you, but she made me swear that I never would. She just wants you to be happy, Keeg. Sparrow is truly happy for you and Kateri. She told me so herself. She thinks you both will be really happy together, and she doesn't want to interfere. She didn't want me to tell you because she knew it wouldn't change the way you feel about Kateri..." Preston paused. I could feel the searing heat of his gaze. "Would it?"

For a moment I just stood there, my heart waging war between my ribs. I could hardly think straight.

*Sparrow still loves me. She still loves me.*

I pressed my eyelids shut, a hot tear streaking down my cheek. I turned around to face Preston. I couldn't answer.

It felt like a dream, what Preston had told me... I could still hardly believe it—I was afraid to believe it. It was everything I'd been longing for months to hear. Thinking back to that night in the District... It all seemed so different now. Everything she'd said and done... It had been because she *loved me*. It had all been to *save me*.

I couldn't stop looking at Sparrow through the firelight that night. My mind was a hurricane.

When Sparrow's eyes met mine, all the other voices around me seemed to fade away, leaving only her and the distance between us.

Hours passed like moments. I barely spoke, barely heard what anyone was talking about. Finally, one by one, everyone turned in for the night, leaving Kateri and me alone at the fireside. For the first time, I felt uneasy in her presence, and for a long time neither of us spoke.

"Keegan," she said at last, "is everything all right?"

My heart pounded as I stared into the flames.

"Mm-hm... Everything is fine."

Her warm fingertips touched my cheek. "Look at me."

I let her hand guide my gaze. Her soft, glimmering eyes narrowed, seeming to probe mine. Fear rose between my ribs—fear that she could see right through me to the war going on inside my chest. I wanted to pull away from her, but I couldn't.

Kateri studied my face like it was a cipher, something troubled and uneasy in her dark, familiar eyes.

"What is it?" I asked softly, taking her hand in my own. "Please tell me."

Kateri shook her head. "It's nothing I can tell you, Keegan. It's... it's something you have to figure out yourself."

"Kateri, I don't know—"

"Shh." She placed a finger against my lips. "No. No, Keegan, don't say anything." She studied my face for a moment before gently leaning in, her lips caressing my own. A soft, still kiss. There and gone like vapor.

She rose to her feet, turning to leave, but I caught her by the hand.

"Please, Keegan," she said, without turning around. "Stop fighting."

"I'm not fighting you, Kateri. I—"

"No, Keegan. Not me..." She turned around to look at me now, the amber glow of the fire reflecting in her eyes. "Stop fighting yourself... for all of our sakes."

Her fingers slipped away from mine, and she left me there by the firelight. My voice faded in my throat as I stared after her.

I heard the canvas flap to the shelter open, then close.

I let go of the breath I hadn't realized I'd been holding, rubbing a hand over my face.

*What just happened? What did she mean? Does she... know?*

I felt sick inside as I sat there, listening to the silence, the stirrings of the night. The moon rose steadily over the mountain peaks, illuminating the woods in soft, milky light. I'm not sure how long I sat there or how much time passed, but when I was sure everyone was asleep, I rose from the dying fire and made my way through the woods to the lookout point, where Sparrow had agreed to meet me. I moved through the shadows like a ghost.

By the time I reached the cliff face where the woods opened to the view of the valley below, my hands were trembling, sheathed in sweat.

God, I was so nervous. I couldn't stop my racing thoughts; in a few moments *I would see her*. Everything inside me was chaos.

I paced, rubbing my unshaven jaw anxiously. I kept glancing at the woods, expecting to see her.

Finally, she appeared, so silently it was as if she had materialized out of thin air. I stopped dead in my tracks, heart in my mouth.

"What?" Her familiar, husky voice was soft. "Did I scare you?"

"You always scare me," I admitted.

Her lips curved, but she remained where she was. "So... what did you want to talk about?"

I took a few steps towards her, stopping close enough to see every detail of her face in the faint light.

"I..." I hesitated. "I had to see you."

She studied me in the moonlight, her night-sky eyes searching my own.

"Sparrow," I began again, trying to steady my voice, "I know I said I would accept whatever you chose—even if that meant that you wanted to leave—but... but I..."

*I can't live without you—don't leave. Don't leave, don't leave...*

Can I tell her that? No. I *can't*.

*God, I want to. I have to.*

Her eyes remained unflinchingly fixed on mine.

"I just... want to know why," I lied, dying inside.

"I already told you," Sparrow replied steadily. "I want to start over. I want to... I want to forget about everything that has happened. I want to be free, and I want you—*all of you*—to be safe."

I stared at the ground between us, unable to look into her eyes.

"But you already knew that..." she said. "So why did you really ask me to come out here?"

Her warm, soft fingers lifted my chin, bringing my gaze back up to meet her own. Her dark eyes were so close—deep and full of moon shadows.

"Keegan." I felt her soft breath on my face. "What is it?"

I fought to hold it all back—but I couldn't anymore. Something inside me had broken.

My hand drifted up to her face, the backs of my fingers brushing over her cheeks and into her hair. I leaned closer, resting my forehead gently against hers.

"Because something inside me is tearing apart, Sparrow." I sighed shakily. "I can't lose you."

"And I *can't stay*. You know I can't stay—they're looking for me right now," she reminded me. "Aaron is out there looking for me. And I'll be damned if I stand by and let them find all of you—I'm not going to let that happen. It's best if I leave."

"What about my father?"

"He'll understand. You can explain it all to him when he returns."

"And... and what about Hawk?"

Something flashed in Sparrow's eyes. She tipped her chin back to look at me. "What about her?"

"They're your parents, Sparrow. They've been searching for you for so long," I said. "Icarus is still trapped there and Hawk is still trying to find *you*. What are you going to do about it?"

"There's nothing I can do—Fin will know what to do."

I studied her. "Maybe he left because he believes the *exact opposite*. Maybe he truly believes that you're the one who's going to bring them back. You're the one who has to come to terms with—"

"The fact that they left me?"

"The fact that they've been *searching* for you," I corrected her. "For years now. Hawk told me so herself."

She shook her head. "I don't want to hear it—I can't, Keegan. You don't know what it feels like. Your parents would have given anything to stay with you. Mine just... mine just *left*."

"Not by choice."

"Everyone has a choice." Her jaw hardened. "Just as I chose to..."

Sparrow didn't finish; she just stared into my eyes. My heart skipped a beat. For the first time, I knew what she meant.

"Sparrow, I know what happened." My voice softened to a whisper as I stepped closer. "I know why you made me leave you in the District. I know why you married him. I know everything."

"No, Keegan. No, you don't know—"

"Preston told me."

She cursed under her breath. "He promised me he wouldn't."

"God, Sparrow, why didn't *you* tell me?" I took her in my arms, looking down into her dark eyes. "All this time I thought—I thought that was what you wanted. I was so... *so stupid*." I leaned my forehead gently against hers, hot tears beginning to blur my vision. "I'm so sorry I left you. I'm so sorry..."

"Don't be," she said softly. "I would do it all again, Keegan. I would do it a thousand times, because I..." She stopped and wiped her hand roughly against her cheek, blinking back her tears. "*I love you*. And that's why I have to leave you now. I have to let you move on—I want you to be happy, Keeg. I know you will be—"

"No." I cut her off, taking her face in my hands. "No, I won't be, Sparrow... How could I ever be happy without you?"

She gazed up into my eyes, tears glistening in her own. I couldn't fight the storm raging within me any longer.

I smoothed my fingers over her hair, kissing her forehead, and then, leaning in, I pressed my lips against hers, kissing her gently, as if she were a ghost—a dream I would wake up from.

My fingers curved around her waist, pulling her closer. Her fingers tangled in my hair. I pressed her back against the tall pine we stood beneath, opening my lips over hers. Her hands slid down my chest and around my body in the darkness. And I was on *fire*.

Tears rolled down my face as her lips moved over mine, and the warmth of her hands pulled me closer. My heart was so full of her it hurt.

When she finally drew back, tears sparkled on her cheeks. I reached up to brush them away with my fingertips.

"I love you too, Sparrow," I said softly, caressing her face. "I love you more than anything."

She gazed into my eyes as I rested my forehead gently against hers.

"Please don't leave me," I whispered against her lips, kissing them again, lingering for a moment. Then I looked into her eyes. "I don't want to live another day of my life without you."

Sparrow gazed up at me. "What about Kateri?"

I shook my head slowly. "She'd already seen in my heart what I've been fighting this whole time... *you*." I sighed. "I wanted so badly to forget you... I was... I was hurt. But I never stopped loving you; I've been lying to myself. And worst of all, I've hurt Kateri..."

"What are you going to do?" Sparrow asked quietly.

"I have to tell her the truth. I think she already knows, really; she all but flat-out told me to stop fighting the way I feel for you." I sighed unsteadily. "She doesn't deserve to be with someone as unstable as me anyway."

"Mm. I agree with you there."

My lips curved in a smile. "I love you."

Sparrow drew back to look at me. "And the baby?"

"I'll love her too," I said, kissing her forehead. "Like she was my own."

Sparrow smoothed her fingertips over my cheek and down my neck. "I'm afraid of what could happen to you if I stay."

I shook my head gently, my forehead still connected with hers. "There is no me or you anymore... There's just us, Sparrow." I kissed her. "Us."

I awoke before the dawn. Lying there, staring up at the ceiling, it hit me full force: Today was the day Kateri and I were supposed to exchange promises.

The sky was soft gray when I emerged from the tent and made my way to the stream in the woods. I knelt at the embankment and splashed the cold water onto my face and neck. A sinking feeling settled inside me as the water stilled, and I met the reflection of my own eyes in its surface.

What would Dad think of me now? He'd probably never betrayed Hawk for anyone else. I'd betrayed Sparrow, and I'd hurt Kateri.

I sighed, pressing my eyes shut, cold droplets of water rolling down my face.

I wished I could have been more like my father: more steadfast and stable and always intuitively knowing what was right—never wavering. He was like a horizon, and I was like a storm.

How could I ever be a leader like him?

Lara's words echoed in my mind: "Not all leaders are made of mountains. Some of them are stormy seas…"

"Like who?" I'd asked her.

"Icarus," she had answered.

Icarus. Lara had described him as a storm.

Maybe that was true. Maybe it wasn't just the light, the good, the peace that made us leaders, but our ability to grapple with the darkness, the storms, the mysteries within us.

I looked back into the gently swirling stream. There I still was.

Then a snap caught my attention.

My gaze shot up, my senses becoming alert. I scanned the woods around me, searching for the source of the sound. The trees loomed, their branches unmoving.

I listened, first with my ears and then with my mind, trying to trace any thoughts lingering nearby.

That was when I caught the thoughts of someone else—someone familiar. And a moment later, I heard her voice behind me.

"Keegan?"

I turned as Kateri stepped into the clearing. Her long dark hair was pulled over one shoulder in a braid.

"You're up early," I said softly.

She walked over to the bank of the stream, sitting down beside me. "I couldn't sleep."

For a moment we both sat in silence, watching the water flow steadily past.

"You went to her last night," Kateri said softly.

I drew a deep breath, turning to look at her. "Yes."

Kateri studied my face for a moment, not even a hint of judgment in her deep brown eyes. "Did you tell her how you feel?"

I swallowed, nodding slowly.

"I'm glad."

"Kateri, I'm so... *so sorry*," I said. "I... I wish I could go back and..."

Kateri shook her head. "No. Don't say that. Everything you have done... *we* have done... has brought you to this moment." Her voice wavered a little. "I'm glad it happened, Keegan. I wouldn't change anything." A lump formed in my throat as I listened. "And I am glad that you are finally listening to your heart's voice—a voice I've heard for a long time now," she went on. "Your heart belongs to Sparrow, Keegan. I've always known that..."

I pressed my eyes closed. "Can you ever forgive me?"

"No. Because there is nothing to forgive, Keegan." She gently touched my cheek. "I will always love you. But I don't need you—or any man. I know who I am—we are gods and goddesses. I don't need anyone else to help me be who I truly am."

Tears blurred my vision as I looked at her. She smiled weakly.

"I've asked Lara to take me back to Section C with her. I can be of far better use there than I can here."

"When do you leave?"

"As soon as Lara is prepared," she said, taking my hand in hers. "Be happy, Keegan, okay? For me."

I studied her for a moment, not even sure what to say. Leaning closer, I wrapped my arms around her.

Her arms closed around me, and for a moment we just held each other. Then she rose to her feet, wiping the tears off her cheeks.

"Goodbye, Keegan," she whispered.

I sat there with a lump forming in my throat, watching her walk away. Then, abruptly, she stopped, going rigid as she scanned the forest.

"Kateri?" I rose to my feet.

She quickly placed a finger to her lips, gesturing for me to come closer. I made my way as silently as possible to where she stood.

"What is it?"

Kateri pointed into the woods. "I saw movement—I heard someone."

I narrowed my eyes, searching the ghostly trees for some sign of life. At first, I didn't see anything. Then Kateri drew a sharp breath, and this time I saw it too.

A rustling disturbance among the leaves in the distance, as if something—or someone—was darting through the brush.

I took off after it, sprinting into the deeper parts of the forest. I watched for the movement in the low branches, and for a moment I was able to keep track of it. I was behind whatever it was—whoever it was.

Finally, I halted. I'd lost it somewhere.

"Dammit," I hissed under my breath. I slowly turned, straining my eyes for some sign of whoever had been there.

"Look!" Kateri called from a little ways behind me. "Footprints..."

I raced to her side, dropping down to examine the depressions in the soil.

"Boots," I said under my breath. "It's got to be one of them."

"Should we follow the prints and see if we can track them down?"

My jaw tightened as I scanned the prints. I shook my head.

"No. No, we need to get back and warn the others," I whispered. "If there's one, there will be more coming." I straightened up to look at Kateri. "We need to get out of here."

# 38

I WATCHED FROM THE SHADOWS OF THE TREES AS KEEGAN spoke with a young woman by the stream—the same woman he was going to marry. I listened as she spoke to him.

"You went to her last night," she said to him quietly.

"Yes."

"Did you tell her how you feel?"

Keegan nodded.

"I'm glad."

"Kateri, I'm so... *so sorry*. I... I wish I could go back and..."

"No. Don't say that. Everything you have done... *we* have done... has brought you to this moment. I'm glad it happened, Keegan. I wouldn't change anything. And I am glad that you are finally listening to your heart's voice—a voice I've heard for a long time now," she went on. "Your heart belongs to Sparrow, Keegan. I've always known that..."

My eyes narrowed, my heart sinking as I listened in silence, in the concealment of the forest. I shivered into my thin coat, my face pressed against the rough bark of a tree as I watched the young woman rise and begin to leave.

Then I stumbled—and she stopped, staring straight into the woods where I was.

I took off at a run, sprinting, dodging around trees. Moments later I heard footsteps behind me.

I melted in with the shadows—became one myself. I ran until I was sure I'd left him behind, tripping, catching myself, digging my heels into the dirt as I slid down an embankment. I crashed to my knees at the bottom.

I didn't bother to get up. I just knelt there as the dried leaves followed me over the top of the ridge, showering down on me. I could see Sparrow standing in front of me as if she were really there, wearing a white dress that clung to her body, wrapping around her swollen abdomen. Those dark eyes, long, thick lashes and fierce brows crowned by nearly black hair.

It was still so surreal to believe that I was a father—or at least that I soon would be if she safely delivered the child. She was better off with them for now, I knew. I couldn't drag her away while she was still pregnant—in danger of death if anything went wrong. And anything *could* go wrong—I wouldn't know what to do for her. I was no medic; I knew nothing of how to bring a child into the world.

I closed my eyes, collapsing back against the embankment as sudden weakness overcame me. I could still see her out of the corner of my eye, the white skirts of her dress billowing in the wind as she wove among the trees. I willed her to vanish, but she would not. She stayed just where she was, a smile forming on her pale lips.

I drew a shaky breath and closed my eyes.

*Does she love him? Does she love him still, even though he loves someone else?*

Still, I had no answer to the question that kept me awake each night: did she want him still? Even if I took her now, would she be longing for him?

Wishing she was wrapped in him, drowning in the very thought of him, just like I was drowning in the thought of her?

I didn't know.

The only way to find out was to wait, but I was *so tired* of waiting.

Would she choose me in the end? And if she didn't... What would I do then? Once she had delivered our baby, would I really just let them both go, just like that? *Never see them again?*

The thoughts ebbed and drifted away until blackness came instead, cold and silent.

When I opened my eyes, it was the middle of the night. The moon was full over my head but concealed behind cotton-thick clouds so that I saw but a faint glow, like that of a candle flame behind a quilt.

Half-frozen and stiff, I lay there for a moment, passing my tongue over my burning lips before I attempted movement, rousing first my fingers and then my arms and legs. I could hardly feel them.

I sat up slowly, fresh cold air spiraling down my back as I separated from what little warmth the ground had offered me. Rubbing the back of my throbbing head, I squinted into the darkness. I saw nothing and heard nothing, yet something didn't sit right with me.

I rose to my feet, moving through the trees like a ghost. I listened with all of my senses. If someone had snapped a twig a mile away, I was certain I would have heard it.

I heard nothing now. I saw nothing in the deep darkness.

I moved forward, shivering into my jacket as a soft breeze passed through the woods, there and gone. Silence reclaimed its precedence.

I walked for at least a mile, all downhill, down the back side of the mountain, on top of which the sliders were encamped. I was at least a few miles from their shelter.

I wove through the trees and up over a mossy knoll, jumping over a log and landing noiselessly. A smudge in the distance caught my eye. I merged with the trunk of a tree, catching my breath.

I leaned out just enough to see what lay beyond it.

A mile or more below me, tucked into the woods, was a faint reddish-orange glow. I struggled to make it out, but I couldn't from here; it was too far away.

I crept closer, scuffling my way down the mountainside in the pitch black, guided by nothing but my weak senses as I tripped over roots of trees and rocks protruding from the ground.

Finally, I slid to a stop near the bottom of the slope, catching myself on a low-hanging branch with both hands. I was just above the camp. A dwindling fire burned, and two sleeping sacks were rolled out on either side of it, occupied by the lumpy shapes of sleeping figures.

RGM soldiers. Barely five miles from the sliders' camp—from my wife. I scanned the small patch of forest bathed in the dim light from the fire, making mental notes.

My fingertips tingled as I stared down at the two sleeping soldiers, their weapons tucked close beside them.

I held my breath, watching them for a moment in silence, debating.

A shrill crack severed the silence. Adrenaline rocketed through my veins as the branch I held onto separated from the tree and dumped me the rest of the way down the slope, thumping me first in the back and then snapping back into my face as I tumbled over the top of it. I landed hard on my face at the bottom of the hill, a few feet from the fire.

The first sound to reach me was the whir of a weapon phasing into firing mode. I froze stiff, staring at the pair of boots that now stood poised near me, the black leather glistening in the soft rusty glow.

"Who's there?" Anand's voice boomed, filling the woods. "Show yourself!"

The other soldier was on his feet within seconds. A soft whir as he too phased his rifle into firing mode.

"What is it?" he whispered after a moment of silence had passed.

"Didn't you hear that?"

"I heard you shouting."

"A branch broke and fell."

My gaze remained fixed on Anand's boots as they moved forward, halting only a few feet from where I was sprawled.

He paused, the light from the fire silhouetting his profile as he turned his head, searching in the darkness for the invisible man who lay at his feet, staring up at him.

He took a quick step forward, leading with the muzzle of his rifle. I quickly folded my legs behind me before the toe of his boot caught on my shins and sent him spilling to the ground.

He strode past me and stopped at the broken branch, bending down to examine it. My fingertips still tingled as I watched him, simultaneously keeping an eye on the soldier still positioned by the fire.

Anand clicked on the light mounted to the rifle. He swept it back and forth, looking for some sign of life.

"Sir?" the other soldier asked uneasily.

Anand lifted a hand for silence. He listened, sweeping the bright beam directly over me and then into the woods to his left as he once again walked straight past me, mere inches away.

Finally, appearing satisfied, he clicked off the light. "There is something ill at play in these woods," he said finally.

After a long pause, he stalked back to the fire, the faint flames illuminating his face.

"Should we patrol, sir?" the soldier asked.

Anand shook his head. "We should be silent." He lowered his voice. "Because we won't see Price. We'll *hear* him."

He spat into the flames and slid out of his rifle's shoulder strap. He lowered down onto his sleeping bag again. The other soldier followed suit, mirroring his commanding officer's actions.

"And god knows, wherever Price is," Anand added, "Sparrow will not be far away."

I lay there, frozen and unflinching. My fingers still tingled; I still wanted to reach out and take their very lives from them, but I couldn't risk making another sound. And the worst part was, though the desire was there, the energy wasn't.

My nose was bleeding from my fall, and the splintering pain in my side indicated that I'd probably broken one of my ribs. It was already taking everything I had to stay quiet and still, never mind channel enough energy into my hand to kill them both.

Trembling and scarcely breathing, I lay there until, after what felt like hours, I heard the patterns of their breathing change to those of deep, slumbering inhales and exhales.

Then and only then did I rise to my feet, so incrementally that the movement was silent. Painstakingly, I backed away from their camp and padded into the woods again.

I wiped the blood off my face with my sleeve and stood for a moment in silence, my mind racing in tandem with my pounding heart.

They were about five miles from Sparrow. And I couldn't take her—not now, not yet. But she couldn't stay where she was.

I licked the blood off my lips, looking back over my shoulder at the fire flickering through the trees.

When I closed my eyes, there she was again. But now the smile was fading from her lips, something else tangling with the darkness in her eyes: desperation. I could still see her thin fingers tracing over her belly, as if she were communicating through her touch with our unborn child.

No matter what happened—no matter what she chose, whom she loved... that child was mine. I couldn't let the RGM find her. I knew Sparrow. I knew she'd never let the RGM take her without a fight—pregnant or not, she would force them to kill her.

I had to make sure they never got that far. I had to delay them.

Glancing back at the distant fire and then ahead at the dark woods, I began to move, pressing into the front of each foot, making sure I left prints. I walked steadily forward, in the opposite direction to where I'd come from.

I walked for miles in a straight line until I reached an alternate, much rockier route leading up the mountainside. I slid my boots off and tucked them into my jacket.

I climbed up the rocks on my hands and knees, gripping at footholds with my numb toes and clawing my way forward with my shaking hands. My body was burning with pain—it felt like there was a knife lodged in my side.

When I reached the top, I had left no tracks to follow.

The sky was light purple with dawn by the time I reached the shelter. I crouched behind it, listening to the sound of her breathing from within its walls. I could single it out easily from the rest. She was asleep, just on the other side of the canvas.

I wiped the blood off my face, a tight lump forming in my throat as I knelt there for a moment like a sinner at confession. I lifted one shaking hand to the canvas, gently touching my fingertips to the fabric, just sitting there, just looking at her behind my closed eyes.

*God, I wish I could tell you... I would never have betrayed you... I promise I...*

It was everything I wanted to tell her—what I would have gladly spent my last breath to declare—but was it even true?

Or was it a lie that even... *even I* wanted to believe?

I forced myself up, swallowing back the pain. I stepped silently into the clearing, where the fire had died. I trod silently to the entrance of the shelter where Sparrow slept. I knelt down on the ground by the door.

In silence, I reached out a finger and traced words on the ground: a message. Then I rose and slipped away.

# 39

KATERI AND I RUSHED INTO THE CLEARING WHERE THE shelter stood bathed in the early morning light. I caught Preston's arm as he emerged from the tent.

"Help us get everyone up. We need to move—now," I told him.

"What's going on?"

"It's the RGM," Kateri explained breathlessly. "We saw evidence of soldiers in the woods, watching us, but we couldn't see them. They must have tracked us down."

Sparrow pushed aside the canvas flap and stepped outside—then she stopped, standing frozen just beyond the door, her wide eyes fixed on the ground.

"Sparrow?" I asked. "Sparrow, what's wr—"

The words died in my throat as I moved to her side, Preston right behind me.

"Holy shit…" I heard him mutter.

On the ground, etched in trembling scratches, were words. A message in the dirt.

*They are not far behind. Escape now or they will find you. I never betrayed you.*

My eyes widened as I lifted my gaze to look at Sparrow.

"Aaron knows where I am," she said, her voice cracking. "He's the one who left this message."

"Why wouldn't he try to take you back with him if he knows where you are?"

"I don't know," she answered. "But if Aaron wrote the message, the 'they' he refers to are the RGM. We have to get out of here."

Lara stepped out of the tent, her eyes already alert. "What's happened?"

I didn't even need to answer her; she came up beside us and read the message scrawled on the ground.

"We need to move camp," I concluded. "As soon as possible."

Lara shook her head. "No."

"No?"

"I'm transporting all of you out of here," she said urgently. "I already told Kateri she could come with me back to Section C, but now I think we all should go."

"What?" I blurted. "But—but Dad's still out there!"

"I cannot allow any of you to stay here any longer, not after this," she shot back firmly. "Your father wouldn't want you to, either."

"*No.*"

"Keegan, this is not open for discussion." Lara's voice was steely. "I'm giving you an order."

"No," I repeated. "No, Lara. Dad will be returning *here*, to this very place. I have no way to warn him. Do you really think I would leave and let him walk into a trap?" I shook my head adamantly. "I'm staying here, and I'm going to go find him."

"But, Keegan, you can't even see them," Kateri protested. "You may walk right into them—you could be killed!"

"Kateri's right," Preston agreed. "Sparrow is the only one who has ever been able to see the RGM forces. You would be guessing in the dark."

"I can read minds—I can sense when they're close," I protested. "I'll be fine. It's a risk I'm willing to take."

"Keegan." Lara sighed and then stopped.

I shook my head. "You already know there's nothing you can say that would stop me. I'm staying to find my father."

Lara drew a long breath. "I can't stop you, Keegan. But I'm against it."

"I know you are," I said. "But I've made up my mind. I'm staying."

I could feel Sparrow's eyes on me as I spoke.

"Everyone get your things together," Lara commanded gravely, her eyes still locked on mine. "We'll transport out in a few minutes."

Preston came up alongside me as everyone dispersed.

"You really think it was Aaron who left the message?" he questioned softly.

"Sparrow is convinced that it was."

"And you?"

I turned to glance in the direction of the girls' side of the shelter, where Sparrow, Janna and Myung were still inside, getting their things together.

"I trust her," I answered. "Once I didn't... and doubting her instincts led to Rafael, Janna, and Sparrow herself being taken by those bastards..." My throat tightened. "If only I'd trusted her back then, it all might have been avoided."

"There's no way to know what might have happened."

"True," I admitted. "But it's taught me to never mistrust her again."

"But if he's looking for her... Why wouldn't he make himself known?" He lowered his voice. "Wouldn't he have tried to take her back by now? Isn't he on the RGM's side? Why would he want Sparrow to escape?"

"I have no idea. But from what I heard the soldiers say, it sounds like Aaron may be more loyal to the RGM than they are to him."

"How so?"

I shrugged. "They're hunting him down like an animal—him *and* Sparrow. They're both fugitives."

"Sparrow, because she escaped..." Preston speculated aloud. "But what about him?"

"Maybe he abandoned his duty to go find Sparrow. Maybe she means more to him than the RGM..." I bit my lip, shaking my head slowly. "Though that wouldn't align with any of his actions the night I was thrown out of the District—he showed his true colors fully: the RGM defines him."

"I wish I could stay instead of you." He sighed. "You should really go with Kateri."

I shook my head, looking him in the eyes. "I... I told Kateri the truth, Pres. The truth I should have admitted to myself long ago."

"That you're still in love with Sparrow?"

I nodded.

"How'd she take it?"

"She was the one who broke it off, Pres," I answered. "She saw it in me before I did."

The group began to gather under an oak tree that Lara had chosen for the transport location. Everyone was there. Everyone except Sparrow.

"Come on, let's go, Sparrow!" Lara called.

No response came from inside the shelter.

"Spar!"

Still Sparrow did not answer or emerge.

"I'll go see what's keeping her," I said, striding toward the tent. I flung aside the canvas flap. "Spar—" My voice broke off as I stopped in the doorway.

Cushions were scattered about the floor, along with the many plants that blossomed and grew as if nothing were happening. They were the only sign of life.

I checked the main living area, then the opposite side of the shelter.

My jaw tightened. Sparrow was gone.

"Sparrow!" I shouted as I sprinted around to the back of the shelter, scanning the woods for some sign of her. "Sparrow, answer me!"

No response came. There was no sign of her anywhere.

I ran back around to the front of the shelter, where everyone still stood at the edge of the woods. Lara's eyes filled with concern when she saw that I was alone.

"Sparrow's gone," I announced. "The rest of you transport out. I'll find her."

"But, Keegan—"

"Lara, I'll be fine," I cut in firmly. "You guys need to transport out now... while you still can."

"Do you want me to stay behind with you, Keegan?" Preston stepped forward. "I can help you look for her—"

I shook my head, clapping a hand on his shoulder. "Help the others. I'll be fine—I promise."

Preston looked reluctant, but I could tell he knew there was no changing my mind.

Lara gave me a long hug, then told everyone to join hands once again. I backed away from the group.

"Transport out as soon as you find Sparrow and your father," Lara instructed, worry filling her voice.

"I will," I assured her. "I promise."

My eyes met Kateri's for a moment before she closed them. Everyone became silent as Lara began to conduct the transport. I watched in stillness, my heart pounding in my chest.

A deceptively serene stillness seemed to hang in the air. Then, suddenly, they were gone. I was alone.

Letting out a low howl, I beckoned Cub to my side.

"Come on," I told her as she padded out from among the trees and came to my side. "Let's find her..."

I didn't finish aloud what I was really thinking—fearing.

*Before he does.*

KEEGAN WAS OUT OF HIS MIND TO THINK THAT I WOULD leave him there alone with Aaron. He still didn't understand how much Aaron was capable of, and Keegan would literally never see it—or him—coming. But I would.

I hadn't gone very far after slipping away from the shelter before I heard the sound of distant voices. I slowed my pace and ducked behind one of the trees, listening.

The slow, soft clomp of boots. A familiar sound, followed up by a familiar voice.

"That branch breaking last night was no accident, I can tell you that much." I recognized Anand's voice immediately. "We're close."

"Or we *were*, since he's probably miles away from here by now."

"He won't be able to go down the mountain—not with the rest of the unit coming up," Anand countered. "He'll have nowhere to go but up or to his own death."

I pulled myself in tighter behind the tree, bracing myself as their footsteps drew nearer.

"Where you find one slider, you often find more."

"Didn't you say the same thing when we found Icarus? That Hawk wouldn't be far behind? Yet she's eluded us."

"Which is why we have to find her daughter," Anand replied. "The only way to get rid of them is all at once, in the same place at the same time, and I can't think of a better way to do that than killing their daughter right in front of them—and giving them the option of trading places with her at the last moment."

My throat tightened, my heart plunging in my chest.

"Do you think they would, though? It would be illogical."

Anand grunted. "When it comes to these creatures, logic has nothing to do with it."

"What about Price?" the other soldier asked as they walked steadily closer.

"Price doesn't matter anymore, not now that we've cloned the samples of his blood. Actually, I shouldn't say *doesn't*—he matters to an *extent*. He knows classified information that could potentially cause damage if used in the right way, but his mental state makes it unlikely... Turner was the undoing of him."

"Turner was the reason he snapped?"

"You heard the charges laid out against him. He's a filthy slider—he killed his own commander and used his powers to slaughter the executioners," Anand reminded him. "Turner leaving him was the last straw."

"Bask had it coming to him in a way, though, just between you and me."

"No, I agree. It was like having a rabid dog in the house—keeping it at bay with treats," he replied. "What happens when the treats run out?"

I listened, but nothing more was said. After a few moments I peered around the side of the tree to check on their location. They had branched off to the left, veering away from my hiding place.

When they were far enough away, I scanned the forest and slowly stepped out from cover. I moved through the woods, searching for any sign of Aaron.

Sudden movement in my peripheral vision snagged my attention—a brown blur of motion. I dropped to a crouch behind some scraggly brush. I couldn't tell what it was at first, and then I knew: it was a cougar. But not just any cougar.

Keegan's frame came into view, walking behind the massive animal padding ahead of him. They were headed down the mountain.

Casting glances over my shoulders, I straightened and moved quickly, leaving cover once more to come up behind him. I reached up and slid a hand over his mouth, pulling him backwards. He stiffened as I leaned into his ear.

"And you think you could have survived Aaron alone."

He pulled my hand away and turned around to face me, his green eyes hard.

"What the hell are you doing, Spar? You could have gotten us both killed running off like that, do you realize that?"

"I realize that *you* would have been killed for sure had I not stayed," I retorted. "There are soldiers in the woods—and you're headed straight for them!"

Keegan shot a glance over my shoulder. "You saw them?"

"And overheard enough to know that heading down the mountain is a shitty idea at this point. They have a unit spread out, combing their way up."

Keegan cursed under his breath. I nodded my agreement.

"The only way out is up," I told him.

"Let's move, then. Which way were they heading?"

"They're about a hundred yards down the mountain from here, and they headed west."

"Toward the shelter?"

"A little past it, but they're doubtless going to spot it through the trees. They'll investigate for a while, which will buy us some time."

Keegan gave a quick nod. "Lead the way, then."

We made our way through the trees, climbing up the incline, which grew steeper and rockier as we went. The woods around us grew scragglier and less dense.

"I overheard them talking, Keeg," I began. "They were going to execute Aaron. That must be why he fled the District, and why they're searching for him now..."

I trailed off, my mind reeling back to all those times I had seen a churning sea in his eyes. Aaron's allegiance to Bask had perpetually come before anything else. They had controlled each other in strange ways. Aaron had the upper hand because it was his blood that enabled everything—the very existence of District Firehole itself—yet he always bent to Bask's command.

For the longest time I'd believed his lies—that he was just playing the game so that one day soon, he and I could escape. But Aaron had never wanted to escape Bask, not really. He had wanted to *be* Bask.

But something had happened since I'd left... something that had caused Aaron to turn his back on everything he had stood for. He had *killed* Bask.

"What do you suspect?" Keegan's voice tugged me gently from the storm inside my head.

Before I could answer, a long, shrill cry pierced the silence. I stopped, my gaze darting through the treetops, my heart rising to my throat.

"What is it?" Keegan asked, stopping beside me.

My tongue clung to the roof of my mouth. "Did... didn't you hear that?"

"Hear what?"

I narrowed my eyes, willing myself to see what I had so clearly heard.

"Never mind." I shook my head. "We need to find a place to hide—and soon. Did you erase the message in the dirt?"

Keegan nodded.

I breathed a sigh of relief. "I would rather the RGM not think we're close by. Or that he warned me to leave. The RGM doesn't even know whether I made it to the shelter, and I prefer to keep it that way."

We climbed for miles, finally breaking through the tree line into a boulder-strewn field. Keegan paused, gazing around uneasily. He took off his baseball cap and ran a hand back through his hair.

"Bad position..." he murmured, gazing around. "We're completely exposed."

"We know for a fact that all the RGM forces are below us currently."

He shot me a wary glance. "Would you stake your life on it? Because that is exactly what we *will* be doing."

I considered this gravely for a moment, then stepped out from the cover of the forest. I kept my head on a swivel as I walked slowly out into the boulder field. The ground was covered in dry grass stubble and littered with massive boulders from rockfalls.

"Spar," Keegan hissed, following reluctantly behind me. I kept walking until I reached a trickling stream snaking its way through the valley.

I dropped to my knees as familiar markings in the dirt caught my eye. My heartbeat quickened as I studied them. *Footprints.*

I motioned to Keegan, who dropped down next to me, taking a closer look at the tracks for himself. Then his gaze lifted to mine.

"These aren't more than a day old," he said. "These are the right shape—and they're not boot prints; they're moccasins. They have to be Dad's."

I swallowed, my heart rising to my throat as my eyes followed the prints forward along the bank. "If they're a day old, we'll have some catching up to do."

Keegan followed my gaze, staring down the valley for a moment before turning to look at me. "You up for it?"

"Of course," I replied without hesitation, shooting him a wry glance. "Are you?"

# 41

I HAD ONE GOAL IN MIND AND ONE GOAL ONLY: FIND Dad and get the hell off that mountain. And now, thanks to Sparrow's tenaciousness, we were on the brink of accomplishing just that.

I glanced over my shoulders constantly, searching the silent woods in every direction as we hiked farther and farther into the boulder field, following the subtle prints of moccasins that edged the bank of the clear, cold stream.

Despite the seriousness of the situation, it felt so good to be with Sparrow again.

"How do you think Fin knew Hawk was here in these woods all along?" Sparrow asked me. "For all he knew, she could have been anywhere else in the world, but it was like he knew deep down that she would be here."

"My dad has loved Hawk for a very long time," I said. "I think they communicate beyond just words. The heart speaks a language stronger than the head. I think my dad believes Hawk is close—is *here*—because he feels her.

Because his love for her connects them. Just as she has appeared to you in your dreams... You and she are connected."

Sparrow sighed. "I don't know about that, Keegan. I've never been able to feel her—or sense her close to me. She and Fin may have that bond, but... I've never felt anything like that."

"Sparrow, have you ever thought that maybe... *you* are the one who's supposed to bring them back?"

"Keegan—"

"You've already found Icarus. You were the one who found him—*you*," I interrupted before she could protest. "Do you really think the RGM would have been able to achieve that without you?"

Sparrow looked over at me. "Keegan, what are you saying?"

"I'm saying that, even though they're forces we cannot see, we should never underestimate our power... our words... our thoughts. It's what we think that pushes and pulls and creates everything around us." I paused, searching for the right words. "I'm... I'm saying that maybe you should forgive them."

"You sound like Fin."

"Thanks. I take that as a compliment."

"I don't know how to get Icarus out of there." She sighed. "I don't know how to find Hawk, or Fin for that matter. Do you actually think I have the answers, Keeg? Because I don't. I have no idea what I'm doing."

"I'm not saying you do," I replied. "But there's something beyond you and me that does. How do you think we found Dad's footprints?"

"Because I have sharp eyes."

I sighed.

"Keeg, look. I just..." She pressed her hands to her forehead. "I just can't... can't stop wondering why."

"Why they haven't come back?"

"Why they ever left me in the first place—" She stopped and sucked in a sharp breath, grasping my shoulder.

"Spar, what is it?" I asked, quickly reaching out to take her arms, supporting her. "What's wrong?"

She remained stiff for a moment, her eyes pinched shut as she drew a steady breath and shook her head. "N-n-nothing. I—it happens from time to time, but it always passes."

"What does?"

"It's just a pain," she replied, her voice strained. "I-it's nothing. We have to keep going."

"Bullshit. We can stop," I said firmly. "You need to rest."

"But—" She didn't finish. An agonized cry ripped out of her throat as she sank to her knees.

Adrenaline filled my veins as I sank to the ground with her, my hands still clasped around her arms. "Spar—Spar, talk to me, okay?"

"I-I... I can't."

"Where's the pain?"

She drew a deep breath, straightening slowly. Her face was drained of color, and her eyes were wild. "My abdomen."

"What does the pain feel like? Is it sharp pain?"

She nodded, biting her lip and squeezing her eyes shut again, her fingers contracting around her belly. "Like knives."

"And you've been having these for a while?"

She nodded, still wincing, still squeezing my shoulder.

"How long?" I asked.

When she didn't answer, I leaned closer, speaking a little more firmly now. "Sparrow, look at me. How long?"

She sucked in a breath, slowly opening her eyes. "Ever since I found out I was pregnant..." Her voice faded, and she trailed off. "Several weeks ago."

I stared at her, retracing her words in my mind to see if I'd misheard. "*Several weeks ago?*" I asked.

She took a deep breath, running a hand back through her hair. "Yes."

"But that's imp—"

"Yes, I know," she interrupted flatly. "But... not with the RGM."

Everything inside me froze. "What are you talking about?"

She pressed the heels of her hands to her eyelids and didn't say a word.

"Spar," I repeated, trying to keep my voice calm, "please tell me—what did the RGM do to you?"

Sparrow drew a deep breath, lowering her hands to look at me. Tears welled in her eyes.

"They drugged me so that I would have sex with Aaron." Her voice came out quiet and raw. "And they gave me a serum that would..." She swallowed back the tears, drying her eyes with the backs of her hands. "They gave me an experimental serum to make the baby develop much faster than it would naturally."

My gaze slid down to the place where her fingers were still clenched around her belly. I could feel my heart pounding in my chest.

"What are you saying?" My voice came out in a choked whisper. "They—"

"They made me their experiment," she replied, not meeting my eyes. "Just like Aaron. That's all I ever was to them..."

I took her face in my hands, staring into her eyes. "My god, Sparrow, why didn't you tell me?"

She stifled another pained sob as she doubled over, her arms wrapping around her torso. I held onto her, not sure what to do, my head spinning and my heart racing.

"Because I don't know if I'll live through having this baby," she said. "That's why I didn't... that's why I didn't tell anyone." She laid her head in my lap, and her fingers clenched a handful of my shirt, her body shaking as she cried. "I'm so scared, Keegan..."

"Sparrow, nothing's going to happen to you—I'm not going to let it." I slid my arms underneath her and got to my feet, lifting her in my arms. "It's going to be fine."

Sparrow didn't respond; her body shook uncontrollably.

"Sparrow, keep talking to me," I said quietly, forcing myself to remain calm as I carried her up the rocky slope. "What are you feeling?"

"It h-h-hurts. It—" She fought back a cry in her throat, pressing her face against my shoulder, her fingers clutching at my chest.

"I know, I know," I said softly, kissing the top of her head. "Just breathe for me, okay? Just breathe..."

My eyes darted back and forth as I wove between the boulders. Then I noticed Cub a little farther up, sprawled below a rocky overhang—the entrance to a cave.

A sigh of relief escaped my lungs. I quickened my pace, dodging around boulders, forcing myself up the incline. I ducked into the cool shadow of the cave, nudging Cub out of the way.

Sparrow sobbed, gasping for air, her shaking hands clutching her abdomen as I gently lowered her to the smooth rocky ground. Her face dripped with tears and sweat as she leaned back against the slanted rock wall.

I looked her steadily in the eyes. "Sparrow, it's going to be fine—you're going to make it through this."

"H-h-h-how do you know?" she gasped, her voice shaking. "You don't know that!"

I shook my head, brushed a sweat-soaked strand of hair out of her face. "You're the daughter of the sunrise and the sunset, Sparrow. You can do *anything*—do you hear me?"

She pinched her eyes shut, her face twisted in pain, tears trickling down her cheeks.

"You can do anything," I repeated, my voice soft but strong. "I believe in you, Sparrow."

She nodded, sucking in a ragged breath. Her fingers wrapped around my hand. I opened my fingers, and hers slid easily into the gaps. Her wild eyes met mine.

"I love you, Keegan," she whispered.

"I love *you*, Sparrow. You're going to be fine," I assured her.

She nodded, squeezing her eyes closed. "I'm so scared," she gasped. "I'm s-s-so scared—I-I can't do this!"

"You can," I told her, my sweat-sheathed fingers grasping hers a little tighter. "You can, Sparrow."

# 42

"I CAN'T DO THIS..."

That was all I could say, all I could think. I felt like I was dying—my skin was on fire, and my insides were tightening and letting go only to tighten again—like my own body was strangling me from the inside.

I was soaked with sweat as the waves of death came and grasped me over and over again, reducing me to cries of agony.

I squeezed Keegan's hand, feeling it beginning to slip from my own. Or was my hand slipping from his? My vision grew fuzzy, and blackness swallowed me.

"Sparrow?" His voice grew fainter. "Sparrow, can you..."

His voice faded altogether.

I couldn't feel his hand in mine, or anything at all except the pain as it struck against me in cold, rough waves.

*Is this it? Is this the end?*

The black tunnel grew tighter and then emptied, leaving me alone inside it. Then that darkness began to clear. I could feel something cool touching my face—cool and wet. I tasted rain on my lips.

I slowly opened my eyes. Above me, trees bent and danced in the wind; beyond them was a soft, cloudy sky, and up in the sky, *wings.*

I heard that same long, shrill cry and then the sound of my name spoken in a voice so familiar yet so far away. My mother's.

I could see her feathers stretched out against the sky, rippling in the wind. Strong, capable.

*Like I am.*

"Sparrow?" I heard my name again, but this time the voice was Keegan's. "Sparrow, can you hear me?"

Thunder rolled outside, and I could feel the faint mist of rain on my skin.

My eyes drifted open, and I looked into Keegan's face. His thumb traced my cheek, tangles of his red hair spilling over his forehead and mingling with his sweat.

I didn't say a word. I grasped his hand, sucking in a deep breath as everything coiled tightly inside me again, sending ripples of pain down my back and around my belly. There was a vise within me, tightening until I couldn't breathe.

I had no concept of how much time had gone by. The light had diminished to purple twilight, and the fabric of my clothes was soaked and heavy with my own sweat.

Tears trickled down my face as I choked on the pain. I felt Keegan's hand slide out of mine, the warmth of his hands on my legs, then his arm looping around my back to support me.

"You're almost there, Sparrow." His voice was firm but gentle as he spoke to me. "You're almost there."

I sobbed, leaning forward, squeezing my eyes shut as I pushed—again and again as the burning sensation within me grew, engulfing me from the inside out. I was a star closing in on itself, a supernova.

"You're almost there—Sparrow, you're almost there." Keegan's voice grew stronger.

I gasped ragged inhales, sweat melting down my burning face. My eyes locked with Keegan's. My fingers curled into fists.

Keegan's hand slipped away from my back as he leaned over me, his hands between my legs. Suddenly the fire, the stranglehold, and the battering waves all crashed to a crescendo and then ceased as I felt the child leave my body. I sank back against the stone, panting and weak. A peaceful stillness enveloped me. Then the sudden quiet was broken by a tiny, whimpering cry.

I opened my eyes slowly, drawing a shaky breath. In Keegan's hands, slick and gasping for breath, was a tiny human being. Keegan's lips parted; his eyes were wide and glistening as he stared, his breath catching in his throat.

"It's a girl." His voice cracked as he half laughed half sobbed. He quickly pulled off his shirt and wrapped it around the delicate little creature, staring down at her. A trembling smile found my lips as his gaze lifted and met mine, a tear spilling down his cheek.

Keegan leaned over me and laid her against my chest. He slid carefully behind me, wrapping himself around me so that I could lie back against him. I stared down at the baby, breathless.

Her tiny head was swathed in black hair, and her little brown hands were already reaching. I brushed one finger gently over her cheek, then down her arm and over her hand. It closed around my finger.

I smiled through my tears as I stared down into the face of the most beautiful being I'd ever seen.

Cradling my daughter, I lay back against the warmth of Keegan's body. Cub crept over and nestled up against my leg, peering curiously at the baby in my arms before settling down to rest her chin on my thigh.

"You did it," Keegan said, peering over my shoulder, gently brushing my hair back. "You did it, Sparrow."

"*We* did it," I corrected him, smiling weakly.

He didn't say anything. He just wrapped me and my daughter in his arms, resting his face in the curve of my neck, kissing it.

For a moment I wondered if it was all a dream. But when I awoke, I was stretched out on my side on the floor of the cave, and Keegan's arms were still wrapped around me. Mine were still wrapped around the baby girl in my arms.

The back of my head rested against Keegan's chest, rising and falling with his gentle breathing. Cub was curled up at the entrance of the alcove, as if guarding us.

I pulled my daughter closer to my chest as she began to fuss, reaching with her arms. I kissed the top of her head.

"Good morning, my sweet one," I whispered.

She responded with a gurgled whine, clinging to my chest. Keegan drew a deeper breath, stirring and pulling me closer in his sleep. I turned my head, resting the side of my face against his chest. His skin was warm against my cheek.

For a long moment I just lay there, lost in it all, watching the light as it spilled down the canyon and leaked into the tiny pocket of the mountain in which we were hidden. From where we were, I could see all the way down the valley—the sparkling stream that cut down the middle, the jagged granite rocks, and the occasional scraggly pine tree. I could see where the light met the shadow of the mountain leaning down over the valley below.

Everything was so still, so quiet. For the first time in my whole life, I felt... at peace. Like there was nothing I lacked, nothing I needed to do or to become. There was no Aaron, no RGM, no bounty on my head.

There was just... *this.*

Keegan stirred, this time awakening. He ran a hand back through his hair, slowly blinking his eyes open.

I watched him without saying a word.

"Good morning," he whispered, his warm breath grazing my skin.

My eyes searched every feature of his face, memorizing it in the early light—his coppery hair, the spattering of freckles on his cheeks and nose, those depthless green eyes...

"Good morning," I whispered back.

Keegan rolled onto his side, propping himself up on his elbow. He gently traced his fingers over the tiny being snuggled against my chest, tucking in a corner of the shirt that covered her. Then he leaned closer and kissed the top of her head, closing his eyes, lingering there for a moment as if he were touching something sacred.

I reached up and brushed the hair off his forehead. His hand gently captured my fingers before they had a chance to drift away, bringing them to his lips. He opened the palm of my hand and leaned his face against it, pressing his lips there, and then to my wrist and my forearm.

He leaned over me, brushing my hair back. His lips melted around the shape of mine, a kiss that was reaching, as if we still weren't close enough, as though we wouldn't be even if we shared the same skin. My fingers closed around a fistful of his hair, my lips parting against his.

My hands wanted him closer; my fingertips drifted over his shoulder, his chest, winding around his back, closing the distance between us until the only space between our bodies was where my daughter was cocooned.

We kissed like a whirlwind, like we weren't sure where it began or ended. He sighed against my neck, resting his face there, his lips caressing my skin.

"Marry me, Sparrow," he said softly. "I love you with all of my being. I pledge myself to you, body and soul. I give myself to you... I am yours: I always have been. I always will be."

I drew back a little to look into his eyes. "Keegan... what about..."

"What is marriage, Sparrow?" he asked, returning my gaze. "Is it not two hearts burning with desire, with passion—running towards the same vision? Isn't it bodies and souls bearing and tangling, fighting, loving, creating—isn't that what it is?"

I nodded. "But, Keegan... I am a storm."

Keegan's eyes probed mine for a moment. "Do you truly think I would wish you to be anything otherwise, when it was the storm I fell in love with?" he asked me, his eyes glistening.

"Keegan, I promise myself to you, body and soul." I exhaled the words against his lips like a prayer. "I give you a storm in exchange for your fire. I love you... I *love* you."

He leaned in to kiss me again just as my daughter began to fuss and squirm. I shifted her into the crook of my arm so that she was looking up at Keegan. He stroked a finger gently over her soft brown skin, a look of awe still lingering in his eyes.

"What are you going to call her?"

I looked down at her, saw her big brown eyes gazing up at Keegan. I smiled.

"I think Hope would be appropriate."

# 43

SPARROW HAD NO IDEA HOW TERRIFIED I'D BEEN. EVERY time she'd yelled "I can't do this," I was thinking the same thing. I had no idea what I was doing, and when Sparrow blacked out for a moment, time seemed to stop altogether.

But Sparrow pulled through. She gave birth to a beautiful baby girl, and I'd helped to deliver her. I'd never experienced anything quite like that moment when I lifted Hope into my arms for the first time. I felt like laughing and sobbing at the same time—I was swept away by awe.

It felt so natural to sleep with Sparrow, to awake with my arms around her and her daughter. It felt so natural for Sparrow to be the first person I saw when I opened my eyes, to kiss her, stroke my fingers over her skin, whisper to her. Nothing had ever felt so right. With the tiny new life and Cub as our only witnesses, we promised ourselves to each other, finally letting go of everything we should have told each other so long ago.

It was strange to think I'd been so close to a completely different life only days before—so sure of myself, so convinced I was doing the right thing. I'd been burying my head in the sand, and even Kateri had seen it. In striving to be right, I'd been more wrong than ever. But somehow that all felt like a lifetime ago.

"What now?" I asked softly, gazing down the length of the canyon sprawled before us. "We're a day behind him, and the rain will have washed away what was left of the tracks."

Sparrow sat down beside me, her dark, curious eyes probing the valley below. "Maybe he's closer than we think... Fin always knows more than we realize—always seems to know what we're thinking before we say anything."

"And so...?"

"So if Fin knew what was going on right now, what do you think he would be doing about it?" she asked. "Where do you think he would be right now?"

"Freeing Icarus from District Firehole."

She gave a single nod. "Who are we to say that he hasn't found Hawk? He wouldn't have stayed away this long if he hadn't found her."

My eyes widened a little. "I... never considered that."

"What if he and Hawk have been in communication since you saw her?" Sparrow went on, smoothing a hand back over her short, messy hair. "What if they both know exactly what's going on? Maybe they aren't even the ones who need to be found—what if *we* are?"

"What if he walks right into them? God, this is the whole reason I stayed behind, and *still* I can't do anything."

"You saved my life," she reminded me. "I would call that something."

"Consider it repayment," I replied, shooting her a glance. "For saving my life back there in the woods."

She studied me for a moment. "It was the reason I stayed behind, you know. I was never going to leave you here."

"I know." I folded an arm around her. "So... let's assume Fin found the shelter abandoned—and didn't get caught in the process. He would have, what? Gone to the District from there?"

"Or maybe he went there first. Or maybe Hawk did." She sighed. "There's no way to know."

I considered her words. "You know, you've mentioned Hawk three times now. Are you starting to—"

She put up a hand, pulling back from me a little. "Don't—don't ask me yet."

Her words were not bitter ones. I could tell from the look in her eyes that something was spinning inside her. I wasn't about to question it.

Instead, I told her something I should have said ages ago.

"You know, Sparrow, I spent so much time looking for you out in the woods before I found you in the District. I..." I paused, considering how to phrase it. "I met someone I barely know how to describe. Someone who showed me myself—spoke to me in words that were so real they made everything else that had seemed real up until then seem like facades that had pulled themselves over my eyes, made me blind to what was always right there in front of me..." I trailed off. "I'm not making too much sense, am I?"

"You wouldn't be were it not for the fact that I met someone just like that too," she replied.

My eyebrows lifted. "An old man?"

"With eyes like the sky, hands like the soft earth... A man who spoke words ancient and new all at the same time?" I nodded. "He appeared to me, too; stayed with me. He's the only reason I survived."

I stared at her, thunderstruck. "He showed me a place in the woods— the waterfall, remember? He showed me... how do I even put it into words..." I rubbed my hands over my face, gazing out at the valley. "Two worlds... One, the land of my father, and the other this one we see with our eyes and touch with our hands. They spilled into one another... I don't even have words to describe it, but it was... a sign."

"A sign of...?"

I shook my head, still at a loss for words to describe it. "What is to come... what already is, whether we realize it or not..."

Silence fell over us as we both sat lost in thought. Finally, Sparrow drew a breath.

"I think that's what Fin's been trying to tell us all since he began training us," she concluded, getting to her feet. I offered her a hand, but she smiled and shook her head. "I'm fine. Would you do me a favor?"

"Mhmm?"

"Watch Hope while I walk down to the stream?"

"The stream?" I asked. "Why?"

"After last night, I wouldn't mind washing up," she explained. "Plus, I want to check out how much damage the rain did. Maybe there's still a trace of the footprints."

"I don't think it's a good idea for you to go down there by yourself…"

"I think you just want to see me take my clothes off."

"That too." I grinned. "But in all seriousness, we don't know how far up they've progressed."

"And we won't until someone's gone down there."

"Then let's all go."

Sparrow shook her head firmly as soon as I started to rise.

"What the RGM would love more than anything else is to capture me and Hope both."

"But they don't even know you had a child."

"And I want it to stay like that," she replied, that stubborn tone in her voice. "Stay here with her, and I'll be back in fifteen minutes."

I opened my mouth to protest, then bit my lip, glancing over my shoulder to the place where Hope was nestled in the blanket, sound asleep alongside Cub, who was curled around her, helping to keep her warm. I looked back at Sparrow. "Fifteen minutes?"

She didn't reply. She stepped closer and looped her arms around my neck, leaning in to kiss me.

"Okay," I said, sighing, when she drew back to look at me. "Just be careful."

"I always am." She kissed my lips again, then slowly melted away. I watched her slip out of the shadows and into the bright daylight. "Fifteen minutes."

I nodded and gently lifted Hope into my arms, ducking back outside with her. I stood at the opening of the alcove and watched Sparrow as she vanished among the boulders and shrubs.

I looked down at the tiny baby in my arms, rocking her gently as I paced slowly back and forth. Her tiny head was covered in black fuzz, and her eyes were clamped shut.

Even if it was true, even if Dad was a step ahead of us... how could he free Icarus from a prison he couldn't even see?

Then I thought of Sparrow's own abilities. Sparrow's own strange and bewildering power to see the things that no one else could see. What if that wasn't unique to her? What if... what if she had inherited it?

*What if Hawk can see, too?*

Regardless, we still had to find Fin somehow and get the hell off this mountain. We were sitting ducks up here, and I wasn't about to wait around for the RGM to come find us. The stakes were higher than ever now.

I kissed Hope's forehead gently, resting her against my shoulder.

I completely understood Sparrow's reasoning—it was paramount to keep her and Hope separate for their own safety. Still, I was uneasy about Sparrow going anywhere alone, even if it was only to the stream farther downhill. I found myself counting down the minutes.

Hope fussed and reached up to wrap her tiny fingers around the strap of my holster. I paced slowly back and forth, bobbing her gently in my arms and shushing her asleep.

"Shhh, it's okay," I whispered to her. "Your momma will be right back..."

It was difficult to remember that she was not my child. Yet somehow, I felt connected to this tiny being I held in my arms. I loved her, though I'd known her barely a day. I loved her because I loved her mother more than life itself, and she was a part of her mother.

When I looked down into her dark eyes, I saw glimpses of Sparrow's there. I stroked my fingertips over the back of her head as her eyelids sank farther and farther shut.

Then an explosive gunshot split the serene silence. My heart leapt to my throat as I scanned the valley below. I could still hear an echo from the shot, but I could see nothing—no one.

I ducked into the shadow of the cave once more, quickly setting Hope down a little farther back, where she had been curled up beside Cub. The cougar had already bolted to the entrance of the alcove, ears flattened against her head.

"Shhh," I soothed Hope as she began to whimper and flail her tiny arms. "Shh, it's okay. It's okay—I'll be right back."

I ducked out of the cave and into the light of day, reaching one of the first boulders in just a few short strides. Cub slid up alongside me in silence. I couldn't see the stream from this vantage point. Giving my surroundings one last scan, I quickly backtracked to the cave to get Hope.

"Screw it, we're going down there," I murmured to myself. "They're closer than we thought."

It took a moment for my eyes to adjust to the cave's dim interior. I stooped down to lift Hope into my arms, then froze.

She was gone.

## 44

I HAD NOT SLEPT OR EATEN IN DAYS, AND I WAS DIZZY from dehydration. My ribs and nose were broken. I had wiped the blood from my face, but I could still taste it in my mouth.

After leaving the message on the ground outside the shelter for Sparrow, I retreated into the woods and watched—waited to see what she would do. At first it seemed as though everyone was heeding the words I had scrawled on the ground; they gathered their things and prepared to transport. Then Sparrow disappeared. Keegan couldn't seem to find her. I listened, crouching in the underbrush, as he searched the shelter and then their campsite, calling her name with greater urgency each time.

I weaved my way back down the hill. I knew the two RGM soldiers I had seen the night before would be combing their way up the mountain. I slid myself between them and Sparrow like a buffer.

I could see them making their way through the trees farther down. I could see Sparrow, too, from where I stood. She was tucked behind one of the big pines about fifty yards from where I hid from her.

She listened to the conversation between Anand and the private, gleaning all the same grave information that I did. More units were coming, making their way from the District to the Tetons.

It was my fault. They never would have tracked her here otherwise, and now she was stuck—we were all stuck, because there was nowhere to go but up, and up only went so far.

*Damn.* Why had she stayed? Why hadn't she left with the others?

Could she... could she have stayed because she knew the message was from me—that I was still out here? Did she stay because she didn't want to leave me behind?

I watched the soldiers as they made their way through the woods, branching out to the left and looping up to the place where the sliders' now abandoned shelter stood. I lifted my hands as they drew nearer, letting the energy surge into my fingertips, forming into a tight spinning ball.

I held back, keeping one eye on Sparrow while I monitored the soldiers' movements, waiting to see if they would turn and make their way closer to her.

After a moment, it became obvious that they weren't coming any closer. They had probably spotted the shelter by now.

Still, I could hear strange footsteps—not Sparrow's.

I peered around the side of the tree behind which I stood and caught a glimpse of red hair. I slid back behind the tree, listening carefully as he passed right by the place where I knew Sparrow was.

I heard her footsteps first, then her voice as she spoke to him. Her words were whispered, but I still heard them, and they still cut as sharp as a knife.

"And you think you could have survived Aaron alone."

Everything seemed to slow down as I sank back against the trunk of the tree. I didn't hear what she said next, or what Keegan said in response. Their voices faded, then moved out of my earshot.

It didn't really matter what either of them said next. It didn't even matter if I was caught by the RGM and shot through the chest.

Sparrow had not stayed for me. Sparrow had stayed for *him*—the man I despised.

I stayed hidden long after their near-silent footsteps had faded into the distance. For a long time, I didn't move. I just stood there, staring straight ahead at nothing in particular.

*Survived Aaron.* Was that what she had done? *Survived me?*

Finally, I took a step forward, forcing myself to follow them up the mountain.

They reached the canyon, hesitating at the edge of the woods. Sparrow was the first to step out into the open. He followed her. I set off after both of them, but at much more of a distance.

They began to follow footprints that ran along the edge of a stream. I waded through the stream, watching each tiny droplet of water as it splashed across the surface of the water, scattering as I walked. Sparrow and Keegan were specks in the distance now, disappearing as they rounded another massive boulder.

The water was icy cold, sending chills fluttering over my skin as it splashed against my shins and then my thighs as it deepened. Ahead, the crystal-clear water turned black, deepening even more. I didn't stop walking, didn't step out of the stream. I just kept walking straight ahead. I felt my foot drop a moment later into a void, with no rocky bottom to catch it. I slipped below the surface.

The world vanished as I went under. Bubbles drifted out of my nose and mouth, a soft whooshing sound filling my ears as the water poured past. The river gripped my body in her icy fingers, rolling me over gently as I sank deeper and deeper.

I saw Sparrow as my eyes closed—saw her like I always did. In a white dress, reaching for my hand. My fingers tingled, going numb from the cold water. My limbs felt heavy now.

I reached for her hand, but there was nothing there; she was, as always, only an apparition.

My lungs burned for air. I heaved for breath but drew in water instead. My body convulsed, my eyelids fluttered open, and I saw the shimmer of gray light on the surface of the stream far above me.

Air.

But did I want any? What did it matter whether I lived or died? My life's meaning had been stripped from me. I was no longer a soldier, and I was no longer Sparrow's lover. She hated me.

God, the only person who had ever really mattered counted herself as fortunate to have escaped my grasp. What I wouldn't give to go back... to do it all differently.

But there was no rewinding life. It was there and then gone, and forever unalterable.

I could never change what I had done. No matter how many times my fraying mind repeated that I would never hurt or betray her—had never done so—I knew it was a lie. It was *all* a lie.

I had turned myself into a person Sparrow could not trust—could not love.

Could it all have ended differently? And if it could have, would it be ending, or only just beginning?

But the past was fading out of my reach, just like the sparkling surface of the stream, as the black water pulled me into her numbing, disorienting embrace. This was it. My final stand, and it was for nothing at all... Nothing. Just what I had always stood for.

My god, how different my life might have been if I had only realized that sooner. If I'd only stood for something—just *one thing* that mattered. *Sparrow*. She was my one thing, the one thing I would forever wish I had stood for.

Instead, the last moments of my life would be spent in regret. In aching, in pain, in grief for what I had lost.

When my eyes closed for what I thought would be the last time, it was not Sparrow's face that I saw. It was a new face.

Small, round, dark eyes; dark hair; soft brown skin covering tiny arms.

It came and went from my head like a vision, there and gone before I could even grasp it. I had seen the face of a newborn baby, and I had no doubt in my mind whose it was. It was mine. It was the child who lived and grew inside Sparrow, a child who would attempt to make its way into the world soon.

What if the experiment succeeded? What if my child lived?

Could I go to my death knowing I would never see their face, never look into their eyes, never hold them in my arms, touch them, speak to them—never watch them grow up, never see who they would become?

Could I really do that?

I hung there suspended in the cold dark water, unable to move, unable to think, to see anything beyond that one image that had burned itself into my brain.

My eyelids opened as I felt my arms already reaching and pulling myself closer to that soft light moving and sparkling on the surface. I stroked hard, fire in my lungs as I kicked harder and harder toward that soft, scattered light.

I broke the surface coughing, sputtering, gasping for air. I dragged myself over to the bank and pulled myself up, coughing up water. I sprawled into the mud on my face, lying there lifelessly. I could hear rain falling, pattering against my skin, though I could barely feel it, I was already so cold and numb.

My eyelids drifted closed.

When I opened them again, it was black as pitch, and I could no longer feel my fingers. I rubbed my hands together, bending my frozen fingers back and forth, trying to get some life back into them.

My teeth were chattering, and my body shook uncontrollably. I slowly pushed myself up to my feet but fell on my face into the mud again as my legs collapsed under my weight.

As I peeled myself up off the ground, I heard a low, rumbling crack of thunder. I struggled up to my knees and then pushed myself heavily back onto my feet. I felt my way along the rocks and boulders in the darkness, trying not to cross paths with the stream again.

Every bone in my body ached. I struggled to remember what had actually happened before I'd awoken on the bank. My brain was filled with fog about as thick as the darkness stretching before me.

Before I could think any further, a cry cut through the tumultuous rain. A cry that stopped me in my tracks only because I knew the voice.

Falling, tripping, clawing my way uphill, I followed the sound. Then, rounding a boulder, I noticed a light: faint, but still there. A flickering fire burning in the shadow of a small alcove hewn into the mountainside.

I could see the outline of two figures even from here, but not well enough to make out who they were. I shrank into the shadows and made my way closer to the entrance. I could make the faces out now: Sparrow's. Keegan's. She was leaning against the cavern wall, crying out in pain. He was in front of her, between her knees, holding her, encouraging her.

I shivered, my teeth chattering as I watched from the shadows, listening to her scream. Wishing I was the one there, helping her deliver our child. But I knew she would never have wished for me to be there instead of Keegan.

I crouched in the darkness and watched, listened, squeezing my eyes shut as the pain poured out of her lungs to mix with the pounding of the rain and the roar of the thunder.

My heart pounded faster in my chest as the hours ticked past, and still the child still struggled inside her. The same words kept repeating in my head:

*My fault.*

*My fault.*

*My fault.*

I should never have touched her. I should have known there was something different about her—that something was wrong. Instead, I'd done exactly what the RGM had wanted me to do—had expected me to do—and now I was in the dark, in the rain, having to face up to the fact that if she died, her blood would be on my hands.

My fingers tightened into hard fists. I leaned around the boulder, staring up at the flicker of light illuminating the alcove, my lips forming around the shapes of silent words, a prayer to a god I had never been sure was there.

The night wore on.

I crouched on the ground against the boulder, my legs pulled tight to my chest and my chin tucked to my knees. I kept whispering to myself in an attempt to stay awake, which was becoming increasingly difficult. Every time my eyes did close, I saw the face of my unborn child, saw Sparrow's hand reaching for mine: a face I would never behold, a hand that I would never grasp. I hadn't known that her feelings for me that night had been caused by a drug. I had thought it was real... that it was honest love. That maybe she had finally fallen in love with me. How foolish I had been.

Nothing in my life had ever been real. Not my rank or worth within the RGM, not my relationship with my wife, nothing...

The only thing that was real was how far I had fallen, and how ashamed my father would be of me if he were still alive. I had become everything he had hated—everything he had fought against.

I cupped my hands around the back of my head, dug my fingernails into my scalp.

Then, at last, the anguish, the sobbing—it all stopped. The rain had lightened to a drizzle by then, and when I peered around the boulder, I could see clearly. Sparrow leaned back against the cavern wall, and Keegan held a child in his arms.

A crying newborn baby. My heart went light in my chest.

"It's a girl," I thought I heard him say.

I watched with burning eyes as he lowered her to Sparrow's chest. He slid behind her, wrapping her in his arms.

I was left alone in the darkness. I told myself it was the rain that dampened my cheeks. But the raindrops had never felt so warm.

The sun rose over the peaks to illuminate the valley. I heard voices—Sparrow's, Keegan's. Then the voice of my child, softly fussing.

I tasted blood as my cracked lips curved into a weak smile, my sore eyes closing for just a moment as I leaned my head back against the cold granite. She was alive. She had made it.

I drifted in and out of semi-consciousness. My limbs were too heavy to move. I doubted I would ever rise from the place where I now sat, waiting to see the soldiers coming through the trees, making their way uphill toward me. They would never find me—no one ever would.

Off to my left, Sparrow made her way down the rocky slope. Her shoulders were bare under the tan dress she was wearing. I'd never seen her in a dress before; she was beautiful. She was heading for the stream that lay below like a bending streak of metal.

I watched her through bleary eyes, willing my weak eyelids to stay open. As she faded from my view, I felt myself slipping back into the arms of unconsciousness. But I wrenched away.

Sparrow had left the cave, and she'd left our baby inside.

I fought my way up to my feet. I drew a shaky breath, my head swimming, dizzy. I checked to make sure Sparrow was still on her way down the hill, that she hadn't turned back. She hadn't.

I climbed slowly uphill toward the entrance of the cave.

Keegan was standing there, his shirt stripped off and wrapped around the tiny being in his arms. God, it was the first time I'd seen her in the light of day.

I could see her head of curly black hair. Her skin was soft brown. Her hands were tiny and reaching, grasping the strap of Keegan's holster.

She was the closest thing I had ever seen to perfection.

I could scarcely breathe for a moment as I stood there, taking her in, too stunned to move right away.

Keegan paced, bouncing her gently in his arms, shushing her, speaking to her with soft words.

A hatred that dwarfed anything I had ever felt before sank its teeth into my heart as I stood there watching. It was everything I had ever wanted... and he had it all.

My fingertips tingled. I swallowed it back.

Just then, a shot sounded in the valley—it was still far away, most likely one of the units signaling to the other.

Keegan was startled. He ducked into the cave and set my daughter down, gently shushing her. His cougar bounded past me and concealed itself behind one of the boulders. I backed away, leaning into the slope, climbing farther up the hill until I was crouched at the cave's entrance.

Keegan bolted out into the light of day, and the cougar ran to his side. He took cover behind a rock where he could get a better vantage point. My daughter's tiny voice echoed inside the cave, tugging at my attention.

I ducked into the cavern, treading noiselessly across the rock floor. I knelt down beside the bundle, which was wrapped in a flannel shirt.

She whimpered and reached with her little arms, trying to move in the fabric that wrapped her. I didn't touch her or speak. I just sat there silently, looking down into her face, my hands trembling and my vision blurry.

She made little sounds and spread her arms out at her sides. Her brown eyes seemed to turn in my direction and stare up at me.

I glanced back toward the entrance of the cave, listening intently for Keegan's footsteps.

My gaze lowered again to my daughter. God, it still felt so unreal to think that she was part of me.

My fingers shaking, I lifted one hand, reaching out. I couldn't bring myself to actually touch her, though. Something about it felt like… sacrilege. My fingers hovered inches from her, trembling, as I looked down at her, tears cresting in my eyes.

She fussed and then quieted, blinking, reaching. Her small hand closed around my finger.

A tear rolled down my cheek as I stared down at the tiny being, whose little dark eyes stared back at me.

She had seen my hand there. She could see me.

My god… she could *see me*.

My heart pounding in my chest, I cast a glance over my shoulder to the entrance of the cave. Still, Keegan had not returned.

I gently lifted the baby into my arms. She was still holding onto my finger. I left the flannel shirt there on the floor and scuttled to the entrance of the cavern. I checked left and right. No sign of Keegan. Then I ducked out into the sunshine and raced farther up the mountainside as fast as my aching legs could carry me, throwing glances over my shoulders as I ran.

When I finally reached the treeline where the pines picked up again, sprawling up the side of one of the escarpments, I slowed to a stop.

I dropped back against the trunk of the tree, squeezing my eyes shut, gasping for breath. I held my daughter tightly in my arms, breathing her in, relishing her warmth against my cheek. I nestled her to my chest, kissing her head over and over again, listening to her little sounds. Tears streamed down my cheeks.

"I loved Sparrow..." I whispered, my voice breaking. "She could see me. She was... she was the only one who ever could, and I lost her..."

I swallowed back a sob, my throat tight and aching as I drew back a little to gaze down at the delicate little human being in my arms.

"But in losing her, I've found you." I blinked furiously, trying to focus through the tears. "And you can see me..."

She blinked her tiny eyes, fussing softly, reaching one hand up to fasten her fingers around my bloodied shirt.

I leaned down and kissed her head again. "You can see me," I whispered, tears burning in my eyes. "*You can see me...*"

I tried to ignore the cold, the pain, and everything else in the world. Trying to burn every last detail of her into my memory. Trying to remember her like I remembered that day so long ago. The look of pride in my mother's eyes, the black confetti as it had rained down from the sky. I tried to remember her like I had remembered and cherished the last normal day of my life—the proudest day.

This child was my new proudest day. She was my redemption.

# 45

DESPITE THE COLD, I PLUNGED MY HEAD BELOW THE surface of the stream. For a moment my ears were numbed by the faint whoosh as the water rolled past. Then I straightened back up, flicking my short hair back, out of my face.

The cold felt good when I remembered the fire the night before, what had felt like flames consuming me from the inside out. I closed my eyes and drew in a deep breath.

I was all right.

We were far from out of the woods, both literally and metaphorically, but I was all right. The unbearable burden of fear I'd been carrying since I'd found out I was pregnant had finally been lifted. Hope had been born. She was healthy. She was beautiful. We had both survived.

*I'm all right.*

A small smile passed over my lips as I dunked my hands into the cold water once again and ran them over my shoulders and chest. I pulled myself closer to the bank and dipped my legs into the clear, icy stream. I could see every pebble that lay at the bottom.

I drew the skirt of my dress up around my waist and washed off my legs. The warm fingers of morning light made their way down the canyon, contrasting with the cold air and sending chills racing down my spine.

I took another deep breath, tilting my head from side to side to stretch my neck. Everything was sore and tender, but strangely, I wasn't tired. In fact, I'd slept better than I had in what felt like years. It felt so normal, so right, to fall asleep next to Keegan, to awaken beside him.

I splashed more water over my face, my gaze resting on the pebbles beneath the surface. They seemed to waver and bend as the water rolled ever onward.

A strange feeling came over me as I looked upstream.

There was nothing there but boulders and shrubs, nothing out of the ordinary. Yet, when I looked back down at the cold water rushing around my legs, the feeling came back stronger than ever. There was something dark in that water; I could feel it as chills raced up my thighs.

No sooner had the thought crossed my mind than I heard the sound of a gunshot. Every muscle in my body tensed. I swung my legs back up over the bank and got to my feet, crouching down and racing to the nearest boulder for cover. I stayed there, listening for a moment, before peering over the top of the rock, scanning the edge of the forest.

My eyes narrowed, my senses opening.

Voices. As distant as the shot had been. More than just two; there was no doubt about that.

I cursed under my breath, dropping back into a crouch, my mind racing. One of the other RGM units had finally caught up to Anand. The shot had been the signal.

I began to run, staying crouched as I took off as quickly as I could, racing up the slope toward the alcove. I rounded a craggy boulder and slammed into Keegan. I gasped, almost fell backward, but he caught me by the shoulders. As soon as my eyes met his wide, wild ones, I knew something was horribly wrong.

"Hope." The word rolled off his lips in a frantic rush. "H-h-hope—she's gone. I left her there for one sec—"

"Gone?" The voice that repeated the word hardly sounded like my own. "She's *gone*? What do you mean?"

"I—she—"

"What are you talking about?" My voice rose, cracking, as I cut him off. "She can't be!"

"Sparrow—"

I raced up the hill, running as fast as my legs would carry me until I reached the entrance of the cavern. I ducked into the darkness, my frantic breathing echoing in the small space as my gaze darted feverishly back and forth.

No... no, no, no, no...

"Sparrow." Keegan put a hand on my shoulder. "Sparrow, I heard the shot and set her down for one second—"

"What happened?" I roared. "What happened to her?"

"There was no one there! I swear to God, I saw no one!" Keegan's voice cracked, his tone every bit as panicked as my own. "I was only a few yards away! I swear—"

Shoving past him, I bolted outside, darting past the cougar, who stared at me curiously from where she was crouched in the grass. I made it to higher ground, then slammed to a halt. The blood rushed to my head, sending my perception spinning. I squeezed my eyes shut, gripping my head in my hands. I couldn't think, I couldn't think, I couldn't *breathe*.

"Sparrow," Keegan panted, coming up behind me. "Sparrow, we'll find her—I promise, we're going to find her."

"You said you saw no one." My voice ached in my throat. I could practically feel the blood draining out of my face. "D-d-didn't you?"

A look of haunting realization dawned in Keegan's eyes.

"Aaron," I began. "I—I knew he would follow us. My god—of course he would follow me... I... I was carrying his child." I glanced over my shoulder, down into the canyon. "We have to find him and get the hell out of here— the soldiers are just beyond those trees. I could hear their voices when I was sitting on the bank of the creek." Panting, I began moving again, gesturing for him to follow me farther up the slope and into the pines, towards the sheer rock at the higher altitudes. "There's no way for him to go but up—he won't put Hope in danger."

"How can you be sure of that?" he shot back. "He's a soldier, Sparrow! He would just as soon kill us!"

"He wouldn't kill me—"

"How the hell do you know?"

"Because I am the only person on the planet who can actually see him!" My voice rose to a frantic shout as I whirled around to face him. "I know he won't kill me, Keeg."

"Lead the way."

"Keep your eyes peeled."

"I won't be able to see him," he reminded me.

"No, but you'll be able to see our daughter," I said, without even thinking about it. A lump formed in my throat. *Our daughter.*

I felt the warmth of Keegan's hand as it slid into my own. My fingers closed tightly around his.

Then two words cut through the quiet, echoing off the rocky escarpments.

"Up there!" a voice shouted.

Keegan stiffened, his head snapping toward the direction the voice had come from. He couldn't see what I did.

"Drop!" I shouted, dragging him down with me as I flattened against the ground. Bullets spattered the trees, sending bits of bark scattering.

Keegan cursed.

The bullets had come from the left, farther downhill. These were not the soldiers I'd heard by the stream; this was yet another of the units sent to smoke us out of the mountains.

"Hurry!" I yelled, already crawling forward on my elbows. I made it to the cover of a jagged rock. Keegan threw himself behind it just as more gunfire blasted through the forest. I braced myself behind the rock, cursing.

When the gunfire stopped, I cautiously peered out from behind the rock.

"Sparrow, get down!" Keegan shouted.

Ignoring him, I pushed my arms out to full extension and sent a hot, white orb sailing through the trees. I dropped down into cover again, heard it impact—and someone scream.

A bullet hit a tree beside us, and another punched into the ground, sending dirt flying.

I rose to my feet again despite Keegan's curses and pleas, my arms wide, sending orb after orb crashing down among the black uniforms dodging back and forth among the towering pines, bounding in and out of cover.

Orbs whooshed from my hands—one, two, and then the third hit a soldier and laid him flat in the dirt. I ducked behind the rock again. Keegan grabbed my face in his hands.

"You're out of your mind."

I nodded. "Yes, I am," I panted breathlessly. "Go find my baby."

"No, I'm not leaving you here."

"Keegan—"

The sickening *brrrat-tat-tat* grew nearer, cutting down shrubs and de-barking the trees. I pressed my forehead to Keegan's.

"I can see them. You can't," I said. "But you can see Hope, and Aaron couldn't have gotten that far, not yet—"

Bullets peppered the trees, one zinging off the top of the rock we were sheltered behind.

"Go," I hissed urgently. "Please."

I lifted to the balls of my feet, formed an orb in the palm of my hand, and sent it soaring through the trees.

"Go!" I screamed to Keegan.

Covering him as he ran, I formed another orb and threw it towards the soldiers—then ducked as more bullets came whizzing my way.

I cursed, gasping for breath, forming another orb in my shaking hands. I stood and threw. What felt like fire scathed the fleshy blade of my hand.

Cursing, hot tears springing to my eyes, I swallowed hard and gritted my teeth against the pain. I curled my fingers into claws and eased them up over the edge of the rock, sending out a blast of energy. The powerful bolts rippled through the air like lightning, shattering bullets in midair.

I heard a few more soldiers howl and go down. I pushed my trembling fingers out to full extension, letting go of everything I had.

Another soldier fell; the other was out of ammo. I could see the sheer terror in his eyes as he dropped back behind the nearest tree. Around him, a few of his comrades staggered back to their feet, only slightly wounded by the energy blasts that had hit them. That would buy me about five seconds, and that was all I needed to take off farther up the slope.

The *brrrrat-tat* started up almost immediately. I dodged behind trees and rocks, staying low, my legs burning as I sprinted farther and farther uphill. I could see Keegan up ahead, a blur as he ran, ducked, waited for me. As soon as I made it to cover, I signaled for him to keep going.

I knelt behind the trunk of a tree, peering around it only enough to turn and throw another orb. It flashed through the trees and exploded against a rock, sending hundreds of piping-hot, deadly shards of stone every which way, punching into tree trunks and skidding across the dirt.

I straightened and took off again. Keegan was already out of the woods, and even from where I was, I could see that we weren't far from where the tree line opened to the rocky peak looming ahead, already blanketed with snow at this altitude. Ash-gray snow clouds were beginning to gather over our heads.

Blood trickled down my arm from my injured hand as I sprinted up the slope. All I could hear was the ringing in my ears, the soft siren that the bullets left in their wake.

Bullets sped past me, but I hardly noticed now. I could barely feel the ground beneath my feet. Hope was the only thing I could focus on; her face filled my mind, blocking out all else. In that moment I realized nothing else mattered: only my daughter and her safety. And I would do anything to protect her, no matter how painful.

And that was when a long, shrill cry cut through the air.

My gaze flashed to the sky as I ran. Above the pine trees soared a hawk, wings outstretched, bright white light shining through her feathers as they spread above me like a protective shield.

*My mother.*

My heart thudded in my chest as I watched the light around her wings morph into orbs that rained down like fire. The first one impacted behind me. Everything flashed, and I was nearly blinded when I looked back over my shoulder. Deafening explosions pulsed through the atmosphere as the orbs fell, exploding one after the other.

Hawk was buying me time to run, covering me as I sprinted the rest of the way up the mountain. Finally, I broke through the trees to the rock escarpment that sloped and dropped into a steep dive off the sheer face of the peak.

I ran a few more yards, then slammed to a halt, my heart lifting to my throat. Keegan stood there, frozen just like I was.

Higher up, on a ledge that jutted out from the rest of the escarpment, stood a figure silhouetted against the morning sky. He stood with his back to me, his eyes fixed on the void before him, his arms cradling Hope. I could just see wisps of her jet-black hair in the crook of one arm.

*Aaron.*

I swallowed, hardly able to breathe. I stepped up to Keegan silently, leaning over his shoulder and putting my lips to his ear.

"Stay here," I whispered.

Keegan flashed me a frightened glance but didn't question me. Cautiously, I began to climb the rock, moving as quickly as I could without making noise. Aaron was up so high I had to use my hands to pull myself up to the top. Blood trickled from my wound as it opened again, but I ignored it. A few rocks split off and rattled down the rock face as I caught myself and hoisted my body up onto the plateau.

Rumbles of explosions echoed in the canyon far below, accentuated by the occasional chatter of fire from the RGM's guns. Aaron's back was still to me as I made my way cautiously closer. I was fairly sure he hadn't heard me over the sound of the firefight in the canyon.

"Aaron?" I said gently.

He didn't move. The wind whipped around us. I could see Hope's face, her cheek resting on his shoulder, her eyes shut tight and her mouth open in slumber. The wind danced through her hair.

"Aaron, can you hear me?" I repeated, my throat tight around the words. "Aaron, please talk to me."

A moment passed in silence. He readjusted his grip around Hope, which nearly caused my heart to stop beating. All I could think of was the drop yawning inches from Aaron's toes.

"Is..." His voice was timid. "Is he still there?"

My eyes instantly swept the plateau, at a loss as to whom he was referring to.

"No," I replied steadily. "No, Aaron, there is no one here but me. It's just me... It's Sparrow."

He remained frozen where he was for a moment before slowly turning. I was struck by how thin his face was now. It was streaked with blood and the tracks of tears. His hollow eyes met mine.

"Aaron, what happened?"

He didn't answer. His almost lifeless gaze drifted over my shoulder and stuck there. "H-h-he's right behind you."

Slowly, and only taking my eyes off him at the last second, I shot a quick glance over my shoulder before my gaze snapped back to his.

"Aaron, there's no one there," I told him, struggling to maintain the same calm tone. "There's no one—it's just me."

But he was still staring over my shoulder into the thin air, his trembling fingers clutching Hope. "He will not leave me alone. He is here because of what I have done." His fevered words tumbled out one over the other. "He's here because I have done wrong."

I stepped incrementally closer. "Aaron... we've all done wrong—I have." My voice sounded raw. "Just because you've done something wrong doesn't mean that you can't change. We can *all* change."

He turned to me as if he were seeing me for the first time. "You wouldn't say that if you knew what I have done. It is you whom I have destroyed."

"No." I shook my head slowly. "You have not destroyed me, Aaron, nor could you ever."

"I was the one who captured you," he went on, as if I had never spoken, as if he couldn't hear me. "I led you there. I captured you. I negotiated the deal to keep you there with Bask, Sparrow. It was me. It was my fault."

"I know."

"I was the one who lied to you—all that time." His voice cracked. "I was… I was the one who betrayed you."

"I know, Aaron. I know what happened. I know what you did," I told him quietly, inching closer. "I forgive you."

Aaron's dark eyes stared hollowly into mine, like two caves, echoing and empty. "How can you say that? I—I have taken everything from you. I almost took him, too."

"Him?"

His lips twitched towards a tortured, miserable smile. "Keegan. The man you love."

My eyes shifted to Hope. I didn't give him an answer.

"I have loved you, Sparrow." His voice cracked as he continued. "I have, in my way, you know."

I swallowed, nodded.

"But I can never have you, because you will never… you will never feel for me what you feel for him." He blinked furiously, sucking back tears, then took a faltering step backward, causing my heart to leap to my throat. I forced myself to be still. "I've lost, Sparrow. I've lost who I was—and now I've lost you." His gaze lowered to Hope. He stroked his fingertips over her soft head. "She's the only thing I have, Spar." He looked up at me again. "She—she can see me!" He let go of a laugh that was more like a sob. "She's all I have now."

I swallowed, stepping closer now. "Aaron, come to me, please…"

"Stop!" Aaron's voice burst out so abruptly I jumped a little. "Just stop saying that!"

He stared over my shoulder as if someone stood just behind me.

"Aaron, *what is it?*"

"I know what I've done!" He was weeping now. "I know what I am! I cannot be anything else. I can't—I—"

He doubled over onto his knees, sobbing, bowing his head to his chest, his arms still wrapped around the baby. I closed the distance between us now and fell to my knees at his side. I looped my arms around Hope, but he didn't release his grip.

"Aaron." I said his name softly, looking into his face. "You can be whoever you want to be... You don't have to be who you've always been. Aaron, look at me."

I still held onto Hope, who was awake now, her depthless eyes looking between the two of us. Aaron's dark, absent eyes lifted slowly to meet mine, bloodshot and shiny with tears.

"Aaron, you don't have to live like this. You can be the man I thought you were," I whispered. "You *can* be that man."

Aaron stared steadily into my eyes as tears rolled down his cheeks. There were signs of frostbite on his fingers. Slowly, his grip loosened, and he let me pull Hope into my arms.

I stood, backing away a few paces.

"The old man," he began. "He's behind you... He stays with me... haunts me. He will..." He sobbed. "He will never let me forget what I have done."

I shook my head. "No, Aaron. He's not the one who won't let you forget—I know him," I said, my voice softening. "I have seen him too, and... and I finally know that love is not like that. Love doesn't rule by fear and torture..." I trailed off, looking at him. "Love forgives."

His face crumpled as he bowed his head to his chest. "I cannot... I will *never* forgive myself," he whispered. "There's nothing left. There's no undoing it."

"Maybe not—maybe you can't undo it, but you can change."

"Sparrow—" Keegan's voice called urgently from far below.

He didn't have to finish. I heard the gunfire. The RGM was closing in on us, and Keegan couldn't see them.

I ran to the lip of the ledge, Hope still in my arms, and dropped carefully to my knees to peer over the edge. I could see the soldiers' outlines as they moved among the trees, see puffs of dirt as their bullets hit the ground around the boulder Keegan was crouched behind.

"Stay down!" I shouted.

I turned back to Aaron.

"You can stop this!" I told him. "Aaron, you can stop them!"

Aaron stared ahead, not at me, not at anything in particular. For a moment I wondered if he could hear the gunfire, the chaos unfolding below. Then, slowly, he stood.

"Yes," he said quietly. "Yes, I can. But not in the way that you imagine."

He stepped backward, closer to the edge of the cliff.

"No, Aaron, no, don't!"

He stopped, his heels at the edge. He looked at me; then his eyes lowered to the baby in my arms.

"I love you, Sparrow," he whispered.

Then he stepped off the cliff.

"No!" The word tore out of my throat in a scream as he vanished over the edge and into the void. I raced to the edge, clutching our child, staring down.

There was nothing there, just fog. Just gray, rolling fog.

I swallowed back tears, forcing myself to snap out of it, then turned and moved back to the slope. Half running, half falling, holding Hope to my chest, I scrambled my way down as fast as I could, one bleeding hand wrapped around Hope, the other clutching at the jagged rocks.

"Keegan!" I shouted as bullets sprayed the trees. Panting, I flattened myself against the rocks, holding tight to Hope, who was now beginning to cry.

Keegan lifted and threw an orb, followed by another and another—each impacting into its intended target, covering me as I moved.

"Keeg!" I sprinted to him in a crouch, lifting my hand and launching a pulsating, clear orb towards the RGM soldiers as I dropped to the ground beside him. "Let me—I can see them! Stay down—"

"So can I!" he cut in.

I stared at him, my eyes wide. "What?"

"I can see them now!" he shouted, lifting again to channel a deadly stream of energy forward into the trees, where the soldiers were gushing out like a river.

"You can see them?"

"I can now—they just suddenly appeared," he panted, shooting me a glance. "Does the invisibility wear off?"

"After a few days. But surely, they would..." My voice faded in my throat. "Oh my god. Aaron knew..."

Keegan crouched down again as bullets showered over us. He lifted an eyebrow. "What do you mean?"

It had worn off. The source of the blood that ran in their veins, the substance that made them invisible, was gone. Aaron's last words echoed in my mind: *"Yes, I can... but not in the way that you imagine."*

I swallowed, staring at him. "Keegan, we can win this."

We waited for a lull; then Keegan threw again while I formed energy in my own hands and blasted it into the oncoming soldiers, scattering them into the trees they had just emerged from with a penetrating *whoosh*.

Suddenly, a shower of hot white orbs began raining down. The remaining soldiers dove for cover.

I squinted up through the snowflakes that were beginning to fall. Time seemed to move in slow motion as I gazed up at the wings spread out above me, soaring over my head.

Hawk's cry seemed to cut through the forest, stirring the trees like wind. Branches began to swirl around me, bending and dancing every which way. I watched in astonishment as deep, emerald-green flecks of leaves began to appear on their branches.

My breath caught in my chest. "Keegan, look."

"What—"

"The trees!" I exclaimed, pointing.

Still crouched beside me, Keegan craned his neck to peer skyward, following my gaze.

The orbs impacted faster and faster now; the trees churned as the forest writhed and grew, the snow falling more and more heavily until it spun like a hurricane around us. Keegan and I grasped each other's hands and cradled Hope between us.

Slowly, the gunshots died away. So did the explosions of the impacting orbs, and, finally... so did the wind.

For a moment we both just knelt there, disoriented; then Keegan lifted cautiously to his feet, peering over the edge of the rock.

"Sparrow..." he hissed. "Sparrow, look."

I felt frozen for a moment, a strange, knowing sort of anticipation welling inside me. I looked down at Hope, then back to Keegan as he crouched to take her in his arms.

Slowly, I got to my feet.

Everything that had been there before was gone. The bullets, the soldiers, the guns, the chaos—it was all gone. The forest even looked different somehow, and not just the fact that it was alive again. Something was different, as if a new world had suddenly merged with this one.

A cloaked figure stood among the shadows of the trees at the forest's edge. He reached up and pushed back his hood, and my lips parted in astonishment as my eyes locked with a pair of emerald green ones. For a moment I just stood there, breathless.

Then I ran to him.

He ran too, meeting me halfway, where we collided into each other's arms. I buried my face in his chest and burst into tears, shaking uncontrollably, holding on to him. A river of emotion poured out of me; I couldn't control it. I held him, and I cried and felt the warmth of his own tears against my skin.

"Fin... I—I'm sorry."

"Shhh. I love you." He stroked a hand over my hair. "It's okay."

"I'm sorry," I sobbed. "I'm so sorry."

"Shhh, it's okay," he whispered. "I love you."

"I'm sorry..."

"I love you."

I pulled him in tighter, tears rolling down my face. "I love you too."

# 46

"AARON..." I BEGAN. "HE STEPPED OFF THE ESCARPMENT. I didn't have time to reason with him, Keegan was down there, and another unit was moving in from the left—soldiers he couldn't even see."

"It was right after I heard you scream," Keegan added, "right after Aaron stepped off the cliff, that everything began to... become visible..." He fell into step beside Fin and me as we began to walk. "Do you think he knew what he was doing? Do you think he was actually trying to... save us?"

I shivered, tucking myself deeper into the crook of Fin's arm. "Yes, I think he did know—he told me he could stop them, but not in the way that I imagined. Aaron did love me, Keegan. He wasn't evil... There was good in him. I tried to stop him. I... Should I have done something different? Would something different have stopped him?"

Keegan shifted Hope in his arms, looking like he wanted to respond but holding back, waiting for Fin to reply first.

"We cannot know what would have happened," Fin answered gently. "What Aaron did has nothing to do with you, Sparrow... It had to do with him. With what he believed about himself and about the world. What we believe is true about ourselves is what makes us who we are."

"Could I have made him believe?"

"You cannot make someone believe, Sparrow. Not even if it's the truth." He glanced down at me. "Not even if you know who *they* truly are."

I studied him as the meaning of his words sank in. "Hawk," I began. "I saw her during the battle. She covered me as I ran."

Fin kissed the top of my head, still holding me close. "Your mother would do anything for you, Sparrow."

"When did you find her?" Keegan asked.

"Days ago. After you already had," Fin replied. "She told me Icarus had been captured. That's where she is now."

"She went to the District?" I asked.

He nodded. "Which is where we're headed now."

I froze. "I..." My voice died in my throat as I shook my head. "I can't go back there. I can't, not after..."

Keegan looked at me wordlessly, sliding a hand into my own. "Their powers are gone, Sparrow," he said quietly. "Their power of invisibility, and their power over you."

I swallowed, lowering my gaze, brushing my shaking fingers back through my hair. "We've escaped them already, Keeg. Why would we seek them out?"

"Because your father is there," he answered gently. "And your mother."

A thousand words warred in my throat, but I said nothing. I just nodded, massaging my fingers over my forehead.

I looked up at Keegan, who still held our daughter cradled in his arms. She reached for my face and smiled, and Keegan shifted her gently into my arms. He lifted my chin with his free hand, brushing his fingers back through my hair.

"What wouldn't you have done to save her?" he whispered, his eyes gazing down into mine. "Wouldn't you have done anything? Even if..."

"Even if it had meant letting her go," I finished for him, a tear trailing down my cheek. "Yes, I... I would."

Keegan smiled as he leaned down and gently kissed my lips. "You have nothing to be afraid of," he said. "You are the strongest person I know."

I smiled, my forehead still touching his. "So are you."

We transported to the woods surrounding the District. My heart had already begun to pick up its pace when we arrived. I took Keegan's hand, and together we followed Fin through the woods. He was taking a turn carrying Hope. I couldn't help but smile, noticing what a natural he was with her. Keegan's hand wrapped around mine, giving it a reassuring squeeze.

We approached the edge of the woods, and Fin gestured for us to follow him out of the trees. "Come."

With each of my footsteps my heart seemed to quicken until at last we stepped out into the open. I stood on the slope, staring down into the place that had been my prison and Aaron's own kingdom of darkness.

"Impossible..." I gasped.

Keegan stepped up beside me. "It's all visible..." he said, awestruck. "I can see it. I can—I can see *everything*."

Below, in the palm of the valley, a thin trickle of the last remaining soldiers trailed listlessly past walls that were shattered, covered in vines, overgrown by the roots of trees. But more noticeable, more astonishing than all of this, was the herd of a hundred or so buffalo that occupied the area now instead of the humans who had once had such a violent stronghold.

Their massive, looming shapes filled the District, or what was left of it, and surrounded it as though they were guarding the ruins. The soldiers barely glanced at them as they stumbled past, empty-handed, their heads hanging low.

I came up alongside Fin, staring wide-eyed at what seemed too surreal to be reality. "What on earth happened here?"

"Earth," he said simply. "Earth happened here."

"You mean this wasn't you?"

Fin shook his head. Then he pointed.

I followed his gesture, shielding my eyes from the sunlight as I squinted down into the valley. I could see a figure walking past the piles of rubble, all that remained of the District's once-impenetrable gates.

I recognized him immediately.

"Icarus..." I began.

I took a step forward, hesitated, then looked back at Fin. He watched me, his eyes soft and glistening.

I turned back to him and reached up to take his face in my hands, looking into his emerald eyes. I swallowed back the lump in my throat, forcing my voice to steady.

"You have always been," I whispered, "and you will always be my father."

Fin said nothing in response, tears glistening in his eyes as he leaned closer to kiss my forehead, wrapping his arms around me. We held on to each other for a moment, and then, slowly, I let go of him.

Drying my cheeks with the backs of my hands, I turned and looked at Keegan, tipping my head toward the beautiful chaos below. A smile twitched at the corners of his lips as he seemed to understand. He stepped forward and lowered Hope into my arms, then wrapped an arm around me.

Together, we set off down the hill.

"Imagine that," he mused, almost to himself, as we made our way down the incline. "A new world. It's... it's exactly what Sensei showed me that day when I was looking for you. A new world invading this one."

I thought about it, then nodded. "I think that was what he was telling me all along," I said softly. "Every time he appeared—every time he proved that he would never leave me..." I tried in vain to swallow back the lump in my throat. "Every time he told me that it wasn't the end. Every time he helped me rediscover hope..."

I trailed off and looked down at the tiny face that rested against my chest.

"And now I've found it," I finished quietly.

Keegan gave my shoulders a squeeze as we walked the rest of the way to the gates just as the familiar figure I'd seen only moments ago appeared through the clearing clouds of dust and fog and shimmering snow.

He stopped at the gates, still wearing black RGM prison clothes, an expression of surprise and awe lingering on his face as his eyes met mine over the distance between us. His steps quickened as he drew closer, and at last Icarus and I were standing face-to-face. His arms encompassed me, his lips pressing to my hair as he wept.

I held on to him, cradling little Hope between us, resting my face against his shoulder, and letting my tears fall.

After a moment, I felt him turn his head, and I turned to follow his gaze. Beyond the gates, another figure emerged from the fog and the snow. A woman dressed in black, with hair the same color as mine spilling over her shoulders. A woman with immense dark eyes that stared toward me as if they beheld something they once had feared they would never see.

For moment I simply stood there, my voice stuck in my throat, and then, holding tightly to Hope, I began to run. I barely noticed the ground passing beneath my feet, the distance closing, and suddenly I was before her, all but blinded by the hot tears that streamed down my face.

Speechless, I stood there and just looked at her. And at last, all those sharp words I had always wanted to say simply melted away like the snow on my skin.

In their place was just one word. Hardly daring to breathe, I spoke it so softly that only she could hear.

"Mom..."

Tears spilled down her cheeks as she threw her arms around me.

I gasped for breath, sobbed, laughed, held onto her like I was never going to let go, whispering that same word once more.

"*Mom.*"

She kissed my head and my cheeks and drew back to look down into my face, tears streaking her own. "*Sparrow.*"

Time seemed to stand still as we stood face-to-face and looked at each other for the first time. Then her eyes softened and lowered to my daughter still sleeping peacefully in my arms.

I smiled and brushed a lock of perfect dark hair away from the baby's forehead. "This..." I began softly, then raised my eyes to look at my mother, my father, Keegan, Fin—and then at the herd and the light and the flowers that were beginning to grow around us in spite of it all. "This is Hope."

# EPILOGUE

EVERYTHING WAS DARK. I COULDN'T SEE OR FEEL. I began to wonder if I was dead, if this was hell, this cold, strange darkness that surrounded and filled me. But gradually I began to feel something with my fingertips. I slowly moved them, caressing something cold and crystalline.

I tried to remember what had happened before I'd awakened—but was I even awake?

I didn't know. All I knew was that I felt cold and numb.

I blinked, and suddenly my eyes burned as bright white light hit my eyes. I lay there for a moment, my heart racing.

*Where am I? What happened?*

Like a memory from a dream, I remembered Sparrow—I remembered the face of our child. I remembered Sparrow screaming.

Then nothingness.

Dragging my hand over what I could now identify as cold, snowy ground, I reached up and pressed my hands to my eyes, sucking in a deep breath.

My god—I could remember it now: I'd leapt from the top of the escarpment. I could remember the foggy mist as it had billowed up around me, seeming to set fire to my skin, knocking me unconscious.

*Surely, I died...*

Slowly, I opened my eyes again. The shapes around me seemed to writhe and twinkle, coming slowly into focus: trees. Massive, looming pines in every direction—a forest all covered in snow.

*... didn't I?*

Blinking feverishly, I rubbed the back of my head and checked the rest of my body, making sure nothing was broken. Nothing was, which bewildered me as much as the strange and silent sanctuary that now encompassed me.

I climbed slowly to my feet, gazing around. All around me was snow that came up to my knees. The trees blurred around me as I slowly spun, looking around, craning my neck to stare up at the treetops.

This was not the same forest—this was not the Tetons. This, I was sure, was not even in Section West.

"Impossible..." I whispered, my breath steaming in the frigid air.

I stepped forward—or tried to. The snow was so deep I tripped and fell headlong into it. I lay there for a moment, my heart in my mouth, a strange and terrible feeling running its fingers down my spine.

A sudden snapping sound caught my attention. I scrambled around to a sitting position, fighting the thick snow.

My eyes searched back and forth between the trees, looking for the source of the noise. I saw nothing but silent, towering pines blanketed in shimmering white.

I gave a quiet sigh of relief.

Then I heard another snap—like a branch breaking.

My entire body braced. The hair on the back of my neck rose as I slowly turned around again, sinking deeper in the snow.

Standing between two trees was a black wolf, its bright golden eyes boring into mine.

It didn't move, and neither did I. I stood there and watched, too fearful to move, unable to breathe as another black wolf stepped out from behind one of the trees farther back.

Like a ghost, yet another black wolf appeared to my left. And another to my right.

I spun around and saw another one behind me, its massive paws making no sound in the thick snow as it padded out from among the trees and began to move toward me.

The other wolves drew closer now, and I could see that there were at least six more, all massive, all cloaked in thick black coats and moving silently through the snow toward me.

I spun back around to face the first wolf, my eyes wide—wild, my head spinning.

I was surrounded. The wolves were all around me, edging closer.

Then a long, low howl split the air like a siren. I spun to face it.

There, standing in the distance, staring at me with piercing blue eyes, was a white wolf.

# About the Author

K.A. Emmons is the author of The Blood Race series and co-host of The Kate & Abbie Show – a podcast she produces with her sister. When she's not writing, you will probably find Kate outside: hiking, surfing, practicing kata or heading to the climbing gym. Visit her online at:

WWW.KAEMMONS.COM

## Also follow Kate on:

youtube.com/kaemmons

facebook.com/kaemmonsauthor

instagram.com/lonehawkwriter